CELIA HARWOOD
lives in Buxton,
the town which has inspired this series.

AUTUMN'S PEAK
THE SECOND BUXTON SPA MYSTERY

CELIA HARWOOD

NEUF NEZNOIRS LIMITED

Published by Neuf Neznoirs Limited
Unit 20, 91-93 Liverpool Road, Castlefield, Manchester, M3 4JN.
e-mail: gemggirg@gmail.com

ISBN 978-0-9933261-1-0

Printed and bound in England by 4edge Ltd. Hockley, Essex
Tel: 01702 200243

For
Darcy

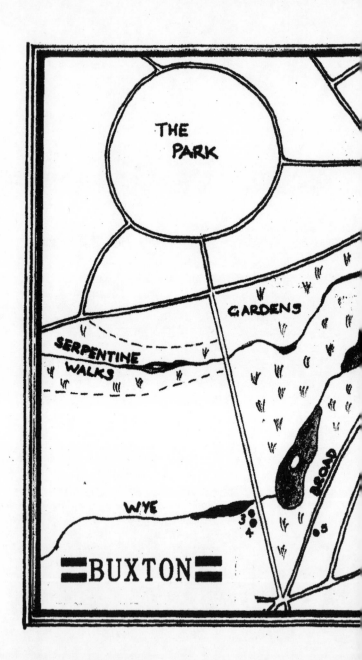

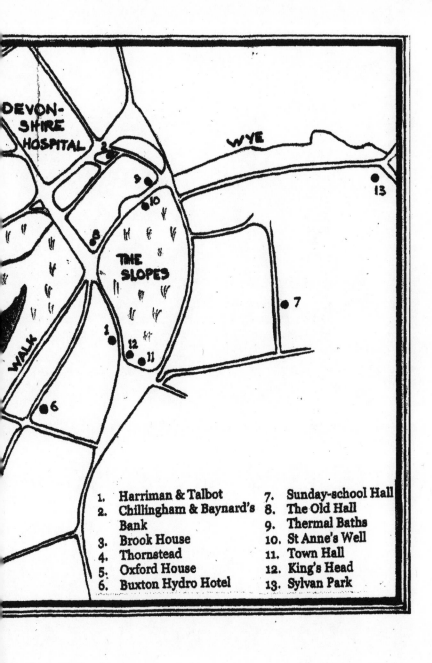

DEVON-
SHIRE
HOSPITAL

WYE

THE
SLOPES

WALK

1. Harriman & Talbot
2. Chillingham & Baynard's
   Bank
3. Brook House
4. Thornstead
5. Oxford House
6. Buxton Hydro Hotel

7. Sunday-school Hall
8. The Old Hall
9. Thermal Baths
10. St Anne's Well
11. Town Hall
12. King's Head
13. Sylvan Park

CHAPTER ONE

Nearly everyone in the spa town of Buxton knew Jon Jon. Nominally, he lived with his aunt at the back of the baker's in Higher Buxton but he was rarely there. He spent most of his day and part of his night in the Market Place or the High Street, moving from one spot to the next, just watching or, if something attracted his attention, migrating to the lower part of the town. All the shopkeepers knew him and the local people greeted him as they went in and out of the shops and pubs. He was just accepted as part of the town. He was well into his thirties but his mind had not grown with his body; he was like a young child with only a limited knowledge of life. He rarely spoke, other than to echo the local greeting of "y'aw reet" when people saw him in the street. Despite his large size and his awkward, lumbering gait, he was a gentle, warm hearted soul. People said of him with affection: 'There's summat wrong wi' 'is 'ead but 'is 'eart's in t'right place.'

No-one had bothered with Jon Jon's education so he was unable to read or write and, being a stranger to newspapers and discussions about politics and unemployment, he was sheltered from the fears and problems that troubled the minds of the other inhabitants of the town, still recovering from the effects of the Great War. However, Jon Jon was very observant and he watched the town's activities and interpreted its events in his own way. Sometimes, when the mood took him and the weather was fine, he wandered further afield pursuing whatever attracted his attention. He frequently walked on the moors which surrounded the town.

He had an extensive knowledge of the plants and wildlife there and, although he did not know their official names, could identify them all by the names he had given them.

Early this morning, Jon Jon was at the bottom of High Street near Mr Morten's dairy. A horse harnessed to one of the milk carts was standing patiently in the street, waiting to begin his daily delivery round and, as he shifted his weight from one foot to another, the metallic scrape of his horseshoes on the road echoed in the stillness. The sun had not yet risen. The air was crisp and turned the breath of the horse into white vapour. Jon Jon loved animals and was standing quietly on the edge of the pavement beside the horse, looking at it intently. The horse turned his head slowly and returned Jon Jon's gaze in a friendly, uncritical way.

It was October and the Buxton season was officially over. Every year, the mountain spa welcomed thousands of visitors who came to drink the water and undergo treatments at the various hydropathic establishments, to take part in sporting activities, or just to enjoy the clear, clean air which their home cities lacked. Those who came to "take the cure" usually stayed for three weeks, sometimes as long as six weeks. Others who came for a family holiday stayed for a week or two. Consequently, a large proportion of the townspeople made a living by offering accommodation to visitors. This year, 1921, the town had been even busier than usual due to the weather. For several months, the whole country had suffered from severe drought and unusually high temperatures. The cooler climate of Buxton, sometimes regarded as a disadvantage, had made the town a particularly appealing holiday destination and the higher than usual temperatures had made bathing in the spa waters less of a challenge. Because of the increase in the number of visitors, it had been a profitable year for the town's traders. Now, with the shorter days and lower temperatures, all except the hardy few had returned to their homes.

With considerably fewer guests to cater for, the proprietors of the hotels and lodging houses had reduced their orders for milk and cream and it did not take as long to load the milk delivery cart as it did during the season. The delivery man came out of the dairy, greeted Jon Jon cheerfully, swung the last container of milk onto the cart, and gave the signal for the horse to walk on. For a while, Jon Jon followed the cart on its rounds watching the milk being poured out into a variety of receptacles. His pace was unhurried. When the cart was moving, he lagged behind and when it had stopped outside a house, he caught up with it again. After a while, he began to lose interest and gradually the cart got well ahead of him. By now they had reached the area of town officially called Buxton Park but generally referred to as The Park. The cart had stopped outside a house named The Elms. Today only one pint of milk was required because the owner, Mrs Hazelwood, was away on holiday in Yorkshire. Unusually, there were no lights on and there was no sign of activity. As there was no need to make breakfast for her mistress, the cook-housekeeper had left the container for the milk out ready the night before and was still asleep upstairs in her room in the attic, indulging in the unaccustomed luxury of a lie-in. By the time Jon Jon reached The Elms, the milk cart had disappeared around a bend in the road. He leaned against one of the stone gateposts of the house opposite The Elms, gazing ahead at nothing in particular. There was nothing to retain his interest so, after a few minutes, he decided to move on but then a sudden movement caught his attention. Somebody was hurrying along the narrow lane which extended along the side of The Elms from the road to the back boundary.

At the far end of the lane, there was a small building which had once been the stables for The Elms, occupied by two horses and a groom, but which was now used as a kennel for Mrs Hazelwood's dogs. For many years, Mrs Hazelwood had been a member of the Kennel Club and was well-known in the Peak

District as a breeder of prize winning Border Terriers. Because the Border Terrier breed had just been officially recognised by the Kennel Club, Mrs Hazelwood was hoping for an increase in her income from the sale of this year's litter of puppies sired by her champion dog, officially named Shorbeck Gillam, but generally known as Jake. Jon Jon watched with interest as two men, one very tall and the other much shorter, came creeping stealthily along the lane from the old stables towards the road. They were dressed in workmen's clothes and each was carrying a cloth bundle which wriggled. The men had almost reached the road when the shorter one spotted Jon Jon in the gateway opposite and stopped. He nudged his companion in order to draw attention to Jon Jon.

The taller man whispered: 'It's alright. It's only Jon Jon. He won't bother us. He can't understand owt.'

They turned into the road and walked briskly away.

They were right. Jon Jon didn't understand what they were doing but that did not stop him from being interested and he did recognise the taller of the two men, although he had not seen him for some time. Jon Jon had no intention of bothering them, but his curiosity had been aroused by the wriggling bundles. Unnoticed by the two men, he followed them at his own pace. When he reached the main road, once the Roman road to Manchester, he could see them a considerable distance ahead. The road climbed steeply and the two men, intent on reaching their destination, walked with their heads down and did not look back. At first, they passed large houses set back from either side of the road then, after several hundred yards, they neared the edge of the town. The bundles of cloth were now making high-pitched yelping noises and the sound carried back to Jon Jon on the still, morning air. He quickened his pace. He empathised with any living thing which was unhappy or distressed. If he passed a pram with a crying baby he would stop and look, frowning with concern.

The road now followed a long, wide curve to the right. Had the two men looked back, they would not have been able to see Jon Jon, even though he was now close behind them. Just as the road straightened out again, the men stopped at a five-barred gate. Above them, nestled into the hillside, was a group of buildings which, until recently, had been a working farm called Red Farm. There were no lights on at the old farm house. The men were made awkward by the squirming bundles and were slow opening the gate. By the time they had gone through it, Jon Jon was close behind but they did not notice him as they hurried up a dirt track towards an old barn at the top of the slope. Jon Jon watched as they disappeared into the barn. For a long time, he stood at the gate looking up towards the barn not sure what to do. He could no longer hear the yelping noise and there was no sign of activity in any of the other buildings. It was now light. Eventually, he gave up and wandered back down the road into the town, puzzling over what he had just witnessed.

Mrs Hazelwood had lived at The Elms since her marriage twenty years ago. She was now a widow, her husband having died of pneumonia in the winter of 1916. Recently, while reading a magazine at the hairdresser's, she had seen an advertisement for Dr Edgecombe's newly opened Vitality Health Resort and Clinic in Yorkshire where one could undergo a seven-day treatment guaranteed to bring youth and vitality back to the body even if, the advertisement assured her, that body was over forty. Mrs Hazelwood had recently crossed that threshold but she had not yet given up hope of finding a new husband to replace the one she had lost. In fact, Mrs Hazelwood already had her eye on a possible candidate but he was proving much slower to respond to her advances than she had anticipated.

It was clear to her that a more intensified campaign was necessary and she thought that there was no harm, before beginning the new offensive, in enhancing her charms with a week of massage, sauna, gentle exercise, gallons of spa water, and healthy food all of which, for a price, Dr Edgecombe was prepared to supply at his Clinic.

To justify the expense, Mrs Hazelwood thought of her stay at the Clinic as an investment rather than an extravagant holiday. Of course, the regime offered by Dr Edgecombe could just as easily have been obtained at home in Buxton which was, after all, a spa town but then she would have had to explain her absence from social occasions for seven days. Given her motive and the ultimate goal of the treatment, that would have been rather embarrassing. Absolute discretion was required and she felt certain that she could rely on Dr Edgecombe for that. So, she had ordered her bags to be packed and, in an optimistic mood, had taken the train north to be transformed. Her dogs and the litter of puppies had been left in the care of the gardener with strict instructions regarding their care and feeding regime. She was due to arrive back from Yorkshire the following day and, unfortunately, the beneficial effects of the seven-day cure were destined to evaporate when she discovered the theft of two of the puppies.

~O~

Just after eleven o'clock that morning, Edwin Talbot walked down Hall Bank and entered the business premises of Harriman & Talbot, Solicitors, Notaries, and Commissioners for Oaths. Edwin Talbot was the younger half of the partnership and looked after the firm's litigation. The senior partner, Mr Harriman, looked after commercial and private client matters. They were assisted by Mr Harriman's daughter, Eleanor, who had joined the firm a few years previously. Her brother, Edgar,

Mr Harriman's only son, had been articled to Edwin Talbot with the expectation that he too would become a partner but, never very keen on law, he had enlisted in 1914 and been killed in France the following year. Eleanor Harriman had replaced her brother and Edwin Talbot, although greatly saddened by the loss of Edgar, was not at all disappointed by the substitution of his sister. He recognised Eleanor's ability and encouraged her to develop her skills. He was an easy-going, happily married man. He and Mr Harriman were both good friends and compatible as partners. Consequently, the atmosphere at Harriman & Talbot was very congenial.

Edwin Talbot was returning from a meeting and as he passed the clerk's room he exchanged a greeting with James Wildgoose, who had been the firm's confidential clerk for over thirty years. James' office was on the ground floor and he was busy copying a letter for Mr Harriman. Messrs Harriman & Talbot was an old established firm and, although they had moved with the times and had had the telegraph and the telephone installed, the partners did not consider that typewriters had a place in a lawyer's office. The court documents and the correspondence were still prepared by James Wildgoose in his perfectly even, copperplate handwriting and were then copied into large leather bound books.

Edwin climbed the stairs to his own office on the first floor. He dumped a pile of papers on his desk, took off his hat and coat, picked up a file and went across the landing into Eleanor's office. Napoleon, Eleanor's large Boxer dog, given to her by her father the second year after her brother's death, got up from his snoozing position under Eleanor's desk. He greeted Edwin enthusiastically and Edwin made a fuss of him. Mrs Clayton, the housekeeper, appeared in the doorway of Eleanor's office.

'Here's your tea, Miss Harriman. I've put yours on your desk, Mr Talbot. Or do you want it bringing in here?'

'No, thank you, Mrs Clayton. I'm going back there in a minute. I only came to give Eleanor a file. By the way, I've just seen Superintendent Johnson. He tells me that there are rumours of a new dog fighting ring in the area. He thought last year that he had seen the last of them but apparently there is a new group operating. People from Sheffield, he thinks, and he is taking the rumour seriously. You haven't heard anything, have you, Mrs Clayton?'

'Funny you should mention it,' responded Mrs Clayton. 'I have, as it happens. Alf was out late-ish the other evening doing a collection, out past the back of Harpur Hill, and he said he thought he heard dogs barking. A lot of them, not just one or two. But quite a way off, mind.'

Mrs Clayton had been at Hall Bank for several years. After her husband was killed at Gallipoli, she was left with two young boys to support. She went to live with her brother, Alf, and his family and then Mr Harriman engaged her as housekeeper. During the day, she came to Hall Bank to supervise the household and prepare meals and then returned to her family in the evenings. Mrs Clayton provided a useful link between Harriman & Talbot and the rest of the town and had a very effective communication network for local information. Food and household items were always purchased from local tradespeople and shopping was done on a daily basis. Mrs Clayton either went to these shops herself or placed an order by telephone, so she regularly heard the latest gossip from the shopkeepers and their customers, or from the men who delivered the goods to Hall Bank. The remarkable thing about Mrs Clayton was the fact that, although she freely shared the news from the town with everyone at Hall Bank, she never repeated anything that she heard at Harriman & Talbot's office and everyone there knew they could rely absolutely on her discretion. Her brother, Alf, was one of the local undertakers. Because of his profession, he travelled widely throughout the area and had an unusual level of access to people's homes. He was a noticing sort of person and kept his eyes and ears open and, as a consequence, was another valuable source of information.

'Alf mentioned it to George from the garage the next day,' continued Mrs Clayton, 'and George said he and his lad had been delivering a motor-car over that way a couple of weeks back and they had heard barking. They wondered if someone was getting together a pack of hounds for the High Peak Hunt again. You know, to replace the ones that they put down because of the War. But it might have been dog fighting, mightn't it? I'll mention it to Alf, about what Superintendent Johnson said. He might hear something more. Right, I'll just take Mr Wildgoose his tea.'

Mrs Clayton went downstairs with her tray and Edwin returned to his office. Eleanor got on with her work, attending methodically to her list of "things to be done this morning" for the files on her desk. After about half of an hour, she went down to James Wildgoose to take him some documents for copying.

James said: 'Ah, Miss Eleanor. I was just about to come up. Lady Carleton-West telephoned.'

Eleanor's eyebrows went up in surprise because it was common knowledge that a firm of solicitors in London had supplied all the legal requirements of Lady Carleton-West and her family for well over eighty years.

'Yes,' said James, seeing Eleanor's expression. 'It is a surprise, isn't it? Lady Carleton-West wondered if you would go up to Top Trees as soon as convenient after lunch, or as she put it, luncheon.'

'Knowing Lady Carleton-West that means after lunch today whether that is convenient for me or not.'

'She suggested three o'clock,' added James, poker faced. Eleanor laughed. 'Oh, did she? You have to hand it to her,

James. Lady C is a passed master when it comes to getting what she wants. I wonder what she does want.'

'I'm afraid that she gave no indication at all.'

'It must be important if she took the trouble to telephone herself and not have Ash or the housekeeper make the call for her. Very well then, three o'clock it shall be. I don't have any appointments this afternoon, do I?' James shook his head. 'Would you please telephone to Top Trees then and let them know that I shall be there at three.'

'Certainly, Miss Eleanor.'

She looked at her watch. 'It's nearly one o'clock. I shall take Napoleon for his walk. Come on, Leon. If we go now, we shall be back in time for luncheon.' She mischievously emphasised the word. 'You stay here while I get my hat and coat.'

Napoleon sat down obediently and waited while Eleanor went back up to her office to get ready. They left for the nearby Pavilion Gardens and James telephoned to Top Trees and left a message for Lady Carleton-West with Ash, the butler.

When Eleanor and Napoleon returned to the office twenty minutes later, James said:

'Mr Norman telephoned while you were out, Miss Eleanor.' Eleanor groaned. 'He was enquiring about the tennis club dance on Saturday and wanted to know if you were going. I gathered that he was intending to offer to be your escort.'

'Oh, bother!' said Eleanor. 'Save me, James!'

'I told Mr Norman that I thought you had not yet decided whether you were going to the dance or not,' said James, with a knowing smile.

'Thank you, James. He is a perfectly lovely man, I'm sure, but I am just not interested in being escorted to the dance by him.'

'Mr Norman did say that he would telephone again.'

'Oh Lord!'

'What would you like me to say if he does?' asked James.

'That I am unavailable. That I have gone to the remotest part of Scotland, or Africa, or even Outer Mongolia, if you like. Unless you can think of somewhere more remote.'

'Very good, Miss Eleanor. Leave it to me,' said James, kindly. He had known Eleanor since she was a little girl and his relationship with her was almost paternal.

'Thank you, James, what would I do without you?' said Eleanor.

As she turned to go up to her office, James said: 'Mr Talbot asked me to give you these documents for checking so that they can be filed this afternoon.'

'Right-ho. I'll do them before I go to see Lady Carleton-West,' she said, taking the pile of papers from James.

After lunch, while Napoleon snoozed, Eleanor carefully checked the Court documents for Edwin and then, leaving Napoleon with Mrs Clayton, took the documents downstairs to James and left the office to go to Top Trees.

CHAPTER TWO

The weather was cold but fine so Eleanor had decided to walk to Top Trees. She had put on her hat and coat and added a scarf because Buxton was notoriously chilly at the tail end of the year. Although it was nestled in a valley, the town was a thousand feet above sea level and surrounded by even higher moorland peaks, which gathered snow in winter. The main part of the town had been built east of the river Wye with the lower, more recent part, strung along the river bank and the older part grouped on the rocky outcrops high above. To the west of the river, occupying land on either side of the Manchester Road, was an enclave of privilege physically and socially separated from the rest of the town. It contained large houses inhabited mainly by gentlemen of independent means, their families and their servants, although some of the properties provided accommodation to wealthy visitors during the season. The gentlemen belonged to a gentlemen's club, formed learned societies on subjects such as literature and archaeology, and attended concerts and performances at the Opera House and the Concert Hall, accompanied by their wives and their older children. Their wives held dinner parties, met for bridge, organised fund-raising events for their chosen charities, and arranged marriages for their daughters. They were the self-appointed arbiters of good taste and regarded it as their duty to monitor the tone and the guest list at all the major events in Buxton's social calendar. Some of them, being new to wealth, guarded their social position jealously and were inclined to be snobbish.

The unchallenged leader of this social set was Lady Caroline Carleton-West. Her husband, Sir Marmaduke Carleton-West, was the grandson of a Sheffield cutlery manufacturer who, during the Crimean War, had turned his factory to making armaments instead, thereby making his fortune and becoming a baronet. Lady Carleton-West was a large, solidly built woman, in her late fifties, of striking appearance and imposing bearing. She had cleverly mastered the art of dressing to suit her face and figure instead of slavishly following the fashion and knew exactly what to wear and how to appear to advantage. The combination of Sir Marmaduke's wealth and her forceful personality had guaranteed her position as the leader of the town's society. Whenever there was a problem to be solved or an event to be organised, Lady Carleton-West immediately formed a committee of ladies which, in theory, formulated a plan of action but, in reality, simply carried out Lady Carleton-West's wishes.

Eleanor was quite used to Lady Carleton-West's ways and not in the least intimidated by her. The Harriman family had once lived in The Park and had been part of its social hierarchy but the two eldest daughters, Amelia and Alice, had married and moved away from Buxton. Then, when the War came, it claimed, first of all, the only son, Edgar, then shortly afterwards, Cicely's husband, Wilfred, and finally Eleanor's fiancé, Alistair Danebridge. Not long after that, Mrs Harriman died, probably from grief at the loss of her son. The remaining three, Mr Harriman, Eleanor and Cicely decided to leave the family home and its memories and try to start afresh. Mr Harriman owned another property, Oxford House on Broad Walk, which he gave to Cicely so that she could support herself and her young son, Richard, by offering accommodation to visitors. Mr Harriman and Eleanor moved to Hall Bank to live above the offices of Harriman & Talbot, where they were fussed over by Mrs Clayton.

~O~

After a fifteen minute walk, Eleanor reached Top Trees, went up the steps to the front door and pressed the bell. The door was opened by Ash, the butler, Top Trees having lost its footman in the War.

'Good afternoon, Miss Harriman,' said Ash, smiling in welcome. 'Her ladyship is expecting you.'

'Good afternoon, Ash. I hope you are keeping well.'

'Yes, very well, thank you, Miss Harriman,' said Ash as he stepped back from the threshold to allow Eleanor to enter. Eleanor followed him across the large tiled entrance hall.

He opened the door to the morning room on the right of the hall and announced in his deep bass voice: 'Miss Harriman, m' lady.' Lady Carleton-West was sitting in a large armchair drawn up to one side of the fireplace, warmed by a glowing coal fire. She signalled to Ash to wait and then extended her hand regally towards Eleanor in greeting, saying: 'Good afternoon, Miss Harriman. Thank you for coming so promptly. Won't you sit down? I think you will find that chair comfortable.'

She indicated a much smaller chair on the other side of the fireplace. Eleanor smiled, said good afternoon, and sat down obediently. When Lady Carleton-West wanted support for one of her causes she always came straight to the point and saw no reason to delay matters by discussing the weather or engaging in small talk first.

'Now, Miss Harriman, I want to speak to you about an urgent matter which cannot be delayed. There appears to be a general disregard for the law amongst the shopkeepers in this town,' she said, forcefully. 'There have been instances of an unforgivable practice which, if not checked, can so easily spread and get out of hand. It must be stopped immediately. You were very clever at resolving that unpleasantness we had at the beginning of the season last year, so naturally I thought you would be just the person to deal with this current difficulty. It is imperative that we root out the offenders.'

Eleanor knew that "we" meant Eleanor Harriman. She was surprised at how indignant Lady Carleton-West sounded but she replied, calmly: 'Of course, Lady Carleton-West. Perhaps you could give me some details as to what you suspect.'

'I think it would be best if you speak to Mrs Kendall, my housekeeper. She can explain better than I can the deception being practised on this household. I gather that other households have been similarly affected. I have a committee meeting in a quarter of an hour, so when you have finished speaking to Mrs Kendall you can speak to some of the committee members as well. I have asked them to make enquiries and they will be able to give you further information. I think you should hear it directly from them.'

Eleanor was well acquainted with Lady Carleton-West's method of operation and, although she was slightly resentful of the way she was being ordered about, she decided that it was easier just to comply with these demands, for the moment at least. Besides, Eleanor was curious to know what unusual phenomenon was troubling the smooth and unruffled world of the society matrons, usually shielded from the workaday world by wealthy husbands. Lady Carleton-West looked across at Ash, who was waiting beside the door, and said:

'Ash, show Miss Harriman to Mrs Kendall's room. I want her to hear from Mrs Kendall the details of the offence which has been perpetrated upon us.'

'Yes, m' lady,' said Ash, his face an impassive mask, as he stepped aside to let Eleanor through the door.

Ash was accustomed to Lady Carleton-West's imperious manner and tendency to dramatize and he managed always to remain unflappable no matter what impending crisis was anticipated. Eleanor dutifully followed Ash as he crossed to the rear of the entrance hall, held open the door into the servants' quarters, and led her to the housekeeper's room. It was quite a large, very comfortably arranged room and had a cosy feel. Mrs Kendall welcomed Eleanor and directed her to a chair by the fire. A china tea service was set out ready on a small table. Mrs Kendall, somewhat hesitantly, offered Eleanor tea. She wasn't sure whether this was the correct thing to do as she did not know quite where to place Eleanor on the social scale.

When Eleanor had been a daughter of The Park, she had been expected to follow the usual path from debutante into matrimony and motherhood. In those circumstances, drinking tea with the servants would have been quite out of the question. Now, however, her social status had changed. She earned her own living instead of being kept by her father and that fact alone placed her lower on The Park's rigid social scale. The Park tried to distance itself from anything associated with trade.

The society matrons had held Eleanor's mother in high regard. She was an Honourable and had all the attributes and connections which they considered someone with a title should have. They were certain that, had she still been alive, Eleanor's mother would not have tolerated her daughter's eccentricities and social decline. Eleanor had become far more worldly wise than was considered appropriate for a young woman of her class. For her mother's sake, they continued to invite Eleanor to their social events, but worried about their daughters coming into contact with such a dangerously independent person. Some of them were slightly in awe of Eleanor because of her intelligence. Some pitied her, convinced that she was ruining her chances of marriage and that, by allowing her to become a solicitor, her father had condemned her to spinsterhood and the lonely life of a stateless, social refugee.

Eleanor cared little for the judgment of the ladies of The Park and found their endless round of social events extremely tedious. For her father's sake, she conformed as much as possible to the strict etiquette imposed by them but she did not allow herself to be constrained by it. She was doing a job that she loved and that was all that mattered as far as she was concerned, even though it did sometimes put her into the company of the sort of people she would not normally meet socially. Consequently, she was perfectly comfortable with Mrs Kendall and gratefully accepted the housekeeper's offer of tea. After they had chatted about the weather and the current issues in the town, Eleanor moved on to the topic of Lady Carleton-West's anxieties.

'Mrs Kendall, Lady Carleton-West referred to a general disregard for the law amongst the shopkeepers in the town. Can you please explain to me what she means?'

'Well, Miss Harriman, there's been a problem with the greengrocer.'

Eleanor tried not to smile. The enormous outrage perpetrated on Top Trees seemed to amount to the actions of just one shopkeeper.

'Just the greengrocer?' she asked.

'Yes,' confirmed Mrs Kendall. 'You see, we normally buy the fruit and vegetables for the household from Mr Dawson, the greengrocer and fruiterer in the High Street. Three weeks ago, Cook asked for five pounds of quinces and I placed the order with him. Cook was making quince paste so she had occasion to weigh the fruit herself to be sure to add the right amount of sugar. She found that she was four ounces short. She brought it to my attention and she said it had made her think back a bit to just before Christmas when she was making her usual batch of pickled pears. She had noticed that the pears weighed a few ounces short. She didn't mention it at the time because there wasn't much of a difference, not four ounces certainly, and she thought perhaps it was just a mistake. And she said that she wouldn't have recalled the incident at all if it hadn't been for the quinces. I thought it best to telephone Mr Dawson and let him know about the order being short and he was most apologetic. He assured me it wouldn't happen again and he sent another five pound of quinces immediately. And he didn't charge us for the first order either. But then, I happened to mention the quinces to the housekeeper at The Gables and she told me that she had ordered currants for redcurrant jelly from Mr Dawson and when they were delivered the order was slightly short.'

'And when would that have been, Mrs Kendall, do you know?'

'Oh, July time. That's when the red currants come in.'

'I'm sorry. I interrupted you with my question, please continue.'

'Well, Cook and I weren't sure what to do so we thought we would weigh everything as it was delivered. Last week, we found the Brussels sprouts were four ounces short, the same as the quinces. It seemed a bit of a coincidence to have both orders short by the same amount, so I thought it probably wasn't a mistake. I telephoned the housekeeper at The Gables to see what she thought and she told me that one of her orders was also short by four ounces that week but she hadn't yet spoken to Mr Dawson about it. I thought perhaps I had better mention it to her ladyship and when I did she said I was to go straight to Weights and Measures and report Mr Dawson. I have to admit I felt bad about it because we've used Mr Dawson's shop for years and there's never been any trouble before. And his fruit and vegetables are of very good quality.'

'So, let me just summarise,' said Eleanor, as she took out her notebook and pencil from her leather document case. 'There have been at least five instances: last December here, this July at The Gables, three weeks ago here, and last week both here and at The Gables.'

Mrs Kendall nodded and Eleanor jotted down the dates and details.

'And what about the other shopkeepers, the grocer or the butcher, for example. Have you had a similar problem with goods delivered by them? Or heard of anyone else having a problem?'

'Oh no, not so far,' said Mrs Kendall. 'When the ladies were here for their committee meeting last week for the Royal Visit, her ladyship did ask them to enquire if their housekeepers had had the same thing happen. I believe that they are expected to report this afternoon.'

There was no time for any further conversation with Mrs Kendall because Eleanor was summoned upstairs.

~O~

Immediately after taking Eleanor to the housekeeper's room, Ash had returned to duty at the front door for the arrival of the committee members. As Lady Carleton-West relied on the same pool of socially acceptable ladies for her various committees, Ash knew each of them by name but he was never entirely sure which committee he was greeting as he opened the door. When all the committee members had arrived, Lady Carleton-West rang for tea. The bell clanged loudly in the kitchen passage and the staff sprang to attention. Everything was ready and only the hot water had to be added to the pot. After the trays had been sent up, Ash came to retrieve Eleanor. She said good-bye to Mrs Kendall and followed Ash to the small drawing room where the committee meeting was being held.

'Ah, Miss Harriman, please sit here,' said Lady Carleton-West, indicating a chair. 'You know everyone here, I think.'

There was a murmur of welcome from the ladies. In The Park, they gained their identity and social status from their husband's standing and importance in the town, therefore, three members of the committee were sitting on one side of the fireplace in proper order, the highest ranking being closest to the fire. On the opposite side, Lady Carleton-West was sitting closest to the fire and a small table had been drawn up by Ash for the benefit of Mrs Hampson who was acting as secretary to the committee. She was sitting on Lady Carleton-West's left hand side, away from the fire. The chair to which Eleanor had been directed was between these two groups and furthest away from the fire. Eleanor found this very amusing. She also noted that the ladies had all been served with tea but she was offered none. Clearly, she was here to work, not to enjoy herself, but that suited her. She felt far more comfortable acting in her professional capacity, than she ever did in the presence of these ladies on social occasions. She sat down, took out her notebook, and waited. Lady Carleton-West sent the parlour maid away and took control of the gathering.

'Ladies, I have asked Miss Harriman to look into the question of dishonest shopkeepers. There seems to be a general practice of giving short weight when goods are sold; we need to make it clear that this is not acceptable. It must cease.'

The ladies responded in strict order of precedence. Mrs Grosvenor-Pike from The Gables confirmed what her housekeeper had already reported to Mrs Kendall and then asked:

'Is it a general practice? We do need to find out how many shopkeepers are involved, don't we?'

Mrs Wentworth-Streate added: 'Yes, are we able to identify them? My housekeeper tells me that she has not experienced any problems.'

Mrs Apthorp said: 'The housekeeper at the Hospital told me that she had telephoned Mr Dawson last week to complain of a short order. He had apologised and assured her that he would look into it.'

Mrs Hampson had no incidents to report. The ladies then exchanged their opinions as to the general standard of shopkeeping in the town. Eleanor listened patiently and resisted the temptation to draw doodles on her notepad.

'Well, Miss Harriman?' said Lady Carleton-West.

'It appears that the problem was first noticed last December. There were only isolated incidents but recently they have become more frequent. At the moment, the evidence points to only one shopkeeper. Therefore, I suggest that to begin with we concentrate our attention on Mr Dawson.'

There was silence while the ladies waited to see if Lady Carleton-West had anything to add.

'Well,' ventured Mrs Hampson, rather timidly, 'I did hear a rumour that Mr Dawson had been cautioned by the Inspector towards the end of last year but I don't know what it was about and it may only be a rumour.'

'Thank you, Mrs Hampson,' said Eleanor. 'I shall make enquiries about that. Lady Carleton-West, if you will give me a few days to look into this matter, I shall report back as soon as I can. In the meantime, perhaps your cooks or housekeepers could be asked to weigh the goods when they are delivered and let me know of any further discrepancies.'

The ladies all agreed that this was a very sensible idea. Lady Carleton-West thanked Eleanor for coming, and Ash appeared on cue to show her out. With relief, Eleanor left Top Trees and walked slowly back to the office, enjoying the fresh air and mulling over the information she now had.

CHAPTER THREE

On her way back to Hall Bank, Eleanor dawdled past the Devonshire Hospital where an extra wing was being added to provide a new kitchen and dining halls for patients and staff. The residents of Buxton were justly proud of the Hospital and the services it provided. They had sent a request to Buckingham Palace the previous year asking for a member of the Royal family to lay the foundation stone of the new wing. The Palace had announced that H.R.H. Princess Mary, the King's only daughter, had graciously agreed to accept the invitation but the visit had been delayed for so long that the building work had now reached first floor level. A foundation stone was out of the question so the town's officials had decided that a commemoration stone would be set in the wall instead, just below the sill of one of the first floor windows. Eleanor noticed that a large platform was being constructed at first floor level, so that the official party could reach the place where the commemoration stone was to be laid. The ceremony was less than two weeks away and there was an air of anticipation in the town.

The Devonshire Hospital was a very impressive building and, whenever Eleanor passed it, she stopped to admire its architecture. Of all of the town's many imposing buildings, she found this the most interesting and she was intrigued by its history and its mix of styles: decorated Imperial Victorian self-assurance, superimposed on perfectly proportioned, simple Georgian elegance. The Hospital was very unusual in that the original building had accommodated horses not patients. In the late eighteenth century, the current Duke of Devonshire's ancestor, the fifth Duke, needed to find an extra source of income to balance the vast sums being gambled away by his wife, the famous Duchess Georgiana. The Duke had wanted to make Buxton the northern rival of Bath, then at the height of its profitability as a spa town. The architect John Carr was commissioned to design luxurious accommodation for visitors and The Crescent was built at the source of the springs. A short distance away, a very large two-storied building, formed of four wings arranged in a square, provided stabling for one hundred and ten visitors' horses on the ground floor, and accommodation for grooms and other servants on the upper floor. In the centre of the square was a colonnaded ring, covering half an acre and open to the sky. Here, visitors could exercise themselves and their horses when the weather was not suitable for riding on the moors.

In 1859, the current Duke of Devonshire, by now the seventh Duke, had allowed half of the building to be transformed into a hospital for the treatment of the poor. Wards and treatment rooms were created on the top floor although some of the stables and the central open air ring remained. Twenty years later when the whole of the building had become a hospital, a local architect, Robert Rippon Duke, was commissioned to design a roof to cover the ring. The resulting dome, at 150 feet in diameter, was the largest unsupported dome in the world and just as stunning as its nearest rival, the Pantheon, in Rome.

Eleanor was certain that Princess Mary and her entourage would be impressed by the Hospital building. She hoped that they would be equally impressed by the work of the Hospital, which in many ways was as unique as its architecture. It carried on a practice which had been in existence in Buxton for centuries. The springs attracted visitors from as early as the Iron Age and were considered sacred by the Celts and the Romans. After the Norman Conquest, the healing effect of the water was attributed to St Anne and rich and poor alike came seeking a miraculous cure for their ailments. After Henry VIII's reformation of the church, St Anne's influence was replaced by a scientific explanation of the springs' power. Thus, instead of making offerings to the saint, visitors had to contribute to a fund, which paid for a doctor to treat poor bathers and provide them with accommodation. The sum payable, calculated according to a visitor's rank, ranged from twelve pence for a yeoman to fifty-one shillings for an archbishop, although it is not known how many archbishops actually visited Buxton. By the eighteenth century, this arrangement had been formalised as a trust, the Buxton Baths Charity, which fund was later used for the Hospital. The Hospital was now funded by public subscriptions from residents and visitors, and the collection taken each year when a special hospital sermon was preached in church.

The Devonshire Hospital specialised in hydrotherapy using water from both the warm spring and the cold spring. Treatment, often lasting several weeks, was offered completely free of charge to three hundred patients at a time, referred there by their local doctor. Priority was given to patients from the smoke-laden industrial towns to the north of Buxton who were suffering from illnesses caused by poor working or living conditions. A dedicated team of doctors and nurses had provided free treatment to tens of thousands of patients since the Hospital had opened. Then, during the War, the Hospital had treated hundreds of injured British, Canadian, and ANZAC soldiers and it was this work that the commemoration stone was intended to honour.

~O~

When she arrived back at Hall Bank, Eleanor noticed a large bunch of chrysanthemums on James' desk.

'Do you have an admirer, James?' asked Eleanor, teasing. 'May one ask her name?'

'They are for you, Miss Eleanor,' said James, solemnly. 'From Mr Norman.'

'Oh no!' said Eleanor.

'Yes,' said James, nodding gravely, 'I'm afraid so. Mr Norman did not telephone again as he said he would, but these were delivered about twenty minutes ago.'

'Goodness,' said Eleanor, 'they are magnificent, aren't they? I hope these aren't the ones he has been nurturing for the Chrysanthemum Society's Annual Show next month! I should feel very badly if he had squandered his prize blooms on me.'

'There is a note,' said James, handing her an envelope. Eleanor opened the envelope and read the note aloud: 'Hoping to see you at the tennis club dance.' She picked up the bunch of flowers and looked at them closely. 'They are very attractive and it was kind of him to send them but I don't really want to feel under any obligation to him.'

'A very determined young man if I may be permitted to say so.' James delivered his verdict with a frown.

'Sadly, yes,' said Eleanor. 'He is proving extraordinarily hard to discourage.' She sighed. 'I'll get Mrs Clayton to deal with these.'

Eleanor went back upstairs wondering how she was going to evade Mr Norman at the tennis club dance. Mr Norman was a surveyor and often referred clients to the firm so Eleanor knew that it was important not to alienate him. He was sometimes also retained by the firm on behalf of clients and this gave him the opportunity to call in to the Hall Bank office in the hope of meeting Eleanor. Eleanor did not find him at all attractive and tried to make it clear that his attention was unwanted but he seemed to be oblivious to her lack of response.

Napoleon welcomed Eleanor back and she handed over the flowers to Mrs Clayton, saying gloomily: 'Mr Norman.'

'Ah,' said Mrs Clayton, raising her eyebrows and tutting. She poured Eleanor a cup of tea and handed it to her without speaking. Then she reached down a vase from the dresser and took it to the sink to fill it with water, shaking her head as she did so.

Eleanor and Napoleon watched as Mrs Clayton began to strip the leaves from the lower part of the flower stems. She was always calm and steady in her movements but she was performing this task with unusual vigour and in silence. Eleanor thought she must dislike chrysanthemums and was about to ask her when Mrs Clayton, unable to contain herself any longer, inhaled deeply and then said:

'I know it's not my place to say so, Miss Harriman, but it's not right.'

'What's not right, Mrs Clayton?'

'Mr Norman,' she said, decisively.

Mrs Clayton put down her scissors and picked up some of the flowers she had just stripped. One by one, she put them into the vase and then stepped back to look at them gaining time while she plucked up courage to speak. Turning to Eleanor, she said: 'He's not the one for you.'

'Oh, I agree. Don't worry, Mrs Clayton, I have no intention of becoming involved with Mr Norman. You can speak freely, I assure you.'

Mrs Clayton looked relieved. 'Then I must say I am very glad to hear it. I know it's none of my business but, all the same, I don't mind telling you it's been bothering me.'

'So, you think it would be an entirely unsuitable match?' teased Eleanor.

'Definitely.'

'It's kind of you to be so concerned, Mrs Clayton, and I appreciate it but please be assured, there is no need to worry.'

Eleanor sipped her tea and then said: 'Do you know something about Mr Norman that I should be aware of? In fact, do you know anything about him at all?'

'Not very much. I know his mother's one of the Watching Brethren,' said Mrs Clayton, resuming the task of stripping the stems.

'You mean the strict religious sect that has the meeting house down on London Road?'

Mrs Clayton nodded. 'Yes, I don't know very much about them. I don't think anyone does. They keep themselves very much to themselves. I only know what Alf has told me. She's a widow and her two youngest died of diphtheria as children. Mr Norman's all she's got left now. He still lives at home.' Mrs Clayton paused while she put several more flowers into the vase. Then she added: 'She's very dour is Mrs Norman. Hardly gives you the time of day. It's a puzzle really when you think of the amount of time they spend at the meeting house reading the Bible and listening to preachers. Religion is supposed to bring people happiness, isn't it? But not theirs, seemingly. Alf jokes about it. Says their religion brings them little comfort and absolutely no joy. He does the burials for them sometimes, you see.'

'And is Mr Norman one of the Watching Brethren?'

'Huh, he's supposed to be and I used to see him going with his mother to the meeting house but she's often on her own now. Alf says it's because of the War. Mr Norman had to go, of course, and it took him away to places he shouldn't have been and he got to know the sort of people he shouldn't have been with. They're only supposed to go to the meeting house and nowhere else and there's lots of things they're not allowed to do. Dancing and drinking and that sort of thing and the men have to keep separate from the women, even in the meeting house. It's not like us, all the family together on a Sunday.' Mrs Clayton stepped back to look critically at the vase and then added more flowers.

27

'I see,' said Eleanor. 'Perhaps that explains why he always seems awkward in social situations. At the tennis club, he never really fits in. His manner is a little bit forced, as though he is trying too hard, if you know what I mean. I thought perhaps he came from a different social background but perhaps it's just that he feels uncomfortable being in contact with people who are not members of the sect. Also, he can be a bit too competitive sometimes, aggressive even, and rather erratic. I did wonder if perhaps he had suffered from shell shock.'

'Guilt more like,' pronounced Mrs Clayton, as she resumed stripping the leaves from the flower stems. 'I'd say he knows he shouldn't be there, playing tennis and enjoying himself. And then there's the Chrysanthemum Society as well. Sam Fidler says he's very competitive about winning the trophy, not that Sam Fidler can talk, mind, but I shouldn't think Mrs Norman would approve of that sort of thing. Time spent growing flowers is probably time best spent on the Bible. And being proud of winning? Puffing yourself up? I'm sure that's not allowed either. But I suppose now that Mr Norman's enjoying himself, he can't stop. He's seen the world outside and he likes it. That must make him feel guilty.'

'Yes,' said Eleanor, thoughtfully, 'I suppose if one is brought up with a very strict religion, one never really leaves it behind.'

'Oh, they won't let you leave! We had one of them at our church not long back, a young girl. She told them she wanted to leave and she came to stay with one of our neighbours. Hounded she was. Visits from the preacher, threats, anonymous letters. She finished up running away to Manchester. No doubt that's what'd happen to Mr Norman if he tried to leave.' With this dire prediction, Mrs Clayton put down her scissors and reorganised the flowers in the vase. As she did so, she considered the situation further. 'Of course, it's not my place to judge what sort of a person Mr Norman is but I've seen him here a few times and I've heard him talking to James. He always puts me in mind of someone who thinks he's been cheated. You know, awarded third prize in life when he thinks he should have been given first.'

Eleanor laughed. 'Yes, he does rather give that impression, I agree.' She thought of Mr Norman and then added: 'Do you know, I don't think I've ever heard him laugh. All he manages is a rather ingratiating smile.'

'You can't trust a man who never laughs,' said Mrs Clayton, sagely. She picked up her scissors and resumed stripping the chrysanthemum stems. Some of the leaves fell onto the floor. 'Now, just you leave those alone, Napoleon,' she said, as he began sniffing at them and nudging them with his nose. 'They're not for you.' She began cutting the flower stems.

Eleanor retrieved the leaves from the floor and put them back on the table. She said: 'Speaking of not trusting people, have you heard anyone complaining lately about being given short weight in the shops?'

Mrs Clayton thought for a minute, scissors poised in the air. 'No, I can't say as I have. Has someone made a complaint?'

'Yes, this afternoon I heard of several recent incidents where goods have been delivered several ounces short.'

'Well, there are some as I could mention in the past, resting their thumb on the scales while they're weighing, and that even after the rationing was brought in during the War, but that was only a little under, hardly enough for you to notice.'

'But what about now?'

Mrs Clayton put down the scissors and thought about this while she arranged the last of the flowers in the vase. 'No. I think if there was a problem, someone would have mentioned it to me by now.' She gave the flowers a final tweak.

'Well, thank you, Mrs Clayton. I had better be getting back to work.'

'Where do you want these putting?' said Mrs Clayton, holding up the finished vase of flowers.

'Certainly not in my office, thank you. Why don't you put them in father's office and he can enjoy them instead,' said Eleanor, laughing as she and Napoleon went back into her office.

CHAPTER FOUR

Frequently, as the office was closing, Eleanor, Edwin and Mr Harriman would gather in one of their offices and discuss issues which had arisen during the day so that they kept in touch with each other and with the firm's business. Whilst Eleanor had been at Top Trees, Mr Harriman had been at a creditors' meeting in Bakewell and when he returned, just after five o'clock, Eleanor and Napoleon were in Edwin's office. Napoleon, hearing Mr Harriman coming up the stairs, went to greet him.

'Ah, Harriman, you're back,' said Edwin. 'How was the meeting?'

'Carnage, I'm afraid. As soon as the meeting opened, the creditors were baying for blood. There was absolutely nothing I could offer them in order to save Pilkington-Thomas. His house will have to be sold.'

Mr Harriman pulled up a chair for himself and, turning to Eleanor, said: 'Pilkington-Thomas made some very ill-advised investments before the War which have now severely reduced his income. He has been living outside his means for some considerable time and, as a result of the death of his father last year, now has a substantial liability for Estate Duty as well. His future is in the hands of the trustee in bankruptcy and his creditors now.'

'Financial difficulty is an all too familiar theme at present, I'm afraid,' said Edwin, gloomily.

'I fear that you're right,' said Mr Harriman, 'and it is affecting all classes of people.'

'Whatever happened to the hope for the future that we celebrated at the end of the War?' said Eleanor.

'Far from becoming a reality at the moment, unfortunately,' said Mr Harriman.

'Well, Eleanor has something that will cheer you up. She was just about to tell me about her encounter with Lady Carleton-West,' said Edwin. 'And we have an ethical problem for you to solve.'

Napoleon, sensing that everyone was going to stay and talk, flopped down beside Eleanor and made himself comfortable. Eleanor gave Edwin and Mr Harriman a description of her visit to Top Trees.

'So,' concluded Eleanor, 'as far as I can gather there appears to be only one shopkeeper involved although Lady Carleton-West managed to give the impression that the whole town is in the grip of a criminal conspiracy.'

'I must say, Lady Carleton-West is good value as far as entertainment is concerned,' said Edwin, 'and the way she manages to manoeuvre everyone into doing her bidding is a lesson in management which a lot of our politicians could benefit from.'

'The way she bosses everyone about is quite disgraceful,' said Mr Harriman. 'I suppose, as usual, she expects us to investigate this for nothing,' he added indignantly.

Eleanor said: 'Lady Carleton-West did make it clear that I was being asked to do this work "for the benefit of the town" and there was certainly no suggestion that anyone would be paying for it. I don't mind spending some time making enquiries but can the firm afford that? What do you think?'

Mr Harriman said: 'This sounds as though it is a matter for the Weights and Measures people and if there really is a widespread problem in the town, surely the Inspector would know about it.'

'Well, Lady Carleton-West is thinking in terms of an epidemic spreading through the town,' said Eleanor, 'but, having established a few facts from the housekeeper at Top Trees, I suspect that the problem is actually confined to one shopkeeper. The only discrepancies detected so far are for goods delivered by Mr Dawson, the greengrocer in the High Street.'

'I see,' said Mr Harriman, 'and what is the ethical problem?'

'If I do undertake this enquiry without being retained by anyone,' said Eleanor, 'I wouldn't have the usual professional constraints or problems about conflicts of interest, would I? Which means I would be at liberty to approach whomever I thought could give me the information I need.'

'You mean,' said Mr Harriman, laughing, 'you would be free to interrogate anyone you want with impunity? People on both sides of the question, Mr Dawson, his customers, and the Inspector of Weights and Measures included.'

'Precisely,' said Eleanor, turning an innocent face to her father and smiling angelically.

'What do you think, Talbot?' asked Mr Harriman.

'When one has been ordered by Lady Carleton-West to sort things out "for the benefit of the town" I think one can justify pretty much anything,' joked Edwin. 'There are no rules governing that sort of thing as far as she is concerned. However, she does have a point. If Mr Dawson is guilty of offences against the Weights and Measures legislation, he shouldn't be allowed to get away with it. It should be dealt with.'

'Which is where the ethical problem becomes relevant,' said Eleanor. 'I can hardly go to Mr Dawson and persuade him to answer my questions and then take that information straight to the Inspector and have Mr Dawson charged with an offence, can I?'

Mr Harriman looked at his daughter and smiled. He said, affectionately: 'But now that you know there is a puzzle, you will not be happy until you have solved it, one way or another. I know you too well to think otherwise.'

Edwin sighed with mock resignation and said: 'I think we both know from experience, Harriman, that if there is something that Eleanor thinks should be investigated, there is no point in asking her not to do so.'

Eleanor pulled a face at Edwin. Mr Harriman laughed. 'I suppose that settles it then,' he said.

'Really, the only issue is whether or not we can find a way for Eleanor to get the information she needs without ruffling feathers. I know the Inspector well enough,' said Edwin. 'I could find out from him which way the land lies, if that will help.'

'Oh, yes, please, Edwin,' Eleanor said eagerly, 'that would be really helpful because it is possible that the Inspector already knows there is a problem and, if so, he might be just waiting to gather enough evidence before he acts. If I go charging in asking a lot of questions as Lady C wants me to, I could unwittingly upset the Inspector's whole strategy.'

'Yes, that's a very good point,' said Edwin. 'I'll have a word with him tomorrow and then we can decide how to proceed from there.'

Having agreed on a plan, the trio went back to their own offices to tidy up and put away their files before closing up for the day. As it was now time for his walk, Napoleon went downstairs and, after checking that there was nothing of interest in James' office, sat beside the front door and waited, just to make sure that Eleanor didn't forget.

~O~

The following day, as promised, Edwin called at the Town Hall. The Inspector of Weights and Measures was just getting ready to leave for the inspections he had to do that day. Edwin came back to the office and reported to Eleanor.

'Eleanor, it's just as well that you suggested a visit to the Inspector. I told him I had heard rumours about shopkeepers giving short weight and asked if he thought there is a general problem in the town. He assured me that, as far as he is aware, there is not. He said that he had received reports of isolated incidents and that he is currently dealing with the case in question.'

'That sounds as though he is investigating Mr Dawson, doesn't it?'

'Yes, it does but, of course, he didn't let on and I didn't get any further with him. I do have something more for you though. I went over to the Court and had a chat with the clerk and discovered that Mrs Hampson's information was correct. Mr Dawson was fined four months ago. The clerk remembered the case and got the file out for me. In July last year, Mr Dawson was served with a notice requiring him to attend at the Town Hall and present his weights for testing. He failed to attend and his explanation was that he did not receive the notice. That was not a defence, of course. The Inspector proved that the notice had been correctly served and Mr Dawson was fined. That notice must have been served for a good reason but there was no information about it on the Court file. However, there was a reference to the caution given to Mr Dawson last December. The Inspector had found that his scales were incorrect. I've made a note of the case for you.'

'Thank you, Edwin. There does seem to be something odd going on. This recent trouble does not fit with a previously good reputation. I think I need a bit more information and Mrs Clayton usually knows what is happening around town, so I shall begin with her.'

Before Eleanor had a chance to consult Mrs Clayton, Mr Harriman came into her office holding a letter.

'Sorry to interrupt, Talbot, but this letter has just been delivered from Chillingham & Baynard's bank. Sutton is in the process of organising a mortgagee sale but he thinks he may have to cancel it. He would like some advice as soon as possible. I have several clients to see today so I shan't get to it straightaway. I was wondering if Eleanor could make a start on it. Draft a letter perhaps and then we can discuss it later on.'

'By all means,' said Edwin.

'Certainly,' said Eleanor. 'I was just giving some thought to Mr Dawson's problem because Edwin got some interesting information this morning. We can discuss that later too.'

'Right you are,' said Mr Harriman and he went back down to his office.

Edwin left Eleanor to get on with the advice and she put aside consideration of Mr Dawson and turned to the letter from Mr Sutton. Chillingham & Baynard's bank was one of the firm's clients and Mr Sutton was the manager of the local branch. At least, thought Eleanor, this is work for the bank rather than for "the benefit of the town" so we shall be paid for doing it.

~O~

At four thirty that afternoon, Mr Harriman was free of clients and Eleanor took the Chillingham & Baynard file downstairs to his office to discuss her draft letter of advice to Mr Sutton. Napoleon followed her and settled down beside her chair, anticipating a long interval before there was any chance of a walk or food, the two things principally on his mind at that time of day.

'Right,' said Mr Harriman. 'What has Sutton got to say for himself?'

'Well, he's provided us with a summary of the facts and the action he has taken so far. He's not sure what to do next. It's a mortgagee sale for a farm.'

'Hmm,' said Mr Harriman, frowning, 'yet another farmer in debt. Where's the farm?'

'Mr Sutton doesn't say,' said Eleanor. 'He just says it is owned by two brothers, John and Frederick Hartshorn, but I get the impression that it is somewhere local. Mr Sutton says the farm was given as security for a loan six years ago. One of the brothers, that's Frederick, doesn't have anything to do with the farm. He lives somewhere else. The other brother, John, works on the farm and he makes all of the loan repayments. In March and June this year, two quarterly repayments were missed. So, when the September quarter's repayment was also missed, Mr Sutton sent a warning letter to both of the brothers saying that, if they didn't pay the debt by the first of October, the bank would exercise its rights as mortgagee and the farm would be put up for auction. Mr Sutton didn't receive a reply from either of the brothers so he began to make arrangements for the sale. Then, yesterday, he received this letter. It's from Frederick Hartshorn. I'll read you what he says.

Dear Sir,
Re the letter from you which I have now received. Please be advised that I know nothing about any loan from the bank and nothing about the farm. It is entirely the concern of my brother, John Hartshorn. I did not reply to your letter sooner because it has only just reached me having been sent to my old address at Harpur Hill and has only just been forwarded to me. You say you have a document signed by me in August 1916 but that cannot be correct. I have never signed any document for the Bank. Also, at that time, I was serving in France with the 1ST/6TH Battalion, Chesterfield Sherwood Foresters.

I remain,
    Your faithful servant,
        Frederick Hartshorn.'

'I see,' said Mr Harriman, 'and because of this letter, Sutton wants to know whether or not he can go ahead with the sale?'

'Yes,' said Eleanor.

'And what do you make of it all?' asked Mr Harriman.

Eleanor said: 'First of all, we shall need to establish whether or not the bank has a valid mortgage. Mr Sutton hasn't sent us the documents but he says in his letter that all of the mortgage documents were signed by both brothers. Of course, Frederick Hartshorn may not be telling the truth. It may be just a ruse to delay the bank proceeding with the sale but I am inclined to believe him. Surely he must realise that it would be very easy to check his military service record and establish his whereabouts on the date in question.'

'Has Sutton written to the military authorities?'

'Yes, but he is still waiting for a reply. I have drafted a letter to go to Mr Sutton, but I am not sure that he will be happy with the advice.'

'Clients rarely are when we tell them the truth about a bad situation which cannot be easily remedied,' said Mr Harriman, resigned by long experience to the unrealistic expectations of some clients. 'They always want us to come up with a miraculous solution even when the problem stems from their own poor decision or folly. Have you found a miraculous solution for the bank?'

'No, I'm afraid not. According to Mr Sutton, all of the documents are in order and the signatures have been properly witnessed. But the bank's rights as mortgagee will have to be clarified before it can consider selling the property.'

'Yes, I agree with you. Was Frederick's signature witnessed by Sutton?'

'No, Mr Sutton was on leave at the time. He says that John Hartshorn applied on behalf of both brothers for the loan and was interviewed by the relief manager. The loan was approved by him.'

'Hmmm. And yet, Frederick denies signing anything...' said Mr Harriman.

'... and if Frederick is telling the truth, who did sign the documents? Someone must be guilty of forgery, mustn't they?'

'And it is possible that someone is also guilty of fraud,' added Mr Harriman. 'John Hartshorn has not replied to Sutton's letters of demand?'

'No. I am wondering if John Hartshorn told the relief manager that Frederick knew about the loan and that he consented to the mortgage.'

'But why would the manager not insist on seeing Frederick as well, just to be sure. It would have been the prudent thing to do,' said Mr Harriman.

'I tried to imagine how it could have happened. If Frederick was away in France with the army as he claims, presumably John knew that. He must have realised that there would be a problem if Frederick wasn't able to sign the documents. Perhaps he made the appointment at the bank for both of them and then when he got there told the relief manager that Frederick had been ordered back to barracks on short notice and couldn't keep the appointment. Something like that. The War did create difficulties for people so a story like that might have been plausible.'

'Hmmm, it's possible, I suppose. A story like that would certainly have received a sympathetic response from the relief manager.'

'Knowing that Frederick was away fighting, the relief manager might have decided not to insist on adhering to the usual formalities,' suggested Eleanor.

Mr Harriman considered this proposition. Then he said, teasing his daughter: 'I must say, Eleanor, you do seem to find it easy to explain people's devious behaviour and think of ways in which they can evade the law. It is just as well that you are a solicitor and have an obligation to stay on the straight and narrow otherwise you could have become a successful criminal. I must watch out for you in future.'

Eleanor laughed. 'Well, devious or not, my suggestions still won't help Mr Sutton, will they? If the documents have been forged, the bank cannot rely on them.'

'Yes, you are right. I suppose Sutton has asked the relief manager for information.'

'No, he is no longer an employee of the bank and it seems no one knows where he is. And we don't know where Frederick is either so we can't ask him. Frederick didn't put his new address on the letter that I just read out. Apparently, before the War, he was working at the Hoffman Quarry but when Mr Sutton enquired there he was told that Hartshorn had left and they thought he was now a porter at the Midland Railway station. I suppose we could ask there.'

'I think we should wait for further instructions from Sutton first. Leave your draft letter with me and I will look over it and get James to send it out first thing tomorrow. I should think Sutton will want to proceed against John Hartshorn before he considers a sale of the farm.'

'And, if so, we will hand the file over to Edwin,' said Eleanor.

'Yes, but don't worry. I'm sure he will let you do his sleuthing for him,' added Mr Harriman, smiling. 'Won't you, Edwin?'

Edwin had appeared in the doorway wearing his overcoat and holding his hat. He looked questioningly at Mr Harriman.

'I just came to say good night. I'm off home. What will I do?'

'Let Eleanor do whatever she wants,' joked Mr Harriman. 'Goodnight, Talbot.'

'Don't I always?' mocked Edwin. 'Goodnight all.'

CHAPTER FIVE

Whilst the Harriman and Talbot families were enjoying a peaceful evening, there was a different atmosphere at the Town Hall where the monthly meeting of the Chrysanthemum Society was taking place. By now, Mrs Hazelwood had returned to The Elms. On discovering the theft of her Border Terrier puppies, she had gone straight to the police station to demand that they be recovered immediately. The desk sergeant had listened patiently, taken down details of the missing dogs, and promised to look into the matter. Fortunately for Mrs Hazelwood's peace of mind, he had not mentioned the rumours of dog fighting.

As well as being a member of the Kennel Club, Mrs Hazelwood was also a member of the Chrysanthemum Society, another club which catered for her interest in breeding things. This evening she had dressed with great care and put on her most flattering hat because she was confident that Mr Aubrey-Mere would also be at the meeting. He was her chosen target for matrimony and the reason for her visit to the Vitality Health Resort and Clinic. As he too was a breeder of dogs and a member of the Chrysanthemum Society, Mrs Hazelwood was confident that they had enough in common for a successful future together. Mr Aubrey-Mere, known to his friends as Mondo, did not live in The Park amongst the members of the wealthy establishment and intellectual elite. However, he was the younger son of a wealthy land-owning Yorkshire family and had been educated at the right public school and Oxford University, so the gentlemen of the town considered that he was "sound" and therefore reliable as a magistrate and the matrons found him trustworthy in the company of their daughters. He had charming manners and was attentive to the ladies. They all sighed and said: 'Isn't it a pity that he has not considered the advantages of matrimony.' A sentiment with which Mrs Hazelwood heartily agreed.

When Mrs Hazelwood arrived at the entrance to the meeting room, she greeted the Secretary at the door and then paused to survey the room.

'Ah, yes,' she said to herself, 'there he is. Three rows from the front with an empty seat beside him. Excellent!'

Just as she was about to make her way to the front of the hall, her path was blocked by two other members, the Misses Pymble. They were the elderly cousins of the vicar and had accompanied him to Buxton nearly thirty years ago, having been left homeless when their father, also a clergyman, died. They still dressed in the style of thirty years ago and had retained the same values and manners. They supported themselves by providing lodgings for visitors during the season and also for the various curates who came to the parish. They were good-hearted souls who knew everyone, were interested in everything, and were always involved in the latest fund-raising bazaar, fête, or good cause.

'Good evening, Mrs Hazelwood. We heard about your puppies.' said Miss Pymble, clasping Mrs Hazelwood's hand sympathetically.

'So dreadful for you,' added Miss Felicity Pymble, her twin sister and five minutes her junior.

'Good evening, Miss Pymble, Miss Felicity.'

'Have you had any news?' asked Miss Pymble.

'It's kind of you to enquire but no, unfortunately, there is no news,' answered Mrs Hazelwood politely, keeping an anxious eye on the empty seat beside Mr Aubrey-Mere.

'We've been asking everyone we know,' said Miss Pymble.

'But no-one has any information,' said Miss Felicity.

'Oh, thank you. That is good of you,' said Mrs Hazelwood, distractedly as she tried to edge past the two ladies. Fortunately, the arrival of another member attracted their attention and Mrs Hazelwood was released. She moved towards the empty seat as quickly as dignity would allow.

'Good evening, Mr Aubrey-Mere.'

'Mrs Hazelwood. Good evening,' said Mr Aubrey-Mere, standing up politely and bowing his head slightly.

'Is this seat taken?' asked Mrs Hazelwood, innocently.

'Not at all. Won't you sit down?' said Mr Aubrey-Mere.

'Oh, thank you,' said Mrs Hazelwood, eyelashes fluttering.

Instead of taking the offered chair, Mrs Hazelwood remained standing and, out of courtesy, Mr Aubrey-Mere was obliged to do the same. If Mr Aubrey-Mere had been allowed to resume his seat, Mrs Hazelwood would have lost control of the situation. Sitting beside her, Mr Aubrey-Mere would have been able to avoid eye-contact and remain silent, a luxury Mrs Hazelwood had no intention of permitting him. Instead, by remaining upright, she was able to look bewitchingly up at him, ensuring that he saw her to full advantage and forcing him to continue talking to her.

Reluctantly, Mr Aubrey-Mere began a conversation, saying: 'I was very sorry to hear about the theft of your dogs. Is there any news of them? I assume that you reported it to the police?'

'Oh, yes,' said Mrs Hazelwood, with a well-contrived sigh, 'but they have not been a great help. Do you think perhaps this is the work of some awful gang? Or is it just one person?' Mrs Hazelwood looked into his eyes and gave him one of her most coquettish looks which she hoped conveyed the message "helpless female looking for male counsel and support" and then added: 'I do hope your dogs are quite safe.'

Mr Aubrey-Mere bred and trained gun dogs. He replied:

'Yes, thank you. There's only Jasper with me at the moment.'

'Oh, and where are the others?'

'All of this year's litter have been sold and Gemma went off yesterday on loan to some friends in Hampshire who are just setting up as breeders.'

'Oh, how lovely to have contacts in Hampshire,' simpered Mrs Hazelwood. 'It is my favourite county. I went there to the seaside as a little girl and enjoyed it very much.' She rearranged her scarf and looked admiringly at Mr Aubrey-Mere. 'Oh, I should so love to see it again.'

Mr Aubrey-Mere was absolved from responding to this opening gambit because the chairman's commanding voice cut through the hubbub of voices.

'Ladies and gentlemen,' boomed Mr Wentworth-Streate. 'Shall we begin?'

Mrs Hazelwood now had no choice but to sit down. Mr Aubrey-Mere also sat down and stared straight ahead for the rest of the meeting.

'Good evening, ladies and gentlemen. Welcome,' continued the chairman. 'We have a lot of items to deal with this evening, in particular the Annual Show, the timing of which is well known to those of you who are aiming to bring plants into bloom exactly on cue.'

There was an enthusiastic murmur from the members. The Annual Show was the high point in the Society's calendar. For many of the members it was the culmination of a year's hard work and these final weeks were filled with anxiety. For months now, they had been in their greenhouses, propagating, potting on, feeding, pinching out, fussing over their plants and boring their families and neighbours with their fears and hopes. When not in their greenhouses, they had been ensconced in their armchairs poring over books of advice on how best to deal with the many problems encountered in preparing chrysanthemums for show. Now though, the time of reckoning was almost upon them. Competition was fierce and every entrant in the Show was looking forward to winning a prize.

Mr Wentworth-Streate called on the Honorary Treasurer to provide a report as to the funds now available for the Show. Mr Sutton, as manager of Chillingham & Baynard's Bank, had been the obvious choice for treasurer and had held that post for many years. He had also collected many trophies for his winning blooms and was hopeful of success again this year. He addressed the meeting in a clear, confident voice, listing the various trophies to be won, the value of the cash prizes being offered, and the names of the local businesses who had agreed to be sponsors. There were murmurs of approval as these names were read out. When Mr Sutton had finished, Mr Wentworth-Streate reviewed the arrangements for the Show and reminded the members of the rules for the different categories in the competition. Then he read out the names of the judges for each category. At this point, one of the members, a keen but not always successful competitor, stood up and interrupted, saying:

'Mr Chairman, I don't want to strike a negative note but I really must emphasise the importance of the judges being both knowledgeable and impartial. In my opinion, the judging last year did not demonstrate a thorough understanding of the correct method of presenting chrysanthemums. As a result some people's entries were marked down because of alleged faults which, in fact, they did not have. I commented on this at the time and, as you will no doubt recall, I wrote a letter of protest to the committee after last year's competition referring the committee to the National Rules.'

'Hear, hear,' said Mr Norman, very loudly, and then sank back in his chair surprised at his own vehemence.

Murmurs of either dissent or agreement mingled with calls of "sit down" and instead of addressing the chairman, members turned to their neighbours and expressed their views to each other. Mr Wentworth-Streate allowed the volume to reach a certain pitch and then called the meeting to order.

'Ladies and gentlemen, please! I do understand the point being made but the decision as to this year's judging is final. It cannot now be revised. The method of judging will be the same as last year and I can assure you that the judges are well aware of the rules. The rule as to the anonymity of the entries will be enforced and that will ensure impartiality. Now, shall we move on to the next item? The list of stewards for each day of the Show. Do we have any volunteers?'

The member who had objected to the judging sat down. Mr Norman glowered at the chairman, folding his arms aggressively across his chest. When the list of stewards had been settled, Mr Wentworth-Streate threw the meeting open. There was a flurry of questions and much animated discussion from the members wanting to clarify the arrangements. Mrs Hazelwood had not been paying attention to the business of the meeting because she was fully occupied in formulating her plan to get Mr Aubrey-Mere to walk her home. Eventually, Mr Wentworth-Streate declared the meeting closed. The members gathered up their belongings and shuffled towards the door. Knots of people formed, dissipated, and re-formed. Members heading home in the same direction grouped together.

Mrs Hazelwood had one last tactic for snaring Mr Aubrey-Mere. She stood up, walked to the end of the row and, before moving into the aisle, turned to face him. As he had been following behind her, he was now trapped between two rows of chairs.

'I wonder,' she said, 'if you would be kind enough to walk me home this evening.'

As she spoke, she realised that Mr Aubrey-Mere was not

listening. He was looking past her, one eyebrow raised, and she turned so that she could see who was standing behind her in the aisle.

'Oh, good evening, Mr Sutton,' she said to the treasurer. 'I didn't see you there.'

'Good evening, Mrs Hazelwood,' said Mr Sutton. 'Please excuse me,' he added as he moved past her, ignoring Mr Aubrey-Mere, and headed towards the exit.

'Oh, that man!' thought Mrs Hazelwood. 'It was very rude to cut Mr Aubrey-Mere like that.' Then she recalled herself to her quest and turned back to her quarry. Mr Aubrey-Mere was now looking at her and she resumed her campaign.

'I don't want to inconvenience you and I do feel very silly asking but the thought that there might be robbers or violent people about is most disturbing. After what has happened to my puppies, one cannot be too careful. Would you mind terribly if I asked you to walk me to my door? I should feel so much more confident with you. Surely, no-one would dare confront a magistrate.'

Mr Aubrey-Mere, whose house was several hundred yards in the opposite direction, sighed inwardly then gallantly agreed to see Mrs Hazelwood home. On the way there, Mrs Hazelwood did her best to be an engaging companion. She tried several topics of conversation, none of which led anywhere and, eventually, she was reduced to silence. Mr Aubrey-Mere was proving impervious to her charms and she was beginning to think that she would have to give the whole thing up. When they arrived at the gate of The Elms, Mr Aubrey-Mere bowed, lifting his hat courteously.

'Good night, Mrs Hazelwood,' he said firmly, making it clear that he did not intend their acquaintance to progress one inch further.

Mrs Hazelwood thanked him as prettily as her disappointment would allow and went up the path to her front door. Mr Aubrey-Mere waited politely until she had opened the door and then, relieved of his burden, strode out for home and freedom.

CHAPTER SIX

The theft of Mrs Hazelwood's puppies had been the first incident to disturb the usual tranquillity of the town. The second incident was The Cow Dung Affair which took place at Chillingham & Baynard's bank. At a quarter to ten every morning the head clerk, Mr Pidcock, arrived at the bank to open up and make sure that the staff were ready for the arrival of the manager and the customers. On Thursday morning, Mr Pidcock arrived as usual only to find something smeared over the front windows of the bank. He inspected it and concluded that the substance was cow dung. In addition, three words had been daubed on the side wall of the bank in lime wash:

ROBBERS   THEIVES DECEIVERs!!

An outraged Mr Pidcock telephoned to the police station immediately. After a constable had viewed the scene, made a note of the offending words and suppressed a smirk, the bank's most junior employee was sent out, armed with a bucket and mop, to cleanse the building. As most people in the town did not keep bankers' hours, there had been four hours between sunrise and ten o'clock during which a great many people had read the message and either laughed or expressed indignation depending on their politics, their social status, or the size of their overdraft. Some simply shook their heads and said: 'Well, whoever it was, he could at least have got the spelling right! What do they teach children in school these days?'

Mrs Clayton had already brought news of the incident to

Hall Bank, having met one of the post-men on her way to work. She reported the details to Eleanor and Mr Harriman as she served breakfast.

'It'll be that Sam Perceval again, I expect,' she said, as she poured Eleanor's tea. 'Same as last time. Remember how he daubed messages on the wall of the bank after his father died.'

'But that was some time ago if I remember rightly,' said Mr Harriman, 'although I seem to recall that the messages were similarly aggressive.'

'I don't think he's a bad lad really,' said Mrs Clayton. 'It's just that business with his father, I suppose. Sam was the one who found him when he'd hanged himself. It knocked Sam for six.' She poured Mr Harriman's tea. 'Or perhaps it's some other poor chap who's got on the wrong side of the bank.' She paused thoughtfully, the teapot poised in mid-air. 'Of course, it could always be Mr Aubrey-Mere, I suppose. Everyone knows there's no love lost between him and Mr Sutton at the bank. No-one would be surprised if those two came to blows again although what Mr Aubrey-Mere would want with putting up a message like that, I don't know.' With this analysis, she returned to the kitchen.

'I know Mr Aubrey-Mere and Mr Sutton don't get on but I can't believe Mrs Clayton's suggestion is right,' said Eleanor. 'I've never understood what their disagreement was about. Do you know what caused it?'

'Oh, it's an old story. Well before your time here in this office. It must be fifteen or sixteen years ago at least. No, probably more like twenty years actually.' He paused, lost in thoughts of the past.

'But what happened?'

'There was a dispute over a boundary and, as you have just witnessed, people in this town have long memories. It goes back to when Mr Sutton moved into the house next door to Mondo. Everything was fine at first. They seemed to be friends but then, after about two years or so, there was an argument about the common boundary between their two properties. I have no idea what started the argument or why it took so long for them to notice the position of the boundary. There wasn't even a wall or a fence between the two properties. There still isn't, only a row of shrubs and trees. But it became a very bitter feud.'

Mrs Clayton reappeared with the toast rack and, hearing Mr Harriman's last words, said: 'Mr Aubrey-Mere took Mr Sutton to Court. I remember my father telling me about it.'

'Yes,' said Mr Harriman, 'proceedings were commenced and, fortunately, they did not proceed. Given their respective positions in the town, a Court case would have damaged those two gentlemen professionally. Eventually a settlement was reached and there has been a truce ever since, neither one speaking to the other, but with occasional flare-ups. The vicar tried to intervene at one point but gave up. Even he couldn't sort things out. It's a shame really. They were good friends at first and they had a lot in common. They were often out on the moors together training the gun dogs that Mondo breeds.'

Mrs Clayton nodded in agreement. 'I've heard it said that Mr Sutton had a rare way with those dogs. Had them properly trained in no time, better than Mr Aubrey-Mere even.'

'And then, of course, there is the Chrysanthemum Society,' said Mr Harriman.

'Oh, yes,' said Mrs Clayton, 'at the Annual Show everyone expects that they will be contenders for the Mayor's Best in Show trophy. It's become a bit of a joke, really.'

'Yes, and years ago they were also rivals for the position of president of the Society. There was a lot of bitterness about the election but eventually they both withdrew and neither of them has ever been elected,' said Mr Harriman.

'Mr Sutton always seems a very affable, level-headed person,' said Eleanor. 'He never seems to get worked up about anything. And as for Mr Aubrey-Mere, he is such a gentleman, I can't imagine him involved in a bitter feud. I don't recall him ever mentioning it.'

'No. No-one ever does mention it now. They just accept the situation and don't bother to comment. At the club, the two of them just ignore each other,' said Mr Harriman.

Eleanor was intrigued by this insight into the lives of these two gentlemen. Mr Aubrey-Mere was a family friend and she and Mr Harriman were due to dine at his house the following evening. Eleanor made a mental note to try and glean more information about the feud. Eleanor could not imagine Mr Aubrey-Mere daubing the walls of the bank and she wondered about Sam Perceval, the other culprit Mrs Clayton had suggested.

For three generations, the Percevals had been saddlers and harness-makers but, with the arrival of the motor-car, the fourth generation had realised that demand for their products would soon decline. Therefore, the fourth Mr Perceval decided that his future lay in supplying petrol and providing repairs and spare parts for the increasing number of motorcars in the town. With a loan from Chillingham & Baynard's bank, he turned his premises into a motor garage. He also purchased a motor-car so as to provide a hire car service for people wanting transport to social events around town in the evenings. He opened his new business at the beginning of the season in May 1913. His judgment had proved to be sound and the business was showing great promise but, unfortunately for him, at the end of the season the following year, war was declared. The supply of petrol dried up and then, as the men left for the Front, the supply of motorists also dwindled. Eventually, the social occasions for which people required motor-cars all but ceased. Mr Perceval found it increasingly difficult to meet the loan repayments and, by the third year of the war, he was persistently in default.

Mr Sutton had been sympathetic and had given Mr Perceval as much lee-way as he could but eventually the unpaid loan attracted the attention of Chillingham & Baynard's head-office in London and Messrs Harriman & Talbot were instructed to commence proceedings. Edwin had taken as much time as he possibly could to prepare the Court documents but ultimately he had no choice and they had to be filed. The day after being served with the Court Summons, Mr Perceval had hanged himself. Eleanor could only guess at the effect his death had had on the Perceval family. She could understand why Sam Perceval had expressed his anger at the time by painting messages on the bank's wall. However, there seemed to be no reason why he should begin again. Eleanor wondered who else might now have cause to be angry with Mr Sutton and his bank.

~O~

When Eleanor had completed the tasks that needed to be done on her other files she turned her attention to the problem of Mr Dawson and Lady Carleton-West's demand for action. She decided to begin her enquiry by consulting James. He had lived in Buxton all his life and his knowledge of its affairs was extensive.

'James, how long has Mr Dawson been at his shop in the High Street, do you know?'

James considered the question. 'Well, let me see. The Deakin family owned the shop before he did. Mr Dawson started as their delivery boy and worked his way up from there. The Deakins moved to their new shop in Spring Gardens in…oh, it must be a good ten years ago now. Yes,…the old King died in 1910 and it was just before that. Mr Dawson was left in charge as manager and then he got a loan from Chillingham & Baynard's bank so that he could buy the business from the Deakins. I remember that because Mr Harriman acted for the bank.'

'Is he a steady, reliable sort of man, would you say?' asked Eleanor.

'Oh, yes. I would say so. He seems to be well-regarded.'

'Thanks, James.'

Eleanor went back upstairs to the kitchen where Mrs Clayton was getting the morning tea ready. Napoleon was sitting outside the kitchen door.

'Mrs Clayton, do you shop at the greengrocers in the High Street?'

'Mr Dawson? Yes, I do. And so does my sister-in-law.'

'And is Mr Dawson good at his trade, would you say?'

'Well, yes. His fruit and veg. are always fresh and he gives good value, if that's what you mean. He's reliable.'

'And you have never thought that perhaps you have been given short weight?'

'No, I don't think so. Sometimes he's not very obliging, a bit off-hand, and he blusters a bit,' said Mrs Clayton. 'But he's honest enough, I'll give him that.'

'How well do you know him? Can you tell me anything about him?'

'What sort of thing do you want to know, Miss Harriman?'

'Anything. Tell me about his family, his shop, who works there, that sort of thing.'

'Well, let's see. There's only Mr Dawson there now. Mrs Dawson died about…' Mrs Clayton paused, reviewing various family events in her mind and then continued: 'Oh, it must be five years ago now. He's got two boys, they've both left home, and two girls. One's married, she lives in Dove Holes. The other one used to serve in the shop but last year Mr Dawson sent her away.'

'And why was that?'

'He sent her out of harm's way. She went to work for Mrs

Dawson's brother, the pork butcher in Spring Gardens. Mr Dawson wasn't happy on account of young Perceval paying her too much attention. Smitten she was.'

'And which young Perceval is that?' asked Eleanor. 'The one who was paying too much attention to her, I mean.'

'Charlie, Sam's brother. He does the deliveries and helps out in the shop.'

'And they're the Perceval family who owned the motor garage on London Road?'

'Yes,' said Mrs Clayton. 'The Mr Perceval who killed himself because his business was taken by the bank. That would have been what? A year ago? No longer than that.'

'Yes, about July or August, wasn't it?'

'About then, yes. Charlie's the oldest. He worked for his father so he lost his job when the motor garage closed. That's when Mr Dawson took him on. The other boy, Sam, he worked with his father as well. He ran off to Sheffield after his father died and nobody's heard anything from him since, although someone did tell me recently that they thought he was back in Buxton, working on a farm out Brandside way.'

'When did Charlie become friends with Mr Dawson's daughter? Is it since his father died, I mean.'

'Oh,' said Mrs Clayton, 'I couldn't rightly say but it's been going on for some time. Mr Dawson didn't know about it at first. Sarah was meeting Charlie secretly and someone saw them. Mr Dawson got an anonymous letter and when he asked Sarah about it she had to own up.'

'And how old is Sarah?'

'She must be about eighteen or nineteen by now.'

'I see,' said Eleanor, 'so what is the situation between Sarah and young Perceval at present? Do you know?'

'She's forbidden to have anything to do with him but my sister-in-law thought she saw them together one Sunday not long back, walking in Grin Low Woods. She asked me if I thought she should mention it to Mr Dawson next time she was in the shop.'

'And did she?'

'Yes, and apparently Mr Dawson gave Charlie a piece of his mind and threatened to put Sarah into service and send her away from Buxton.'

'That's interesting. How long ago was that, do you remember?'

'Hmm, I'd say it would be about three weeks ago.'

'So obviously Mr Dawson's solutions have not had any effect on his daughter. Do you have any idea when Sarah went to work in her uncle's shop in Spring Gardens?'

'Oh, now. Let me see. When did I last see her in Dawson's? It would have been towards the end of last year, December probably, yes, because she definitely wasn't in her father's shop at Christmas.'

'Is she still working for her uncle?'

'No. She left there a while ago. A customer reported seeing Sarah with Charlie again and Mr Dawson packed Sarah off to live with her sister in Dove Holes to help with the children. Her sister had a new baby at the time, only a few weeks old.'

'How long ago would that have been, do you think?'

'It was the summer time. I'd say June? July perhaps? A good three months ago, anyhow.'

'I see. And did Mr Dawson employ someone else to replace Sarah in the shop?'

'Not permanent, like. His sister, Sam Fidler's wife, helps out at busy times, serving in the shop. I suppose he hopes Sarah will come to her senses and then she can come back to the shop and he won't need to employ someone else.'

'Well, thank you, Mrs Clayton. That has been most helpful.'

'The tea's ready. I'll bring it in to you when I've done Mr Harriman.'

'No, it's all right, Mrs Clayton. I'll take it with me now.'

Eleanor went back to her office followed by Napoleon

who flopped down beside her desk. She took out the notes she had made during the meeting at Top Trees. She added the information she had just gleaned from James and Mrs Clayton and then she sat and thought about Mr Dawson. He had been in business for many years and all the evidence she had so far suggested that he had never been in any kind of trouble before.

Eleanor said: 'Why would Mr Dawson suddenly begin to cheat his customers? What could have happened to cause him to do that?'

Napoleon raised his head and looked up at Eleanor as she spoke and then, not being interested in Mr Dawson's problem, flopped his head down again and contentedly resumed his snooze. Eleanor watched the steady rise and fall of his chest as she reflected on the general state of trade in the town. Although a few national companies had arrived in Buxton, most of the town's commerce was still carried on by independent traders, many of them family businesses established fifty or more years ago. Spring Gardens, The Quadrant, the Market Place, and the High Street were all lined with a huge variety of shops and, despite the adverse effects of the War and the financial difficulties of the three years since it had finished, there was still an air of determination and activity.

'No,' said Eleanor, firmly, 'this change in behaviour is not due to the state of trade. If Mr Dawson was in financial difficulty, giving short weight to his customers a few ounces at a time would certainly not solve his problems. Something else must have happened. But what?'

Eleanor was good at seeing patterns, even in a mass of detail, and often was able to identify the one vital piece of information which was out of keeping with the rest. That "out of place" fact often proved to be the key to a puzzling case. So, as always when confronted with a problem such as this, Eleanor got a sheet of paper and made a list, in chronological order, of all of the facts which she had gathered. When she had finished this chronology, she read through it again. Then, she sat looking out of the window while she considered the facts. She frowned, looked at the chronology again and, after a minute, nodded her head.

'Yes, Napoleon,' she said. 'This does make sense and I think I am right. Each time Mr Dawson makes a stand and forbids his daughter to see Charlie Perceval, he has trouble with his scales. Once might be a co-incidence, twice even, but I am sure that three times is not. The question now is, what do I do next? Will my theory be accepted or will I be branded an empty headed female interested only in romance?'

Napoleon did not respond. He had other things on his mind. It was getting close to the time for his walk, so he got up and stretched and went to the door of Eleanor's office. Eleanor took the hint and put on her hat and coat.

Chapter Seven

When James was closing up the office for the day, Eleanor pulled out the notes she had made regarding Mr Dawson and went into Edwin's office. Napoleon followed her and stood in the doorway looking in.

'Edwin, can we discuss the information I have gathered on Mr Dawson. Have you got time before you leave?'

'Yes, of course,' said Edwin. 'Bring your papers in.'

Napoleon, assuming that he was included in the invitation, went in and settled at Eleanor's feet.

'I must say I find it all a bit baffling,' said Edwin. 'Dawson doesn't seem to be the sort of chap to be on the wrong side of the law. I can't understand how he has got himself into trouble like this. What are your thoughts?'

'I've made a chronological list of the information we have so far and I think I can see a pattern.'

'Excellent,' said Edwin, always pleased when his star pupil showed initiative. 'Tell me what you think.'

Before Eleanor could begin, Napoleon got up and watched as Mr Harriman climbed the stairs. He was coming up to Edwin's office having seen off his last client for the day.

'Pull up a chair, Harriman. Eleanor's just about to tell me her ideas about Dawson, the greengrocer.'

'Ah, good. I'm curious to know what Lady Carleton-West has got us involved in,' said Mr Harriman as he settled himself on one of the spare chairs. Napoleon sat beside him resting his chin on Mr Harriman's knee, and they both looked at Eleanor expectantly.

'Where do you want me to start?' she asked.

Edwin smiled and said: 'Take the advice of the King of Hearts to Alice: Begin at the beginning and go on till you reach the end: then stop.'

Edwin sat back in his chair, folded his arms, and listened attentively. Mr Harriman looked on proudly.

'Well, Mrs Clayton seems to think Mr Dawson is honest and reliable. And I asked James what he thought and he says he has never known Mr Dawson to be in any trouble before and he's been in the business for a long time. James remembers Mr Dawson from when he was a delivery boy. Now, all of a sudden, since last December there have been several incidents, some of them quite serious, and all involving the inaccurate weighing of goods. So I asked myself, why? What is different? What has brought about that change? Something unusual must have happened.'

'And what answer did you come up with?' asked Edwin.

'A love triangle.'

Edwin's eyebrows shot up. 'Go on,' he said, smiling.

'The triangle involves Mr Dawson, his daughter Sarah, and a young man called Charlie Perceval. Apparently Sarah used to work in the shop with her father but Sarah is, to use Mrs Clayton's expression, smitten with Charlie Perceval. Mr Dawson doesn't approve of this Perceval fellow.'

'Is this the Percevals from the motor garage?' asked Mr Harriman.

'Yes, Charlie is Sam's older brother,' said Eleanor. 'Mr Dawson employed Charlie in his shop after Mr Perceval died. Now, I have noticed that the incidents in Mr Dawson's shop occur at the same time as events in the life of Sarah and her relationship with Charlie Perceval.'

'So you think that the timing of these incidents must be more than coincidence?' asked Edwin.

'Yes,' said Eleanor. 'According to Mrs Clayton, when Mr

Dawson found out about the relationship he sent Sarah to work in her uncle's shop in Spring Gardens, to get her out of Perceval's clutches. That was some time just before Christmas. Now, you will remember that the first incident, the caution mentioned by Mrs Hampson, occurred just before Christmas.'

'So in December, the only people working in the shop were Mr Dawson and Charlie Perceval,' said Edwin.

'And Mr Dawson's sister, Mrs Fidler. She came to work for Mr Dawson to replace Sarah but only when the shop is busy,' said Eleanor. 'So if we eliminate Mr Dawson and Mrs Fidler, that just leaves Charlie Perceval.'

'Is it safe to eliminate Mrs Fidler?' asked Mr Harriman.

'I think so,' said Eleanor. 'I accept that her presence in the shop is one of the things that has changed but, given that she is only there to help her brother out, there seems to be no motive for her to tamper with the scales. Whereas with Charlie Perceval, things are very different. Apparently, the strategy of sending Sarah to her uncle's shop didn't work so Mr Dawson sent her to stay with her sister in Dove Holes instead. Mrs Clayton thinks Sarah was sent away in June or July this year. In July, Mr Dawson was fined for not presenting his weights for checking at the Town Hall. The timing of this incident also seems to coincide with Sarah being sent away.'

'I think Eleanor might have a point here, Talbot. What do you think?' asked Mr Harriman.

'Yes, I see what Eleanor's getting at,' said Edwin. 'So what about the latest incidents?'

'My guess is that the relationship between Sarah and Charlie has continued and that they have been meeting up in secret. It is easy enough to get between Dove Holes and Buxton. Mrs Clayton's sister-in-law saw Sarah and Charlie up at Grin Low Woods recently and she mentioned it to Mr Dawson. That was three weeks ago. According to Mrs Clayton, when Mr Dawson found out, he gave Charlie Perceval the benefit of his opinion.

Three weeks ago, Top Trees received an order for quinces which was four ounces short. Then last week another order at Top Trees and one at The Gables was short four ounces. It seems curious that the shortfall is consistently four ounces rather than a random amount. I am wondering, therefore, if a false weight is being used.'

'Yes,' said Edwin, 'that's possible, I suppose.'

'I think that is perhaps another reason for eliminating Mr Dawson's sister. I suppose it would be possible for her to obtain a false weight but, again, it is hard to see a motive,' said Eleanor.

'I wonder where one gets a false weight from?' said Mr Harriman, puzzled.

'Some acquaintance in the pub, I should think,' said the more worldly-wise Edwin. 'Good work, Eleanor, I think your hypothesis is entirely credible and well done for spotting the pattern of coincidences. The question now, Harriman, is what do we do? Just report back to Lady Carleton-West and assure her that this is an isolated incident and not a general outbreak of crime? Or do we interfere and make further enquiries for the sake of Mr Dawson?'

'I suspect that I already know Eleanor's preference,' said Mr Harriman, smiling at his daughter.

'Well, if my theory is correct, I think it is a bit unfair for Mr Dawson to be penalised in this way,' said Eleanor.

'I'm inclined to agree but it is getting late,' said Mr Harriman, consulting his pocket watch. 'I'm due at the club and it's time you were getting home, Talbot. Let's discuss it again tomorrow morning, shall we?'

'Right, I'll be off then. Well done, Eleanor, goodnight. Goodnight, Harriman.'

Edwin went home to his family and Mr Harriman went off to his club where he had arranged to dine with a friend. James had closed up the office and gone home. Mrs Clayton, having left Eleanor's dinner ready for her, had done the same. Eleanor sat down contentedly in front of the fire with a book and Napoleon settled on the hearthrug with an old gym shoe that he was methodically taking apart.

~O~

Breaches of the Weights and Measures legislation, such as selling short, or possession of false weights, were very serious offences and attracted a heavy penalty. Every establishment where scales were used was visited at least once a year by an Inspector of Weights and Measures. Many of the shops in Buxton still had the old-fashioned mechanical scales, which used weights stacked into a pyramid and depended solely on balance. A dishonest shopkeeper could tamper with the balance mechanism so that the scales "weighed light" and the customer would pay for more than he received. The weights used on these scales were verified when they were manufactured and stamped to certify that the weight was correct. Every Inspector of Weights and Measures had a set of certified weights against which to test the shopkeeper's weights. A shopkeeper caught in possession of weights which did not match the Inspector's or which had not been stamped, could be prosecuted and the penalty would be a fine or even imprisonment.

The following morning, Edwin came into Eleanor's office and said: 'Well, Eleanor, it looks as though we might get paid for investigating this business about short weight after all. Mr Dawson has been charged on two counts: possession of a false weight and possession of an unstamped weight. He's just telephoned to ask if we would act for him.'

'Oh dear!' said Eleanor.

'I'm afraid,' said Edwin, 'Mr Dawson might be facing a prison sentence rather than a fine this time, so he needs our help. He'll be in for a conference first thing on Monday.'

'If we are now instructed by Mr Dawson, what about Lady Carleton-West? What shall I tell her?'

'I don't think we need to worry about that for the moment,' said Edwin. 'We are satisfied, aren't we, that this problem is confined to Mr Dawson and is not the general outbreak of lawlessness imagined by Lady C?'

'Yes, and if my theory is right it doesn't seem to be Mr Dawson's fault either. If that is the case, I should like us to be able to resolve this issue for him.'

'In any event, Lady C has not formally retained us to act for her so I see no reason why we should not act for Mr Dawson.'

'Good,' said Eleanor.

At that moment, Mr Dawson and the weight of his fruit and vegetables was the last thing on Lady Carleton-West's mind. She was fully occupied with a far more important matter.

CHAPTER EIGHT

The planning and anticipation surrounding the visit of Princess Mary for the dedication and laying of the commemoration stone at the Devonshire Hospital had been going on for many months. As soon as the request had been made to Buckingham Palace, an official committee of civic leaders and the town's most prominent business men had been formed. The committee meetings sometimes became very heated because, naturally, everyone had a different view as to the parts of the town which the Princess should be invited to visit, and what entertainment should be provided for her. However, a great deal of this energy had been expended in vain because, ultimately, most of the committee's suggestions had been vetoed by the Palace officials. From a programme full enough to occupy a whole day or more, the Palace had chosen only four venues and had limited the visit to a mere two hours, to be conducted according to a strict timetable.

The Royal Visit was always referred to at Top Trees in reverential tones and capital letters. Inevitably, Lady Carleton-West had formed her own committee for the purpose of scrutinising the official arrangements. She had also adopted a proprietorial air regarding the Princess. A distant cousin of her husband's grandfather had once, very briefly, been considered for appointment as one of Queen Victoria's household staff and, although the appointment was never made, this amounted to a "connection" with the Royal family as far as Lady Carleton-West was concerned and endowed her with the authority to judge what was appropriate. She was convinced that no arrangements could safely be made without the advice and support of her committee, in other words, Lady Carleton-West herself.

The much anticipated Royal Visit was now imminent. A number of the ladies of The Park were privately practising their curtsey, just in case they came within sighting distance of The Royal Person. This afternoon at Top Trees, Lady Carleton-West and the members of The Royal Visit committee were meeting for the last time. There were now only two subjects left for discussion and interference. Mrs Hampson, acting as secretary as usual, reminded the meeting of the first topic which was the afternoon tea to be provided for the guests at the Devonshire Hospital. Mrs Apthorp, the wife of one of the doctors at the Hospital, had been asked by the official committee to make suitable arrangements and she had been quietly doing so for some time. However, Lady Carleton-West did not consider Mrs Apthorp equal to the task and had now turned her attention to this subject. Mrs Apthorp was due to provide a report to the meeting.

'Now, Mrs Apthorp,' said Lady Carleton-West, 'the arrangements for refreshments at the Hospital. I need hardly stress how very important this occasion is for the town. There must be no room for criticism, no possible suggestion that this town is not capable of entertaining Royalty. The tea must be organised to the very highest standard.'

Before the meeting, Mrs Apthorp had not been at all daunted by the task which the official committee had assigned her. Now, she felt her self-confidence ebbing away completely. She said nothing.

Lady Carleton-West continued: 'I know that you will need all the help you can get and I shall certainly do my best to see that you get it.' She paused.

Mrs Apthorp, well-trained after many such meetings, knew that this was her cue to express gratitude and she said meekly:

'Thank you Lady Carleton-West. I knew I could rely on you.'

'How many people are to be catered for?' asked Lady Carleton-West. 'Apart from the Royal Party, that is. How many people will be at the Hospital?'

Mrs Apthorp had been temporarily reduced to silence and Miss Pymble said: 'I believe that there will be about a thousand people there.'

'Yes,' joined in Miss Felicity. 'Four hundred subscribers have already applied for tickets to the galleries. Isn't that marvellous!'

'And all of the patients are going to occupy the floor area under the dome,' added Miss Pymble, 'and they will see the Princess which will be so beneficial for them.'

'That's at least another three hundred people,' said Miss Felicity.

'And some of the nurses will be with them, of course,' added Mrs Frampton.

'Well, you can't possibly cater for a thousand people,' stated Lady Carleton-West. 'Some people will have to be left out. The patients can be given their tea by the nurses and the nurses can look after themselves. We need not trouble about them,' she said, dismissively. She looked at Mrs Apthorp and asked: 'How many official guests?'

'Two hundred,' said Mrs Apthorp, meekly.

'So, that makes about six hundred altogether. Then it is obvious that for such a large number it will be necessary to engage caterers...' Mrs Apthorp leaned forward nervously, trying to find the courage to speak. Lady Carleton-West charged on: '...and the only caterers that I could confidently recommend will be...'

Mrs Wentworth-Streate took a deep breath and interrupted. 'If I may, Lady Carleton-West, I should like to remind the meeting that the King has expressly asked that no public money be spent on this occasion. He is very mindful of the difficult financial situation that the whole country is in. Unless the catering is paid for by private citizens that would surely be going against His Majesty's wishes.'

There was an audible intake of breath among those present, surprised at the courage shown by Mrs Wentworth-Streate in disagreeing with their leader. Mrs Apthorp sank gratefully back in her chair and waited. Fortunately, the mention of the King had the desired effect on Lady Carleton-West. She relinquished her look of indignation and outrage at this opposition to her ideas and transformed her features into a suitable look of Respect for the Wishes of His Majesty.

'Yes, you are quite right, Mrs Wentworth-Streate.'

The committee members breathed again.

Mrs Wentworth-Streate continued: 'Also, from what Mr Wentworth-Streate has told me, I understand that Her Royal Highness and her party do not intend to stay for refreshments, so it is only the officials and possibly the subscribers who will need to be catered for.'

Mrs Apthorp nodded vigorously but remained silent. Lady Carleton-West realised that she was at a disadvantage. Sir Marmaduke did not involve himself in the affairs of the town, being interested only in hunting, shooting on the moors, fishing, or, when the weather was inclement, snoozing in front of the fire either at home or at his club. He was not a source into which Lady Carleton-West could tap for information about the town's affairs. Mr Wentworth-Streate on the other hand was on the official committee and, being fond of his wife, shared his knowledge of the arrangements with her. In any event, if the Princess was not to be included in the refreshments, the subject no longer held any interest for Lady Carleton-West.

'Ah,' said Lady Carleton-West, decisively taking back control, 'in that case I think we should move on to the other item for discussion. The bouquets.'

It was inevitable that a bouquet of flowers would be presented to Princess Mary at each venue. It was also inevitable that there would be disagreement as to who should make that presentation.

'A woman clearly has a better understanding than a man as to the appropriate person for this role,' said Lady Carleton-West. 'The official committee, as it is made up of men, is very likely to choose purely on appearance, whereas a woman's choice would be based on the overall quality of the person, her manners and demeanour as well as her appearance.' She paused to allow time for a general murmur of assent. 'For the sake of the town's reputation, it is our duty to see that the correct person is chosen, so let us consider those eligible.'

'I think,' interrupted Mrs Apthorp timidly, 'that for the presentation of the bouquet at the Hospital the town committee has suggested the daughter of Mr Harrison, the Hospital's superintendent.'

'On what grounds?' demanded Lady Carleton-West, directing a cold stare at Mrs Apthorp as though this irresponsible decision had been hers and hers alone.

Mrs Hampson joined the fray and came to the rescue: 'Mr Hampson mentioned to me that the general feeling of the official committee was that it should be someone connected with the Hospital.'

'Fiddlesticks,' said Lady Carleton-West. 'It should be someone with the right breeding, and the necessary level of poise and sophistication to carry it off confidently. Someone who has been properly finished and is not likely to be overawed by meeting Royalty.' These were all qualities which Lady Carleton-West detected in herself. However, she accepted that the task should be performed by a much younger person and, therefore, had not put herself forward. She continued: 'Everything connected with the Royal Visit must be perfect. The national press will be there. It is vital that we create the right impression. I am sure I have your support on that. Now, what name should we propose?'

There was a general stirring amongst the ladies, feet were shuffled, hands re-arranged on laps, while gazes remained firmly fixed on the floor. Then Mrs Wentworth-Streate bravely mentioned a name which, she hastened to add, was merely a suggestion for the purpose of opening the discussion. The ladies debated, in turn, the merits of each of the eligible daughters of The Park. Expertly guided by Lady Carleton-West, they naturally came to the conclusion that there was only one person who had all the required qualities and she was, of course, Lady Carleton-West's youngest daughter. The meeting closed with the unanimous resolution that Lady Carleton-West should write to the official committee and advise them that her daughter was willing to undertake this duty.

~O~

Lady Carleton-West was not the only person occupied with planning. Mrs Hazelwood was also engaged in the same activity. On Friday morning, it was cold and windy and beginning to rain. As she opened the door of No. 6 Spring Gardens, Mrs Hazelwood was greeted with the comforting aroma of Collinson's freshly ground coffee and the tempting sight of pastries and cream cakes. The café was a haven of comfort and elegance and, pushing aside thoughts of Dr Edgecombe's regime, she planned to spend a pleasant half hour indulging in these delights while she considered the problem of Mr Aubrey-Mere. A very capable waitress, dressed in a crisp, starched apron and cap, and with manners to match, came to take her order and then Mrs Hazelwood was free to think.

While she sipped her coffee, Mrs Hazelwood considered her progress. She had to admit that since the Chrysanthemum Society meeting, there had actually been no progress at all. Time was passing and she could not wait forever, even for Mr

Aubrey-Mere. She came to the conclusion that one final assault should be attempted and, if that failed, she should withdraw from the chase and choose another quarry. She realised that lack of opportunity was her main enemy. Mr Aubrey-Mere did not come within her normal social sphere. That was partly what made him attractive as a matrimonial prospect but it also meant that there was no opportunity for her to meet him socially. He was part of that exclusive circle of people who dined at houses in The Park but Mrs Hazelwood was not. He divided his time between sitting on the Bench as a magistrate, presiding at the gentlemen's Literary Society meetings, relaxing at his club, reading in his study, pottering in his greenhouse with his chrysanthemums, and training his dogs out on the moors. All of these activities took place either in his own home or in the masculine world from which Mrs Hazelwood was barred. The Chrysanthemum Society meetings were the only occasions on which their paths crossed and it would be another two months before the next meeting because of the Annual Show.

It seemed to Mrs Hazelwood that the only viable option would be to contrive a "chance" meeting, preferably more than one, but to engineer that she would almost have to stalk the magistrate which seemed rather ludicrous. Then, as she finished her cream cake, it occurred to her that she could station herself in the road where he lived and be "just passing by" as he left his house or when he was returning home. To make that look like the most natural thing in the world, all she needed to do was change the usual route she took when walking her dogs and, instead of going into the Gardens, walk along Burlington Road where Mr Aubrey-Mere lived. Predicting the most effective times for carrying out this plan would not be too difficult and, as she had several dogs in need of exercise, she realised that if she took them out in relays, two at a time, she would have several reasons to be in Burlington Road at different times of the day. Satisfied with her plan, she paid her bill and went out into Spring Gardens, eager to begin. However, a new hat was essential to the success of her scheme so, putting up her umbrella, she headed to Madame Esme's, her favourite milliner's shop.

~O~

Mr Aubrey-Mere lived at Brook House, which was the right-hand half of a semi-detached pair. Thornstead, the left-hand half of the pair, was occupied by Mr Sutton. Brook House and Thornstead had been designed in the last years of the nineteenth century by a local architect who had abandoned the customary Buxton design, a rectangular building with bay windows on either side of a central door, and ventured instead into an eclectic mix of the newer asymmetrical Arts and Crafts style to which he had added Queen Anne style Dutch gabling and a touch of Scots baronial for good measure. The entrance porch was located over to one side and the front façade was broken up into a series of protrusions designed to bring the house into closer contact with the garden in accordance with the newest fashion. However, as the houses were built entirely of stone and each half was the mirror image of the other, they still managed to look solidly Victorian.

Brook House had a branch of the Wye river running along its western boundary and this formed a major feature of its garden. In the summer, an abundance of plants rambled along the edge of the garden in a profusion of colour and tumbled down the bank towards the river. From the summer house on the bank, guests could enjoy watching sparkling, clear water rushing past and bubbling over the stony river bed, with ducks splashing about in the shallows under dappled shade. Now though, in late October, the energy of the flowering plants was spent, leaving only sparse clumps of dried stalks and spiky seed-heads as food for the birds. The focal point of the garden had moved upwards to the colourful trees: beech, chestnut, and ash trees formed a backdrop of red, brown, and golden-yellow, which was doubled by the reflection of the leaves in the river.

~O~

Mr Aubrey-Mere, known as Mondo to his friends, was one of those people who, when they enter a room, manage to capture everyone's attention. Although not physically large, he seemed able to take up more space than the people around him. He was a stylish gentleman who dressed elegantly and with care. His clothes were well-tailored and fitted his lean figure perfectly. He was usually formally dressed in a suit and waist-coat, his shirt immaculately pressed and his collar well-starched. The only time he ever wore anything as casual as a jumper was on the golf-course, and he never appeared in shirt-sleeves, even in his own garden. When, as a magistrate, he sat on the Bench, his waist-coat was as sombre as his suit but when he was not on duty he wore extravagant waistcoats made of expensive coloured silk, patterned or embroidered, elegant or flamboyant, depending on the occasion. His silk ties, held with a gold tie pin, were of such variety that no-one could remember him wearing the same one twice. His hair was trimmed every fortnight by the barber and firmly controlled with a daily application of Blue Pomade Hair Wax, supplied from Jermyn Street in London.

Everything about Mondo and his house was measured and meticulous and yet the atmosphere was welcoming and relaxed. His house was filled with exquisite hand-made furniture, valuable pieces of porcelain, and original works of art but it did not have that cluttered appearance which many collectors have to contend with. Each piece had been carefully placed and given the space it needed to be properly appreciated. Mondo was a generous host and had a great sense of humour. He lived a contented, and it must be admitted, somewhat selfish, bachelor life without any of the distractions and disturbances that a family brings. For over twenty years he had been looked after by Mr and Mrs Rowland, a husband and wife team who, between them, covered the duties of valet, butler, chauffeur, house-keeper and cook. This left him free to spend a great deal of time reading, walking on the moors with his dogs, propagating his prize winning chrysanthemums, and pottering about in the garden at Brook House.

CHAPTER NINE

It was still raining that evening as Eleanor and Mr Harriman walked the short distance from Hall Bank to Burlington Road where they were dining with Mr Aubrey-Mere. They were often invited to Brook House and enjoyed evenings of lively conversation and witty repartee which, not infrequently, turned into an animated discussion on some moot point of law. Dr McKenzie, one of the local general practitioners, was a frequent guest at Brook House as was Philip Danebridge. He was the cousin of Eleanor's fiancé, Alistair, who had been killed in France. When Eleanor and Mr Harriman arrived, Dr McKenzie's motor-car was parked in the driveway of Brook House and just as they were walking through the entrance gates, Philip arrived in his Bentley. They waited for him and walked to the front door together.

The front door was opened by Rowland. Eleanor, Mr Harriman and Philip were expertly relieved of hats, overcoats, umbrellas and, in Philip's case, driving coat and gauntlets and shepherded towards the sitting room. Eleanor noticed Dr McKenzie's medical bag in the hall and concluded that he was on call that evening. In the sitting room, they were welcomed with a pre-dinner glass of sherry and a well-stoked coal fire. Dr McKenzie shook hands all round. Jasper, the black retriever, was sprawled in front of the fire and he sat up and wagged his tail in greeting as Eleanor bent down and stroked him.

Mr Harriman, fully aware of Mondo's current preoccupation, began by enquiring:

'How are those prize blooms of yours getting on, Mondo,

are they going to be ready in time for the Annual Show? Competition will be fierce this year. Mr Norman was telling me yesterday that he is expecting to carry off the trophy for the Cut Blooms category and he also has his eye on the Mayor's Best in Show trophy.'

Fortunately for the guests it was now too dark for the magistrate to propose a tour of the large greenhouse at the far end of his garden. He had to be content with describing the finer points of the various specimens on which his hopes were pinned. This took some time because he had entries in several classes. He expressed his hopes for the competition and spoke disparagingly of the current efforts of the previous year's prize winners.

'But what about last year's winner, Mondo?' said Dr McKenzie. 'Sutton with his Russet Sunset. Now, that was a magnificent effort, even you must admit that. I gather he has several entries in preparation this year.'

'Bah! I'm not afraid of the competition. In fact, I have a spy who visited at Thornstead yesterday and he informed me that Sutton's blooms are not as far on as mine. In fact, Sutton is concerned that they will not reach their peak in time for the show, particularly the one called Autumn's Peak which, given its name and the season, is a little ironic, don't you think.'

'Sutton has had other things to worry about lately,' said Mr Harriman. 'I imagine the incident of the cow dung on the bank's windows has distracted him. And it is not the first time either. Someone has clearly got it in for the bank.'

'Or the bank manager,' said Dr McKenzie.

'Yes,' said Mondo, darkly. 'It is very worrying. I gather that the police have not been able to identify a culprit so far. They are doing their best but, for them, it is not really an urgent matter. Sutton has decided to do some surveillance himself. He is down at the bank at the moment, as a matter of fact.'

'I doubt whether anyone will be interested in writing messages on walls in this weather,' said Philip.

'You are probably right but, you see, the committee organising Princess Mary's visit is worried that messages might appear on the day of her visit,' said Mondo. 'Sutton's on the committee, you know.'

'But Mr Sutton's bank is not on the route that the Princess will be taking,' said Eleanor.

'That's true,' said Mondo 'but until the committee knows who is responsible for this damage, they cannot be sure that Sutton's bank will be the only target. It took several hours to clean the windows and the walls and the committee doesn't want to take any risks. It is hoped that surveillance now will discourage the culprits from attempting anything further, particularly on the day of the visit.'

'Well,' added Mr Harriman, 'I expect Philip is right about the weather being a deterrent tonight. Sutton will probably just get a thorough wetting for nothing.'

Mondo laughed and Eleanor thought about the feud between him and Mr Sutton and she wondered idly how Mondo knew so much about his neighbour's activities. She supposed it was always important to be aware of one's enemy.

'Now, Philip, before we go in to dinner,' said Mondo, 'I would very much value your opinion on this piece of china being offered for sale, if you don't mind.' He handed Philip an auction catalogue. 'It's listed here for sale next week in Derby. What do you think?'

For the next few minutes, the two enthusiasts discussed the merits of the potential purchase and the other guests, cosily installed in front of the fire, discussed the weather. They thought of Mr Sutton and his lonely vigil in the rain and, although they sympathised with him, they agreed that the current rain was very welcome after the exceptionally dry summer they had just experienced. That led to comparisons with the weather in previous summers and Eleanor, Mr Harriman, and Dr McKenzie were still engaged on this topic of conversation when Rowland announced dinner. With no dependant wife and children, Mondo Aubrey-Mere was in a better position than most to maintain the pre-War standard of dining. Rowland and Mrs Rowland served an excellent dinner and throughout the various courses the guests engaged in lively general conversation and some good-natured teasing, which Rowland and Mrs Rowland pretended not to hear but, nevertheless, found entertaining.

~O~

After dinner, Mondo Aubrey-Mere and his guests returned to the sitting room and, in the absence of the staff, could give their views on more confidential and controversial topics. They began with the state of the economy.

'It certainly isn't easy for some people at the moment,' said Mr Harriman, 'and I do not see things improving in the immediate future.'

'We are all still suffering from the effects of the War,' agreed Philip, 'especially the farmers, and the drought this summer has just added to their burden.'

'Nevertheless,' said Eleanor, 'there is no doubt that, for them, the worst damage has been done by the government. The farmers have completely lost confidence in Westminster, and I think they are right to consider this last piece of legislation as The Great Betrayal.'

'Eleanor!' teased Mondo. 'You'll be joining the Bolsheviks next!'

Eleanor smiled, unconcerned. Philip said to her, jokingly: 'Ah, observe, Eleanor. A typical Establishment reaction.' Then, turning to Mondo, he said with mock severity, 'You, sir, have no proper answer to the problem so you fall back instead on the old "fear of the revolution" bogey. That is typical of the conservative classes.'

'In any event, I don't think one needs to be a Bolshevik to see that the farmers are right,' said Eleanor, firmly. 'Last year, in order to guarantee that farmers could cover their costs of production, the government fixed prices for farm produce for a specified period. The farmers were entitled to expect that those prices would remain fixed for the whole period. But now, after only six months and without any warning, the government has taken away that protection. The prices have dropped alarmingly. They've almost halved in some cases. It is not surprising that so many local people are suffering financially.'

'Eleanor's right,' said Mr Harriman. 'During the War, the farmers lost a large part of their work force to the Army, and many of them have either lost sons or had their sons returned injured and unable to do physical work. Now they have this added burden of low prices. Some of our clients have been asking for advice as to what they can do about the new policy. I saw one client a few days ago who invested in cattle last year at the government's guaranteed prices, expecting that when it was time to send the cattle to market this year, those prices would continue. If they had done, he would have made enough profit to keep going. But now, with the change of policy, the market price has fallen and the animals are only worth half of what he paid for them. If he sells them, he will actually lose money. Even if he holds on to the animals, there is no way of knowing what will happen to prices next year. He might get even less. So he is in a quandary as to what to do.'

'And as to the wool prices, some of the farmers are practically giving away their clip,' said Eleanor.

'You can hardly blame the farmers for turning to other avenues for income,' said Mr Harriman, 'and I have no doubt that is what has encouraged this latest outbreak of dog fighting. Unscrupulous people from the towns have seen an opportunity and the farmers have realised that they can rent out their barns for a tidy profit. The barns are well out of the way and there is little chance of the activity being noticed. Edwin was talking to Superintendent Johnson this week about the latest reports of dog fighting in this area. He thinks his informant is reliable, but he's not yet sure where the fights are being held. Have you heard anything, Mondo?'

'Not at the moment,' said Mondo. 'Although, I understand that there have also been some thefts of dogs recently, household dogs reported missing. An acquaintance of mine had two puppies stolen last week. She lives in The Park and whoever it was obviously had no fear of coming into a built up area and risk being seen.'

'Edwin tells me that even if Superintendent Johnson finds out where the fights are being held, he doesn't have enough men available to mount the sort of large-scale operation needed. The people involved in this type of activity are not likely to be intimidated if only one or two policemen turn up and try to stop a fight,' said Mr Harriman. 'Apparently the Superintendent has put out a call to neighbouring forces for assistance.'

'So no doubt it won't be long before the culprits appear before me,' said Mondo. 'As will whoever is daubing messages on the bank's walls.'

'On the last occasion,' said Dr McKenzie, 'the messages at the bank coincided with the bankruptcy and death of Albert Perceval. I wonder if the motive for this new message is another impending bankruptcy.'

'I shouldn't be at all surprised, given the current state of things,' said Mr Harriman.

'Yes,' said Mondo, 'last time it was Sam, the younger Perceval boy. It was just unlucky for him that someone was in the vicinity at the time and reported him to the police. He was only cautioned, otherwise, he would have been up before me.

I think he's been out of trouble since and I had hoped that was the end of it but perhaps not.'

'According to our housekeeper, he's been in Sheffield but may have now returned,' said Eleanor.

'Oh, then perhaps my hope is in vain,' said Mondo.

'What was it last time, though? Not cow dung. It was only lime wash, wasn't it?' asked Dr McKenzie.

'Yes, the medium was different but the message was the same,' said Mondo. 'If I remember correctly the word murderers was scrawled over the windows last time.'

'Yes, and, as in the present case, that accusation also included the word *deceivers*,' added Eleanor. 'I remember thinking at the time that at least the spelling was correct. The curious thing about this recent message though is that the word *deceivers* is spelt correctly but the word *thieves* is not.'

'Perhaps it's someone who failed to understand the "i" before "e" except after "c" rule and errs on the side of caution with "ei" every time, just in case,' joked Mr Harriman. 'Should we be looking for someone haunted by the wrath of a rigorous spelling teacher and a cane across the knuckles?'

'Perhaps,' said Philip, 'the words were painted by two people: one who can spell and the other who can't.'

'That's an interesting thought,' said Eleanor.

'How is Sam Perceval at spelling, I wonder?' said Philip. 'I suppose the police can always give a spelling test to any suspects.'

The others laughed and Eleanor pulled a face at him.

'If Sam Perceval is involved, I have no doubt that it is connected with his father's bankruptcy,' said Mr Harriman. 'When Chillingham's foreclosed on Albert Perceval's garage, he was left without any means of supporting his family. He was an honest man and his family had a good reputation as saddlers. It was unfortunate for him that he decided to change his business just before the War. It ruined him.'

'It wasn't his fault,' said Mondo, 'and I know Sutton was reluctant to act. He delayed for as long as he could but finally his head office gave him no choice.'

'But unfortunately the shame of the bankruptcy was too much for Perceval,' said Mr Harriman, 'and that seems to be why he took his own life. I know the coroner's verdict was accidental death but everyone seems to refer to Perceval's death as suicide. I didn't conduct that inquest; it was one of Taylor's so I was not privy to all the details, although I did read the report.'

'The whole business of Perceval's death was most unfortunate,' said Dr McKenzie, 'and it was handled very clumsily. It affected both of the Perceval boys very profoundly. It was bad enough for Sam finding his father as he did, and he was only sixteen at the time, but to then have suspicion thrown on him needlessly made a bad situation even worse.'

Four pairs of eyes looked at him in surprise.

'I wasn't aware of that,' said Mondo. 'Why was he under suspicion? Suspicion of what?'

'It was a case of misdiagnosis,' said Dr McKenzie, 'due to an unfortunate sequence of events. Sam was under suspicion for a couple of days while the police considered whether or not his father actually had committed suicide. Sam was subjected to some rigorous questioning, although it was not common knowledge at the time. That was probably very fortunate for Sam because he left town immediately after the inquest and, if there had been any rumours going around, some people would have interpreted his leaving town as a sure sign of guilt.'

'But how could hanging be misdiagnosed? Surely such a case is obvious,' said Philip.

'Yes, that is difficult to understand,' said Mondo. 'Perhaps you had better explain, old chap. You can't just leave us in suspense like this. Just let me top up everyone's glass first.'

'Well,' said Dr McKenzie, 'in a case of anoxic encephalopathy, in lay terms hanging, death is caused by the blockage of blood to the brain, but that type of blockage can also be caused if someone turns the head of their victim and applies the right degree of pressure. Before accepting that someone has committed suicide, one always has to consider all the evidence and eliminate other possible explanations. First, there is the question of intention. Did the deceased set out deliberately to kill himself? Did the deceased leave a note providing evidence of that intention and, if so, is it credible? Secondly, if there is no note, might the death have been self-inflicted but accidental? Thirdly, was there a deliberate act by a second party, coupled with an attempt to make the death look like suicide? I need not go into detail here but, by careful examination of the neck bones, it is generally possible to distinguish between a suicide by hanging and a murder made to look like suicide. However, one certainly needs to know exactly what one is looking for because the signs can sometimes be inconclusive. The decision one comes to is of particular interest to both the police and the insurance companies. Unfortunately, I cannot comment confidently on the case of Mr Perceval because when he died, I wasn't here. I'd gone off to Dovedale for a couple of days of fishing.'

'Yes,' interrupted Mr Harriman, 'I remember now. Your locum gave evidence at the inquest, a doctor from Stockport, wasn't he?'

'That's right. Ferguson. Charles Ferguson. Nice fellow, but quite young and very cautious. I don't think he'd seen a case of hanging before. When I came back I looked over his notes just to bring myself up-to-date and I discovered that he had refused to sign a death certificate which is why the police were questioning Sam. When I asked Ferguson about it he said he couldn't be satisfied as to the cause of death because a few things had struck him as odd.'

'Nothing odd was raised at the inquest, was it?' asked Mr Harriman.

'No, because by then there was nothing to raise. The death certificate had been provided. One of the difficulties Ferguson had was that the body had been moved before he arrived so he did not see it in situ. It had been cut down and an attempt made to revive Mr Perceval. Ferguson was concerned that vital evidence had been destroyed. The usual plan for someone wanting to make murder look like suicide is for the culprit to find the body, in this case, Sam. This affords the best opportunity for removing incriminating evidence or planting a note.'

'But what possible motive could Sam Perceval have had for killing his father?' asked Eleanor.

'And how could the police seriously consider a sixteen year old capable of planning a murder and making it look like suicide?' added Philip. 'That is scarcely credible.'

'If that is the way Sam Perceval was treated at the time, it certainly explains why he was so angry and possibly still blames the bank for his father's death,' said Eleanor.

'As I said, the whole incident was very unfortunate. Either the physical evidence was equivocal or Ferguson was too inexperienced to interpret whatever evidence was there, but suggesting that Mr Perceval may have been murdered was probably quite unnecessary. The one genuine difficulty was the fact that there was no suicide note. People who commit suicide usually leave an explanation of some kind. I suppose they feel the need to justify their action. In my opinion, Albert Perceval was a brave man, very optimistic, a forward looking man. That is why he was able to conceive the change of business that he borrowed so heavily to accomplish. He seemed to be the sort of man who would have had the determination to keep going and to pull through somehow, not the sort of person to give in or to commit suicide.'

'Even though the bank was threatening to foreclose?' said Mr Harriman.

'Yes. That might have meant him losing all his possessions but he would not have given in,' said Dr McKenzie. 'At least, that was my impression of him. Nevertheless, the general opinion in the town seems to be that he did, in fact, kill himself. I have to admit that I was troubled by the absence of a note but that does not mean that it was not suicide. And, of course, it is always possible that there was a note and that it had been deliberately removed.'

'Why would someone do that?' asked Philip.

'Because of the insurance,' said Mr Harriman. 'A life insurance policy will generally exclude death by suicide. If someone is aware that their relative had a life insurance policy, there is always the temptation to destroy any evidence of suicide on which the insurance company can rely in refusing payment. A verdict of accidental death is preferable.'

'Unfortunately though, if someone is aware that a relative has a life insurance policy, there is always the temptation to dispose of that relative, accidentally or deliberately,' said Dr McKenzie.

'But was there anything else?' asked Mr Harriman, turning to Dr McKenzie. 'Apart from your own impressions, I mean. Any evidence that should have been given at the inquest.'

'It was difficult to form an opinion but on the evidence available I expected that the verdict would be either suicide or accidental death so I was able to persuade the police to wait until the inquest before charging Sam with murder. The verdict was accidental death so, of course, he was never charged.'

'Ah,' said Mr Harriman, smiling, 'so, the Coroner might have come to the right verdict after all.'

'Certainly,' said Dr McKenzie, 'and I do not wish to be unduly harsh on Charles Ferguson. People in professions such as ours cannot always be right and it does not become us to crow when our fellow practitioners overlook or misinterpret a fact.'

'People in glass houses, eh?' said Mr Harriman.

'Quite,' said Dr McKenzie, and he turned his attention to his whisky.

'You know, I have always been puzzled by that expression,' said Philip. 'If one lived in a glass house why on earth would one ever consider throwing stones? Or is it something to do with other people throwing stones at one.'

'Perhaps,' suggested Eleanor, 'the proverb as we know it simply means that, if one lives in a glass house, one is more exposed to the scrutiny of others and therefore more vulnerable to attack or criticism.'

'It is rather curious, isn't it?' said Mr Harriman, accustomed to examining words and giving them their precise meaning. 'Most people do use the expression to warn against hypocrisy. What they mean is "don't criticise in others what you are guilty of yourself" but if that is their intended message, surely the more appropriate phrase would be: Let he who is without sin, cast the first stone.'

'Actually, in one of my moments of idle curiosity, I did try to track down the origin of the expression,' said Mondo. 'I learnt that a seventeenth century poet had created a book of foreign proverbs translated into English and "people in glass houses" was included. I wondered if the proverb, in its original language, did actually make sense and had been mistranslated. Then, a few months afterwards, I happened to be reading Chaucer and I did find a much earlier version which does make sense. It is a rather lovely passage so I will read it to you.' He went over to a bookshelf and found the volume he wanted. He flipped through the pages and then said: 'This is it. It's in Old English but you will understand the gist of it.'

When he had finished reading, he closed the book and added: 'So, Chaucer is denouncing people who condemn love without having ever experienced it for themselves. Then he warns those who are not strong enough to cope with love's consequences to have nothing to do with it. He says that people whose heads are made of glass should stay out of the way of passing hostile stones. Very good advice, I think.'

'So, in that case, it would be more accurate to say "People who have glass heads should not throw stones." For fear of retaliation, that is,' said Mr Harriman.

'Or, perhaps he is saying that if you have a weakness or a vulnerability you should beware of things which may damage you,' said Philip.

'I couldn't agree more,' said Mondo. 'One always has to be alert.'

Before they could discuss the issue further, Rowland appeared at the door to announce that Dr McKenzie was wanted at The Claremont Private Hotel because one of the guests had been taken ill. The doctor made his apologies and bid them farewell.

'Thank you for a splendid evening, as usual, Mondo. And may I say it was refreshing to have spent a whole evening with only one fleeting mention of the Royal Visit. I congratulate you all,' said Dr McKenzie jocularly as he made them a deep bow.

The other guests took this as a signal that the dinner party was over and also prepared to depart. Mr Harriman said: 'Now that the topic has been mentioned, are you taking part in the Royal Visit, Mondo?'

'Unfortunately, yes. It has been made clear to me that my presence as one of the town's officials is mandatory which is most inconvenient because I have also been invited to attend the inaugural meeting of the newly formed Magistrates Association which will take place at Westminster the day before the visit and sadly I cannot attend both.'

'Oh, that is most unfortunate, I agree. But I suppose the town must come first,' said Mr Harriman.

As they were leaving, Mondo said: 'And Philip, please don't forget that I want that piece in the latest catalogue. Do your best for me, won't you.'

When everyone had gone, Jasper resumed his place on the hearthrug. Mondo refilled his whisky glass and sank into an armchair by the fire. He continued to browse through Chaucer's text, brooding on what Philip had said about vulnerability.

~O~

Just after twelve o'clock the following morning, Mrs Hazelwood, armed with her new hat and two of her dogs on leads, crossed over St John's Road to the top of Burlington Road. There was no-one about. When she passed Brook House, she could see no sign of anyone being at home. She walked as slowly as she could, pausing occasionally to look at the remnants of summer flowers in the gardens of the houses she passed and allowing the dogs to meander. They were used to being walked at a brisk speed designed for exercise not entertainment so they were a little puzzled by today's slow pace. They took full advantage of the opportunity to investigate every possible scent, allowing Mrs Hazelwood to dawdle satisfactorily.

When she reached the end of the road, she turned and walked slowly back towards Brook House. There was still no sign of life so at the entrance to the river path known as The Serpentine Walks, she turned off and walked along the river. This enabled her to loiter unobserved for a time and then, still keeping an eye on Burlington Road, she sat for a while on a seat facing the river, where the water rushed over the miniature rapids created by Victorian improvers to "enhance nature" and provide a focal point. Eventually, she looked at her watch, called the dogs to order, and returned to Burlington Road. She walked to the end of the road again and back still without success and then decided to give up and return another day. What she did not know was that Mr Aubrey-Mere had left home very early that morning in order to spend the day far away on the moors engaged in his favourite pastimes of climbing and walking.

CHAPTER TEN

On Saturday evening, Eleanor and her youngest sister, Cicely, had arranged to go to the tennis club dance which was being held at the Buxton Hydro Hotel in Hartington Road, a very large hotel where there was an elegant ballroom with a superb dance floor. Lawn tennis was very popular in Buxton and the facilities were excellent. During the season that year there had been several tournaments for professional players, including a match between England and Ireland. There was also the Duke of Devonshire's Challenge Cup and the All England Ladies Doubles Championships. The local amateur players were inspired by watching these events and, as a result, the standard of their competition was very high. But now the season was over. The trophies had been presented and the dance was the last social event of the year, a fundraiser designed to get the next season off to a good start. Edwin Talbot and his wife, Helen, who were also members of the tennis club, had arranged to call at Hall Bank for Eleanor and Cicely, on their way to the dance. The hotel was only a short distance from Hall Bank but the evening was far too cold for walking in light evening dress.

Eleanor and Cicely were gathering up cloaks and gloves and checking their evening bags to make sure they had their tickets, clean handkerchiefs, and small change for the cloakroom attendant. Cicely's son, Richard, was spending the evening at Hall Bank with his grandfather. Mr Harriman had recently given Richard a copy of *The Wind in the Willows* for his seventh birthday and had promised to read it with him that evening. While Eleanor and Cicely were getting ready, Richard and Napoleon were standing at the front window watching for Edwin's motor-car to arrive.

During the War when it was necessary to conserve resources, it had been considered both bad form and unpatriotic to dress extravagantly. In any event, with so many deaths, plain black had been the norm for much of the time. Immediately after the War, Eleanor and Cicely had lived very quietly but the previous year, they had made a pact. They had agreed to be positive about the future and to move their lives forward, despite their losses. The pact included buying new clothes whenever their finances permitted, so tonight they each wore a new evening gown in the latest style.

Eleanor's gown featured a sleeveless top and full-length straight skirt of black silk velvet over which was loosely draped a long-sleeved, knee-length tunic of transparent faille printed with a pattern of roses in red and gold. The tunic, secured at the waist with a wide belt, had an uneven hem. A border of tiny gold and black beads on the hem ensured that the light fabric draped in order to form the latest fashion feature known as a floating fringe. Cicely's gown was a drop-waisted blouse of pale apricot tulle, stamped with a pattern of silver ferns and decorated with silver beads. This was worn over a camisole top and a long straight skirt, both made of heavy crêpe in a deeper shade of apricot. Each of the sisters had matching hair ornaments in the latest style involving feathers and beads.

Richard announced that Edwin had arrived and he and Napoleon raced downstairs to open the front door. Edwin complimented Eleanor and Cicely on their elegant appearance and escorted them downstairs.

~O~

When they arrived at the hotel, Edwin left his motor-car with the attendant and the foursome deposited their cloaks at the cloakroom, collected their dance programmes, and went up the flight of steps leading into the impressive ballroom. It had a deep coffered ceiling, carved and decorated, from which hung huge inverted glass domes of light. Floor to ceiling mirrors along one wall reflected the coloured glass in the tall windows opposite. At one end of the ball-room was the stage where the hotel's own orchestra was playing and, at the opposite end, there was a balcony from which one could watch the dancers below.

The dancing had already begun and about twenty couples were energetically Fox Trotting around the floor. Swirling flashes of brightly coloured evening gowns were interspersed with the black and white of the gentlemen's evening dress. Edwin and Helen joined the dancers and Eleanor and Cicely, spotting a group of friends, went to chat with them for the duration of the dance. This group included two of Eleanor's mixed doubles partners. One of them asked for the next dance which was a Waltz and the other claimed a later dance. Eleanor pencilled their names into her programme and walked onto the dance floor with her first partner. The organisers, mindful of the preferences of some of the older members of the club, had put together a mixed programme which included traditional favourites as well as the newer dances. When the Waltz finished, Eleanor and her partner returned to their group of friends and, after a short pause, the Master of Ceremonies announced:

'Ladies and gentlemen. Please take your partners for the Pride of Erin.'

Mr Norman suddenly appeared at Eleanor's elbow and she heard the unwelcome words: 'Miss Harriman, may I have the pleasure of this dance?'

Eleanor was not already engaged for that dance and, being well-brought up, knew that it would be discourteous to refuse.

Etiquette demanded polite acceptance, therefore, she turned to Mr Norman as graciously as she could manage, and bowed to her fate. She decided not to mention the chrysanthemums. The dance involved a complicated set of manoeuvres and for most of the time they were either moving side by side or facing each other with only their hands touching.

'At least,' thought Eleanor, 'there are only two Waltz steps which require close bodily contact and they are mercifully brief.'

Mr Norman was not light on his feet; rather, he was heavy on his partner's toes. He tried valiantly to engage Eleanor in conversation but the flow of words was constantly being interrupted either by silence while he concentrated on the steps or by his apologies for his clumsy feet. They had exchanged the usual pleasantries about the orchestra and the number of people present and Mr Norman had moved on to commenting on the winners of the year's trophies when the music stopped and the dance was over.

Eleanor said politely: 'Thank you, Mr Norman,' intending to go back to her friends but the Master of Ceremonies announced that they would go straight into a One Step and Eleanor did not have the chance to escape.

'Oh, how fortunate. Our partnership can continue!' exclaimed Mr Norman, delightedly.

Eleanor smiled fixedly and resigned herself to another three minutes of torture in Mr Norman's company. The One Step involved bodily contact of a much closer kind than Eleanor desired with Mr Norman. She was in complete agreement with those early Victorian matrons who, when the Waltz was introduced from the Continent, declared that it was indelicate and unseemly, indecent even, for people to dance in such close proximity to each other. As with the previous dance, the One Step was proving to be beyond Mr Norman's dancing skills even though, as the name implied, it simply involved taking one step with each beat of the music, progressing in a straight line until they reached the corner of the dance floor, turning, and then repeating the whole process again until the music stopped.

As they moved around the floor, Mr Norman began to perspire, overheated by the exertion of dancing and the excitement of being with the object of his matrimonial hopes. His gloves became clammy and began to smell of cleaning fluid. The heat also brought out the scent of his shaving cream and his hair lotion, an overpowering combination. He began a conversation about the club's success in this year's tournament and, forgetting to pay attention to his feet, caused his partner to stumble. Eleanor gritted her teeth and responded as politely as she could to his conversation and at the same time mentally formulating words of escape.

When the music stopped, Eleanor said in her best Victorian debutant's manner:

'Thank you, Mr Norman, it was very kind of you to offer to be my partner but I'm afraid I am an indifferent dancer and quite overcome with the exertion of it all. Please excuse me but I think I shall rest for a while and sit the next dance out.' She turned and walked to the edge of the dance floor.

Mr Norman following her solicitously, said: 'Oh, I am so sorry to have tired you. How thoughtless of me. I should have realised that two dances in a row would be too much for a lady. Please, let me find you a seat.'

Eleanor cleverly headed for a single free seat between two occupied ones and sat down, fanning herself with her dance programme. Mr Norman hovered indecisively for a moment and then asked if Eleanor would like some water or some lemonade. Eleanor would have enjoyed a glass of lemonade but was anxious not to give Mr Norman any further reason to linger so she refused politely. People were milling about in front of her, waiting for the next dance to begin, claiming partners, greeting each other and exchanging banter. Mr Norman somehow got swept up in the mêlée and disappeared out of sight. Eleanor stared blankly at the crowd in front of her, seeing people only at waist high level. A gentleman in immaculate evening dress came into view and a familiar voice said:

'What ho, Eleanor! If you are not already engaged, may I have the pleasure of the next dance?'

'Good evening, Philip,' said Eleanor, looking up and smiling. 'You certainly may.'

'And one or two more, if you can bear it and your programme is not already full.'

She took the pencil attached to her programme and wrote "Philip" next to the Tango and the Veleta in her programme and also wrote his name next to the supper dance which was a Fox Trot.

'Ladies and gentlemen. Partners please for the Tango,' announced the Master of Ceremonies.

As Eleanor stood up she noticed Mr Norman easing his way through the crowd towards her. His surprise at her decision to continue dancing after all was evident. Eleanor gave him a quick smile as Philip steered her away to the edge of the dance floor.

While they waited for the music to begin, Eleanor said: 'Have you just arrived?'

'Yes. There was company at dinner, some important business colleague of the pater, and I have only just managed to get away. I arrived in time to see you dancing with that Norman fellow,' said Philip. 'Should I be jealous?' he added mockingly.

'Certainly not! You are indeed the relief party. Mafeking could not have been more grateful than I am.'

'That is a charming new gown you are wearing,' said Philip. 'The design and the fabric are just right for you.'

Eleanor accepted the complement graciously. The music began and they glided out on to the floor. After Alistair had been killed in France, Eleanor and Philip had become firm friends, united by loss, and they were companions at many of the town's social events. They had danced together so often that their steps were perfectly attuned. They moved effortlessly around the floor, executing the complicated steps of the Tango confidently and at the same time carrying on a conversation, although that was slightly disjointed due to the necessity of turning their heads when they abruptly changed direction as required by the dance.

'Norman is still pursuing you, then?' said Philip as they took several steps forward.

'Relentlessly,' said Eleanor as they paused and turned their heads.

'I should warn you. His intentions are serious.' They took several steps in the opposite direction.

'What do you mean?' They paused and turned again. 'He was in the shop this morning with a friend looking at brooches. I overheard his conversation and it was about you.'

'What a liberty!'

'I certainly thought so.'

'What did he say?'

'That he was choosing a brooch for a very special lady and his future wife. He went on to praise you to the skies.'

'Oh no!'

'He's fairly confident that his addresses are welcome. He asked me to put the brooch aside for him.'

'Bother!' said Eleanor, crossly. She missed her step and Philip paused in his backward movement so that she could regain her balance. 'You couldn't mislay the brooch, could you? Or sell it to another customer?'

'You shouldn't lead him on,' teased Philip.

'Oh, but I don't. I've tried everything I know to make it

clear to him that his attention is not welcome but I don't seem to be able to discourage him. What else can I do?'

'Well, you are well brought up and you are naturally very gracious. Perhaps he is not used to that and does not realise that you are just being polite.'

'He tries so hard to be agreeable and I don't want to hurt his feelings. In a way, I feel sorry for him although he is a great nuisance.'

'Obviously he has mistaken your concern for genuine affection. I don't think he is very sophisticated or very bright. I also think he is very self-centred and therefore incapable of being able to step back and assess the situation rationally.'

'You think I should be brutally honest with him?' Philip nodded. 'What? Say to him that I want him to leave me alone?'

'Well, either that or put about a rumour that you are engaged to me.'

Eleanor laughed: 'That would certainly stop him.'

'Yes, although his feelings would probably be even more hurt than if you just told him to go away.'

'What a mess.'

They danced in comfortable silence until the music finished. Philip said: 'That's our lot. Thank you Eleanor. A beautifully executed tango as usual.'

'Thank you, Philip. And thank you for rescuing me. I've got you down for the Veleta and the supper dance. Is that all right?'

'Perfectly. I shall look forward to it. Who is your next partner?'

'Mr Sutton, our esteemed treasurer.'

'Right. Shall we go over to where Edwin and Helen are? Cicely's there too. I can leave you safely with them until Mr Sutton claims you and I'll go and circulate for a bit. I noticed Catherine was sitting out during the Tango. I shall go and annoy her.'

Dr Catherine Balderstone was one of the local doctors and she and Eleanor and Philip were good friends. During the dancing, Catherine and several other ladies had been left without partners. There was always a general shortage of younger gentlemen on social occasions such as this as a result of the losses caused by the War and, as a consequence, all of the gentlemen present were expected to dance as much as possible. However, no-one took exception to the fact that Philip did not.

When Philip was in France during the War, his lungs had been damaged by gas. He had recovered reasonably well but was unable to engage in very strenuous exercise for any length of time. He was a generous, very affable person and well-liked at the tennis club so there was no shortage of strong players willing to be paired with him and he was still able to take part in the competitions. He made up for his inability to dance every dance by joining the ladies who were sitting out and entertaining them with his conversation instead. Before the next dance was announced, Mr Lionel Sutton joined Eleanor's group and he and Eleanor chatted happily for a few minutes. They knew each other well. Edwin had pursued several mortgage debts for Chillingham & Baynard's bank on instructions from Mr Sutton and Eleanor and Mr Sutton met frequently at the bank for the completion of property sales for Mr Harriman's clients.

Mr Sutton was in his forties, handsome and always immaculately dressed. He had impeccable manners and a wonderful sense of humour. He was interested in the theatre as well as tennis and was a member of the Buxton Amateur Dramatic and Operatic Society. Possessing an excellent tenor voice and very competent acting ability, he often took the leading role. He was also the perfect dinner guest, charming to the ladies and considerate of his hostess, sociable, witty, able to talk intelligently or listen sympathetically on any topic. He was greatly in demand at the tables of the ladies of The Park, although they all knew not to invite Mr Sutton if Mr Aubrey-Mere was on their guest list. Even though their falling out was long ago, the embargo remained. For many years, the matrons of The Park had earmarked Mr Sutton as a suitable match for their daughters but, much to their regret, he had managed to evade them and remained a bachelor. By the age of forty, an unmarried woman was expected to have given up the idea of marriage, but a man of that age could safely contemplate embarking on it without causing his friends any anxiety, so the matrons had not yet given up hope.

The Master of Ceremonies announced another Waltz and Mr Norman, who had been hovering in the background moved forward but, before he could reach the group, Mr Sutton stepped in front of Eleanor, made an exaggerated and very deep bow with many flourishes of his hand and said in a loud stage voice:

'Miss Harriman, you have done me the inestimable honour of consenting to include my name on your dance programme this evening and I am, therefore, emboldened to seek your company for this next dance.'

He came upright again and held out his hand to Eleanor. She took it, laughing, and allowed herself to be whirled on to the dance floor. Mr Norman turned on his heel, and walked away. Eleanor and Mr Sutton glided gracefully around the dance floor, enjoying themselves. Eleanor caught occasional glimpses of Mr Norman glowering in a corner of the room. As she and her partner passed close to a group of ladies sitting along the edge of the floor she heard one of them say: 'Don't they make a lovely couple?' and she hoped that Mr Norman had also heard. When the music stopped, Mr Sutton escorted Eleanor back to the chairs at the side of the dance floor and sat down with her. Philip, whilst talking to Catherine and a couple of other friends during the dance, had been keeping a watchful eye on Mr Norman. Seeing him now approaching in Eleanor's direction, Philip invited his group to join Eleanor and Mr Sutton and they crowded Mr Norman out. Once again, his amorous endeavours were frustrated.

Eleanor was down to dance the next dance with Edwin and he whisked her on to the floor for a lively Fox Trot. When it finished, Edwin and Eleanor regrouped with Philip, Cicely, Helen, and their other friends and chatted animatedly until the next dance was announced. This was the Veleta which Eleanor danced with Philip. When the dance finished, Philip left Eleanor with Catherine, and went off to find his next partner. Eleanor and Catherine did not have partners for the next dance and stood contentedly chatting.

Catherine said: 'Philip says Mr Norman is serious about you.'

'I am very conscious of that fact and I have tried to discourage him, honestly I have. He sends quite a few clients to us so I am careful not to offend him but I realise now that I have been too polite. The hints I sent out were obviously too subtle. Anyone else would have seen straightaway that I am not interested but he seems incapable of picking up the signs.'

'Or else he is just deliberately ignoring them.'

'Possibly, but he just doesn't seem to have a sense of awareness of anyone other than himself and it is so difficult to have a proper conversation with him. He's very serious about everything and so intense. One cannot afford to be flippant. He takes everything literally and doesn't understand when one is joking.'

'A couple of my patients are members of the sect his mother belongs to and I can assure you they don't approve of frivolity or of pleasure even. They certainly would disapprove of tennis. And dancing, well, quite out of the question! In fact, I am surprised Mr Norman had the courage to come here this evening.'

'I wonder if his mother knows that he is here,' said Eleanor. 'If she does I am certain she wouldn't approve.'

'There is just something about him that ...'

'That what?' asked Catherine.

'Oh, I don't know,' said Eleanor, frowning. 'There's an undercurrent. It's nothing I can put my finger on. What do you think of him?'

'I've been his partner from time to time during this last season and I've heard various comments about him from others. I am sure that being in the company of women at the tennis club has been a revelation for him. He's probably discovered that, contrary to what he has been taught, we are not all harpies or temptresses,' said Catherine. 'I suspect, therefore, that he is trying to live in two worlds and that in itself must create a certain amount of tension. That's perhaps the undercurrent you detect but can't quite define.'

'You sound like Mrs Clayton,' laughed Eleanor. 'She says he is suffering from guilt because he is supposed to belong to the Watching Brethren but would rather join the outside world.'

'Mrs Clayton may well be right. I imagine that currently he is struggling to balance his obedience to his mother and his attraction to you.'

'Oh dear,' said Eleanor. 'That sounds very grim. I never wanted him to be attracted to me. I was not even conscious of inviting his attention.'

'I know that, and I'm sure you did nothing out of the ordinary. All you did was play tennis skilfully, the same as you do with all your mixed doubles partners, without any thoughts of seduction. Perhaps, being inexperienced with women, he saw more in it than just the tennis. But, without wanting in any way to detract from your undoubted charms, Eleanor, I do think his attraction to you is merely infatuation, and immature infatuation, at that.'

'You mean, the more something is forbidden, the more one desires it?' said Eleanor, putting one hand on her waist, the other behind her head, and pushing her hips to one side in order to adopt the supposedly alluring pose currently favoured by women appearing in newspaper photographs.

'I'm afraid so,' said Catherine, laughing at Eleanor's demonstration of "desirable female."

'So, what do I do?' asked Eleanor, moving her hips back to normal and shrugging her shoulders.

'Ignore his advances and stay out of his way as much as you can. I think that really is all you can do.'

Eleanor nodded in agreement and they moved on to other topics until they were claimed by their partners for the next dance.

~O~

Eleanor danced with several of her mixed doubles partners, eventually losing sight of Mr Norman.

'Ladies and gentlemen, please take your partners for the Fox Trot and this will be the supper dance,' called the Master of Ceremonies.

Philip re-appeared at Eleanor's side.

'Are we sitting this one out?' asked Eleanor, knowing that by now Philip would be starting to tire and not up to foxtrotting.

Philip smiled at Eleanor. 'I think so, old thing, if you don't mind. Besides, we must consider the chaperones. We don't want to exceed the permitted number of dances together and give them cause for anxiety, do we?'

Eleanor laughed: 'I shouldn't worry. I expect the tongues have already been wagging. That Tango wouldn't have done anything for my reputation.'

'Then, let's see who we can gossip about instead.'

Most people had chosen as a partner the person they intended to take into supper and, as almost everyone was dancing, the floor was crowded. Eleanor and Philip sat contentedly watching the swirling dancers, noting with interest which tennis club members were dancing together.

'I say,' said Philip, 'speaking of pairing off, look at Miss Wilkins. She's managed to snare Mr Sutton for the supper dance.'

'She's been following him about all evening. All season, in fact,' said Eleanor. 'The poor man.'

'I know. I've been watching her. Most amusing,' said Philip.

When the music stopped and supper was announced, Mr Sutton and his partner were close to where Eleanor and Philip were sitting.

'Oh, good,' simpered Miss Wilkins, fanning herself. 'I'm quite desperate for a cup of tea. Dancing is quite exhausting isn't it?' She clearly hoped that good manners would compel Mr Sutton to take her into supper.

'Yes,' agreed Mr Sutton, 'Almost as exhausting as tennis. If you will excuse me, Miss Wilkins. May I return you to your friends? Unfortunately, I have already agreed to take someone else in to supper.'

They moved out of earshot.

'She's wasting her time,' said Philip sagely.

'Oh?' Eleanor looked at Philip questioningly.

'Yes,' said Philip firmly. 'Shall we, Miss Harriman?' he said, standing up and offering his arm to Eleanor in true Victorian style.

'Certainly, Mr Danebridge.' Eleanor mockingly fanned herself with her programme and fluttered her eyelids at him as she took his arm. They joined the crowd moving towards the supper room, meeting up again with Edwin and Helen. Then Catherine and Cicely found them and they all went in together.

Philip looked around the room and said to Edwin: 'I don't

see Norman anywhere.'

'I wonder if he has left,' said Edwin. 'I certainly hope so.'

'So do I,' agreed Edwin. 'At first, we regarded his attention to Eleanor as a bit of a joke but he seems to be making rather a pest of himself lately. Eleanor says you have been rescuing her all evening.'

Philip laughed. 'I've done what I can.'

'He's a hopeless dancer,' said Eleanor, 'although I have to admit he is a very good tennis player.'

Edwin added: 'Yes, very strong. I have partnered him several times although one does always have to remember to keep on the right side of him.'

'Actually,' said Catherine, 'I remember someone commenting to the Club Secretary that you and Mr Norman made an excellent team, Eleanor. Perhaps that's what gave him ideas.'

'Perhaps he bribed the Secretary to fix the draw,' laughed Philip.

Mr Norman was not seen again that evening. Eleanor was left in peace and, by eleven thirty, had danced with all her other tennis partners of the season. Philip arrived to claim her for the last dance and they took to the floor for the final Waltz.

CHAPTER ELEVEN

On Sunday afternoons, Eleanor and Napoleon generally called on Cicely and Richard at Oxford House and during the season they went into the Pavilion Gardens and listened to the band, sometimes taking a picnic. If, as today, the weather was not suitable for sitting in the park, they went for a walk along one of the many paths leading through the woods surrounding the town. Richard was curious to know the names of the trees and the birds so their walk usually turned into a nature ramble. Now, as it was autumn, he had taken up collecting fallen leaves and trying to identify them. This afternoon they had decided on a walk up to Grin Low Woods.

When everyone was suitably clothed and booted, they set off along the footpath towards Poole's Cavern. At Green Lane, they joined the track which led across the fields and through the woods up to Solomon's Temple at the top of Grin Low. Richard and Napoleon raced ahead across the fields occasionally stopping or zig-zagging to examine something that caught their attention. Eleanor and Cicely followed at a slower pace, climbing steadily up through the woods and chatting about the week's events. They reached a flat grassy expanse at the top of the hill and the stone tower which was known as Solomon's Temple. The original tower had been built in 1834 on the initiative of a local man, Solomon Mycock, using unemployed men disadvantaged by amendments to the Poor Law but the structure fell into disrepair and, in 1896, a new tower was built to provide a new generation of visitors with a panoramic view of Buxton and the hills of the Peak District beyond.

Richard climbed to the top of the tower and Eleanor restrained Napoleon who was eager to follow. She put him on his lead and stood with Cicely looking out past the rooftops of Buxton to the surrounding peaks. On a clear day it was possible to see as far as Kinder Scout but today the sky was overcast and the view was more restricted. To the right beyond Fairfield, they could just make out Mam Tor, once an Iron Age fort. In the foreground below Brown Edge was the huge dome of the Devonshire Hospital and near it the splendidly ornate Palace Hotel. They stood contentedly waiting for Richard.

'I never get tired of this view,' said Eleanor. 'No matter how many times I come up here.'

'It is wonderful, isn't it?' agreed Cicely.

'Even on a day like today, the hills are magnificent. And there is so much variety.'

'I wonder if the first visitors to The Crescent ever came up here. Although, nearly all of what we can see wouldn't have been built then. It would have been mostly fields and hills.'

'If they had, I'm sure it would have been just the sort of view to send the Georgians into raptures and reaching for their sketching materials. Just like Henry Tilney and his sister in *Northanger Abbey* admiring the view of Bath.'

They lapsed into silence and eventually Cicely said:

'Father told me this morning that Mr Norman had chrysanthemums delivered to the office last week. He did make rather a nuisance of himself last night, didn't he? Surely he must see that you are not interested.'

'Apparently not,' said Eleanor. 'Anyway, if I was interested in matrimony it would certainly not involve Mr Norman.'

Richard came clattering down the stone steps of the tower exclaiming about the view and headed back at full tilt down the slope towards the woods. Eleanor let Napoleon off his lead and he was half-way down the slope after Richard by the time that she and Cicely left the tower and started to follow them.

'Of course, if you were to get married, you would have to give up being a solicitor,' said Cicely.

'Exactly. And why should I ever want to do that? I might have given it up for Alistair but certainly not for Mr Norman.'

Cicely laughed: 'You wouldn't have given it up for Alistair, you enjoy it too much. Anyway, you mightn't have had the choice. It was only because Edgar was killed that father let you take his place. But for that, you would have had nothing to give up.'

'That's true. Life would have been very different for all of us if Edgar hadn't been killed,' said Eleanor sadly.

'If Edgar hadn't been killed, he would have finished his articles and become a partner with father and Edwin. I wonder what you would have done. You certainly would not have had the opportunity to discover your talent for the law.'

'I expect I would have married Alistair and been a devoted wife and mother,' said Eleanor. She paused and then added: 'I find that hard to imagine now. It sounds a bit disloyal to Alistair to say so but it would have been a much more restricted life than the one I live now.'

'Yes, and you are very good at what you do. Far better than Edgar would ever have been. His heart was never really in it. He was only trying to please mother.'

'The War has changed our lives so much. In ways that we just could not have imagined when we were growing up. In fact, sometimes I find it hard to remember what we were like in that last summer of 1914.'

'It does seem such a long time ago, doesn't it? We were very different people then.'

They had reached the woods again and walked along immersed in their own thoughts about the past and what might have been.

~O~

Richard called to them to look at a hole that Napoleon had found. When that had been thoroughly examined and the identity of its likely occupant had been discussed, they started walking again. Richard was gathering autumn leaves to take home and giving them to Cicely to carry. Napoleon was trotting contentedly along, well ahead as usual. They were descending along a path and had come to a small clearing when Eleanor caught a glimpse of a female figure just as it disappeared behind the trunk of a large tree. Eleanor stopped and looked around to see if there was anyone else about. She could detect no movement, no sound of broken twigs or rustling leaves. Cicely, realising that Eleanor had stopped, turned and waited with Richard a few paces ahead.

'What's the matter?' asked Cicely.

Eleanor walked towards her. 'I think there is someone hiding behind the trunk of that big beech tree. Over there. It's a woman.'

Cicely looked, but could see nothing. Napoleon, up ahead, had glanced back mid-trot and realised that the rest of his party had fallen behind. He had turned and started back towards Eleanor at a gallop but then, picking up a new scent, he diverted his attention from Eleanor and headed towards the beech tree. He bounded up to the tree, halted at its base, and raised himself up onto his hind legs. There was a high-pitched scream.

Eleanor called loudly: 'Napoleon, come.'

Cicely called out: 'He won't hurt you. It's all right.'

Napoleon was well-trained and although for a few seconds he was torn between fun and obedience, he dropped back down onto all four paws, bounded back to Eleanor and sat attentively in front of her, waiting to be rewarded. As soon as Napoleon had moved away from the tree, the woman rushed out from behind it and ran, terrified, without once looking back, stumbling over tree roots and hampered by her long skirt. Fearless Richard said scornfully: 'Fancy being afraid of a dog,' and resumed his search for autumn leaves. Eleanor saw that there was nothing more to be done.

'Whatever was she thinking of, hiding behind a tree like that?' said Eleanor.

'I recognised her,' said Cicely. 'It was Sarah Dawson. The greengrocer's daughter. I used to see her in the shop sometimes.'

'Ah, then I think I can guess why she was up here,' said Eleanor. 'She seems to have been alone but I suspect that either she was waiting to meet her young man or she was with him and was hiding from us because she did not want us to see them together.'

'Oh, dear!' said Cicely.

'I wonder if he is still here somewhere.'

'Are they not supposed to meet? Will she get into trouble?' asked Cicely.

'Yes,' said Eleanor, 'and the question is: Should I tell Mr Dawson or not?'

'I think we should say nothing,' said Cicely. 'Who are we to stand in the way of young love? They might end up separated like Romeo and Juliet if we tell.'

'You are a hopeless romantic, Cicely,' teased Eleanor. 'Well, I think I shall just tell Edwin and he can decide.'

'Is Mr Dawson one of Edwin's clients?'

'Yes.'

'Then, yes. I think that would be best. Now, let's get home. It will be dark soon and it's nearly tea time.'

They set off again, Napoleon and Richard running ahead, but Eleanor was sure that, somewhere to her left higher up the hill, she heard a twig snap. She thought it very likely that Charlie Perceval was still there, out of sight, but she didn't bother to turn around and look. The rest of their walk was uneventful and they arrived at the end of Broad Walk, tired but contented with the world, just as it was starting to get dark.

'Here's the lamplighter,' said Cicely to Richard.

'And Jon Jon,' added Eleanor.

All along Broad Walk, there were large gas lamps which the lamplighter looked after, igniting them every evening at sunset and returning every morning to extinguish them. One of these lamps was directly outside Oxford House and Richard loved to watch this nightly ritual. He never saw the lamplighter return at dawn because he was always still fast asleep in bed. He often saw Jon Jon following the lamplighter and knew him well. Napoleon also knew Jon Jon and he and Richard went to greet him. Richard held out his hand and said: 'Good evening, Jon Jon,' and they solemnly shook hands. Jon Jon patted Napoleon and then turned his attention back to the lamplighter. When the gas was ignited, a soft light appeared and then gradually increased in brightness. The lamplighter and Jon Jon moved on to the next lamp-post and the others all went indoors. While the sisters made a pot of tea and toasted muffins in front of the fire, Napoleon took possession of the hearthrug and Richard spread his autumn leaves over the floor and admired them one by one.

CHAPTER TWELVE

On Monday morning, Eleanor and Mr Harriman had finished breakfast and Mrs Clayton was about to clear the table. Mrs Clayton said:

'I was talking to the Misses Pymble yesterday and they told me that some puppies had been stolen from The Park last week. Mrs Hazelwood at The Elms. Apparently she breeds Border Terriers. The Misses Pymble were wondering if the puppies had been taken by the same people who are organising the dog fighting. Do you remember we were talking about the rumour that it had started up again?'

'Yes. Has Alf heard anything more?'

'Not that he's mentioned,' said Mrs Clayton, 'but I'll ask him again tonight. I don't like to think of dogs being used in that way. Perhaps the puppies were stolen by someone who wants to sell them. I suppose they are valuable.'

'I'm sure they are. Let's hope that whoever has them realises that they are more valuable alive,' said Eleanor.

'I think we should keep an eye on Napoleon though,' said Mrs Clayton. 'You never know. He's just the sort of dog people would think of using to fight. He looks fierce enough, although he's a big softie. He hasn't got a vicious bone in his body and he'd certainly come off worse. We don't want anything happening to him.'

'We certainly do not,' agreed Eleanor, as she went towards the door. 'Leon, come on, this way. Mr Dawson is due shortly so I need to take you upstairs out of the way.'

Napoleon stood up obediently.

'You can leave him with me if you like,' said Mrs Clayton.
'I'm sure he would prefer that.'

Napoleon sat down again, making his preference clear. He was sitting to attention, facing towards Mrs Clayton, body upright, haunches square, head alert. Rigidly holding that pose, he let his eyes stray casually sideways to look at the table where he knew there were bacon scraps. Eleanor, trying not to laugh, left him to it.

~O~

When Mr Dawson arrived, Edwin went down to meet him and took from him the Information which had been filed at the Court and served on him. Edwin sent Eric, the messenger boy, up to Eleanor's office with the document so that she could read it before Mr Dawson came up to her office.

'Now, Mr Dawson,' said Edwin, 'I want to introduce you to one of the other solicitors in this firm, Miss Harriman. She has recently been given some information which may be relevant to the offence with which you have been charged and I asked her to look into this matter. I think that what she has discovered will be very useful to your defence.'

Without giving Mr Dawson time to protest, Edwin ushered him upstairs to Eleanor's office and introduced him to Eleanor. He offered Mr Dawson a seat, and then took one of the visitors' chairs for himself. Mr Dawson sat stiffly upright, glanced sideways at Edwin, and looked intently at Eleanor. She was amused to see the confused look on his face. The sight of a woman occupying the chair behind an office desk was clearly not what he was used to.

Edwin said: 'Right, Miss Harriman, where would you like to begin?'

Mr Dawson, a bit nonplussed at this novel experience, Humphed and Aarghed a good deal at first but, as Eleanor conducted the interview efficiently and with confidence, he soon forgot his initial reservations about dealing with a female.

'Mr Dawson, according to this Information, you have been charged on two counts: possession of a false weight and possession of an unstamped weight. The charges relate to the same item: the two pound weight being used in your shop. Am I correct in thinking that the weight is four ounces light?'

Mr Dawson looked very surprised. 'By Jove! How did you know that? Where does it say so? It's not on that paper there.' He pointed to the document which Eleanor was holding.

Eleanor went on: 'And the false weight wasn't your property?'

'Nay, it were not one o' mine. Hmph! Never seen it afore,' he said forcefully.

'Mr Dawson, I know that recently you have had other problems with the Weights and Measures department...'

Mr Dawson shuffled his feet and leaned forward. He puffed out his cheeks and exhaled loudly. Eleanor could see that he was becoming uncomfortable.

'...but several people have assured me that this is most unusual,' she added, trying to reassure him.

'Aye. I've never had no trouble afore,' said Mr Dawson, defensively, still on the edge of his chair. 'And I can't understand it now, because I checks the scales regular, like.'

'So we need to find an explanation.' said Eleanor, calmly. 'I have looked at the facts in order to understand what has been happening and why, and I think I can see where the problem lies but I do need you to provide me with some more information first.'

'Aargh,' said Mr Dawson. He moved back in his chair and folded his arms across his chest.

'Now, can you tell me, please, when you first started having this trouble.'

'Well, it were December last year, nigh on Christmas. The Inspector were in town for the annual inspection. He checked the weights. All correct. Tested the scales. Out of balance. Now, that were a surprise because I'd checked the scales only that morning, and I told the Inspector so. And he said to me: "Mr Dawson, he said, I've been coming here nigh on twenty years and these scales are always right." And I didn't know what to say. I check my scales regular. Then he said as how he did have to give me a caution, official like, but he didn't need to give me a fine.'

'And the scales were not faulty in any way?'

Mr Dawson was shaking his head. 'Just needed to be adjusted, that's all. They must have been bumped or something but I don't quite know how.'

'Mr Dawson, when there is an annual inspection, do you know that the Inspector is coming or what day he is going to call?'

'Not exactly,' said Mr Dawson. 'If the Inspector's in, say, Bakewell or Hartington, word gets round and we expect to see him here within a week or two. I always check to see things are in order before he comes.'

'And anyone who works in your shop with you would be likely to know that a visit was expected?'

'Aye,' agreed Mr Dawson.

'Now, I believe you also came to the attention of the Inspector again a few months ago but that was not during an annual inspection. That was a special visit.' Mr Dawson's eyebrows shot up in surprise and he wondered how Eleanor knew this. 'Could you tell me what happened on that occasion?' she asked.

'Well, I were fined and I were right cross, an' all. It were in July. The Inspector, he reckoned he'd sent a letter saying I were to present the weights at the Town Hall for checking and I said to him I never got the letter so I never did take them.'

'So, when and how did you find out about the letter?'

'The Inspector arrived at the shop, without any warning like, and he says why haven't I been to the Town Hall as ordered. I said I didn't know about any order. He said it were in a letter and I said I didn't know about any letter neither. Then he gives me a copy of it but I hadn't seen it afore and I told him so. He said it didn't make any difference because he had proof it were sent and that were that. And then he checked the weights and the scales and found that they was right.'

'And you were fined for not complying with the notice?'

Mr Dawson nodded: 'Aye. But I swear I never saw that notice afore and I said so to the Inspector,' said Mr Dawson, firmly.

'And apparently the reason that the Inspector sent the notice was that there had been a complaint and he wanted to check the weights you were using?'

'Aye, two pounds of red currants, it were.'

Eleanor mentally matched this up against the information she had received from Mrs Kendall. The housekeeper at The Gables had complained because the order of redcurrants was short.

'And yet, while the Inspector was in the shop, he tested your scales and your weights, and they were accurate.' Mr Dawson nodded. 'Now, what can you tell me about this latest trouble? I understand that you have been receiving reports recently from customers about goods not being the correct weight when they were delivered.'

'Well, yes. How did you know?' Mr Dawson moved awkwardly on his chair and was clearly uncomfortable remembering these affronts to his reputation.

'The housekeeper at Top Trees telephoned and said her order for quinces was short and then it was the Brussels sprouts. And each order was four ounces short.'

Mr Dawson again showed his surprise at Eleanor's knowledge of his problems. He nodded.

'Now,' continued Eleanor, 'I would expect that the usual reason for selling goods short and making the customer pay for more than he receives is to give the dishonest shopkeeper a greater profit. Unless a customer becomes suspicious, this practice could go undetected for some time. But you see, Mr Dawson, I have noticed that, with the exception of the most recent incident, all the orders were for the sort of ingredients used for pickles or jam which meant that the short weight would be discovered immediately. The person using the fruit is bound to weigh it beforehand to make sure that she adds the right amount of sugar.' Mr Dawson's eyebrows went up in surprise at this revelation. 'So, it looks to me that whoever is responsible for these orders being incorrect is deliberately choosing items which he or she knows will be weighed by the customer, presumably in the hope that the customer will discover the short weight and complain to you and perhaps ultimately report the incident to the Inspector. That, of course, causes trouble for you.' Mr Dawson rubbed his hands up and down his thighs in indignation. 'The other thing which I find odd is that, recently, the orders seem to be always four ounces short, which suggests that a false weight is being used. It is not someone randomly altering the quantity of goods sent out.' Mr Dawson's jaw dropped at this point. 'Again, the purpose of the deception appears to be to put blame on you. To give the Inspector the impression that you are in possession of a false weight.'

Mr Dawson looked at Eleanor so intently that Eleanor wondered if he thought she was a witch with special powers of divination.

'By 'eck,' he said, 'you're right. I see that now.'

'Of course, it is possible that, as well as the instances we know about, goods weighing light have been sent out to other customers but it is only these particular orders that have been discovered.'

Mr Dawson was now speechless and all he could manage

was a snort of indignation as he loudly exhaled. Eleanor moved his attention on to the latest incident.

'You had another visit from the Inspector a few days ago.'

'Aye, he came to the shop and checked all the shop weights against his. The two pound weight were four ounces light and he took it away with him.'

'And it was also unstamped.'

'Aye, and for the life of me I can't fathom how it's happened. That weight he took away were not mine. I know that. My weights have always been properly stamped and the Inspector knows that. He's checked them every year and they've always been right.'

'And you have no idea where this false weight could have come from?'

'None. And I haven't found my proper weight neither. I've looked all over the shop for it but it's not there.'

'Can you just describe for me exactly what happened when the Inspector arrived at your shop?'

'Well, I were not there. I were at the bank across the road, only for a few minutes like, and when I got back, the Inspector were there, in the shop testing the weights.'

'So, who was left in charge of the shop while you were out?'

'Charlie Perceval. He does the deliveries. And when I got back the Inspector said the two pound were short.'

'So, the two pound weight only weighed one pound twelve ounces and also did not bear the official stamp.'

'Aye, the Inspector said he had to report it and it would mean Court and being as how I had already been fined he thought it might mean prison and not just a fine.'

Mr Dawson looked at Eleanor and she could see that he was hoping she would contradict the Inspector.

'I'm afraid the Inspector is right, Mr Dawson. Being in possession of a false weight or an unstamped weight is a very serious offence and a jail sentence can be imposed.'

Eleanor paused. 'If you are convicted of this offence, that is. But, as you say, these recent incidents are the first time you have ever had any trouble with Weights and Measures and that will count in your favour. I believe you when you say you have no explanation for what has been happening; nevertheless, there must be an explanation and I think we should look for it. I can't promise anything, of course, but I do think it is worthwhile investigating a bit further before you decide whether to plead guilty or not. What do you think?'

'I'd be right pleased if you would, Miss Harriman. I can see that you understand what's what and I'm happy to leave it to you.'

'Thank you, Mr Dawson. I need some more information. First of all, does Charlie Perceval serve in the shop or does he only do deliveries?'

'No, not in the shop. He does the deliveries and he helps out with putting the orders together.'

'Ah, then, yes, I think that both the pattern and the motive are beginning to emerge. Let me explain what I have noticed.'

Eleanor began by drawing Mr Dawson's attention to the dates on which the incidents had occurred and the timing of Mr Dawson's actions in relation to his daughter. Mr Dawson became red in the face immediately Eleanor mentioned Charlie Perceval's interest in his daughter. He became progressively redder as Eleanor worked her way through the pattern of events and suggested that Charlie Perceval had been tampering with the scales or substituting a false weight as acts of revenge for being cut off from contact with his daughter.

'You see, Mr Dawson, the false weight that the Inspector took away must have come from somewhere and Charlie is the obvious source. It is not something one can obtain on the spur of the moment. It takes planning and presumably he intended to use it as often as he could until a customer complained or reported you to the Inspector. It was a piece of luck for him that you happened to be out of the shop when the Inspector arrived and he could substitute his weight for yours.'

Mr Dawson was now apoplectic with anger and ready to convict Charlie Perceval immediately without any further proof. Had the town still had stocks, Mr Dawson would have dragged Charlie there immediately and secured him in them without waiting for the constable or any form of due process. He opened his mouth to speak but could find no words to express his rage.

'Charlie has had plenty of opportunity to tamper with the scales and the weights and he certainly has a motive to do so. I know that you have forbidden your daughter to see Charlie and that you have taken steps to keep them apart, but I have reason to believe that your daughter is continuing to meet Charlie secretly even now and, of course, with you out of the way in prison he could do as he likes.'

'I'll...I'll..,' was all that Mr Dawson could manage, as he clenched and unclenched his fists.

Eleanor gave him a moment to calm down and then changed tack.

'Forgive my asking, Mr Dawson, but, after you became aware of Perceval's preference for your daughter, why did you keep him on?'

Mr Dawson took a deep breath and exhaled loudly. 'For his father's sake. He were a good man. And as a favour to his mother. Charlie worked for his father until the bank took the business away. The poor woman, with four other children to feed and no husband, she needed Charlie to have a job. The other boy went off to Sheffield and the others are still too young to work and anyway they're girls. They can't earn much.'

'I see,' said Eleanor. 'So, do you agree? Is it possible that Charlie Perceval may be the cause of your troubles since last December?'

119

'These problems have been a mystery to me. I've never had this happen and I'll be honest with you, Miss Harriman, I've not known where to turn. I've been at a loss. But if what you say is true…well…I don't know what's to be done, apart from getting rid of Charlie, that is. But that still doesn't clear my name, does it?'

'No, it doesn't and that is why I think it would be better for you to keep Charlie on, for the moment, and say nothing about our suspicions.' Mr Dawson wriggled in his chair in disagreement. Eleanor continued: 'It is important to get proof of what has been going on and I have had an idea. Let me explain what I am proposing. I want you to provoke Charlie into further action so that we can demonstrate to the Inspector that you are not to blame. The idea is to tempt Charlie to tamper with the scales or the weights again and catch him at it. To do that we need two things. We need to make him think that this current prosecution is not going ahead. That way he will believe that this latest tampering has been for nothing and he will be tempted to try again. At the same time, we need to make the temptation really strong. Could you send your daughter away for a few days? Somewhere where Charlie will not be able to contact her so that he will have no idea where she is?'

'I certainly can. In fact, if what you tell me about her continuing to meet him is true, it will be for her own good anyway and not just for a few days neither. She will soon find out where disobedience leads,' said Mr Dawson, ominously.

'You must understand,' said Eleanor, calmly, trying to get Mr Dawson's attention back to the matter in hand and away from the question of disciplining his daughter, 'that this may not alter your position in relation to the offence…'

'I'll send her to Great Aunt Cooper in Bolton. That will do very well,' said Mr Dawson, still not listening to Eleanor.

'…although it might help you to avoid a jail sentence. It

will depend a great deal on the evidence and the attitude of the Inspector,' continued Eleanor.

'Yes, yes,' said Mr Dawson, still not paying attention. 'I'll send her tomorrow.'

Changing tack and focussing on Sarah instead of the offence, Eleanor said: 'Well, you must instruct this aunt in Bolton that Sarah is not to have any communication with Charlie whatsoever. That is vital. Would she be reliable in that regard?'

'Oh, yes. Never fear,' promised Mr Dawson. 'You don't know Great Aunt Cooper! She were born last century and she keeps to the old ways. She'll have Sarah reading her Bible and mending linen all day. She doesn't hold with unmarried girls going about unaccompanied so there will be no chance of meetings or posting of letters. And any letters that are sent to Sarah will be opened and read by Great Aunt Cooper first.'

'Very well…' said Eleanor, feeling slightly sorry for Sarah given the punishment about to be inflicted on her. Then she paused because she could see that Mr Dawson was thinking and she waited for him to speak.

'This is how I'll work it, Miss Harriman. I'll take Sarah on the train and tell her we're just going to Stockport for some shopping. I'll arrange for Great Aunt Cooper to meet us at the station and she can take Sarah back to Bolton. By the time Sarah realises where she is going, it will be too late for her to tell Charlie.'

'Then as soon as your daughter is safely out of Buxton, you should keep an eye on Charlie and see what he does,' continued Eleanor. 'Perhaps, you could put temptation in his way. If you could give him some orders to make up and then leave him unsupervised, you could check the weight of each item yourself before the orders go out.'

'Now that is a grand idea. I tell you what I'll do. First thing tomorrow, I'll write down some orders, I'll say they've been rung through and I'll give them to Charlie to make up. I can't thank you enough, Miss Harriman. You've taken a weight off my shoulders. Now, I have just one more question, I know you can't speak for the Inspector but do you think there is any chance he really will stop this Court case?'

'Mr Talbot is better able to answer that, Mr Dawson, because he will be dealing with this prosecution.'

Edwin said: 'I do understand your position, Mr Dawson, and I shall explain to the Inspector what has happened. I shall certainly try to persuade him not to proceed but unfortunately it will be a decision for him. There is a good chance that he will decide not to. I am sure he is aware of your good reputation and that will count in your favour and he has told me that these recent occurrences have puzzled him. If we can provide him with evidence of what has been happening, I am sure he will try to resolve things in your favour but I cannot stress enough, our success or failure depends on us getting the evidence we need against Charlie Perceval.'

'Thank you, Mr Talbot. I know you'll do your best.' Mr Dawson stood up and went towards the door, thanking Eleanor again as he did so. Edwin accompanied him downstairs to the front door.

When he returned to Eleanor's office, Edwin said: 'Well done, Eleanor. I think you had Mr Dawson completely convinced.'

'I hope that he will be calm and play his part without giving the game away. I can understand how angry he must be if Perceval has done this deliberately but it won't help if he loses his temper,' said Eleanor.

'Well, it is worth a try.'

'I think Mr Dawson is telling us the truth. Or am I being naïve?'

'No, he does seem genuinely perplexed at what is happening. Your theory is perfectly plausible and I think he is a victim not a guilty party.'

'When he said that he had not received the notice telling him to present his weights at the Town Hall for inspection, I believed him. He knew that the Inspector had proof that the notice had been served and he had been told it would make no difference to his defence, so why would he bother to make up a lie and pretend that he hadn't received the notice?'

'So what are you suggesting?'

'If the notice had arrived while Mr Dawson was out, it could easily have been removed and destroyed by someone else in the shop.'

'Someone like young Charlie Perceval, you mean?' said Edwin.

'Yes. If I am right, he appears to be a determinedly vengeful young man. I wonder if Sarah Dawson knows anything about this,' said Eleanor. 'I don't imagine that she would be very impressed with Perceval if she knew that he was the cause of her father being prosecuted.'

'No. Certainly not,' said Edwin.

'I didn't tell Mr Dawson, because I didn't want to get him any more worked up than he already was, but Cicely and I saw Sarah Dawson up at Grin Low on Sunday. I didn't have time to tell you before Mr Dawson arrived. I think she might have been there with someone, probably Charlie, although I didn't actually see who it was. She went to great lengths not to be seen so I assume she was not there on her own.'

'Well, Eleanor, I think your explanation of these events is very persuasive. Let's hope Mr Dawson can provide the evidence we need.'

'But even if I am right,' said Eleanor, 'I still haven't solved Mr Dawson's problem, have I?'

'No,' said Edwin. 'I'm afraid not. He may still be prosecuted. We certainly should be able to keep him out of jail so, even if he is left with a fine, at least he will be able to keep his shop open and his family fed.'

'I hope we will be able to clear his name and save his reputation,' said Eleanor. 'Mr Perceval seems to have had a good reputation in town when he was running the motor garage and Mr Dawson clearly thought highly of him. Do you have any idea why Mr Dawson is so fiercely against Charlie Perceval?'

'No, although Mr Dawson pays Perceval's wages, so I suppose he is in a better position than anyone to know whether or not Perceval can afford to get married and keep his daughter in the manner accustomed and all that.'

'Yes, that's a point,' said Eleanor.

Edwin went back to his own office. As Eleanor was tidying up the papers on her desk, Mrs Clayton came in bringing with her Napoleon and Eleanor's morning tea.

CHAPTER THIRTEEN

The Post was delivered to Harriman & Talbot's office several times a day and James, as confidential clerk, opened all correspondence. He sorted the letters and documents according to which solicitor they were for, then took them all up to Mr Harriman, as senior partner. After Mr Harriman had glanced through the pile, he kept the letters relating to his own files and gave the others to James to deliver to Edwin and Eleanor. So, while Eleanor and Edwin were in conference with Mr Dawson, James was sorting the morning's second delivery. He opened the first envelope and was shocked by the letter it contained. He stood for some time just staring at it, wanting to destroy it immediately and not mention it to anyone, but dedication to his duties as clerk overcame his desire to protect his employers and he knew that he must take the letter to Mr Harriman and leave him to deal with it. He recovered his composure, sorted the rest of the letters, and went into Mr Harriman's office. He shut the door behind him and this was such an unusual occurrence that Mr Harriman looked up immediately, knowing something was wrong.

'Is something the matter, James?'

James approached the desk in silence and, putting the pile of letters on Mr Harriman's desk, handed him the offending letter separately. Mr Harriman frowned as he read it. He uttered a snort of indignation.

'Well, really!' He shook the letter angrily. 'I suppose this quotation is intended to refer to Eleanor.'

'That is what I took it to mean,' said James, 'but it is quite unjustified. It is insulting.'

'Libellous!' added Mr Harriman. 'What about the envelope. Was it addressed to me or to her?'

'To the firm,' said James, 'and typewritten, like the letter.'

Across the centre of a plain sheet of paper, there was one typewritten line of text. An extract from the Bible:

Do not profane your daughter by making her a harlot:
Leviticus 19:29

'Of course, my first instinct was to destroy the letter,' said James, 'but that would not have been proper and also, you may wish to keep it as evidence so that you can trace the culprit.'

'Quite right, James. I agree with you. My instinct is the same as yours. However, for the moment, will you put the letter and its envelope in a sealed envelope and lock the envelope in the safe out of harm's way. Let's just see what happens.'

'Very good, Mr Harriman,' said James taking the letter back.

'I don't think there is any need to mention it to Eleanor at the moment, do you?'

'No. Nothing would be gained by that.'

'I shall mention it to Mr Talbot, of course.'

'Of course. I shall put the letter out of sight immediately.'

'Thank you, James. I know I can rely on you.'

James bowed and left Mr Harriman to contemplate the message, its possible source, and how best to protect his daughter from this unwarranted criticism. Mr Harriman waited until Eleanor took Napoleon out for his lunchtime walk and then he consulted Edwin.

'Do you recall some time ago you had occasion to act in connection with a series of anonymous letters?'

'Yes, I do. Why?'

'What form did the letters take? My recollection is that they were quotations from the Bible.'

'They were. A plain piece of paper, typed message, just a verse or two. Has there been another one?'

'Yes, there has. Addressed to the firm but directed at me, actually.'

'Oh Lord! What are you accused of?'

'Not regulating my daughter's behaviour properly. It is implied that she is a harlot.'

'Well, that description won't stick for a start. Absolutely no truth to it.'

'I've asked James to put the letter in the safe for the moment. I'm not going to mention it to Eleanor.'

'No, best not. It certainly sounds like the sort of thing my client received. In her case, the source turned out to be the Watching Brethren. They should just mind their own business but apparently they think it is their duty to scrutinise the behaviour of others and then threaten them with eternal damnation. But, Eleanor...why her? Leaves a bad taste, doesn't it.'

'It does indeed. Of course, I realised that by letting her join this firm I would be exposing her to criticism, at least from some more conservative sources, but this sort of thing is completely unwarranted and unacceptable. I will not have my daughter hounded in this way.'

~O~

At lunchtime, Eleanor and Napoleon generally walked in the Pavilion Gardens. When he was free, Philip joined them. The shop he managed for Willis, Wise and Campbell, a firm of antique dealers, was only a short walk away and it closed for lunch. Today, Eleanor and Napoleon had reached the stone steps to the Pavilion when Eleanor saw Philip walking along the path beside the plant conservatory. She waited as he reached the top of the steps and came swiftly and gracefully down them.

'What ho! Eleanor. Hello, Napoleon, old chap,' he greeted them.

'Good afternoon, Philip. Do you have time to join us?'

'With pleasure, although you must promise not to talk about the Royal Visit. I am very tired of that subject. It appears to be the only topic of conversation that the customers and my parents have. The whole town is agog.'

'Yes, it does seem to be getting a lot of attention. Father's a subscriber to the Hospital so he has applied for tickets for himself and Cicely. Will your parents be there?'

'Oh yes. Weeks ago my mother began worrying about what she was going to wear and she has already changed her mind several times and no doubt will do so several times more before the day. I pointed out that there will be at least a thousand other people there and, consequently, it is unlikely that anyone will notice what she is wearing. She said that was not reassuring and that I had missed the point. According to her, it is respectful to wear something really smart for the Princess whether one is going to be within the royal range of vision or not. And, of course, "something really smart" means one's entire outfit must be new and expensive. You're not going to the Hospital?'

'No, I volunteered to mind Richard. He's going to be waving a flag with the school children who have been chosen to wait outside the Thermal Baths. I expect I shall go and watch the Princess arrive there. Cicely tells me that she will be staying at Chatsworth House and the Duke and Duchess will be bringing her. Apparently there will be a house party staying there and they are all coming, I suppose as moral support for the Princess. They're going to arrive in a cavalcade of motor-cars which will drive along Spring Gardens to the Thermal Baths, so I am planning to watch from The Slopes after I have made sure Richard is in the right place. What are you planning to do?'

'I have no plans. I have orders. Apparently, I am to be one of the accessories my mother has chosen as part of her new outfit so I shall be accompanying her to the Hospital because Father will be in the official line up at the Thermal Baths. Did you know that they are presenting the Princess with a Blue John vase while she is at the Baths? It's absolutely magnificent. All the gifts are on display at Mr Woodruff's shop. I went there yesterday to have a look. Actually, I prefer the inlaid table. The craftsmanship is superb. It's…'

'Philip,' interrupted Eleanor, 'you said you didn't want to talk about the Royal Visit, and yet you've managed to make it the sole topic of conversation of our walk so far.'

'Oh dear, so I have.' Philip laughed delightedly. 'I consider myself justly rebuked. As a penance, I shall walk in complete silence from now to the end of this path.'

CHAPTER FOURTEEN

The third incident which disrupted the usual calm of Buxton occurred the following morning. Mondo Aubrey-Mere had finished his breakfast and was eager to visit his greenhouse. He wanted to monitor the progress of his chrysanthemums and assess their prize winning qualities. He put on his overcoat and went through the conservatory, followed by Jasper. It was a beautiful morning and man and dog paused at the door into the garden, Mondo to admire the garden, and Jasper to sniff the air. There had been a frost last night and now there was bright sunshine, as well as that clear crispness which autumn brings to the air. There was a large greenhouse near the back boundary of the garden and the path which lead to it took a winding course, passing first through a shrubbery and then through the vegetable garden. The path was uneven in places and Mondo was conscious of the need to watch where he was walking so it wasn't until he was amongst the cabbages that he looked up and saw his greenhouse for the first time that morning. He stopped, midstride, and remained rigid like a pointing dog. Jasper came to an abrupt halt behind him and adopted a similar pose. Mondo stared in disbelief. Every pane of glass had been covered in white paint.

When his brain had fully comprehended the enormity of this outrage, Mondo began walking slowly towards the greenhouse. He suffered a mixture of emotions and then logic came to the fore. Being a magistrate, he knew better than to rush into action and disturb the scene of the crime. Instead, he balanced the urgent need to salvage his chrysanthemums against the risk of destroying the evidence that would convict the culprit. He stood and considered the problem. He reasoned that, at this stage of their development, the chrysanthemums would not be affected unduly by having the light blocked out, even though they would by now have missed several hours of full sunshine. The real enemy of chrysanthemums at this time in their development was humidity. It caused fungal infections on the petals, known as damping off, two words dreaded by the chrysanthemum competition enthusiast. Mondo feared that, if the heating had been turned off during last night's frost, moisture would have collected on the inside of the glass and dripped onto the plants. The paint made it impossible to see from the outside of the greenhouse whether or not moisture had already collected on the inside.

There was a keyed lock on the door into the greenhouse and also a bolt secured by a padlock. The door was still secure. Mondo undid the padlock, slid the bolt aside, and then unlocked the top keyed lock. In trepidation at what he might find, he took a deep breath and opened the greenhouse door. The air was warm and he let out his breath in relief. The temperature inside was just as it should be. Even with the reduced light, he could see that above him the greenhouse roof was dry. Leaving Jasper outside, he stepped into the greenhouse, closing the door behind him, and then carefully examined his competition candidates one by one. They were all quite safe. After some time, he went out of the greenhouse and locked the door. He walked a few paces away and then turned to look back at the greenhouse. He stood thinking, then he looked at Jasper who had been sitting patiently on the path while the inspection of the greenhouse had been going on.

'That's very puzzling, Jasper. You didn't bark, did you, old chap?'

Jasper put his head on one side and looked at Mondo.

'If someone was in the garden last night, why did you not

hear him? And another thing. If someone wanted to damage my plants why go to all that trouble with the painting and yet leave the heating on?'

Jasper, having no answer, lay down on the path and put his chin on his paws.

'If he wanted to kill my chances in the competition, all he had to do was cut the heating pipe and save himself the bother of climbing on the roof with a pot of paint.'

Mondo shook his head and went back to the greenhouse. He scratched at what he thought was white paint. It was quite dry so it had been there for some time but, to his relief, he found that it was only lime wash.

'That shouldn't be too hard to get off,' he said, 'but if the blighter really wanted to ruin my chances why the devil didn't he use proper paint and black paint, at that? By the time we got that off, the plants would really have suffered.' Mondo was impatient with fools. 'Can't even do a deliberate act of vandalism properly! Incompetent, as well as being destructive!' he added, contemptuously. He turned back to the path where Jasper was now lying basking in the sun, indifferent to the crisis. 'Come on,' said Mondo and he turned back towards the house, intending to telephone the police. Jasper followed at his heels.

Mondo walked slowly, paying attention to the uneven path but still puzzling over the identity of the culprit. He went through the vegetable garden and he had just reached the edge of the shrubbery when, out of the corner of his eye, he caught a glimpse of something odd. Something that was not there yesterday. He stopped and stared, frowning as he tried to comprehend. Then, as he realised what it was, he smiled and then he began to snigger and then the snigger billowed out into great roaring, joyous laughter which caused Jasper to look at him in alarm. Nestled beside a holly bush was a stone lion with a blue bow tied around its neck.

It was only visible to someone walking back towards the house which is why Mondo had not noticed it on his way out to the greenhouse. When Mondo had stopped laughing enough to recover his equilibrium, he removed the lion from the shrubbery and put it in the garden shed. Then he considered what to do about the greenhouse. The gardener, Mr Wardle, only came to Brook House three mornings each week but, fortunately, today was one of his days. When Mr Wardle arrived with his young assistant, Joe, just after ten o'clock, Mondo explained about the lime wash and took them down to the greenhouse for a conference as to the best way to remove it.

'It's vital to get that lime wash off quickly,' said Mondo, supressing a smile. 'I don't want the chrysanthemums to lose too many hours of daylight.'

The gardener nodded in agreement as he stood looking in dismay at the greenhouse.

'My word,' he said, 'it's a bit of a liberty to be taking, that is.' He pushed back his cap and scratched his head as he weighed up the options. 'It's too big a job for me and the lad but with the season over, the livery stables won't be busy. I expect they'll be glad to spare a couple of stable hands to help out. I could send the lad over there to see, if you like. Although it'll be an expense, o' course.'

'Yes, that is an excellent suggestion, Mr Wardle. Pay whatever it takes. Just get rid of the lime wash as quickly as you can, there's a good chap.'

Mondo went back into the house, sat down at his study desk, still chuckling, and began to deal with the paperwork associated with being a magistrate. The gardener sent Joe to the livery stables for reinforcements and, by twelve o'clock, he and Joe and the two stable hands had cleaned all of the lime wash off. Mr Wardle knocked on the back door to say that the job was finished and Rowland went to tell Mondo. The gardener normally only worked for Mondo during the mornings and it was now time for his dinner but he had not been able to do any of the usual tasks scheduled for the day. Mondo inspected the greenhouse and expressed himself satisfied.

Mr Wardle said: 'I'll be off then, unless you want me and Joe to come back and do the things we should've done this morning.'

'If you have time,' said Mondo. 'I'd be most grateful. Tell Rowland to pay you for the extra time, of course.'

The gardener nodded and then hesitated. 'There's an ornament of some sort in the middle of the garden shed. Did you want it putting in the garden?' he asked.

Mondo spluttered, trying to suppress his mirth. 'Why not?' he said. 'But leave it for today, there's a good chap. It can wait until next time. I haven't quite decided where to put it yet.'

Mondo returned to the house for his lunch, still smiling. He knew that as soon as the four witnesses had left the garden and gone home for their dinner, the story of the painted greenhouse would begin to spread around the town.

~O~

Just before four o'clock that afternoon, Eleanor went down to Chillingham & Baynard's bank. Mr Harriman needed Mr Sutton to sign some documents which had to be posted that evening and as his signature had to be witnessed by a solicitor it was more convenient for Eleanor to take the documents to the bank instead of waiting for him to come to the office. Eleanor entered the banking chamber and asked for Mr Sutton. Mr Pidcock, the head clerk, came out from his office.

'Good afternoon, Miss Harriman, Mr Sutton is engaged at the moment. Today's cheque clearing process has just finished. He only has to check the balances, so he should be free in a few minutes if you care to wait.'

Eleanor took a seat and looked around the banking chamber. The last customers of the day were concluding their transactions. With dismay she recognised Mr Norman standing with his back to her at the grille of one of the tellers. Eleanor knew that the moment he turned around he would see her and there was nowhere to move to, nowhere to hide. She hoped that his attention would be fully occupied by the woman who was standing beside him, an older woman wearing a long black dress and bonnet in a style not fashionable since the turn of the century. However, as Mr Norman turned away from the teller, he saw Eleanor immediately. He abandoned the woman and walked towards Eleanor, smiling and holding out his hand, saying: 'Miss Harriman, what an unexpected pleasure!'

Eleanor stood up and shook hands with him, inwardly shuddering at the proprietorial way he looked at her and the controlling clasp of his hand. Mindful of Philip's comments at the tennis club dance she said, as indifferently as she could manage: 'Good afternoon, Mr Norman.' She did not smile and she made no further attempt at conversation.

'And what brings you here today?' asked Mr Norman, adopting what he thought was a bantering tone but only managing to sound patronising. 'Withdrawing funds to go shopping? A new hat, perhaps? Or some shoes for those dainty feet of yours?'

'No, Mr Norman,' said Eleanor frostily. 'I am not going shopping. I am at work.'

Mr Norman, undeterred continued: 'Miss Harriman, about the Royal Visit. Mother and I are intending to watch from my office window as the Princess arrives along Spring Gardens. If you would care to join us, you would be most welcome.'

'That's very kind of you to offer, Mr Norman, but unfortunately I have already made arrangements for that day and I am needed elsewhere.'

'I suppose you will be watching the events with Mr Sutton,' he said, sharply.

Eleanor was puzzled by this remark but did not have time to reply because the clerks who had been engaged in the cheque clearing process came into the banking chamber, followed by Mr Sutton. Seeing Eleanor, he moved quickly forward and said:

'Ah, Miss Harriman, good afternoon.' He nodded to Mr Norman. 'I'm sorry to have kept you waiting. Mr Pidcock informed me of your arrival but, as you see, I was already occupied. Please come this way.'

Eleanor smiled at Mr Sutton gratefully and then said good-bye to Mr Norman. As she followed Mr Sutton into his office, she heard the abandoned Mr Noman say: 'This way, mother.'

~O~

When Mr Wardle visited the Bakers Arms that evening and ordered his usual pint he related to all those present the story of the greenhouse. Many of his listeners were also chrysanthemum growers and some were members of the Chrysanthemum Society so the subject was of general interest and the conversation went on for some time.

'It's th' show in a couple o' weeks, Magistrate's bin a winner wi' 'is Chrysanths sev'ral year now. It were one of 'is rivals, fer sure.'

'Aye, if th' police looks for 'is best rival, happen they'll find th' culprit.'

'Th' police ought to ask Mr Wentworth-Streate for th' list of prizes fer last year. That'll give 'em th' names of people to 'vestigate.'

'Well, it's bound to be someone fit, like. Prepared to climb roofs in th' dead o' night.'

'Not th' women then.'

'Nor anyone over forty.'

There was loud laughter at this suggestion.

'Eh but, magistrate, 'e were laughin' an' all. What d'yer make o' that then?' asked Mr Wardle.

There was much speculation as to the habits and mental capacity of the class of persons to which the magistrate belonged but no satisfactory explanation was arrived at. What none of them knew was that between the end of April and the beginning of November, Jasper occupied a kennel outside and on the night in question he had not detected an intruder in the garden or, if he had, he had chosen not to alert the household.

CHAPTER FIFTEEN

By mid-morning the following day, news of the Prize Chrysanthemum Incident had spread completely throughout the town and had been thoroughly discussed in all the shops and pubs without enlightenment. News reached the offices of Harriman & Talbot at Hall Bank via the usual source. The gardener's assistant, Joe, lodged in Church Street and the previous evening had gone to The Wheatsheaf for ale. He had just happened to mention the story of the painted greenhouse to Percy from Mr Morten's dairy, who had just happened to mention it to Alf the following morning when the milk was delivered, who had just happened to mention it to his sister. So Mrs Clayton was able to relay the story to Eleanor and Mr Harriman together with their breakfast.

Mr Harriman said: 'I must telephone to Mondo and see whether or not his plants have suffered. I know how important they are to him.'

'I wonder whether this incident is connected to the bank incident in any way,' said Eleanor, and turning to Mrs Clayton, she asked: 'Were there any words painted on the greenhouse, do you know?'

'Alf didn't mention it,' said Mrs Clayton. 'Are you thinking it might be Sam Perceval again?'

'Possibly. But I'm not sure what interest Sam Perceval would have in chrysanthemums. I suppose it might just as easily be one of Mr Aubrey-Mere's rivals for the chrysanthemum trophy. Some of them do take winning very seriously.'

'Oh, they do,' said Mrs Clayton emphatically. 'Sam Fidler

next door's been fussing for weeks and his wife is that sick and tired of him and his chrysanthemums. He's in that greenhouse of his day and night, trying to breed a new flower or something and he talks about nothing else. He got a second prize last year and he's set his heart on winning this year. I don't see what all the fuss is about myself. They're just flowers, after all.' With this, Mrs Clayton returned to the kitchen.

~O~

Since the day she learnt that Princess Mary would be visiting Buxton, Lady Carleton-West had been planning a function which she had decided to call the Royal Evening Reception. She was not the doyen of Buxton society by accident. She understood the social needs of the town perfectly. Therefore, this was a social occasion entirely of her own invention intended to fill the void, which she was confident would arise after the Princess had left town to return to Chatsworth and the excitement of the afternoon had started to fade. At the Royal Evening Reception, Lady Carleton-West's guests would have the opportunity to discuss their impressions of The Royal Visit and would have the enjoyment of hearing from Lady Carleton-West herself all the details of what she anticipated would be her own Encounter with Royalty.

Lady Carleton-West spent a great deal of time organising events in support of local charities and had raised a significant amount of money for the Devonshire Hospital. Although she did not mention it to anyone, she naturally hoped that one day her efforts would be recognised with the newly created award for civic service: the Most Excellent Order of the British Empire. In the meantime, however, she had to be satisfied with an invitation to sit on the official platform within curtseying distance of the Princess during the ceremony of laying the commemoration stone. Consequently, she would be able to give her guests a detailed first-hand account of the afternoon's proceedings.

As the Royal Evening Reception was an event which had no precedent, Lady Carleton-West had to consider carefully how to indicate to her guests what to expect. The first difficulty was the time at which the reception should begin. The Royal Evening Reception was neither a dinner or a ball. A dinner invitation would normally be for 8.30pm but she did not intend to offer dinner to such a large group of people. An invitation to a ball would specify 10.00pm which allowed guests time to dine beforehand. But such a late start was most inappropriate for her Reception. If the guests were allowed to dine somewhere else beforehand, they would have had ample opportunity to discuss the Royal Visit and exhaust that topic of conversation before they arrived at Top Trees, thus depriving the Reception of its purpose. However, to invite guests for any time other than the two socially acceptable times might suggest an ignorance of the rules of etiquette. This was unthinkable and Lady Carleton-West shuddered at the thought of appearing like a society novice or a parvenu.

Unable to resolve this dilemma of social etiquette, she had decided, in desperation, to put the question to Sir Marmaduke. One evening after dinner some weeks earlier, she had explained the difficulty to him or, more accurately, she had soliloquised in his presence as he dozed fitfully in his armchair. Some of her words had filtered through to his brain and, thinking only of his own comfort, he had roused himself sufficiently to say gloomily: 'I should think dinner's going to be a very scrappy affair that evening. The servants are sure to want time off to go and see this royal person and there will be nobody to serve food.'

Lady Carleton-West had stared at her husband in surprise because, for once, he had made a contribution.

'Yes,' she said as she imagined the scene in her dining

room, 'you are absolutely correct. Our servants will all want to desert us for a glimpse of the Princess and, of course, it is our patriotic duty to let them go. But when they do get back, they will be too busy chattering about the importance of what they have just witnessed to concentrate on serving dinner. Under those circumstances, my guests will be grateful to get away from their tables early.' She paused then added, decisively. 'I think it will be safe to specify 9.00pm, carriages at eleven thirty, and make it clear on the invitations that a proper supper will be served. Thank you, my dear. You are a genius.'

Sir Marmaduke had accepted this as a statement of fact and gone back to sleep. Having settled on a time for the Reception, Lady Carleton-West had then considered the difficult question of dress-code. The anticipated turmoil in the servants' hall would probably also extend upstairs to the ritual of dressing. Guests who had been abandoned by their staff might not arrive at the Reception in the right mood if they had had to struggle unaided with the rigours of white tie dressing. Although it pained her to lower her standards, she decided to be prudent and mark the invitation cards, Black Tie.

As the Reception was to be a static event and did not require the amount of space needed for dancing, Lady Carleton-West could afford to be generous with her invitations. The Oak drawing room, connected with the Green drawing room by double doors, would accommodate a considerable crowd. In addition, there was the morning room on the other side of the main hall for less important guests. The link between the morning room and the drawing rooms would be made by a string quartet positioned in the main hall amongst floral decorations and potted palms. All those of appropriate social status had been invited. Most had meekly accepted. As it was obvious that they were all going to be in town for the Royal Visit, it was difficult for them to think of a convincing reason for declining. In any event, they too realised that they would be at a loose end once the visit was over and were grateful to have something to do at someone else's expense. Even Sir Marmaduke had been deprived of all his usual excuses for avoiding his wife's social occasions and had been ordered to attend.

Now, with only three days before the Royal Visit, Lady Carleton-West was sitting at her desk in the morning room with her many lists of things to be done, imperiously reading out each item to Mrs Kendall and nodding with satisfaction or giving directions as Mrs Kendall informed her of the present state which each of the arrangements had reached.

~O~

Just after four thirty that afternoon, Mrs Hazelwood summoned another two of her dogs for their walk. Since her first unsuccessful visit to Burlington Road, she had made another attempt to encounter Mr Aubrey-Mere but without result, and her many social engagements had prevented her until now from returning again. As she reached the top of the road, she and her dogs began their slow progress to the end of the road, turned, and returned to their starting point. Then they detoured to dawdle along The Serpentine as before, returning to Burlington Road for another slow promenade to the end of the road and back.

It was beginning to get dark and Mrs Hazelwood thought there was now a greater chance of Mr Aubrey-Mere either coming home or leaving to go out for the evening. Rather than risk finding herself at the far end of the road and out of reach if the magistrate did make an appearance, she decided to take up a position on the opposite side of the road from Brook House. By standing there, she could give the impression that she had just reached that spot and stopped in order to cross the road and them if the magistrate did arrive, she could cross over and greet him with "Oh, good afternoon, what a lovely surprise to meet you so unexpectedly" and her most winning smile.

On the opposite side of the road from Brook House, almost level with the gates of Thornstead, there was a large tree with a thick trunk and overhanging branches, low to the ground. Mrs Hazelwood thought that would be an ideal place to stand unobserved. She was about to cross the road and take cover when she realised that there was already someone standing next to the tree trunk. There was sufficient light still to see that it was a man, not very tall, dressed in dark clothing, and he was looking towards the side of the road where Mrs Hazelwood was standing, although he didn't appear to have noticed her. She stopped, uncertain what to do. Then, confronted by the sight of another person seemingly spying, lying in wait for someone just as she had planned to do, she was overwhelmed with a sense of the absurdity of her position. She turned abruptly and walked quickly away, tugging at the dogs' leads to make sure they followed her.

~O~

Later that evening, after dinner, Superintendent Johnson called at Brook House. Mr Aubrey-Mere was occasionally interrupted at odd hours when the police needed authorisation for something or wanted a warrant signed, so for Rowland this was nothing unusual, although he noted that the Superintendent was not in uniform. Assuming that the policeman had come on official business, Rowland left him in the hall, saying: 'I shall inform Mr Aubrey-Mere that you are here.'

The magistrate was in his study reading the paper and Jasper was sprawled in front of the fire.

'Show him in, Rowland, by all means,' said Mondo. 'And bring us some whisky, would you?'

Rowland relieved the superintendent of his hat and overcoat

and showed him into the study. The magistrate greeted him cheerily and noted that the policeman was frowning and looking ill at ease.

'Have you come for a warrant, Superintendent,' asked the magistrate, cheerfully, 'or is this about my greenhouse? Have you news of an arrest?'

'Well, yes,' said the Superintendent. 'And no. As a matter of fact I am not sure which.'

'Let's have it then. What's the story?' asked Mondo.

'I understand that at some time on Monday night or early Tuesday morning someone covered your greenhouse in lime wash.'

'That's correct,' said Mondo, trying not to smile. 'My greenhouse was assaulted.'

Rowland returned carrying a tray.

'Have a whisky while you're here, won't you?' said Mondo.

'Very kind of you, sir,' said the superintendent. 'Thank you.'

'Not at all. On such a miserable night, it's the least I can do to repay you for your trouble in coming here.'

'Mr Wentworth-Streate and Mr Wall, the Mayor-Elect, came to see me today. As they are on the committee in charge of the arrangements for Princes Mary's visit, they are very worried about this current spate of damage to property. First the bank, and now your greenhouse.'

'I can assure you, Superintendent, the two incidents are not connected in any way, at least, not in the way you might imagine.'

'All the same, the committee is probably right to be concerned. This event will provide some much needed publicity for the town. A lot of people depend on the income they earn from visitors and the committee does not want people getting the wrong impression about what sort of town this is. I'd like to know your thoughts on the matter.'

'I see, well. At first I thought it was someone who doesn't

know anything about growing chrysanthemums but then I realised it must be someone who knows a great deal about the subject, enough to know that the damage inflicted on the greenhouse would not harm the plants. Fortunately, I was at home that morning and so discovered the lime wash first thing. Also, it was a day on which my gardener usually comes, so I was able to have the lime wash removed before condensation had a chance to cause damage. Perhaps the perpetrator knew that it was my habit to inspect the greenhouse first thing and, therefore, was certain that I would get to the greenhouse quickly.'

'Mr Wentworth-Streate has been thinking along similar lines,' said Superintendent Johnson. 'When he heard the facts, he suggested that the culprit was knowledgeable about chrysanthemums, perhaps even a rival member of the Chrysanthemum Society, although he was reluctant to think so. But, all the same, the competition does get fierce just before the judging and we have had incidents of sabotage before. Mr Wentworth-Streate did look through the list of members just in case. He came up with three likely candidates but I won't name them in case he's wrong. The question is, sir, what do you want me to do about it?'

'Do you want to do anything, Superintendent?'

'Well, I need to know whether or not you want to press charges. It's up to you, sir.'

'But I sense from your tone that you are against pressing charges.'

'Not at all.'

'Then what is preventing you from proceeding, Superintendent?'

'Well, sir, it's just that, if Mr Wentworth-Streate's list is correct, well, it doesn't look good for the town, does it? It would be different if it was one of the lads who are known to be a bit wild and skylarking but...' He stopped and took a sip of whisky.

'Hmmm. No, it's dashed awkward when respectable citizens go about damaging other people's property instead of setting an example, isn't it?'

'Exactly, sir.'

'Yes, I see your point, Superintendent. Reprehensible and irresponsible behaviour,' said Mondo, lightly, brushing the problem away with a gesture of his hand. He gave his full attention to his whisky. 'So you think making an arrest would only draw the public's attention to this incident?'

There was a pause and the superintendent wondered where this conversation was going. He seemed suddenly to be adopting the opposite position from the one he had intended to take when he arrived. He was confused. The two men sipped their whisky in silence. Jasper stood up and turned around so that his other side could be toasted by the fire.

Eventually Mondo said: 'Anyway, Superintendent, you will be pleased to know that my chrysanthemums have not been harmed by their little adventure and, apart from the cost of cleaning the lime wash off, I have suffered no damage. And I don't think there is the least fear that the culprit will interfere with the royal visit in any way.'

The superintendent nodded. After another silence in which they contemplated the fire and sipped their whisky, the magistrate topped up the superintendent's glass and changed the subject to the reports of dog fighting, asking if there had been any progress. Superintendent Johnson explained the enquiries that were being made and the information he had received from Sheffield. He concluded: 'There are definitely fights being held. It's my view that people in the town know more than they're letting on but someone, sooner or later, will talk out of turn and provide a clue to the location where these fights are taking place.'

Having finished his whisky, the superintendent got to his feet saying that he had better go. The magistrate rang for

Rowland, and said: 'So what do you suggest, Superintendent?'

The superintendent was still confused.

'About the greenhouse?' asked Mondo.

'Well sir, on reflection, perhaps we can let it go just this once.'

Mondo nodded. 'Yes,' he said. 'I think that would be best, just this once. Thank you very much for coming, Superintendent. Good night.'

'Good night, sir,' said the Superintendent.

Rowland saw the Superintendent into his coat, handed him his hat, and opening the front door, wished him good night. The Superintendent had come fully expecting the magistrate to want to press charges and he went away perplexed.

Despite the fact that no arrests were made after the Prize Chrysanthemum Incident, popular opinion insisted that the culprit was Sam Perceval simply because of his previous history, although no-one could suggest a plausible reason why he should have been interested in chrysanthemums.

CHAPTER SIXTEEN

At eleven o'clock on Thursday, Mr Dawson telephoned James and asked for an appointment with Eleanor and Edwin as soon as possible. He said that he would come to Hall Bank whenever they were free. After checking with Eleanor and Edwin, James arranged the appointment and, just before midday, Mr Dawson arrived at Hall Bank holding a reluctant Charlie Perceval firmly by the arm. When James announced their arrival, Edwin went downstairs to meet Mr Dawson and the two of them returned to Eleanor's office leaving Charlie sitting on a chair in the waiting area under the watchful eye of James. After greeting Eleanor, Mr Dawson sat down squarely, hands on knees, and said to her:

'Well, I have to hand it to you, lassie, that idea of yours worked a treat.'

'That is very good news, Mr Dawson,' said Eleanor smiling.

Mr Dawson turned to Edwin saying: 'What do you think, Mr Talbot? I caught Charlie cheating with the scales this morning. I've brought him here because I want to know what's best to do next.'

Edwin said: 'I am pleased we have been able to get to the bottom of this so quickly, Mr Dawson. Now, tell us exactly what has happened.'

Mr Dawson turned back to Eleanor: 'I took Sarah off to her Aunt Cooper straightaway, like you said, and I told Charlie that she had left town. I said I'd heard he'd been seeing her and I'd arranged for her to go into service, like I'd threatened. Then I watched Charlie like a hawk. I saw him last night just as I were shutting up shop. Fiddling about with something behind some boxes of apples on one of the shelves in the storeroom. He didn't see me and when he'd gone I had a look. Sure enough, he'd hidden a weight there. Eight ounces. Ready for the morning, I expect. False, of course. I checked and it only weighed six. And unstamped.' He paused, nodding and rubbing his hands up and down on this knees in satisfaction.

'And Charlie used the weight today?' prompted Eleanor.

'He did, that. When he got to the shop and went out front to do the sweeping up, I looked in the storeroom for the weight. It had gone so I knew he were planning to use it. I'd thought about how I could catch him out. I didn't want him using the false weight on customers so I worked out a plan.' Mr Dawson paused and rubbed his hands gleefully. 'I wrote out an order, a pretend one, and I made sure he'd need to use the eight ounce weight. I told Charlie the order had been rung through last thing the night before, which of course it hadn't. I said I had paperwork to catch up on as it were a quiet time for the shop and I asked him to make up the order. I went and sat at the desk in the back of the shop and left him to it. He just couldn't resist the chance I'd given him.'

'That was very clever of you, Mr Dawson. So Charlie used the false weight?' asked Eleanor.

'Must have,' said Mr Dawson. 'When he'd finished I sent him off to the bank to get some change and while he were gone I checked the order. All the things he had used his weight for, of course, they were all light. I looked for the false weight but there were no sign of it. He must have taken it with him when he went to the bank.'

'And did you mention the order to Charlie?' asked Eleanor.

'No, I telephoned Mr Wildgoose straightaway and made this appointment and I just let Charlie carry on as normal. Then, when it were time, I got my sister to mind the shop and marched him down here. So what do we do now, Miss Harriman?'

149

'Well, we shall certainly speak to the Inspector about this latest charge against you,' said Eleanor. 'The Inspector will want to investigate Charlie's activities.'

'He will also be very interested to know where Charlie got the false weights from,' added Edwin.

'I think we will start by having a word with Charlie, don't you?' said Eleanor.

Edwin went downstairs. When a truculent and crosslooking Charlie Percival appeared on the threshold, Eleanor greeted him politely and asked him to sit down. He did so awkwardly and noisily, ignoring Mr Dawson completely and then folded his arms across his chest, fists clenched. Edwin resumed his seat. Charlie was putting on a good show of bravado and Eleanor thought that, as he was glaring at her defiantly, it probably was intended to intimidate her but she also noticed that Charlie was nervously tapping his heel on the floor.

'I think you know why you are here, Charlie,' said Eleanor, calmly.

Charlie remained silent and continued to glare at her.

'Mr Dawson has told me about an incident in his shop this morning and he has brought you here so that you can give me your explanation.'

'He's got no right,' said Charlie, loudly and aggressively.

Mr Dawson opened his mouth to speak and then thought better of it. He decided to leave things to Eleanor and remain silent for the rest of the interview.

'If what Mr Dawson tells me is true, and I have absolutely no reason to doubt him, he has every right to ask for an explanation of your behaviour this morning,' said Eleanor, quietly. 'Mr Dawson has told me that he discovered that the weight of some of the items in the order that you made up for him this morning was incorrect. In particular, the items for which you would have had to use the eight ounce weight. Those items all weighed short.'

Charlie continued to glare at Eleanor but said nothing.

Eleanor went on: 'Mr Dawson has reason to believe that when you weighed out the goods this morning, you substituted a false eight ounce weight for his correct one. And I have reason to believe that it is not the first time that you have used a false weight. You have done the same thing on previous occasions and you have done other things as well which have caused Mr Dawson to be accused of weights and measures offences. Offences he did not commit. You have stood by and allowed him to be falsely accused and incur punishment he did not merit. I can, if you like, list all of your offences but I think you know only too well already what they are.'

'He's the one responsible. It's his shop,' said Charlie, defiantly. He glanced in the direction of Mr Dawson.

'Well, unfortunately for you, that is not the case,' said Eleanor. 'Mr Dawson is not the one responsible. You are.'

'I know my rights,' said Charlie fiercely. He leaned back in his chair assertively.

'Perhaps you do, but you must also know that what you did today and on previous occasions was wrong, against the law. In fact, it was you who committed the offences for which Mr Dawson has recently been charged.'

'You can't touch me, I'm only an employee,' said Charlie and he uncrossed him arms and gripped each side of the chair seat, leaning forward as he did so.

'And where did you get that idea from?' asked Eleanor.

'That's got nothing to do with you,' said Charlie, rudely.

'Well, let me explain something to you, Charlie. Wherever you got your information from, it is incorrect. You see, normally, an employee is protected when there is a problem with weighing goods. He is not held responsible if the scales are faulty. That responsibility falls on the employer and he is the one who is charged...'

'That's what I just said,' interrupted Charlie.

'...but,' continued Eleanor, and she paused and looked directly at Charlie, 'if the employee knows that the scales are faulty or that the weights are false or, worse still, has himself caused them to be inaccurate, the defence of "only being an employee" is not open to him. He is the one responsible and he alone is the person who will be charged with the offence. Not the shopkeeper.'

Eleanor watched Charlie carefully to see what effect this piece of information had on him.

'You wouldn't know,' said Charlie, staring at Eleanor aggressively. 'You're only a woman. You're just trying to trick me.'

'No, Charlie. I am not trying to trick you,' said Eleanor, calmly, shaking her head. 'I am telling you the truth.' Eleanor returned Charlie's stare steadily and then she said: 'You seem to be intelligent enough and I am sure you can understand the law if I show you the relevant section of the Act.'

Charlie watched intently as Eleanor picked up a volume from the desk in front of her, checked the index and turned to the page she wanted. She turned the book around so that it was facing Charlie and put it down on the desk in front of him, resting her index finger at a point half way down the page.

'Read that, where my finger is.'

Charlie leaned forward so that he could see the book and read, slowly and carefully, his lips moving as he followed the words indicated. He frowned and then sat back in his chair, folding his arms across his chest again but, this time, not quite so aggressively.

'You see, Charlie. That is what the law says. You are not exempt. You knew that the scales were faulty and that the weights were false and you used them knowing that they were inaccurate. Unfortunately for you, there are two, or possibly three, offences involved: first, possession of a false weight, which I suspect is also unstamped, so that is the second offence, and thirdly, using an inaccurate weighing mechanism, knowing it to be incorrect.'

Eleanor looked at Charlie and waited for his response. Edwin and Mr Dawson watched as Charlie glared back. The room was silent, except for the creaking of Charlie's chair as he moved restlessly. Then Charlie dropped his gaze and took a deep breath.

'Because of your actions, Charlie, Mr Dawson has been prosecuted and fined. He is now facing two additional very serious charges, made all the more so because of his previous conviction. Also, his reputation has been damaged. He has suffered all of this because of you and, it appears to me that the motive for your actions, is simply anger and vindictiveness towards Mr Dawson.'

Eleanor paused. Charlie looked up and stared at Eleanor with contempt.

She continued: 'I suspect that you have the false weight in your possession now.'

Eleanor noticed with amusement the slight, defensive movement of Charlie's hand towards his pocket which he checked abruptly as soon as he realised what he was doing.

'Very shortly,' said Eleanor, 'you are going to be taken to the police station so that you can hand the weight over. My advice to you is to tell the truth so that your co-operation will count in your favour when you are charged. You could start by telling the police where you got the weight. I am sure that is something that will interest them greatly and it may mean that they can charge a second person with an offence. That will also count in your favour. The Inspector of Weights and Measures will be given the full story so that Mr Dawson does not suffer any further injustice.'

Eleanor waited to see if Charlie would respond but he remained silent, now avoiding eye contact.

'You may think,' said Eleanor, 'that your actions were

justified because Mr Dawson has forbidden you to see his daughter.' Charlie started and glanced briefly at Mr Dawson. 'Mr Dawson is quite within his rights to protect his daughter, particularly if the person from whom he is protecting her is engaging in criminal activity. I am giving Sarah the benefit of the doubt here, Charlie, because I am assuming that she has not been involved in this scheme of yours and knows nothing about it.'

Mr Dawson, who had remained admirably silent until now burst out angrily with: 'By heaven, if you have involved her in any way…'

Charlie began to look seriously alarmed.

Eleanor interrupted: 'I wonder, Charlie, whether you have considered what her feelings will be towards you when she finds out what her father has suffered as a consequence of your actions, and when she understands that the humiliation he has suffered by being falsely accused has been caused by you. I cannot believe that, as a loyal daughter, she will want to have anything to do with you after she hears the truth. And if that is the case, all of the action you have taken against Mr Dawson will have been in vain. You have got yourself into trouble for nothing and I doubt you will ever see her again.'

Mr Dawson said loudly: 'He certainly will not. My Sarah is a good lass, and she's never given me any trouble until she met this good-for-nothing wastrel.' He turned to Charlie and added, his voice rising in anger: 'I only gave you a job to help your mother and I trusted you to repay the kindness, not betray me! And what is your mother going to think when she finds out? Hasn't the poor woman been through enough, losing her husband and being left with all those mouths to feed? You're a disgrace, Charlie Perceval, a disgrace. And even though I have the greatest respect for your mother, from now on you're fired.'

Mr Dawson sat back in his chair and folded his arms decisively in front of him. It was all over for Charlie. He had

had enough and knew that he was beaten. He looked from Eleanor to Edwin and back again at Eleanor and said:

'If I tell you what you want to know will you agree not to take me to the police station?'

'No, I'm sorry,' said Eleanor, firmly, 'we can't make deals with you. Besides, Mr Dawson already has all the information he needs to clear his name. He watched you today and he knows exactly what you did. The order you put together for him this morning has provided all the evidence he needs. Also, Mr Dawson now understands how he came to be prosecuted on the previous occasions, so any information you may have will probably not be news to him. Your best course of action is to tell the truth to the police in order to give yourself a chance.'

'Tell the truth! To the police!' Charlie was almost shouting. 'Why would I be fool enough to do that? My brother told the truth and it never gave him no chance. They never believed a word he said. Hounded him out of town. You're all the same, you lot, bossing us about with your money and your laws, and making ordinary people's lives a misery.'

As he looked angrily at her, Eleanor could see in his face the depth of hatred and the hurt. Then, he frowned fiercely and looked down at the floor, as though he was afraid that he had given himself away with this outburst.

Eleanor said quietly: 'As I said, Charlie, the best thing is to tell the truth.'

'They'd kill me,' he mumbled.

Eleanor could barely hear what he said. 'Who? The people who told you that, as an employee, you could not be prosecuted?'

Charlie said nothing.

'Or the ones who provided you with the false weights that you used?'

Charlie hesitated and then looked up again and stared defiantly back at Eleanor.

'Then we need to get this straightened out,' said Eleanor. 'I have some sympathy for you. You have foolishly put yourself into this difficult situation and it could have very serious consequences for you. Mr Talbot will take you back down to James and you are to sit and wait there while I speak to Mr Dawson.'

Charlie stood up and looked at Eleanor, still with hatred in his eyes. Then he turned and meekly followed Edwin downstairs. He was returned to the custody of James.

Edwin returned to Eleanor's office and said to Mr Dawson: 'I think that you may now consider Sarah safe and, if so, perhaps we should do what we can to assist Charlie. He is clearly in deeper than he realises and the consequences for him could be quite serious. What do you think?'

'I have no love for Charlie Perceval,' said Mr Dawson forcefully, 'and I want him to suffer all the punishment he deserves, but I feel for his poor mother. She was a good friend to my wife and if my wife were still here I know what she would want me to do, so for her sake and for his mother's sake, please do what you can for the lad.'

'Thank you, Mr Dawson.' Eleanor looked at Edwin and said: 'I suggest that we should take Charlie to the police station and give them all the information they need.'

Edwin said: 'Yes, I think that would be best. I will do that now.' He looked at Mr Dawson and said: 'The police will want you to make a statement, Mr Dawson, so if you can spare the time now, perhaps you could come with me.'

'Certainly,' said Mr Dawson, 'and what about the charges against me?'

Edwin said: 'I suggest that we go and see the Inspector as soon as we can. Now that there is an explanation for what has happened, you should be able to clear your name.'

'Let us hope so,' said Mr Dawson. He turned to Eleanor: 'Thank you for all your help, Miss Harriman. I'm right pleased to have got this sorted out and it's thanks to you.' He shook hands with Eleanor.

Eleanor accompanied him downstairs while Edwin went to put on his overcoat and his hat. Charlie Perceval was sitting on a chair, hunched over, with his head in his hands.

~O~

Superintendent Johnson kept Charlie Perceval at the station while he took a statement from Mr Dawson. Eventually, Charlie was formally charged with offences under the Weights and Measures Act. He was bailed on condition that he remain at his mother's address and report to the police station twice a day. He now had no job and was dependent on his mother for food and somewhere to sleep, and he suffered the further indignity of having his mother come to the police station to fetch him home. In deciding to allow bail, Superintendent Johnson had formed the view that Charlie was unlikely to abscond but it was a decision he was destined to regret. The following morning, Charlie failed to report to the police station in accordance with the conditions of his bail and, after futile enquiries at his mother's house, the Superintendent was forced to make an application for a warrant for Charlie's arrest.

When Edwin returned to Hall Bank from delivering Charlie to the police station he found Mr Harriman and Napoleon settled in Eleanor's office. Eleanor was giving Mr Harriman an account of the interview with Charlie Perceval.

'Well,' said Edwin, 'I don't think there is anything much we or anyone else can do for that young lad. By the time he reached the police station, he had resumed his belligerent attitude. He simply refused to answer any questions and he was very rude to Superintendent Johnson.'

'It is a most unfortunate situation,' said Mr Harriman. 'The Percevals have always been a respectable family with a good reputation. It seems that Charlie has let resentment take hold of him. Perhaps also he has fallen in with the wrong sort of people.'

'I fear you may be right, Harriman, and unfortunately I don't think there is anything we can do to help. I shall, however, do what I can to help Mr Dawson clear his name. So, Eleanor, that just leaves Lady Carleton-West,' said Edwin, looking pointedly at Eleanor.

'I know, I know. I shall have to report to her and explain that Buxton is no longer in the grip of criminals. I think a letter will suffice, don't you? I don't want to take up her precious time with this insignificant matter.'

'Especially not while she is planning the Royal Visit,' said Edwin.

'And the Royal Reception Evening,' added Eleanor.

'Very wise,' nodded Mr Harriman.

CHAPTER SEVENTEEN

A s well as the Royal Visit, the town was also preparing for Armistice Day, the anniversary of the day the War ended. In addition to the Remembrance Sunday parade and memorial service, there was to be a two minutes' silence at eleven o'clock on the eleventh of November, which was a Friday. The purpose of these two events was to remember and honour those who had died. There were, however, thousands of disabled ex-soldiers no longer able to work, who had been forgotten despite the promises of the government who sent them to fight. In addition, there were thousands of widows struggling to support themselves and their children. One soldier, when he returned to Manchester from the Front in the early years of the War, was so concerned at the government's failure to act that he had set up an organisation to help relieve their suffering. Others had followed his example and, by the end of the War, there were several voluntary organisations doing this work.

After many months of negotiation and under the guidance of Earl Haigh, these organisations had agreed to amalgamate and, a few months earlier in May that year, the British Legion had been formed. Very shortly afterwards, the Buxton branch of the Legion had been formed under the leadership of one of the town's residents, Mr George Williams, a thirty year old ex-soldier who had survived the War. Buxton had its own share of local war heroes and widows but, in addition, the many injured servicemen who came to the Devonshire Hospital for treatment provided the townspeople with a constant reminder of the extent to which the War had affected people's lives. The Legion was now actively supporting the first Poppy Appeal, the Remembrance Poppy having just been adopted as a way of raising money for Earl Haigh's Fund for Ex-Servicemen. The poppies were a symbol of hope as well as remembrance.

The wife of the retiring Mayor of Buxton, the Marchioness of Hartington, had sent out a message urging everyone in Buxton to buy a poppy and the idea had been enthusiastically embraced. Poppies were already on display in the shop windows in Buxton and were being used to decorate the traders' delivery carts. Harriman & Talbot were supporters of the Legion and the poppies were available at the Hall Bank office. Lady Carleton-West had, of course, also added her support to the appeal and poppies would be on sale at the Royal Reception Evening. Poppy sellers had now begun to appear in the streets and they provided a new source of interest for Jon Jon. On the Friday before the Royal Visit, he had spent most of his time following one or other of them around and watching with interest as people stopped to buy a poppy.

~O~

At Top Trees that Friday, Lady Carleton-West's attention had been fully occupied in directing the arrangements for her Reception. She moved from room to room like a general scrutinising the preparations of an army before battle. At nine o'clock, the gardener and his boy had arrived to begin the task of hanging one hundred and fifty paper Chinese lanterns in the trees along the carriage driveway and around the front of the house. At ten o'clock, a floral artiste had arrived in a van loaded with flowers and wire structures for the several large floral arrangements to be constructed for the two drawing rooms, the main hall, the conservatory, and the dining room. A second van had arrived full of potted palms and ferns. The caterer's van had arrived bringing all the extra glasses, plates and paraphernalia required for serving supper. Tomorrow afternoon, the caterers themselves would arrive with several vans of food for the lavish supper which had been ordered for the guests. In relation to her own celebrations, Lady Carleton-West had, of course, entirely ignored the King's request that expense for the Royal Visit be kept to a minimum.

~O~

Late that afternoon, as James was opening the final delivery of post for the day, he was very displeased to find another typed letter addressed to Mr Harriman. The format was exactly the same as the previous one and contained another quote from the Bible.

And of Jezebel also spake the Lord, saying: 'The dogs shall eat Jezebel by the wall of Jezreel.' 1 Kings 21:23

As before, James took the letter to Mr Harriman.

Mr Harriman said: 'This makes me very angry, James. I was inclined to dismiss the first one but now I am beginning to be concerned for Eleanor. I am not sure how seriously we should take this, but the tone certainly seems to be threatening.'

'It could be someone who does not like the idea of a lady being a solicitor,' suggested James. 'It's not a very usual thing.'

'You could be right, James.' Mr Harriman looked at the letter with disgust.

'Some people do express surprise when I suggest making an appointment to see Miss Eleanor but no-one has ever been critical of her and no-one has ever refused an appointment.'

'No, in fact, Mr Talbot and I have been pleased as to how well she has been accepted by the clients. And she is developing a good reputation in town. I don't think we need to mention this to Eleanor just yet. Show the letter to Mr Talbot, will you, and then lock it away in the safe with the other one. We must try to get to the bottom of this.'

~O~

During that Friday, Eleanor had spent the day working and then, just before eight thirty in the evening, she left Napoleon at home and walked up to the Sunday-school hall in Hardwick Square where she had arranged to meet Dr Catherine. They were attending a meeting which had been convened with a view to forming a walking group. Eleanor, Catherine and two other women friends already had their own group and generally spent one afternoon a month walking in the local area. They welcomed the opportunity to join a larger group as it would allow them to go further afield.

The meeting was well attended. There was a variety of people and the discussion was lively. Inevitably, there had been more women than men and Dr Catherine had been very eloquent and witty on the subject of surplus women. She had made an impassioned plea for the gentlemen present to do their bit and join in. Mr Sutton, also a keen walker, had addressed the meeting and made an equally eloquent and witty defence on behalf of the gentlemen.

One of the local curates, until recently a keen sportsman at an Oxford college, stood up and said, forcefully: 'In my opinion, two segregated groups would be preferable because the ladies will be frequently in need of assistance on tougher routes and that will necessarily slow the gentlemen down. Being hampered in that way would prove very annoying to the gentlemen. After all, the purpose of this walking group is pleasure not duty.'

This aroused energetic disagreement from the ladies and when the noise had subsided, another gentleman, Commander Wilkins, who was a retired naval officer, got to his feet and said: 'I support this suggested segregation although for a different reason. It is unseemly for women to go walking in the countryside with gentlemen in the way proposed. If I had a wife or a sister, I certainly would not permit them to do so. I urge everybody to vote for segregated walks or, better still, a men only club.'

'Hear, hear!' called several of the gentlemen present and one of them added: 'There are some men, I will not refer to them as gentlemen, with whom it is entirely unsuitable for ladies to go walking.'

There was then a heated debate as to whether there should be one walking group or two. Commander Wilkins had the final word: 'I would urge the ladies to remember that their true role in life is that of wife and mother. They should refrain from gallivanting about the countryside for no valid reason.'

Eleanor could not resist a response and got to her feet. 'I should like to remind the meeting that if the ladies had not been prepared to leave their homes during the War and go "gallivanting" into nursing and ambulance driving, many soldiers would have been much worse off.'

The audience applauded. Eventually, all that was resolved was the election of office bearers and the date for a further meeting. Nevertheless, everyone was optimistic and in good humour despite the heated exchanges that had taken place. Eleanor had noticed Mr Norman sitting at the back of the hall and she made a determined but unsuccessful effort to keep out of his way as the crowd was dispersing. He approached her and offered to see her safely home. As always, she found his over-protective attitude annoying, presumptuous even, and only her innate good manners stopped her from saying angrily that she was perfectly capable of getting herself home, particularly as it was only a few hundred yards. Instead she refused politely, saying that someone had already arranged to walk with her.

This was not strictly true but she anticipated that Mr Sutton would be walking towards Hall Bank and she thought she could easily accompany him and give the appearance of a previous arrangement.

Eleanor and Catherine stopped outside the hall to chat with some friends for a few minutes and Mr Sutton joined them. Eventually, the group broke up. Catherine and some of the group turned right down Hardwick Square and Eleanor, Mr Sutton and a few others turned left towards the Market Place. Eleanor and Mr Sutton left the others and crossed the Market Place to Hall Bank. They chatted about the meeting as they went, laughing as they recalled parts of Catherine's speech. Then Mr Sutton said: 'I thought Commander Wilkins was rather extreme in his views, quite out of date really.'

'Yes, he does rather seem to be clinging to the last century. I suppose being in the Navy has kept him out of the company of women and he doesn't realise that times have changed.'

By now they had reached Eleanor's front door. Mr Sutton said: 'Well, rest assured, Eleanor. You are a great asset to this town, as is Dr Catherine, and people think highly of both of you. Despite what Commander Wilkins might think, no-one would consider you less suitable as a wife and mother just because you went walking, or should I say gallivanting, about the countryside with a group which includes gentlemen. I look forward to seeing you at the next meeting of the walkers' club and to accompanying you on our first outing.' He gave her an extravagant bow.

'Thank you, kind sir,' said Eleanor, laughing and bobbing a curtsey. 'I shall look forward to it.' She gave him a friendly pat on his arm. 'I shall see you on Monday,' she added and then turned to open the front door. She waved to Mr Sutton.

He waved back and continued walking down Hall Bank. Later she was to recall that, although she had not been aware of anyone being behind them as they walked, she had a vague impression that there was someone on The Slopes who had quickly disappeared behind a tree. She closed the front door firmly and, with a mixture of annoyance and amusement, said: 'Bother.'

CHAPTER EIGHTEEN

Jon Jon was probably the only person that Saturday morning who was unaware of the day's importance to the town. Nearly everyone else in Buxton was anticipating an unusual day. Today was the day of the Royal Visit. At a quarter to ten, Eleanor and Napoleon were returning from their morning stroll. Napoleon had been let off his lead after they left the Gardens and went bounding ahead as usual. As he reached the end of Broad Walk, he spotted Miss Pymble and Miss Felicity outside The Old Hall, a building where Mary Queen of Scots had sometimes stayed whilst being held a prisoner. The Misses Pymble were old friends so Napoleon crossed the road to greet them enthusiastically.

Eleanor followed.

The Misses Pymble were looking forward to the day's events and, this morning, they were in an even more heightened state of flustered excitement than usual. They helped to run the local group of Girl Guides. Princess Mary was Chief Guide and the honorary president of the organisation so about five hundred Guides from Buxton and the surrounding area would be assembling in The Crescent and forming a guard of honour for her at St Anne's Well. The Pymble sisters were providing accommodation for some of these visiting Guides and they were also involved in preparing the afternoon tea at which the local Guides were to entertain the visiting Guides later in the afternoon. Also, Pauline, their most senior Guide, was to be presented to Princess Mary. The Pymble sisters were ecstatic on Pauline's behalf.

Right now though, Miss Pymble was looking very agitated,

and Miss Felicity only slightly less so. Each sister extended the back of a gloved hand towards Napoleon in greeting and he nudged them in turn. Then, after circling the two of them a couple of times, he went back to stand beside Eleanor.

'Miss Pymble, Miss Felicity, good morning,' said Eleanor as she approached them.

'Good morning, Miss Harriman,' said the Misses Pymble in unison.

'You look worried. Is anything wrong? Are the preparations for the Royal Visit getting out of control?'

'Oh, dear, no. They are all in hand, thank goodness,' said Miss Pymble.

'Well in hand,' confirmed Miss Felicity.

'No. It's Jon Jon,' said Miss Pymble.

'He's over there,' said Miss Felicity, pointing to the stone retaining wall at the end of The Slopes. Jon Jon was sitting on the wall, with his feet dangling over the edge, frowning as he stared at the pavement a foot below.

'We were on our way to The Quadrant to see Miss Swindells,' said Miss Pymble.

'The confectioner,' added Miss Felicity, helpfully.

'About the catering for the afternoon tea, but we met Jon Jon and he tried to tell us something,' said Miss Pymble.

'We couldn't understand what he wanted and he went to sit over there,' added Miss Felicity.

'He seems very upset that we couldn't understand what he was saying,' said Miss Pymble.

'Perhaps you could try, Miss Harriman?' suggested Miss Felicity.

'Of course. Don't worry,' said Eleanor. 'Napoleon knows him. Come on, Leon, let's go and see Jon Jon and find out what the problem is.'

Eleanor, followed by the Misses Pymble, crossed the road to where Jon Jon was sitting. Napoleon got there first and,

167

raising himself up on his hind legs and resting his front paws on the top of the wall, he nudged Jon Jon with his nose. Jon Jon reached out his hand and stroked Napoleon's head clumsily but affectionately.

'Good morning, Jon Jon,' said Eleanor. 'How are you?'

'He fell,' said Jon Jon without looking up. He was still frowning and started shaking his hands up and down vigorously in the air. Napoleon watched him intently, moving his head up and down as he followed Jon Jon's hand movements.

'Who fell, Jon Jon?' asked Eleanor.

Jon Jon stopped shaking his hands and resumed stroking Napoleon's head. 'Fell down,' he said, addressing Napoleon.

In one quick movement, Napoleon slid his front paws down to the pavement, leapt up on to the grassy bank behind the wall, turned around and flopped down beside Jon Jon, his paws dangling over the edge of the wall, mimicking Jon Jon's legs. Jon Jon put his arm around Napoleon and hugged him. Eleanor looked at them and waited.

'Saw him,' said Jon Jon, nodding.

'I see,' asked Eleanor. 'Who was it that you saw, Jon Jon?'

Jon Jon said nothing.

'It's no good, Miss Harriman,' said Miss Pymble. 'I've already asked him that several times and he just won't answer.'

Eleanor said: 'Do you know the man who fell, Jon Jon? Do you know who he is?'

Jon Jon grinned and nodded.

'Do you know his name?' asked Eleanor.

There was a shake of the head and the same grin.

'Can you tell me anything about him?' asked Eleanor.

Jon Jon looked at Napoleon for inspiration. Napoleon licked Jon Jon's hand.

'The poppies,' said Jon Jon.

Eleanor looked puzzled. 'The poppies,' she repeated.

He nodded.

'Oh,' squeaked Miss Felicity, 'perhaps he means the Remembrance poppies.'

'Perhaps he means that one of the men selling poppies fell down,' interpreted Miss Pymble. 'Some of them are still suffering from injuries.'

'That's possible, I suppose. But there are at least a dozen people selling poppies,' sighed Eleanor.

'It could be just one of his fantasies,' said Miss Pymble.

'But it might mean something,' said Miss Felicity.

'Fell down,' repeated Jon Jon, and he nodded vigorously, frowning again.

'Can you tell me where he fell down, Jon Jon?' asked Eleanor.

Jon Jon stared at her without responding and then he said: 'Poorly.'

Eleanor could tell by the look on his face that he was exasperated with their lack of comprehension but it seemed that having unburdened himself thus far he was content. He stopped frowning and continued to stroke Napoleon.

'I should take him home, Miss Pymble,' said Eleanor. 'He has been very upset by something that he has seen.'

'Don't worry, Miss Harriman. Felicity and I will see that he gets home,' said Miss Pymble.

'Yes, Miss Harriman, don't worry. We can take him home now and then go back to see Miss Swindells,' reassured Miss Felicity. 'We have plenty of time.'

'If you are sure. Thank you, that is good of you. I have to be in the office shortly for an appointment. Perhaps whatever it was he wanted to say will eventually become clear. Goodbye, Jon Jon. Come on, Napoleon.'

As Eleanor headed across Hall Bank, Napoleon reluctantly left Jon Jon and followed her back to the office. As she went, Eleanor thought about the poppies and tried to understand what Jon Jon had meant but nothing came to mind.

169

~O~

Due to their detour with Jon Jon, when the Misses Pymble finally arrived at The Quadrant they had missed the action at Chillingham & Baynard's bank. In the absence of Mr Sutton who had taken leave to go to Chester for a family christening, Mr Pidcock had arrived a little earlier than usual to see that everything was in order before the customers arrived. As he walked up The Quadrant towards the bank he saw, to his consternation, that words had been daubed on the wall again.

THiS BANk DESTRoys Li

Although this was not part of the official route that the Princess's motor-cade would take, other visitors would see the wall and Mr Pidcock was concerned for the reputation of the bank as well as the town. Mr Pidcock let himself into the bank and telephoned the police. As soon as the junior staff arrived, he would have the wall cleaned and later he would set about finding the culprit.

~O~

The Royal Visit had been well-publicised and, although Princess Mary was not due to arrive until 2.45pm, people had already started arriving from the villages and towns outside Buxton, clambering off buses or pouring off excursion trains, and making their way down the hill towards the town like a human lava flow. There was plenty for them to look at. The windows of the shops all along Spring Gardens and the High Street had been decorated with special displays and the windows of the houses at first and second floor level above the shops along the motor-cade route were also decorated and had flags flying.

By half past twelve, the street sweepers were out clearing the streets of litter and horse droppings, policemen on point duty were diverting traffic from the roads which were to be closed off. The staff at the Thermal Baths were sweeping corridors and polishing all available brass even though that task had already been done thoroughly the day before. In households all over the town, shoes were being polished, suits and hats brushed. The Mayoral chain and the mace had been buffed up to a shine ready to be carried by the Sergeant at Mace. Those taking part in the official ceremonies were nervously rehearsing to themselves their moves, where to stand, what to say, when to bow or curtsey. The members of the brass bands from Burbage and from Fairfield had checked their uniforms, polished their instruments, and sorted their music.

A number of children from the local schools had been selected to assemble with their teachers opposite the Thermal Baths so that they could cheer and wave flags as the Princess walked across the road from the Baths to sample the water at St Anne's Well. These children were now under the hands of proud mothers having their hair plaited or slicked into place with water and their faces scrubbed till they shone. Richard had been chosen as one of the children to represent his school and he was receiving similar treatment at Oxford House.

Eleanor had arranged to take Richard to the assembly point at the Well and, at one o'clock, he arrived at Hall Bank, suitably polished and pressed. The family gathered to eat the sandwiches which Mrs Clayton had left ready for them, she having expressed the view that on civic occasions such as this, things did not always go according to plan. One never knew how long it was going to be between meals so it was best to be prepared and go well fortified just in case. She had already gone home to fortify her own family before putting on her best hat and coat and taking her two boys to join the rest of the school children who had been chosen to be at St Anne's Well.

CHAPTER NINETEEN

By a quarter past two, the town was on tenterhooks and the committee members were beginning to get anxious.

A huge assortment of people was milling around, assessing the best vantage points, changing their minds, and trying not to lose belongings, children, or aged relatives in the confusion. Along both sides of Spring Gardens and the entrance to The Crescent, every available window in the hotels, houses and flats above the shops, was already jammed with people eagerly waiting for the Royal party. Mr Harriman and Cicely had left for the Devonshire Hospital and Eleanor entertained Richard with a game of cards until it was time to leave. Then she took him to The Crescent where he joined his classmates, each clutching a Union Jack, and milling about in an excited swarm.

Admission to the area in front of The Crescent was by ticket only so Eleanor joined the rest of the crowd on The Slopes overlooking The Crescent and, as she waited, listened to the buzz of conversation around her. She could see Richard amongst the crowd of schoolchildren and, across at the Thermal Baths, the welcoming party of civic officials which had been ordered to be in place by two thirty. Most of them had arrived well before that time and had already arranged themselves in strict order of precedence at the entrance to the Thermal Baths. Having by now run out of small talk, they were standing about awkwardly, unable to decide what to do with their hands and tweaking nervously at their robes or regalia. Eleanor recognised all of them: Mr Wall the Mayor elect. who was about to replace the Marquis of Hartington, the deputy Mayor, the rest of the aldermen, the town clerk, the vicar of St John's Church, the magistrates and justices of the peace. Mr Aubrey-Mere should also have been with them but there was no sign of him at the moment.

The schoolchildren had just begun to get restless and fidgety when the sound of cheering from the crowd down at the far end of Spring Gardens signalled the entrance of the motor-cade into the town. A surge of waving flags and handkerchiefs rippled along the crowd as the motor-cade passed slowly by and the cheering reached its crescendo as the motor-cade entered The Crescent. The line of open-topped cars came to a halt in front of the Thermal Baths. The gentlemen stood up, each grasping the brim of his top hat to prevent it falling off as he bent forward to climb down from the motor-car. The ladies adjusted their furs and descended from the cars in order of rank.

The Marquis of Hartington who had been in one of the cars with the Marchioness, took up his position at the head of the line of civic officials. Performing his last duty in his role as Mayor, he formally welcomed the Princess and her party to Buxton. The Princess then passed along the line-up of civic officials as each was presented in turn. Eleanor noticed that Mr Aubrey-Mere had still not arrived. Ignoring the advice of Lady Carleton-West, the official committee had chosen a girl from the Fairfield Infants' School to present the first bouquet to the Princess and she managed the task very gracefully. Finally, the Princess was welcomed by the Baths Manager and the party entered the Thermal Baths to be given a tour of the premises. After a tour of the Baths, the Princess was to be asked to sign the visitors' book, which contained the signatures of several of her forebears from previous Royal visits.

With the disappearance of the Princess and her party into the Baths, the crowd subsided into idle chatter, exchanging rumours and discussing what they had heard or read about the proceedings inside the Baths and what was going to happen next. Fifteen minutes had been allowed for the inspection, after which the Princess and her party would leave the Baths and cross the road, through the guard of honour formed by the Girl Guides, and sample the water from St Anne's Well. Eleanor, from her position on The Slopes, viewed the tableau below her with interest. The long wait became tedious for the school children and they began to fidget. Several of the older boys began a mock fight using their flags as swords and were firmly reprimanded by their teachers. By contrast, the Girl Guides forming the guard of honour remained stiffly in line, waiting in silence. At the head of the line, hiding their nervousness as well as they could, were the Guides Commissioner and the Deputy Commissioner who were to be presented to the Princess. They in turn would present Pauline, the Guide standing at the head of the guard of honour.

Eleanor spotted Miss Pymble in the crowd. She was standing close to the guard of honour and anxiously looking at her watch and then looking back at the entrance to the Thermal Baths. There was no sign of Miss Felicity. Eleanor's attention wandered to the rest of the crowd and when she next looked at the Girl Guides she noticed Miss Pymble checking her watch again. Miss Felicity had now joined her and while Miss Pymble watched the entrance to the Baths, Miss Felicity was looking back into the crowd behind her as though trying to spot someone she expected to see. She too looked anxious. Then the crowd, detecting movement at the entrance to the Baths, began to stir and move slightly forward, necks craned in anticipation. The Princess re-appeared at the entrance to the Baths and paused to wave and acknowledge the cheering of the crowd. Eleanor saw the Girl Guide at the head of the guard of honour look back at Miss Pymble who was shaking her head.

To the accompaniment of music provided by the brass bands, the Princess crossed the road and passed through the

175

guard of honour. The bands continued to play while the crowd waited patiently for a further fifteen minutes. Eventually, having sampled the famous Buxton spa water, the Princess and her party resumed their places in the various motor-cars which would now take them to the Devonshire Hospital for the laying of the commemoration stone. After the ceremony the motor-cade would leave town via Higher Buxton and Harpur Hill. There, at the Buxton Lime Firms' quarry, one of the most important businesses in the town, a charge was to be fired in honour of the Princess.

~O~

The motor-cade departed along Broad Walk, taking a circuitous route to the Devonshire Hospital along which it was cheered enthusiastically by the huge crowds lining the streets. The crowd at The Crescent dispersed and some of it headed up the hill to watch the ceremony from the Manchester Road. Eleanor went down the steps from The Slopes in order to wait for Richard and, as she reached the footpath, she encountered the Misses Pymble. The Girl Guides were beginning their march along Broad Walk and up Bath Road to the school where their afternoon tea was to take place. The Misses Pymble were walking alongside the Guides but stopped to greet Eleanor. Seeing their worried faces, Eleanor asked if anything was amiss.

Miss Pymble said: 'Yes, Miss Harriman, we are puzzled and slightly alarmed. Pauline, our most senior Guide, was to be presented to the Princess but she did not arrive.'

'Someone else had to take her place,' explained Miss Felicity.

'And we haven't been able to find her,' said Miss Pymble.

'No-one has seen her,' added Miss Felicity.

'She will be very disappointed,' said Miss Pymble.

'She was so looking forward to meeting the Princess,' said Miss Felicity.

'I do hope she has not met with an accident,' said Miss Pymble.

'Oh dear,' said Eleanor, when she could get a word in. 'She will be very upset to have missed such an opportunity.'

It was now clear to Eleanor why Miss Pymble had been looking so anxiously at her watch while they waited for Princess Mary to leave the Thermal Baths. She said, in her most reassuring tone: 'I am sure there will be a perfectly ordinary reason for her absence. Perhaps she got caught up in the crowd and could not get through. There seem to be hundreds of people here today.'

'I do hope you are right, Miss Harriman,' said Miss Pymble, 'and please excuse us if we rush away. We have to get on…'

'…to help with the afternoon tea.' Miss Felicity finished the sentence for her.

Eleanor bade them farewell and went to meet Richard. He was accompanied by one of his school friends, Alice, and her mother. Eleanor greeted them and asked Richard and Alice if they had enjoyed themselves.

'Yes,' said Richard, without much enthusiasm. 'But there was a great deal of waiting, and that was rather dull.'

'And,' added Alice, indignantly, 'the Princess wasn't wearing her crown. She wasn't even wearing her proper long frock and her fur cape and golden slippers. How were we meant to know she was really the Princess?'

'P'raps it wasn't really her,' said Richard, indifferently. 'There are people who pretend, you know. I forget what they're called. Possters, I think.'

Alice looked shocked and said: 'Oh, but I saw her.'

'Yes, that's right, Alice, you did. That wasn't an imposter,' said Eleanor, reassuringly. 'But a long frock wouldn't have been very practical today so I imagine Princess Mary had to wear something else instead.'

177

Eleanor and Alice's mother exchanged looks over the heads of the children, trying not to laugh, and parted smiling.

'May we have afternoon tea now, please, Aunt Lella?' asked Richard. 'I'm famished.'

They returned to Hall Bank where they were greeted by Napoleon who had been sitting at the window in Eleanor's office watching the activity on The Slopes. Richard went off to play a game of tug with Napoleon. Eleanor began putting out cakes and sandwiches for tea ready for the arrival of Mrs Clayton and her two boys. When they arrived, Mrs Clayton began helping Eleanor in the kitchen and Eleanor sent the boys off to join Richard. She knew that Richard was anxious to demonstrate to them his new interest in dog training.

For his birthday last month, Eleanor had given Richard a copy of a newly published book, J M Barrie's *Peter Pan and Wendy* and Richard was very impressed with Nana, the Newfoundland dog. She was able to do all sorts of useful tasks, including carry things in her mouth, and Richard saw no reason why a Boxer could not do the same. Therefore, he had decided to teach Napoleon to carry things, beginning with his grandfather's newspaper. He wanted Napoleon to bring it from the front door to the sitting room upstairs. Napoleon, not being a retriever, had a very different idea of his role in life and it certainly did not include fetching things. Although dogs of his breed were classed as "working dogs" he was built purely for pleasure. His idea of work was to join enthusiastically any group of people doing something that interested him. So he, in his turn, was teaching Richard; he was helping him learn the lesson of patience. Eleanor could see that Napoleon understood exactly what Richard wanted him to do but he showed no inclination to do it despite many repeated demonstrations by Richard. Eleanor had decided not to interfere in these "training sessions" and watched the mismatch of goals with amusement.

178

Eleanor asked Mrs Clayton if she had found a good vantage point. As she made the tea, Mrs Clayton gave her opinion as to the events at the Thermal Baths. Finally, she said:

'I wonder what the Princess is going to do with that Blue John vase they gave her at the Baths,' said Mrs Clayton. 'I saw it on display at Mr Woodruff's shop last week.'

'I don't suppose she'll get to keep it,' said Eleanor, 'as this is an official visit.'

'That doesn't seem very fair. I mean, when she's the one who's gone to all the trouble of coming here and laying the commemoration stone.'

'I suppose one gets used to it when one is a member of the Royal family.'

'Someone standing near me in the crowd said that one of the gentlemen in the Royal party is going to marry Princess Mary,' said Mrs Clayton.

'Oh, I didn't know that,' said Eleanor, 'which one?'

'The tall one. I've forgotten his name. Older than she is. Didn't look much of a catch.'

Eleanor laughed at Mrs Clayton's verdict, and said: 'Well, I suppose it's difficult for an English princess to find the right sort of husband now that the supply of European princes has dried up. They were the usual source. And, since the Revolution, the Russian princes are no longer an option either. I suppose it doesn't leave one much choice, does it?'

'No, well,' said Mrs Clayton, 'I don't think she wants a foreign husband anyway. I read in the paper that she doesn't want to leave England if she gets married and she wouldn't have any choice would she, if she married a foreigner. They always have to go and live in their husband's country, don't they?'

'Then I suppose she will have to settle for whichever English aristocrat is available, even one that is aged or infirm.'

'Oh, I don't think he's that. Just a bit older than her, that's all. But I'm sure even if the choice was only between aged or infirm it's preferable to being packed off abroad.'

'I'm sure you are right, Mrs Clayton. Of course, she could choose not to get married at all.'

'Oh no,' said Mrs Clayton, shocked, 'not with her being the King's only daughter. No, she has to get married.' Mrs Clayton shook her head as she took the kettle off the stove and filled the teapot. 'And anyway, we could do with a royal wedding. We all need cheering up. Especially with the worry over these strikes that the workers are threatening.'

'Yes,' said Eleanor, nodding, amused at how easily the nation's ills could be cured, 'a royal wedding would be just the thing.'

'Well. I know one thing,' added Mrs Clayton, firmly, 'I wouldn't be her for all the tea in China. Having to traipse all over the country, meeting all sorts of people, always having to smile even if you're worn out and dying for a sit-down and a cup of tea. And I certainly don't envy her today. After she's been at the Hospital, she's got to go up to the Quarry. I can't see the point of that.'

'Well,' said Eleanor, 'the Buxton Lime Firms is one of the most important businesses in the town and this visit will be reported in all the papers. It will be very good for them.'

'I dare say,' said Mrs Clayton, 'but I don't suppose she'll be all that interested in seeing a load of old rock coming down, although it is a powerful sight, I'll grant you. The gentlemen will no doubt find it interesting, but I expect she could do without it. And I suppose they'll want her kitted out in all that protective clothing they make you wear. That won't do her fur or her hat any good, that's for sure.'

'I don't know. I imagine that they will all be in the blast protection shelter. Speaking of kitting out, did my evening shoes come back from the menders, do you know? I shall need them for tonight.'

'They did. I've put them in your room. And that's another thing we could do without. Royal Evening Reception, indeed!' She put the teapot down on the table with an emphatic thump. 'Now, where've Master Richard and my boys got to? Their tea's ready.'

CHAPTER TWENTY

Over at the Devonshire Hospital, the officials and the crowd were consulting their watches and anticipating the arrival of the Royal party. Lady Carleton-West was seated with the other invited guests who were making up the official party. They would all be presented to the Princess as she left the platform after the ceremony. It was true that Lady Carleton-West had been allocated a seat towards the rear of the group but she was consoled by the thought that her rank had prevented her from having to mingle with the unsorted mass of subscribers in the gallery. She sat contentedly waiting for the arrival of the Princess, examining critically the hats and costumes of the other ladies as they arrived. Her clothes, ordered from London especially for this occasion, were impeccable as usual. A perfectly tailored, three-quarter-length black coat made of cashmere, draped with a glossy sable fur tippet, and worn over a dress of dark grey silk Crêpe de Chine and taffeta, lavishly trimmed with jet beads and small water pearls. Her hat, swirled with black and dark grey silk chiffon, was secured by a truly extravagant chased-silver hatpin ornamented with a cluster of three, very large pearls. Lady Carleton-West was confident that she would be better dressed than anyone else that day, except perhaps for Princess Mary or the Duchess of Devonshire, although when those two ladies did eventually appear, Lady Carleton-West was able to make very pleasing comparisons in her own favour and congratulated herself on once again having put herself into the secure hands of Monsieur Raymond at Maison Christophe.

When the Princess arrived at the Hospital she was presented with a second bouquet, this time by the daughter of the General Superintendent and Secretary of the Hospital, the official committee having, once again, ignored Lady Carleton-West's advice. The Princess and the rest of her entourage were then conducted into the dome where almost a thousand people were gathered: subscribers, staff, and patients. To begin her visit, the princess was invited to witness a demonstration by the Duke of Devonshire of the unusual acoustic effect of the dome. Standing on one side of the dome, he spoke words of welcome. Princess Mary heard an echo of his voice and replied from the other side. She was then invited to inspect the Hospital.

A wooden walkway had been constructed between the Hospital and the building site and the nurses, immaculate in their uniforms, starched white aprons and veils, were lined up along it, awaiting the arrival of the Princess. She passed along the walkway and each nurse in turn curtseyed as the Princess drew level. When Princess Mary arrived on the raised platform, the large crowd which had gathered along the Manchester Road began cheering loudly and waving their flags and handkerchiefs. There followed speeches, prayers and hymns accompanied by the band and the commemoration stone was lowered into place. As she left the platform, Princess Mary walked along the line of official guests and they were presented in turn. Lady Carleton-West's fifteen seconds of fame had arrived and she made her carefully rehearsed curtsey with great satisfaction.

~O~

Cicely and Mr Harriman returned to Hall Bank and entertained Eleanor with their impressions of events at the Hospital. They had all received cards for Lady Carleton-West's Royal Evening

183

Reception, which Philip had irreverently christened the Right Royal Bean-feast. Cicely had been keen to go, so they had all decided to make the effort and go in full fig. Philip had arranged to call for them in his Bentley. He could easily have walked the few hundred yards from his parents' house to Top Trees, leaving Mr Harriman to drive the others there but he was always glad of an excuse to use his motor-car and thought nothing of having to drive to Hall Bank and back twice that evening. Mrs Clayton, leaving her boys in the care of Alf and his wife, had returned to Hall Bank to look after Richard and Napoleon for the evening. Eleanor was certain that they were both in grave danger of being over-fed and having their every whim catered for.

As Philip turned the Bentley into the long carriage drive at Top Trees, they admired the effect of the Chinese lanterns flickering amongst the trees. The house was ablaze with light. They joined the queue of other motor-cars and eventually arrived at the front steps of the house. Mr Harriman helped Eleanor and Cicely out and the trio waited accommodatingly while Philip parked the Bentley. The party re-assembled and went up the steps to the front door, where they were greeted warmly by Ash, who looked particularly pleased and polished and was wearing a new suit for the occasion. He directed them to the Oak drawing room and they made their way across the main hall, admiring the floral decorations and greeting friends and acquaintances as they went. They knew most of the people present so the task of mingling was easy and, the choice of topic for conversation having been predetermined, no-one was at a loss for something to say.

The Royal Evening Reception was indeed a glittering affair. The gentlemen wore impeccable evening dress and the ladies displayed the very latest fashion in evening gowns, together with their most lavish jewellery. Lady Carleton-West, no novice when it came to publicity, had invited her favourite journalist to view the rooms and take photographs of the decorations before the guests arrived. Now, that same journalist, strategically placed behind a potted palm, was busily scribbling the names of the more important guests as they arrived and making notes as to what the most socially prominent ladies were wearing. Most of the ladies had chosen the same fashionable style of gown, so it was inevitable that the journalist's vocabulary was going to prove inadequate to the task. The words sash train, broken hemline, flying side panels, French ornaments together with tasteful, elegant, and stylish were going to be much overworked in the newspaper report.

Everyone complimented Lady Carleton-West on the taste with which the Reception had been arranged and congratulated her on being so perceptive regarding the social needs of the town. The guests confessed that when the Princess had left town and they realised that the much anticipated Royal Visit was actually over, they had been left feeling quite flat and this evening's reception was just the thing to lift their spirits again. Lady Carleton-West graciously accepted their praise and thanks as her due and only mentioned about fifty five times how charming she had found Princess Mary to be when she had been presented to her.

Philip, who had been mingling with several of the members of the official committee, returned to stand beside Eleanor.

'I say, have you heard? There's been another attack on Chillingham's Bank.'

'No. What was it, another message?' asked Eleanor.

'Yes. I gather the head clerk found it this morning when he went to open up. He had it cleaned off straightaway, of course, because of the Royal Visit.'

'What did it say?'

'Well, it's a bit odd really. The message was a partially finished sentence as though the culprit had been interrupted while writing it. Apparently, the bank is accused of destroying something but, as the sentence was unfinished, we shall probably never know what that something was.'

'Was it cow dung or lime wash this time?'

'Lime wash, I believe. And it must have been put there some time after about ten on Friday night. I was just talking to Mr Furniss. He was on his way home to Marlborough Road when he passed the bank just after ten o'clock and didn't notice anything amiss. He did notice Jon Jon at the top of Spring Gardens but Jon Jon wouldn't be the mystery message writer.'

'No, of course not,' agreed Eleanor, 'but he might have seen something.'

'What's the matter? You're working on a puzzle,' said Philip. 'I know that look.'

'I've just remembered something. Something Jon Jon said this morning...'

Before Eleanor could finish the sentence, Ash announced that supper was being served and Lady Carleton-West began marshalling her guests. Mr Harriman and Cicely joined Philip and Eleanor as they all complemented Lady Carleton-West on the success of the evening. Lady Carleton-West thanked them and then added:

'I am sorry that Mr Aubrey-Mere has not yet arrived. He was one of the first to accept my invitation and he has not contacted me to say that he has been prevented from coming. I am at a loss to explain his absence.'

'That is most unusual,' said Philip. 'He is always very correct.'

'Perhaps he has been detained by some unexpected business associated with his being a magistrate,' suggested Mr Harriman.

'Yes, perhaps. I do hope nothing unpleasant has befallen him,' said Lady Carleton-West, and she moved on to another group of guests.

Philip turned to Eleanor and said: 'I'm sure he would have telephoned if he had had to change his plans.'

Eleanor said: 'Absolutely. It is odd though. When I was at The Crescent this afternoon, I noticed that he was not with the other officials waiting outside the Thermal Baths. I know that he was supposed to be there. I wondered if perhaps he had been asked to go to the Hospital instead.'

'I didn't notice him at the Hospital when I was there with my mother,' said Philip.'

'I didn't see him there,' said Mr Harriman. 'Did you Cicely?' Cicely shook her head.

'There is still time. Perhaps he will arrive soon,' said Eleanor.

'Perhaps not,' said Philip. 'I've just had a thought. Do you remember when we were last at dinner at Brook House he said he would have preferred to go to that conference in London, some inaugural event for a magistrate's association, wasn't it?'

'Yes, it was. Maybe he decided to go to that instead,' said Eleanor.

'But surely, he would have made his excuses to Lady C,' said Cicely.

'I think the meeting was actually yesterday,' said Mr Harriman. 'Perhaps he went to London intending to be back today and has been delayed. If he is stuck on a train somewhere he would not be able to let anyone know.'

Mr Harriman and Cicely turned to speak to someone else and the matter was left unresolved. Philip turned back to Eleanor.

'Incidentally, I think you may consider yourself safe from the advances of Mr Norman in future,' he said.

'That is very good news but how do you know?' asked Eleanor.

'You remember when we were at the tennis club dance, I told you that he had been in the shop with a friend? He said he was choosing a brooch for someone who was going to be his wife and then went on to praise you to the skies.'

'Yes,' said Eleanor, with loathing.

'He asked me to put the brooch aside for him and I did. But this morning, I had a rather strange telephone call from him. He said that he no longer wanted the brooch. I said that was perfectly all right, I would put it back on display. But then he said "It isn't all right, not at all." And then he said something that I didn't catch properly but I think he said "It's been stolen" and then the line went dead. He didn't even say good-bye.'

'What do you suppose he could have meant?' asked Eleanor.

'I've no idea,' said Philip.

'Perhaps he no longer wanted the brooch because he thought it was stolen property,' suggested Eleanor.

'Goodness, I hope not! I don't want to be accused of being a receiver. I was a bit concerned about him though because he sounded rather agitated.'

'I am sorry about that,' said Eleanor, 'but it is very good news that he has come to his senses at last. I am very relieved.'

CHAPTER TWENTY-ONE

On Sunday the town reluctantly returned to normal and, although people still found things to say about the Royal Visit, there was a sense of anti-climax. For the Misses Pymble there was also a sense of foreboding because there was still no news of Pauline, the missing Girl Guide. In the afternoon, when Eleanor and Napoleon arrived at Oxford House for their Sunday outing, Richard was putting on his boots and expressing the view that they should go up Gadley Lane in case there were any chestnuts to be collected. Eleanor and Cicely thought this unlikely but nevertheless agreed and, when everyone was ready, they set off along Broad Walk, Richard and Napoleon well ahead as usual.

On Burlington Road, as they passed the gates of Thornstead, Richard stopped and called back to Cicely and Eleanor:

'Look, a message.' He pointed to one of the stone pillars beside the gates.

As Eleanor and Cicely got closer they saw that the word "Thief" had been painted on one of the stone gateposts.

'That's odd,' said Eleanor. 'I hope that wasn't there when the Princess drove past yesterday.'

'I'm sure that if it had been, someone would have noticed and cleaned it off,' said Cicely. 'In any event, the Princess would not have seen it because there was quite a crowd along this road and someone was bound to have been standing in front of it. I wonder if it was done by the same person who painted the words on the bank.'

The walking party continued on its way. They followed

The Serpentine Walks, pausing at the little bridge so that Richard could look into the water in case there were any trout. Napoleon went on a quest of his own, sniffing for rabbits or foxes and then caught up with them again at the end of the path. In the park at the lower end of Gadley Lane, Eleanor and Cicely waited while Richard inspected leaves and chose some to collect. From there, the path rose steeply through the woods until they arrived at Manchester Road. As they had not found any chestnuts, Richard was keen to go on searching and asked if they could detour through Corbar Woods before returning home. They began walking down Manchester Road to reach the footpath which went through the woods. As they rounded the curve of the road, they saw Jon Jon a few yards further down the road, walking towards them. Napoleon bounded ahead to greet Jon Jon, with Richard following closely behind.

'Good afternoon, Jon Jon. Where are you off to then?' asked Eleanor.

'Poppies,' said Jon Jon.

'What poppies, Jon Jon?' Recollecting the conversation she had had with him the previous day, Eleanor asked: 'Do you mean the man with the poppies?'

Jon Jon frowned. Eleanor turned to Cicely and explained: 'I met Jon Jon yesterday morning. Something had upset him. He seemed to be saying that a man had fallen down and was poorly. It was someone with poppies or, at least, I think that is what he meant and I wondered if it was one of the poppy sellers.'

'Want to see,' said Jon Jon, impatiently moving past Eleanor. He began walking up the hill again.

'Let's just follow him,' said Cicely, 'and see if we can work out what he means.'

They followed behind Jon Jon for a few yards, surprised at how fast he was moving, and then caught up with him again.

'Poppies,' said Jon Jon, looking earnestly at Eleanor.

'But there aren't any poppies here,' said Eleanor.

'Poppies,' repeated Jon Jon.

'No, Aunt Lella,' said Richard, tugging at Eleanor's coat sleeve. 'Not poppies. Puppies. Jon Jon's saying puppies.'

Eleanor stopped and looked at Richard. 'Puppies?' she said. Richard nodded.

Jon Jon was walking away again. As Eleanor considered this idea, she recollected the information about the theft of Mrs Hazelwood's puppies and an idea slotted into place.

'All right,' she said. 'Let's follow him, shall we? I want to see where he goes.'

After about fifty yards, Jon Jon stopped at the gate of Red Farm where he had last seen Mrs Hazelwood's puppies. Eleanor called to Jon Jon.

'Jon Jon, are you looking for some puppies?'

Jon Jon nodded, looking eagerly at Eleanor and shaking his hands up and down. Then he turned to look up the track which ran beside the farm house to the barn.

As Eleanor reached the gate, she asked: 'Are the puppies in the barn there?'

Jon Jon nodded, grabbing the gate in front of him and shaking it.

'I think we had better go to the farm house first, Jon Jon, and ask to see the puppies. Will you come with me?' Eleanor turned to Cicely and said: 'We need to get to the bottom of this. It is just possible that Jon Jon knows where Mrs Hazelwood's stolen puppies are. You stay here with Richard and I will go to the farmhouse with Jon Jon.'

'All right,' said Cicely. 'There doesn't appear to be anyone about.'

Eleanor opened the gate cautiously and she and Jon Jon went through. He stood still for a moment and then began lumbering up the track to the barn as fast as he could.

Napoleon had also slipped through the gate and was

following Jon Jon. Eleanor decided not to call Napoleon back thinking that if Jon Jon met with an angry reception at least he would have Napoleon for protection. The two of them disappeared into the barn and, abandoning the idea of going to the farm house, Eleanor hurried after them, leaving Richard safely at the gate with Cicely. As Eleanor reached the top of the track, Jon Jon emerged from the barn triumphantly carrying two puppies. Napoleon beside him was jumping up enthusiastically. The puppies were Border Terriers and Eleanor had no doubt that they belonged to Mrs Hazelwood.

'Well done, Jon Jon. You've found the stolen puppies.' There was still no sign of anyone about. Eleanor continued: 'We had better take them back to Mrs Hazelwood. Shall I carry one for you?'

Jon Jon lurched away from Eleanor and clutched the puppies to his chest.

'All right, you carry them but be very careful. We must take them back to their home, where they belong.'

Jon Jon marched confidently down the track and out through the gate, holding the puppies in his great hands as carefully as if they had been eggs. Eleanor put Napoleon on his lead and they followed Jon Jon. On the way down the hill, Eleanor was silent, thinking about her conversation with Jon Jon yesterday morning and, now that she knew he had been referring to puppies and not poppies, she was trying to make sense of what he had said. On Saturday, he had obviously seen something that upset him. A man had fallen and somehow that event was connected, in his mind at least, with the puppies. Jon Jon had clearly known where to find the puppies and Eleanor wondered how he knew. Perhaps, she thought, he knew something about their disappearance. When they reached The Elms, Eleanor had still not made sense of the information she had. Leaving Cicely and Richard to look after Napoleon, she went to the front door and rang the bell. When the housekeeper answered the door and Eleanor asked to see Mrs Hazelwood, the housekeeper hesitated because callers were not welcome at the moment.

'I'm sorry, madam isn't...'

Then she caught sight of the puppies and, with a surprised 'Oh, goodness!' You'd best come in,' she opened the door wide. Eleanor guided Jon Jon into the entrance foyer and they stood and waited. Mrs Hazelwood's expression as she entered the hall changed from annoyance at being interrupted in a game of bridge to joy as she saw what Jon Jon was holding. She rushed forward, reaching out to take them but Jon Jon jerked sideways and refused to relinquish them. Eleanor intervened. While Jon Jon held the puppies, she explained the part he had played in their recovery and pleaded his case. As he was clearly enamoured of them and she had cause to be grateful to him, Mrs Hazelwood gave in. She agreed to let Jon Jon stay with the puppies until the game of bridge finished and her guests had left. The housekeeper took Eleanor and Jon Jon to the converted stables. Eleanor left Jon Jon sitting happily with all the puppies and their mother, acting as their self-appointed guardian. She was sure that eventually he would tire of his role and something new would attract his attention but, for the moment, he was blissfully happy. So, too, was Mrs Hazelwood.

Chapter Twenty-Two

On the Monday morning following the Royal Visit, Mr Harriman came into Eleanor's office with a file, saying:

'Here you are, Eleanor, the Belfield purchase file. James has checked the documents and everything is in order for the completion. By the time you get back, I shall have left for the train so, I'll see you this evening.'

Eleanor already had her hat and coat on and she took the file from her father, saying: 'I'm on my way.' She went downstairs followed by Napoleon and said to James on her way out: 'Keep an eye on Napoleon for me, please James. I shouldn't be long.'

'Of course, Miss Eleanor,' said James as he steered Napoleon away from the front door.

Eleanor arrived at Chillingham & Baynard's bank just before eleven o'clock and asked for Mr Sutton. Mr Pidcock, the head clerk, came out of his office to meet her. Eleanor thought that he looked worried.

'Good morning Mr Pidcock.'

'Miss Harriman, good morning. Please come this way.' Eleanor followed Mr Pidcock into the small, woodpanelled office next to the banking chamber.

When they were seated, Mr Pidcock said:

'Miss Harriman, this is most embarrassing. I didn't want to say anything in the banking chamber as we might have been overheard. You have come to do the Belfield completion, I know, and I am afraid I am unable to provide the documents. Mr Sutton has not yet arrived and one of the documents still requires his signature.'

'Oh. I am certain that the appointment was for eleven o'clock.'

'Yes, it was,' said Mr Pidcock, looking troubled, 'and this is most unusual. Mr Sutton is always here on time when the bank opens and I would have expected him to send word if he was going to be delayed. He didn't arrive this morning and I thought I would wait until eleven o'clock before making enquiries. I hoped he would arrive in time for your completion but as he has not I shall telephone to his house now. Please wait here.'

Mr Pidcock left his office and Eleanor sat and waited. She heard the clock begin to strike the hour and counted the eleven strokes. She listened to the voices of people coming in and out of the banking chamber and talking to the tellers. Mr Pidcock did not re-appear. She wondered whether she should cancel the appointment and make another time instead of sitting here idly waiting but decided to give Mr Sutton ten more minutes. She gazed at the ceiling and speculated on the possible reasons for his absence.

'Miss Harriman, I am awfully sorry but Mr Sutton appears to have gone missing.'

Eleanor looked at Mr Pidcock with concern. 'Oh dear,' she said. 'I saw Mr Sutton on Friday evening and he told me that he was going to Chester but I am sure he expected to be back this morning.'

'Yes, that is what I thought. I have spoken to his housekeeper but he is not at home and she has not seen him this morning. When she arrived, Mr Sutton was not there and she assumed he had left early for some reason and was already here.'

'But that is most odd,' said Eleanor. 'Perhaps he is still in Chester, detained for some family reason, but I am sure, if that were the case, he would have telephoned you to explain.'

'Yes, it's completely out of character. He is usually most

reliable. I am not sure what to do. I must notify head office. Can I offer you tea while I do so?'

Eleanor focussed her attention on the reason for her visit to the bank. 'No, thank you Mr Pidcock. If one of the documents has not been signed, we can't complete so I will return to my office. My clients were expecting to hear this morning that everything was in place and I must let them know as soon as possible that there will be a delay. I don't want to appear insensitive in the circumstances but do you think it would be possible to arrange to have the document signed so that we can complete later this afternoon? My clients are about to travel abroad and they are anxious to have everything settled today.'

'Certainly, Miss Harriman. I am sure something can be arranged. The business of the bank must not be neglected. If you would leave it with me, I shall telephone to your office as soon as I have sorted things out.'

~O~

When Eleanor got back to the office, she explained to James what had happened and asked him to arrange a new time when Mr Pidcock telephoned. She decided to get on with other work in the meantime and she was at her desk drafting a document when James appeared in the doorway.

'I am sorry to interrupt, Miss Eleanor, but Miss Pymble is downstairs and wonders if she might have a word. She is reluctant to disturb you but she says it is urgent.'

'Yes, of course. Please show her up.'

Miss Pymble arrived with her usual flurry of rustling silk and rapid speech and was greeted by Napoleon.

'Good boy, Napoleon,' said Miss Pymble, giving him a pat. 'Oh, Miss Harriman, good morning. Thank you for making the time to see me. I'm sure you are very busy.'

'Not at all, Miss Pymble. Good morning. I am very pleased to see you,' Eleanor reassured her. 'Please do sit down and tell me how I can help.'

Miss Pymble perched on the edge of the chair which Eleanor placed for her, clutching the handles of a large handbag which she rested on her lap. Napoleon settled down on the floor beside her.

Miss Pymble said: 'Thank you. Well, I won't keep you more than a minute it's just that…it's Pauline, you see. I'm very worried about her.'

'Pauline the Girl Guide who was missing on Saturday?' asked Eleanor.

'Exactly,' said Miss Pymble, nodding vigorously. 'She should have been there, and I know how much she was looking forward to Princess Mary's visit, and she was so excited and so proud, and I know that she would not have let the Guides down, and that is why I am sure that there is something dreadfully wrong, and she is not at home, and she is not at work, and I didn't know who to turn to for help, and then I thought of you, and I knew that you would be able to think of something, and be able to sort this out, what do you think?'

Eleanor, who was used to Miss Pymble's long sentences had waited patiently until Miss Pymble came to an abrupt stop.

'You say she is not at home. Where is that?' asked Eleanor.

'You see,' said Miss Pymble, 'Pauline lives with her aunt and uncle. I called there late on Saturday afternoon after we had all finished and Princess Mary had left. I spoke to a man there, a very surly individual, but he wasn't at all helpful. I called again yesterday after church but there was no-one there. I spoke to the vicar and asked him what he thought and he suggested she might have gone home to her father's but Pauline would never have done that, not with the Royal Visit, so that is how I know that something dreadful has happened but I couldn't do anything about it yesterday, being Sunday.'

In her anxiety, Miss Pymble was twisting and untwisting the handles of her handbag.

'And where does Pauline's father live?' asked Eleanor, when Miss Pymble paused for breath.

'At Clough End Farm, it's out Brandside way. Pauline's mother died about five years ago and last year, when Pauline was old enough to go out to work, she came to live with her aunt and uncle in town so as to be near her work. It was more convenient for her, you see. They had only just moved into town themselves but recently Pauline said they were moving again and we were considering, that is Felicity and I were considering, asking Pauline to come and stay with us. There's room at Waverton House now that the season is over. Pauline's a maid at the Grove Hotel but she is not there.'

Eleanor mentally sorted through this jumble of information and asked: 'So you've already checked at the Grove?'

'Yes. I called there first thing and the receptionist told me Pauline hadn't arrived for work this morning. She is supposed to be there by seven. Now I don't know what to do, so I thought I should consult you because you are always so good at knowing what to do.'

Eleanor thought for a few seconds. Then she asked: 'Where do Pauline's aunt and uncle live?'

'At Red Farm on Long Hill. Only it's not a working farm now.'

Eleanor realised that this was where Jon Jon had retrieved Mrs Hazelwood's puppies yesterday. In order to be sure, she asked: 'Is that the last building on the right after you get past the end of the houses.'

'Yes, that's the one.'

'Does anyone else live there apart from Pauline's aunt and uncle, do you know?'

'Well, perhaps the man I spoke to there, but I don't really know.'

Eleanor wondered if it was coincidence or cause for concern that there now appeared to be three people missing: Mondo, Mr Sutton, and Pauline and that Pauline lived where Mrs Hazelwood's missing puppies had been found.

'Do you think it would help if I made enquiries?'

'Oh, would you, Miss Harriman? That would be so kind.'

'Well,' said Eleanor. 'I have an appointment which I must keep this afternoon but I can begin straight after that. Will that be all right?'

'Oh yes. Thank you so much.'

'Perhaps if I go to Red Farm, someone may be there by now and I may be able to find out more. If not, it would seem that the only other likely place to look would be the farm out at Brandside. If she is not there, they may know where she is. I could drive out there and make enquiries.'

'Thank you so much, Miss Harriman. It has put my mind at rest knowing that you will be looking for Pauline. I am so sorry to put you to all this trouble but Felicity and I are very worried and we could not just sit back and do nothing.'

'No, of course not,' said Eleanor. 'I understand why you are worried. I will let you know how I get on.'

With further thanks and a farewell pat for Napoleon, Miss Pymble went downstairs where she had an animated conversation with James about Princess Mary's visit. Eleanor went back to work and, just before lunch, James informed her that Mr Pidcock had telephoned to say that, in Mr Sutton's continued absence, he had arranged for the unsigned document to be taken over to Chapel-en-le-Frith where it had been signed by the bank manager there. The completion had been re-scheduled for two thirty.

Mr Harriman was still in Manchester and during lunch Eleanor discussed Mr Sutton's absence with Edwin. They speculated on the possible reasons without reaching any conclusion. Eleanor also described Miss Pymble's visit and explained to Edwin her intention of going to Red Farm and, if necessary, Clough End Farm to make enquiries for Pauline. Edwin was sorry not to be able to help but he had appointments all afternoon.

CHAPTER TWENTY-THREE

After lunch, Eleanor went to the bank to complete the Belfield transaction and then returned to the office. Leaving Napoleon with Mrs Clayton, she went around to the garage and collected Mr Harriman's car. She drove up Long Hill to Red Farm and, as the gate at the bottom of the track was open, drove up the track, turned the car around so that it was facing the road, and parked outside the front door of the old farm house. No-one answered the door when she knocked and, after knocking again and waiting some time, she gave up. She returned to the motor-car and started the engine. She was on a farm track and not on a public street but, from force of habit, she glanced behind her to check for traffic before moving off. As she did so, she detected a fleeting movement somewhere behind her. She turned and looked towards the stables, which were a little further up the track and to the side of the barn where the puppies had been. She got out of the motor-car and walked up to the stables calling out as she did so to attract attention. A man appeared at the half door. His face was unshaven and his expression was surly. He opened the door and stood in the doorway. He wore clothes that were ill-fitting, torn in places, and caked with mud. He was gripping the collar of a large, battle-scarred mastiff who seemed as surly as himself and was clearly looking for an excuse to attack. Eleanor wondered if this was the man Miss Pymble had mentioned.

Eleanor said, in as neutral a tone as she could manage: 'Good afternoon, I am looking for a young lady called Pauline. I believe she lives here. Do you know if she's here?'

The man said: 'She's not 'ere.' His voice was rough. The mastiff looked intently at Eleanor and took a step forward.

'Do you know where she is?' asked Eleanor, trying to ignore the dog.

'She's not 'ere, I tell yer,' said the man gruffly. 'You'd best be going.' He yanked fiercely at the collar of the dog and bellowed: 'Down.' The dog immediately sank to the ground and as it did so, the man let go of its collar.

Eleanor decided to retreat. She walked at a steady pace back to the motor-car, got in, and drove off down the track towards the road. Eleanor wondered how Pauline could bear to live at that place. At the main road, she paused undecided as to what to do next. She recalled how truly worried Miss Pymble was about Pauline and was beginning to be concerned for her as well. Having promised Miss Pymble that she would look for Pauline, she felt obliged to go out to the farm at Brandside. She thought that the visit would be just as fruitless as the one she had just made and that her enquiries there would be met with the same hostility. She drummed her fingers on the steering wheel as she considered the options.

Brandside was only four miles away. She opened the glove compartment and took out the Bartholomew's motoring map Mr Harriman kept there. Clough End Farm was marked on the map. Miss Pymble had said Brandside but the farm was actually closer to Dale Head and not very far from Buxton at all. There were two ways of getting there and Eleanor decided to take the longer route, the road suitable for motor-cars, rather than the shorter route which she knew was little more than a cart track. She looked at her watch and calculated that she had plenty of time to get there and back before dusk. Making a mental note of the farm's location, she put the map back in the glove compartment and headed back down Long Hill. When she reached St John's Road, she headed towards Burbage and on to the Leek Road.

Very soon, Eleanor had left the town behind and was out on the top of the moors. Even though it was treeless and uninteresting to some, Eleanor never tired of this wide, expansive landscape where the views extended for miles. She knew that she needed to turn off just as the road began to curve as it skirted along below the ridge known as Axe Edge. When she reached that junction, Eleanor could not resist stopping for a few minutes to look back towards Buxton and the landscape beyond. This was one of her favourite views and she was reminded of the times when she and her sisters and brother had walked with Mr Harriman to the top of Axe Edge, where they could sit and enjoy an uninterrupted view over a variety of undulating peaks and ridges towards Kinder Scout, Edale and the Hope Valley, fifteen or so miles away. Today the weather was fine and the air was clear so it was still possible to see for miles even though this viewpoint at the roadside was lower than the summit.

After a few minutes, Eleanor recalled herself to the task in hand and drove along the narrow side road, hardly more than a rough lane and only just suitable for motor vehicles. It climbed steadily through empty treeless moorland and then, after about two miles, there were fields marked by dry-stone walls on either side of the road. Eventually, after another mile or so, Eleanor saw on her left the entrance to Clough End Farm and she turned the motor-car onto the rutted track which led to the house and farm buildings.

Eleanor surveyed the scene in front of her. She was in a U-shaped cobbled yard. On the far end, facing her, was a farm house of the usual design: a south-facing, stone building with two windows either side of the front door and three windows in a row on the floor above. To the right of the farm house was a stable building, and, at right angles to that and forming an L shape with the house and stables, was a large barn. On the left of the yard opposite the large barn was a smaller barn. Little had been done to make the farm attractive and there was a pervasive air of neglect. The timber of the doors and window frames had once been painted but what little remained of the paintwork was now peeling and ragged. The gutters were full of moss. There were no flowers or shrubs to soften the cold effect of the dark grey stone used in the construction of the farm buildings. Weeds sprouted thickly between the cobbles in the yard. In the left hand corner of the yard, various pieces of discarded metal and parts of old farm implements formed an untidy pile. There was no sign of life, not even the usual barking dog to greet or warn off the visitor. The doors and windows of all the buildings were closed and there was no smoke coming from either of the house's two chimneys. And yet, Eleanor had the uneasy feeling that she was being watched.

Eleanor sat for a minute or two, waiting to see if anyone appeared. She then considered whether or not to turn around and just leave. Telling herself not to be a coward, she got out of the motor-car and walked to the front door of the farm house. Using the door knocker, she knocked firmly and listened. The house seemed to have that empty feel that unoccupied houses have. Eleanor knocked again and waited. There was still no sound from within. She wondered if perhaps someone was at home but was upstairs. She took a step backwards and looked up at the windows on the floor above. She caught a brief glimpse of a face at the window on the left and she was taking a further step backwards to get a better view, when a blow to her head caused her to sink to her knees and lose consciousness. Distracted by the face at the window, she had not sensed that someone had stealthily walked up behind her.

Eleanor regained consciousness after a few seconds. There was an overwhelming smell of foul breath, stale sweat, and manure. Someone was gripping her tightly under her armpits and she was being dragged along. Her feet were bumping over the cobbles of the yard. She struggled to get free but the arms tightened their grip and she was dragged across the yard to the smaller of the two barns. She was shoved through the doorway. Then, in one quick, rough movement, the man flipped her over so that she was tossed face down on to the barn floor and before she could turn to see who her attacker was, he slammed the door closed.

Eleanor sat up gingerly and took stock. Physically she appeared to be unharmed except that her head was throbbing. She remembered the face at the window and thought that the person watching must have seen what happened and might call for help. Eleanor wondered if it was Pauline. She stood up warily, feeling a bit shaky, and looked around her. She tested the door, without any real hope that it would open. Small slivers of light were coming through splits in the timber of the door, although they did not penetrate very far into the barn. She stood with her back to the door and examined the barn. She wondered if there was anything that she could use to force open the door.

Eleanor moved towards the left hand corner of the barn where there was a pile of old farm equipment and contemplated the tangle of metal. It was difficult to discern anything that would be useful as a tool. At the far end there was an old cart and there appeared to be little else. She moved across towards the right hand corner. She could make out a couple of sacks propped up against the wall. They appeared to be full of something lumpy, possibly potatoes. Beside them were some empty sacks, tossed randomly in a heap. There was a strong smell of damp hessian and another odour, strong but difficult to place. Then, at the far edge of the pile of sacks, Eleanor saw a shoe. It was not lying on its side or placed flat on the floor as a discarded shoe would be; it was balancing on its heel, toe pointing upwards. The shoe was on a foot. Eleanor stared at the shoe, trying to avoid the thought which was intruding into her mind. She moved closer to the pile of sacks and saw another foot, wearing only a sock, and pointing upwards parallel with the other foot.

Eleanor told herself to remain calm but that was difficult. She was looking at a pair of feet and there was no escaping the fact that the body attached to the feet was lying hidden under the pile of sacks. Eleanor knew better than to disturb the scene so she touched nothing. She continued to stare at the feet and considered the situation. The fact that one foot was wearing a shoe and not a boot suggested that the person lying under the sacks was not a farmer or someone who lived or worked in the countryside. This style of shoe was worn by townspeople. Above the shoe she could see a small portion of cloth, the bottom of a trouser leg. The intrusive thought could no longer be ignored. This was part of a business suit which belonged in the town not the country.

Eleanor walked back to the barn door and leaned against it to steady herself. She tried to think but her head was throbbing and she was feeling dizzy. She looked at her watch but there was not enough light to see what time it was. Nevertheless, she knew that it would soon be getting dark. The side effect from the blow to the head was combining with the shock of finding the body and Eleanor was beginning to feel extremely drowsy. Her knees gave way and she sank slowly to the ground, her back sliding against the barn door as she went down. She wanted to remain alert and ready for whatever danger might be coming next but she was finding it hard to keep awake. Within a few minutes, she fell asleep.

CHAPTER TWENTY-FOUR

Philip Danebridge had been to an auction in Derby that afternoon to obtain the piece of china that Mondo had seen in the catalogue and he had also found some items for the shop. When he arrived back in Buxton, instead of going straight home, he parked his motor-car in Hall Bank intending to call in on Eleanor. He wanted to show off the pair of very fine Chinese porcelain vases that he had bid for successfully. They were a bargain that he was particularly proud of. As he greeted James he deposited a large carton containing the two vases on the clerk's desk. When he asked for Eleanor, James explained that Eleanor was absent and that he and Mrs Clayton were getting worried. Mr Harriman had not yet returned from Manchester and Edwin was out of the office at a meeting. As James was explaining the situation to Philip, Edwin arrived back.

'Good afternoon, Edwin.'

'Philip, good afternoon.'

'James has just been telling me that Eleanor is missing.'

'What! What do you mean, missing?' said Edwin, looking at James.

'Do you have any idea where she might be?' asked Philip.

'She went to look for a Girl Guide,' said James.

'Yes,' said Edwin, 'Eleanor told me at lunchtime that Miss Pymble had been here. Apparently she is quite worried about a Girl Guide who was missing on Saturday. Eleanor had agreed to go to Red Farm to enquire after her and I think she was intending to go out to Brandside to the girl's father's farm

if she had no luck at Red Farm. Now, what was it called…
umm…Clough End, that's it.'

'Miss Eleanor left here straight after she came back from the bank. She has been gone a good two hours and it is only a short drive to Brandside,' said James.

'I've got the motor outside,' said Philip. 'Do you think we should go and look for her?'

'Yes, I think we should,' said Edwin. 'Perhaps we should start at Red Farm and then go out to the farm.'

James added: 'I did expect that Miss Eleanor would be back much earlier than this. I admit that I am getting worried.'

Hearing voices, Mrs Clayton came downstairs followed by Napoleon.

'Good afternoon, Mr Danebridge,' she said. Then, turning to Edwin, she said: 'Mr Talbot, I know for sure that Miss Harriman was expecting to be back by now, and if you don't mind my saying so, I think it would be a good idea if you and Mr Danebridge were to go and look for her. Being as Mr Harriman isn't here. I'm sure that is what he would want and his train from Manchester is not due for another hour.'

'Don't worry, Mrs Clayton,' said Edwin. 'Mr Danebridge and I were just about to form a search party.'

'I'm only too glad to help,' said Philip, opening the front door. Napoleon went outside and sat on the pavement, sniffing the air. 'I'll leave that box there if that is all right with you, James. There are two Chinese vases in there and I don't think they would survive the roads out at Brandside.'

'Very good, Mr Danebridge,' said James.

'Mr Talbot, Miss Eleanor may return in your absence. I will wait here in case, and let her know where you are, if that would be convenient.'

'Thank you, James,' said Edwin, as he went through the front door, 'I would appreciate that, if that doesn't put you out too much.' Edwin looked at Napoleon. 'Coming, old chap?' he asked.

Philip and Edwin drove up Long Hill to Red Farm and when they reached the end of the lane, Edwin said: 'There's no sign of a motor-car. I don't think she's here. In fact, it doesn't look as if anyone is here.'

Philip said: 'I agree. Let's not waste any time here. Eleanor must have gone out to the farm to see if the girl is there.' As he turned the motor-car around, he said: 'There's a map on the back seat. Can you reach it? I know the road to Brandside but I'm not sure exactly where the farm is that she was going to. What's the name of it again?'

'Clough End,' said Edwin as he consulted the map. 'Right, that's it there. It's not as far as Brandside.'

Philip looked at the map and decided on the best route, which was the one taken by Eleanor. They headed back down the hill. By the time they reached the turn off to the farm it was dark. The only light was from the headlights of Philip's car.

When they turned off the main road, Edwin said: 'Keep on this road. We have a little way to go yet. Clough End should be about four miles along.'

After a few minutes, Philip said: 'We must be nearly there but I can't see a thing in this blackness.'

As they drove, Edwin scanned the bank alongside the road looking for a gate and Philip drove slowly so that the beam from the headlights could pick up the entrance to the farm. Napoleon had his head over the side of the motor-car keeping watch and sniffing the air.

'That's it! There,' said Edwin. 'On the left.'

Philip turned the motor-car onto the track to the farm house and parked in the cobbled yard. The headlights lit up the front door of the farm house but the rest of the farm was in darkness. Napoleon was keen to get out but Edwin restrained him. Philip and Edwin looked about them, assessing the situation.

'I don't think there is anyone here,' said Philip, barely above a whisper.

'The place certainly looks deserted,' agreed Edwin, in a low voice.

Although there appeared to be no-one about, they felt compelled to speak softly. They were surrounded by complete silence as they sat, listening intently. No-one came out of the house and no dogs barked.

'I'll go and knock on the front door just in case and then we'll have a look around,' said Philip. 'There's a torch in the glove compartment if you wouldn't mind getting it out. I'll take that as well. No, Napoleon, you stay put.'

Philip got out of the motor-car and began walking towards the front door, staying in the beam of light from the motor-car's headlamps. After a few paces, he stopped and shone his torch into the darkness on either side of the beam of light. Then, instead of continuing to the front door, he returned to the motor-car and said to Edwin, trying to sound calm and hide his concern: 'There's a motor-car parked around the corner there. I couldn't see properly but I think it's Mr Harriman's.'

Edwin and Napoleon got out of the motor-car and joined Philip.

'In that gap between the barn and the stables,' said Philip, as he shone the torch to his right.

'That's Harriman's car, all right,' said Edwin, also trying to remain calm. 'Eleanor must be here somewhere.'

They walked quietly over to the motor-car and checked that it was empty. Napoleon stood with his head raised, looking around and sniffing the air. He too recognised the motor-car.

Philip said, confidently: 'Right-oh, Napoleon. Where's Eleanor? Find!'

Napoleon started casting around for a scent.

'Let's knock on the front door just in case Eleanor's inside,' said Edwin.

They walked towards the front door. Napoleon stayed behind, sniffing and circling the ground around the motor-car.

Edwin used the door knocker and waited, listening intently. He was about to knock again when Napoleon pushed past and began sniffing around the door. Having picked up Eleanor's scent from the motor-car, he had followed it to the front door. He then turned away from the door, head down, casting about from side to side following the scent. Edwin and Philip watched as he zig-zagged across the cobbled yard, in and out of the beam of the headlights from Philip's motor-car. Then he disappeared out of the light and became invisible. They waited in silence. Napoleon headed confidently towards the small barn on the far side of the cobbled yard. He sniffed at the bottom of the barn door, sucking in great gulps of air, and then he began barking.

Eleanor had heard a motor-car arrive and, fearing the worst, had sat listening intently, trying to decide what was happening. After a minute or two she had heard a metallic banging some way off and realised that someone was knocking on the front door. She hoped that was a good sign because people who lived at the farm would just let themselves in rather than knock. Although she had been confident that someone from Hall Bank would come looking for her eventually, she was torn between calling out for help, hoping that the people knocking on the door were her rescuers, or remaining silent, fearing that the newcomers were friends of whoever had attacked her. She was focussing her attention on the banging at a distance, when a sound close to her made her jump. A dog was sniffing at the gap between the ground and the bottom of the barn door. She froze convinced that her enemies had returned. Then the dog barked and she knew at once that it was Napoleon. She called to him and his big paws began scratching forcefully at the door.

When Edwin and Philip heard Napoleon barking, they ran over to the barn. Napoleon was lunging at the door and clawing at it frantically.

'Well done, Napoleon,' said Philip, 'good boy! Eleanor, are you there? It's Philip and Edwin.'

Napoleon's barking was masking any sound from inside the barn and Philip restrained him.

'All right, old chap,' said Edwin. 'Move out of the way while I get this door open.'

The barn had a double door secured from the outside with a bar, which was sufficient to prevent the person inside from opening the door. Philip shone the torch as Edwin lifted the bar and started to pull one side of the door towards him. Impatiently, Napoleon squeezed through the emerging gap and disappeared into the barn. He and Eleanor greeted each other enthusiastically and came out of the barn together.

'Are you all right?' asked Philip, anxiously, taking Eleanor's arm. 'You haven't been harmed?'

'No,' Eleanor assured him. 'I am just a bit sore from having been dragged into the barn. I am very glad to see you both.'

After they had recovered from their relief and excitement, Edwin said: 'There's no-one here at the moment but I don't want to risk someone coming back. Let's get moving, shall we?' As he turned to go back to the car, he added: 'We can save the explanations until we get back to the office.'

'No, wait!' called Eleanor. 'There are two things we must do first.'

'What is it? I don't think we should delay any longer than we have to,' said Edwin.

'What's the matter?' asked Philip.

'First of all we have to find Pauline. That's why I came here. I am sure I caught a glimpse of her when I arrived and I think she is in the house, in the room upstairs on the left. The other thing is that there is a body, in there. Lying on the floor on the right-hand side. I only saw the feet but I'm sure it is a man.'

'Oh dear. Right. I'd better have a look,' said Edwin and taking the torch from Philip, he went into the barn. He returned almost immediately. 'The light from this torch is not very bright so I haven't been able to see very clearly but I think you are right, Eleanor, it is a man and I am very much afraid that it is Mr Sutton. This is most unfortunate.'

Eleanor said: 'I thought perhaps it was him but I didn't want to believe it.'

Edwin stood thinking. 'We need to get you back to Hall Bank and then I need to call Superintendent Johnson but I am loathe to just leave without securing the scene.'

'But that means you would have to stay here alone,' said Philip. 'I don't think that is a good idea.'

'I agree with Philip,' said Eleanor.

'Very well,' said Edwin. 'It will probably only take about twenty minutes for me to bring the police back here. I think we can risk it. Right, Philip, you take Eleanor back to Hall Bank and I will drive Harriman's motor and go straight to the police station.'

Eleanor said: 'No, no, please. We really must look for Pauline. We can't just leave her here. She may be in danger.'

'Are you sure it was Pauline that you saw?' asked Edwin.

'Yes, at least, it was a young woman, and I assume it was her. I don't actually know her. Let's just go back to the house and try and make her hear us,' suggested Eleanor.

'We knocked earlier but no-one came to the door,' said Philip. 'I'll try again. You stay here for the minute.'

He walked over to the front door and knocked again. As he did so he looked up and saw someone move quickly back from the window. He walked back to Eleanor and Edwin.

'You're right, Eleanor. There's definitely someone there,' said Philip.

'Why doesn't she come down and open the door?' said Eleanor.

'Perhaps she is afraid to,' said Philip. 'Or perhaps she is locked in.'

Edwin said: 'I noticed a ladder over by the stables where Harriman's motor is. I'll get it and we can reach the window. It's not very high.'

Edwin returned with the ladder and rested it against the house, tested it, and was about to climb up.

Eleanor said: 'Wait! Pauline doesn't know you. She might be startled if a strange man suddenly appears at the window. She will probably hide when she hears a noise and that will just waste time. She might be more reassured seeing a woman and also I think she saw me earlier on. I should go up.'

Edwin and Philip looked at each other. They had to agree that what Eleanor said made sense and they also knew better than to try to dissuade her when she had a plan in mind. Edwin handed her the torch and wondered what he would say to Mr Harriman if she had an accident. Philip consoled himself with the thought that fortunately farm houses of this kind did not have high ceilings so the first floor was not very far off the ground. He grabbed hold of the ladder to keep it steady. Napoleon sat at the foot of the ladder and watched, unwilling to let Eleanor out of his sight.

When Eleanor reached the top she tapped softly on the window and waited. The window itself was small and difficult to see through. It was the old style with nine small panes of glass. There was a layer of grime on the glass as well. Eleanor tapped again and then shone the torch into the room but she couldn't tell whether the room was empty or not. She could just make out a wardrobe and an iron bedstead. The bed had been made and there was what looked like a coat lying across the bottom of the bed. Eleanor tapped on the window again. Nothing.

Eleanor called out: 'Pauline, are you there? It's Miss Harriman. I am a friend of the Misses Pymble.' Still nothing.

'They asked me to come and find you. They were worried because you were not there on Saturday to meet Princess Mary.'

Eleanor waited and was about to give up when the beam of her torch caught the top of a head on the far side of the bed and then a pair of eyes appeared.

'Pauline?' said Eleanor.

The rest of the face appeared and looked intently across to the window. Pauline had been hiding in the space between the bed and the wall. She stood up and came across to the window.

'I came to see if you are all right,' said Eleanor. 'I have two friends here with me as well. The Misses Pymble were very worried about you because you didn't come to the Thermal Baths on Saturday. They know how much you were looking forward to being presented to the Princess.'

Pauline was fighting back tears. 'I couldn't....my father said...the dogs... I'm so sorry I let them down. But I'm locked in, Miss Harriman.'

'I see,' said Eleanor.

'Oh, please, Miss Harriman. Will you help me?'

'Of course. Can you open this window?'

'No. It's stuck. I tried before because I thought I might be able to get out that way but it wouldn't budge.'

'If we get rid of one pane of glass that is not going to be a big enough space for you to crawl through,' said Eleanor. 'We are going to have to break the glazing bars as well. It will cause a fair bit of damage to the window, I'm afraid. Is there no other way out?'

'No. The door is locked and I have tried to get it open but I couldn't. I don't care if the window has to be broken. I just want to get away from here.' Pauline sounded desperate.

Philip, hearing this conversation, hurried across the yard to his motor-car and came back with the tyre lever to break the window with. Eleanor looked down and said: 'Philip,

I'm coming down. It will be much quicker if you do this job, I think.'

Philip waited for Eleanor to climb down and then quickly took her place. He introduced himself and asked Pauline to get two blankets.

'Pauline, stand well back from the window while I do this. Watch out down below.'

Eleanor moved away from the ladder and took Napoleon back to the Bentley so that he would not tread on any broken glass. As she turned to go back to the house, she noticed a faint light in the distance. It seemed to be in the fields across on the other side of the road from the farm. She thought at first it was another farm building but then the light moved. As she watched, it bobbed about and she realised it was someone walking. It seemed to be moving sideways and not coming any closer but Eleanor thought that they should leave as soon as possible. Telling Napoleon to stay, she went back to Edwin and drew his attention to the light.

The timber of the glazing bars was rotten and came away easily, sending a shower of glass flying. Pauline spread one of the blankets over the broken glass on the floor and Philip spread the other blanket over the jagged edge of the window sill.

'Do you think you can manage to climb out, Pauline?'

'Oh, yes. Girl Guides can manage any difficulty,' she said proudly.

Philip smiled. 'Down you come then.'

'Can I bring my bag? I don't want to leave my things here?'

'Yes, hand it to me though.' Philip took the bag and went part of the way down the ladder to allow Pauline room to climb out of the window.

When Pauline reached the ground, Eleanor said: 'Pauline, this is Mr Talbot, my father's partner. Your rescuer is Mr Danebridge. Gentlemen, this is Pauline. I'm sorry, Pauline, I don't know your last name.'

'Hartshorn,' said Pauline, 'Miss Harriman, I'm ever so sorry you were hit on the head. I couldn't warn you in time.'

'When did that happen?' asked Philip, anxiously.

'What do you mean?' said Edwin simultaneously with Philip.

'Somebody hit me on the back of the head before dumping me in the barn,' said Eleanor. 'I passed out.'

'Eleanor,' said Edwin sternly, 'if I had known that, I would never have let you climb that ladder. What will your father say to me when he finds out?'

'Sorry,' said Eleanor, grinning, 'but I'm fine.'

'We shall discuss that later. Now, we should leave as quickly as we can,' said Edwin. 'Pauline you go with Eleanor and Philip and they will take you back to Buxton.'

'Ooo,' said Pauline, distracted from her troubles by the novelty of a ride in a motor-car.

As Eleanor and Pauline moved away, Edwin said to Philip, 'Pauline hasn't mentioned the barn so I assume she knows nothing about Sutton. Best to keep it to ourselves for the moment. I'll take Harriman's motor and go straight to the police station.'

Philip nodded. 'Right oh. I'll see you back at Hall Bank.'

Constrained by the presence of Pauline, Eleanor and Philip avoided the topics they really wanted to discuss. On the way back to Buxton, Eleanor occupied the time by giving Pauline a description of the visit of Princess Mary, answering her many questions about the event, and commiserating with Pauline on her misfortune at having missed it.

CHAPTER TWENTY-FIVE

Ten minutes later, Eleanor, Philip, Napoleon and Pauline reached Hall Bank. Mr Harriman had returned from Manchester and he, James and Mrs Clayton formed a very relieved welcoming committee. Napoleon bounded in and greeted them. James, after expressing his pleasure at Eleanor's return, left for home. Mrs Clayton headed for the kitchen to make a pot of tea. Eleanor asked her father to take Philip and Pauline up to the sitting room while she telephoned Miss Pymble. She gave the simplest explanation possible to Miss Pymble regarding Pauline's imprisonment and made arrangements for Pauline to stay at Waverton House. When everyone was assembled in the sitting room and the fire had been banked up, Mrs Clayton plied everyone with tea and Mr Harriman plied Eleanor and Philip with questions.

Eleanor began by explaining to her father how she came to be at Clough End Farm. She and Philip were part of the way through describing the rescue of Pauline via the farmhouse window when Edwin returned from the police station. They had not yet mentioned the body in the barn.

Edwin, gratefully accepting a cup of tea from Mrs Clayton, said: 'When I arrived at the police station, Superintendent Johnson was about to leave with some of his men on an assignment of some sort, he couldn't say what. He said he would send someone out to the farm as soon as he could. He asked the constable on duty to contact Alf and let him know he would be needed first thing tomorrow morning.'

Mrs Clayton looked surprised at the mention of Alf but said nothing.

Mr Harriman said: 'What's this all about?' but nobody answered him.

Edwin said: 'Pauline, please tell us how you came to be out at the farm. Do you know anything about what is going on there?'

Pauline looked at Eleanor for reassurance and Eleanor said: 'It's all right, Pauline. You are not in any trouble. You are safe and among friends now.'

'Oh,' said Pauline. 'Thank you. I'm never going back to Clough End, not now.'

'No,' said Eleanor, 'that is completely understandable after what has happened.'

'Will somebody please tell me what, in fact, has happened,' said Mr Harriman, sternly.

Eleanor said: 'Perhaps we should start at the beginning starting with Saturday. Pauline, why were you not there to meet Princess Mary?'

'I couldn't. I was locked in you see,' said Pauline.

'At the farm,' asked Edwin. 'Where we found you?'

'Yes,' said Pauline.

Eleanor said: 'I understood from Miss Pymble that you usually stay at Red Farm so that you can work at The Grove.'

'Yes, with Auntie May and Uncle Fred. I usually go out to the farm once a fortnight on Saturday to see Father, just to tidy up and keep things sorted like, since Mother passed away and there's no-one there to look after him. Mr Tunnicliffe, the carrier from Longnor, takes me as far as Harpur Hill and I walk from there. It's not far.'

'But, why were you at the farm on Saturday when you should have been meeting Princess Mary?'

'Well, I didn't mean to be there but Father and I, we had a falling out, see. About the dog fighting and…'

'The dog fighting?' interrupted Mr Harriman.

'Yes, there's some men come from Sheffield. They organise the fights and Father lets them use one of the barns. I think the man in the stables at Red Farm is one of them.'

'Superintendent Johnson will be interested to hear this,' said Edwin. 'Tell me about these fights. How did you find out about them?'

'A few weeks ago, I was out at the farm and I was sorting things in the kitchen and Father must have forgotten that I was there. Father was in the passage near the back door and I heard him talking to someone about a fight they were planning. At first I thought he meant men but then I realised it was dogs.'

'Do you know who that was that your father was talking to?' asked Edwin.

'No, I couldn't see. Then, when Father came into the kitchen I asked him about the fighting and we got into an argument. He said it was none of my business. He was only making a bit of money out of the farm seeing as how proper farming doesn't pay anymore. He said it was only to be that once and I was to forget all about it. But he lied to me.'

'But why were you at the farm last Saturday afternoon when you were supposed to be with the Guides,' asked Eleanor.

'Well, I'd been out at the farm the Saturday before that and when I was there Father said he was going to sell the furniture in the upstairs rooms that we don't use, to tide him over and make ends meet, like. Some of my things were still there in my old bedroom and he said if I wanted them I had better move them sharpish before Saturday or I'd lose them. But I knew I wouldn't be able to get out there on Saturday as usual because of meeting Princess Mary so I begged some time off work and went on Friday afternoon instead. Father didn't know I was coming and I was passing one of the barns and I heard him. He was talking to someone about a dog fight that was being planned and how many men were coming, and that's how I knew he had lied to me. About it only happening once, I mean.'

'Perhaps they had a fight arranged for Saturday,' said Edwin. 'They may have thought no-one would be about because of the Royal Visit.'

'Yes, they could have counted on all of the police being in Buxton for Princess Mary,' said Eleanor. 'No doubt it was an ideal opportunity.'

'I don't know when the fight was to be,' said Pauline, 'but I don't hold with dog fighting and I was very cross with Father because he had lied to me and because I heard him saying that he'd got money on the fight. When Father came in from the barn, I had it out with him. I told him he shouldn't be doing that sort of thing and he said I didn't know what I was talking about and how did I expect him to make ends meet otherwise. So I said that if he wouldn't agree to stop the fight I would go to the police and they would stop it. He was very, very angry. He said I were only a useless girl, that I was all talk and he weren't afeared of me. He said the fight would go on even if he had to stop me going to the police. Then he said other things, dreadful things.'

'Things such as what?' asked Eleanor.

'That if he'd had a son instead of a useless daughter there would have been someone to help on the farm and that he wouldn't be in the trouble he was in and he wouldn't have to sell the farm and how it was all my fault.'

'Oh, Pauline, that is so unfair,' said Eleanor. 'You must not believe that, not for one moment. None of this is your fault. Your father has been affected like many other farmers because of the economic situation and there is nothing you could have done to make it different.'

'And did you go to the police as you threatened to do?' asked Mr Harriman, steering the conversation back to the main point.

'No, because Father was that angry. He slapped me hard and I fell down. He grabbed hold of me and dragged me up to my room and locked me in. He said he'd show me who was in charge.'

Mrs Clayton expressed her indignation with a loud 'Oh!'

'And that was where we found you,' said Philip.

Pauline nodded.

'And I don't suppose anyone fed you either,' said Mrs Clayton, crossly, always concerned for people's dietary needs.

'*Did* anyone give you food?' asked Eleanor, with concern, realising that she had not considered this.

'Father left me some bread and cheese but I finished that this morning,' said Pauline.

Mrs Clayton tutted and Eleanor said: 'You must be very hungry? Can we offer you something to eat?'

'Yes, please,' said Pauline, shyly.

Mrs Clayton could bear no more of this conversation. She bustled away to the kitchen, saying, 'I didn't start dinner because I wasn't sure when you would get back but I made some sandwiches in case. I'll get them right away, you poor thing.'

'So you had been locked in all that time until we arrived?' asked Eleanor.

'Yes. Father wouldn't let me out. He said I had to stay there until I learnt not to meddle in things that didn't concern me. And I was so worried about the Guides and letting Miss Pymble down and I tried to get out but I couldn't.' Pauline was on the verge of tears.

Before Eleanor could continue, Mrs Clayton returned with a plate of sandwiches and a table napkin for Pauline.

'Thank you, Mr Danebridge,' Mrs Clayton said, as Philip placed a side table next to Pauline's chair. 'I don't suppose any of the rest of you have eaten either, have you?' She looked around accusingly. 'I shall get some more sandwiches.'

Napoleon left the hearthrug and placed himself strategically within sight of Pauline's sandwiches. Eleanor gave him a warning look.

'And, do you think there was another dog fight last Saturday?' asked Eleanor.

'I don't think so. I thought I heard someone in the yard on Friday night but not a fight. I didn't hear anything at all after father left on Saturday afternoon. I didn't see anyone at the farm until today.'

'When I was at the front door of the farm house,' said Eleanor, 'it was you that I saw when I looked up at the window, wasn't it?'

'Yes,' said Pauline, 'and I'm ever so sorry, Miss Harriman, about what happened to you. About being hit, I mean. I saw them coming up behind you but I couldn't warn you.'

'You saw who hit me?'

'What!' interrupted Mr Harriman. 'You were hit? Did someone attack you, Eleanor?'

'Yes,' said Philip, 'she was hit over the head by some brute and if ever I see him I shall return the compliment.'

'Oh dear,' said Mrs Clayton as she returned with more sandwiches and began to distribute plates and napkins.

'This should be reported to the police,' said Mr Harriman.

'It has been,' said Edwin, 'and I would advise Eleanor to see Dr McKenzie tomorrow because she did lose consciousness.'

'Good grief! We must keep an eye on you, young lady,' said Mr Harriman, looking at Eleanor with concern, 'because you could easily suffer from concussion.'

Eleanor smiled at her father. 'I will be fine, don't worry.'

Pauline had been quietly enjoying the first of her sandwiches and was startled when Mr Harriman said, sternly: 'Pauline, you said you saw who hit Eleanor. Do you know who it was?'

Pauline nodded, unable to speak with a mouth full of sandwich.

'Who was it?' asked Mr Harriman.

'Charlie Perceval,' she mumbled and then swallowed.

'Are you absolutely sure?' asked Mr Harriman.

'Oh, yes. I know all the Percevals. I went to school with one of Charlie's sisters.'

Edwin said: 'So that's where he absconded to.'

Mr Harriman said: 'And the other man, do you know who that was? Have you seen him at the farm before?'

'Yes,' said Pauline, 'that was my cousin.'

'You didn't see Charlie or your cousin when you arrived at the farm on Friday?' asked Mr Harriman. Pauline shook her head.

'And after Charlie had hit me over the head, was it your cousin who dragged me into the barn?' asked Eleanor.

'Yes,' said Pauline. 'And I couldn't do anything to help.'

'Was that the barn where you had heard your father talking to someone?' asked Eleanor.

'No,' said Pauline. 'Father was in the big barn then. That was the cart shed where you were.'

'And what did Charlie do while your cousin was dragging Eleanor into the barn,' asked Edwin.

'He walked away. I think he went back to the stables.'

'And where was your father, do you know?' asked Mr Harriman.

'I don't know. I didn't see him there.'

'When did you last see him?' asked Mr Harriman.

'I know he was in the house on Friday night and Saturday morning because I heard him and he brought up some bread and cheese at lunchtime on Saturday. He said I was to stay in my room until he got back. I don't know where he was going but I'm sure he didn't come back after that. In that house you can hear every move and I would have known if he was in the house. Of course, he might have been somewhere else on the farm.'

'Had you seen Charlie or Sam Perceval at the farm before?' asked Eleanor.

'No, but I did hear that Sam had been doing some work for Father, getting the sheep to the sales and that.'

'Well, we shall certainly have to get to the bottom of this and deal with whatever is going on there,' said Edwin.

Mr Harriman looked at his daughter with concern. 'So, after being knocked out, you were dumped in a barn?'

Eleanor nodded. She was anxious to deflect the conversation away from the barn so she held out her cup and said: 'May I have more tea, please Mrs Clayton.'

'Certainly. Anyone else?' asked Mrs Clayton, tea pot poised.

'Yes, please,' said Edwin, 'and those sandwiches are excellent, Mrs Clayton, thank you. Just what was needed.'

'Pauline, are you sure you saw no-one at the farm on Monday,' said Eleanor. 'Apart from Charlie Perceval and your cousin, that is.'

'No,' said Pauline, looking worried. 'I didn't see anyone. Of course, I wasn't looking out of the window all of the time so someone else might have been there.'

Edwin assumed Eleanor was thinking of Mr Sutton and realised that she was following a line of enquiry.

'Pauline, you referred to your uncle earlier on as Uncle Fred. Is his name Frederick Hartshorn?'

Pauline nodded.

'And is your father's name, John?' 'Yes.'

'And does Clough End Farm belong to both your father and your uncle?'

Pauline nodded. Mr Harriman and Edwin exchanged looks, knowing where Eleanor was going with her questions. Philip looked on with interest, sensing that Eleanor was now at work.

'How long have your aunt and uncle been living at Red Farm?' asked Eleanor.

'I'm not sure.'

'When did you go to live with them?' continued Eleanor.

'At the beginning of the summer. That's when I left school and got the job at The Grove.'

'And where were they before that? Do you know?'

'Harpur Hill. Uncle Fred was working at the Hoffman quarry but then he got the job with the railway so they had to move.'

Eleanor said: 'Do you happen to know who owns Red Farm?'

'Oh, yes. My cousin does. It belonged to grandfather once, when it was a proper farm. Grandfather left Clough End to Father and Uncle Fred and he left Red Farm to Uncle Robert but Uncle Robert was killed in the War, so now my cousin owns it.'

'And does your cousin live there?'

'No, he works with Father now. Red Farm isn't a working farm any more so he's out at Clough End most of the time, especially since the upset.'

'And what upset would that be?'

'I'm not really sure. Auntie May told me it was about the farm, Clough End, that is, but she wouldn't tell me anything much. She said Father had cheated Uncle Fred out of the farm and it had something to do with the bank but she wouldn't tell me anything more. And also, Auntie May didn't like having that man living in the stables. That was my cousin's idea.'

'I see,' said Eleanor. 'How long has he been there? The man in the stables.'

'Not long, a few weeks, that's all,' said Pauline.

'And do you know his name?' asked Eleanor.

'Wilkinson. I don't like him at all.'

'I see,' said Eleanor. 'I think I might have met him when I was at Red Farm earlier today. A short man, dark-haired, rather rough looking.' Pauline nodded. 'There didn't seem to be anyone else at the farm, though.'

'Auntie May said last week they were looking for somewhere else to go and Miss Pymble said I could go and stay with her and Miss Felicity. I'd rather not go back to Red Farm.'

'Don't worry. Miss Pymble told me that you are welcome to stay at Waverton House as long as you like,' said Eleanor.

'But I don't expect them to keep me. I pay board to Auntie May so I can pay the same to them if that will be acceptable.'

'I'm sure it will be, Pauline,' Eleanor reassured her. 'I know they will be happy to have you and it's getting late so I will take you there now.'

'No,' said Philip, 'it's time I was going so I'll take Pauline if you like. I'll just collect my vases on the way out. I'll show them to you another time, Eleanor.'

Eleanor accompanied Philip downstairs to retrieve his vases from James' office and she thanked him for coming to find her. He promised to look in on her the following day. Eleanor then explained to Pauline that it would be better not to talk to anyone about the events at the farm just yet even though she would have to explain to the Misses Pymble why she had missed being presented to Princess Mary.

Mrs Clayton, satisfied that everyone had been properly nourished, also went home after having been thanked by a grateful Mr Harriman for raising the alarm and then holding the fort. There was no need to remind Mrs Clayton not to talk about what she had heard that evening. They all knew that they could always trust her never to repeat anything she heard at Hall Bank.

CHAPTER TWENTY-SIX

Eleanor, Mr Harriman, and Edwin settled in the sitting room and tried to make sense of the few facts that they had. Napoleon climbed onto the sofa beside Eleanor, which was normally forbidden but which he was sure would be overlooked tonight. He was right, of course, and as there was no protest from Eleanor he leaned up against her and made himself comfortable. She said to him: 'Good old, Napoleon. You rescued me didn't you? I can always rely on you.' She stroked his back gently and he dozed off, his chin resting on Eleanor's knee.

'Assaulting my daughter is a serious matter,' said Mr Harriman, and turning to Edwin he added, 'and you say you have reported it to the police but I am surprised that you think it necessary for Superintendent Johnson to go out to the farm at this time of night. Can it not wait until tomorrow?'

'No,' said Edwin, 'that's not because of what happened to Eleanor. That's for the body.'

'What body?' said Mr Harriman, with a look of surprise. 'Is that why Alf is being called out?'

'Yes. I'm sorry, we haven't told you all of the story yet. We thought it best to keep the details from Pauline. She doesn't seem to know about it so we didn't mention it while she was here. When Eleanor was locked in the barn, she discovered a body there.'

Mr Harriman looked at Eleanor and she nodded.

'Heads will roll,' said Mr Harriman, ominously.

Edwin said: 'I'm afraid it was Sutton. I can't think what he could have been doing out there.'

'Well,' said Eleanor, 'you remember that Mr Sutton asked for advice about a mortgagee sale. He didn't name the farm although he said it was at Dale Head. I didn't make the connection when I went out to the farm to look for Pauline but I realise now, from what Pauline has just told us, that the mortgaged property must be Clough End Farm. Pauline's Uncle Fred is Frederick Hartshorn, one of the brothers, and her father is John Hartshorn, the presumed forger. Is it significant that Pauline's father seems to be missing?'

'And Red Farm seems to be deserted so it is possible that the aunt and uncle have moved on as well,' added Edwin. 'Are the two brothers involved in this together?'

'John Hartshorn must surely have realised that if the farm went up for auction, his deception over the mortgage would be discovered. He would be exposed as a forger unless, of course, Frederick decided to co-operate and go along with the deception so that John would not be punished,' said Eleanor. 'Pauline did say there had been a falling out between her father and her uncle. I assumed that it was because Frederick found out about the mortgage but perhaps John was trying to persuade Frederick to say that he had signed the documents. It is possible that Frederick has disappeared to avoid pressure from his brother.'

'Perhaps Frederick has disappeared simply because he is not sure what has been going on and does not want to risk being caught up in it,' said Mr Harriman.

'Perhaps Sutton was aware of the dispute between the brothers and went out to the farm to ask questions,' suggested Edwin.

'And then things turned nasty?' said Mr Harriman. 'That's possible. There are strong motives there.'

'If Sutton wanted to put the farm up for sale,' said Edwin,

'I suppose it is possible that he was just out there doing a valuation, although I admit that seems unlikely.'

'If he had been out there on Saturday morning, surely Pauline would have seen him,' said Mr Harriman.

'No, he wouldn't have been there on Saturday morning. Mr Sutton left Buxton early on Saturday morning to go to Chester. He told me that he was going to a family christening on Sunday and he was not due back until Sunday evening. I teased him about missing the Royal Visit and accused him of being unpatriotic.' Eleanor paused and fought back tears as the reality of the situation began to sink in. She took a couple of deep breaths and continued: 'So he couldn't have gone out to the farm any earlier than this morning.'

'But why this morning? The Belfield completion was booked for eleven today,' said Mr Harriman. 'Even if he had left the bank straight after ten, it wouldn't have given him much time to get there and back before eleven.'

'But Mr Pidcock said that Mr Sutton didn't come in to the bank this morning,' said Eleanor. 'And Mr Pidcock told me that Mr Sutton had already left home when his housekeeper arrived this morning. Perhaps he went straight out to the farm and that is where he was at eleven o'clock. He may have intended to be back at the bank in time and been prevented from returning.'

Edwin said: 'If that is the case, it means he was killed sometime earlier today.'

'Eleanor,' said Mr Harriman, 'when you arrived at the farm, those who killed Sutton may still have been there. You may have had a lucky escape. I am very pleased to have you safe here with us and I am very grateful to Philip and to you, Edwin, for having had the sense to go and look for Eleanor straightaway. I shudder to think what might have happened if you had not.'

They were silent for a moment, each thinking of the possible endings that Eleanor's visit to Clough End Farm might have had.

230

'Hmmm,' said Edwin, 'and I wonder just who was at the farm, first of all when Sutton got there and then when you got there, Eleanor. It certainly seemed to be deserted when Philip and I arrived. We know that Charlie Perceval and Pauline's cousin were there earlier. I wonder if they are involved with Sutton's death in some way.'

'And I wonder where Pauline's father is,' said Eleanor. 'Do you think perhaps that Mr Sutton heard about the dog fighting and went out to investigate that? He was very fond of dogs remember.'

'I think that is unlikely,' said Mr Harriman. 'I cannot imagine how he would have known what was happening at the farm and, if he did, surely he would have mentioned it to someone. Besides, he wouldn't have thought of dealing with it himself. He would most likely have informed the police.'

'Yes,' said Eleanor, 'I suppose you are right.'

'Wait a minute, though,' said Edwin. 'How did he get out to the farm?'

They looked at each other, puzzled. Eleanor frowned as she tried to picture the farm when she arrived.

'Of course, yes. I should have thought of that. There was no other motor-car there when I arrived,' she said. 'I am certain of that. Unless it had been hidden somewhere. Perhaps the police will find it. When I got to the farm it was completely deserted. There was no sign of life at all. Although I realise now that Charlie Perceval and Pauline's cousin had seen me arrive. Pauline said she thought Charlie went back to the stables so perhaps they had heard the motor-car and gone in there out of sight when I arrived.'

'It is possible that Charlie thought you knew more than you did,' suggested Edwin. 'You would not normally have visited the farm so perhaps he thought you knew that Sutton had gone there and had come to look for him.'

'Although we don't know whether Charlie knew Sutton was

there in the barn. If he had known, surely he wouldn't have put you in there,' said Mr Harriman.

'No, but Pauline said it was her cousin who dragged me to the barn not Charlie. Perhaps her cousin didn't know Mr Sutton was there.'

'He could have put you in the other barn,' said Edwin.

'But if that was set up for dog fighting he wouldn't have wanted me to see that,' said Eleanor.

'Either way you would have seen something they wanted to hide. I don't understand what he intended to do with you,' said Mr Harriman. 'It doesn't bear thinking about.'

'Perhaps Charlie just attacked you on the spur of the moment, out of revenge, without thinking of the consequences,' said Edwin. 'He no doubt blames you for losing Sarah because of the way you exposed him.'

'I think you are possibly right, Talbot, but this is all speculation and it is not getting us anywhere,' said Mr Harriman. He sighed deeply. 'All I can say for certain is that I am very glad that you are all right, Eleanor.'

'Hear hear,' said Edwin.

'I don't think we can achieve anything further tonight,' said Mr Harriman.

'When I was at the police station earlier this evening,' said Edwin, 'I told the sergeant briefly what had happened at Clough End Farm and said I would come back and report properly tomorrow morning. I will go straight there and see Superintendent Johnson. He will probably want to speak to you as well, Eleanor.'

'Yes, but before you go anywhere else you must go and see Dr McKenzie to make sure that there are no side effects from that blow on the head,' said Mr Harriman, firmly.

CHAPTER TWENTY-SEVEN

The following morning, after a sound night's sleep, Eleanor presented herself at Dr McKenzie's rooms. Dr McKenzie had already been out to examine Mr Sutton's body before Alf removed it. After she had been examined and pronounced fit, Eleanor explained the circumstances of her visit to Clough End Farm and asked about Mr Sutton.

'Well,' said Dr McKenzie, 'as yet I have only carried out a very brief examination and in poor light at that. We shall have to wait for the post-mortem to determine the cause of death. However, I can tell you for certain that he did not die on Monday. He had been dead for some time before you arrived at the farm, possibly as early as Saturday. Therefore, the person who hit you on the head may not be the person who killed Mr Sutton.'

'But Mr Sutton was in Chester on Saturday and Sunday.' Eleanor looked at Dr McKenzie in bewilderment.

Dr McKenzie shook his head. 'No. I don't think so. There is no doubt in my mind that when you found him, Mr Sutton had been dead for some time. It is possible to deduce that from the state of the body. The barn would have been very cold and that certainly has to be taken into account in calculating the time of death but I estimate that he was killed at least in the early hours of Saturday morning.'

'So we need to know who was at the farm then,' said Eleanor.

'Now,' said Dr McKenzie as he wagged his finger at Eleanor and smiled at her. 'I know it is no use my telling you to rest when you go back to Hall Bank but I would like you to avoid strenuous exercise at least, just to be on the safe side. Your father would never forgive me if you suffered any unfortunate complications from your adventure so, if only for my sake, please obey my orders.'

Eleanor thanked him, promising to do as he suggested. She returned to Hall Bank and went in search of Napoleon. She found him sitting at the kitchen door supervising Mrs Clayton. Eleanor did not feel in the mood to start work immediately so she sat down at the kitchen table with Mrs Clayton and had a cup of tea. They chatted about their respective plans for Guy Fawkes Night. Mrs Clayton described the bonfire that her boys were building with their cousins and the fun they were having making a guy out of the cast off clothing they had scrounged from their families and the neighbours. Having been cheered up by Mrs Clayton, Eleanor and Napoleon went back to work.

~O~

Later that morning, Philip closed the shop for the usual midday break and called at Hall Bank to see how Eleanor was. Eleanor had just finished her lunch and was about to take Napoleon for a walk so Philip accompanied them into the Gardens.

'I can't stop thinking about Mr Sutton,' said Eleanor. 'He was so much fun and such a gentleman. I liked him very much.'

'So did I,' said Philip, 'and I cannot imagine why anyone would want to kill him.'

'Who could possibly have done such a thing? He was very popular. I'm sure he didn't have any enemies.'

'Except Mondo, of course,' joked Philip. 'Everyone knows they don't get on. And, after all, they are rivals for the Mayor's Best in Show Trophy and it is nearly time for the Annual Show. Anyway he must be guilty. He's left town.'

'What do you mean? Left town. When?' said Eleanor.

'Well, you remember when we were up at Top Trees for the Right Royal Bean-feast and Lady C was saying how disappointed she was that Mondo hadn't turned up. He hadn't sent an apology or any explanation...'

'...and he wasn't with the official party to meet Princess Mary either.'

'That was because he had already left town.'

'How do you know?' Eleanor stopped walking and looked at Philip. Napoleon looked back at Eleanor and then sat down to wait.

'Because this morning I telephoned to Brook House. You remember when we were at dinner he asked my advice about a rare piece of china. Well, I managed to get it for him at the auction in Derby and I telephoned intending to let him know. Rowland said that Mondo had been called away suddenly on Saturday. Rowland couldn't or wouldn't say when Mondo would be back. He sounded very cagey.'

'But surely you are not suggesting that Mondo has run off because he killed Mr Sutton? That's absurd. I simply refuse to believe it.'

Eleanor started walking again striding out crossly, Napoleon trotting by her side.

When Philip caught up with her, he said: 'I'm sorry, Eleanor. I was just joking.'

'But it's not something to joke about.'

'I didn't mean to upset you and I apologise. Am I forgiven?'

'Yes,' said Eleanor, punching him gently in the arm. 'Anyway, if you think the culprit is someone who has left town, you might try Pauline's father. He's not at Clough End Farm and seems to have disappeared. And so has her uncle.'

They walked in silence for a while. Philip looked at his watch and said: 'I'd better be getting back.'

'All right. Don't forget you promised to bring the Chinese

vases to show me. If you are free, come this evening and you are welcome to stay to dinner.'

'Oh, thank you, I'd love to join you but unfortunately my mother is expecting me home for dinner this evening. She has guests who need to be entertained by my banter. But I shall bring the vases this evening after I close the shop if that will suit.'

'Yes, please do.'

~O~

When Eleanor and Napoleon arrived back at Hall Bank, Mr Harriman and Edwin were just leaving the dining room having lingered over their lunch. Before lunch, Edwin had been to the police station to make his report and explain how Mr Sutton's body came to be found. He had also heard news of a further development.

'Well, Eleanor,' he said, 'I found out where Superintendent Johnson was last night. He and his men and the extra police from Chesterfield were at a dog fight. They were able to get to it while it was still in progress and they rounded everybody up. When the Superintendent hauled in his net, he found some very interesting fish in it, including Pauline's father and her cousin, someone from Sheffield called Gerard Wilkinson, that's probably the man at Red Farm Pauline mentioned last night, and also Charlie and Sam Perceval.'

'Oh dear,' said Eleanor. 'Those Perceval boys are just getting in deeper and deeper.'

'The Superintendent heard a rumour, last week apparently, that there was to be a fight out at Clough End Farm and he was planning a raid there but on Sunday he heard another rumour that the venue had been changed and the fight had been moved to a barn out towards Flagg and was to take place last night. One of the Superintendent's informants heard something in a pub and passed the details on to him. He thinks that because of the sudden change of venue, word had to be spread very quickly and the need for haste made people less cautious than usual.'

'As we now know that Sutton died before Monday, is it safe to assume that the change of venue is linked to Sutton's presence at the farm?' asked Mr Harriman.

'I would think so,' said Edwin. 'I gather a lot of money had already been placed in bets for the fight so it was not possible to cancel it and that is why they looked for another venue.'

'That's probably where Pauline's father went on Saturday when he left Pauline locked in,' said Eleanor. 'Looking for another venue.'

'Obviously he knew that Sutton's body was at Clough End Farm and didn't want to risk anyone finding it,' said Mr Harriman.

'Yes,' said Edwin, 'I gather that Pauline's father is being asked to explain why Sutton was found in his barn.'

'Where does that leave Charlie Perceval?' asked Eleanor.

'So far, he has admitted nothing. There was already a warrant out for his arrest because he had breached his bail conditions so he is in custody. Sam Perceval's in custody as well and I think it is unlikely he will get bail. I've told Superintendent Johnson that he should also be charging Charlie with assault. The Superintendent would like you to provide a statement and he asked me to tell you the sooner, the better.'

'Of course. I'll go now,' said Eleanor.

~O~

Constable Goodwin had been told to take Eleanor's statement. She had been hoping that Superintendent Johnson would delegate this task to someone junior because she wanted to get more information about what was going on at Clough End

Farm and she knew that Superintendent Johnson would tell her nothing. When Constable Goodwin had finished taking her statement, Eleanor asked him about the dog fighting. He was very young and eager to impress the public so he answered Eleanor's questions readily.

Eleanor returned to Hall Bank with the information that the outcome of the dog fight on Monday night had been fixed. She explained to Mr Harriman and Edwin that Pauline's father intended to use a dog which had appeared in previous fights and had the reputation of not being much of a fighter. The dog was to be given drugs to make it more aggressive and keep it fighting to the end.

'Constable Goodwin told me that Pauline's father and her cousin had put a lot of money on this dog. I assume they were intending to win enough in bets to make a payment to the bank and stop the sale of the farm,' said Eleanor.

'That is no doubt why he had to arrange a change of venue instead of cancelling the fight,' said Edwin. 'He must have realised that Sutton would eventually be found but he needed the fight to go ahead. He probably wasn't concerned about what happened after that because he would have had the money to pay his debts.'

'I suppose that Eleanor was put in the barn for the same reason that Pauline had been locked in her room,' said Mr Harriman. 'No doubt as a temporary measure so that no-one could alert the police in time to put the dog fight in jeopardy.'

'I wonder if the same thing had happened to Sutton?' said Edwin.

'Well, John Hartshorn had a very good reason to want Mr Sutton out of the way. I wonder if his callous attitude towards dogs also extended to bank managers,' said Eleanor.

'Perhaps he was hit with more force than was necessary and unintentionally killed,' said Edwin.

'And perhaps we shall eventually get to the truth,' said

Mr Harriman. They returned to their own offices to get on with some work.

~O~

Eleanor was finding it rather difficult to concentrate. There were too many thoughts whirling around in her head. An hour later, she was rescued from feeling guilty about her idleness when Mrs Hazelwood arrived with a very large bouquet of flowers, which included some of her best chrysanthemums. She had written a note for Eleanor intending to leave the flowers with James but he, aware of Eleanor's current state of mind, assured Mrs Hazelwood that Eleanor would be pleased to receive the flowers herself and would not at all mind being interrupted. Mrs Hazelwood was shown up to Eleanor's office and, as she was a dog lover, Napoleon was allowed to stay. After Mrs Hazelwood made a fuss of him, he sat down beside her and listened to the conversation. Eleanor and Mrs Hazelwood had a cup of tea and quite a chat. Mrs Hazelwood was, as yet, unaware of the departure of Mr Aubrey-Mere. She was, however, aware of the death of his neighbour. That topic began or ended every social conversation in Buxton that week. Mrs Hazelwood expressed her regret at the news and, in the course of the conversation, happened to mention that she had been walking her dogs in Burlington Road recently. Naturally, she did not say why.

Mrs Hazelwood said: 'I have been thinking about an incident which occurred last week and wondering if I should report it to the police.'

'What was that, Mrs Hazelwood?'

'Well, I had occasion to stop outside Mr Aubrey-Mere's house, one of the dogs was loitering, and I remember noticing someone on the other side of the road opposite Mr Sutton's house. It is Thornstead, isn't it?'

'That's right.'

'The person I saw was standing beside a tree and I can only describe it as lurking. He appeared to be watching Mr Sutton's house. It was extraordinary which is why I remembered it, I suppose. It may just be co-incidence but one never knows, does one?'

'Perhaps it would be wisest to mention it to the police, just in case,' said Eleanor.

Mrs Hazelwood nodded in agreement. 'Of course, it could have something to do with that attack on Mr Aubrey-Mere's greenhouse. Yes, I think I shall report it.'

After a few more minutes, Mrs Hazelwood left, once again expressing her profuse thanks for Eleanor's assistance in rescuing the puppies.

CHAPTER TWENTY-EIGHT

Later that day, after the office had closed, Eleanor and Napoleon were in the sitting room, when Mr Harriman came in and poured himself and Eleanor a pre-dinner glass of sherry. This had become a custom for them which would have been unthinkable for Eleanor if the Harrimans had still lived in The Park but at Hall Bank it was a mark of their equality as colleagues. As he sank into an armchair, Mr Harriman noticed the large vase of flowers. 'Mr Norman again?'

'No,' said Eleanor, 'Mrs Hazelwood. She came to say "thank you" for returning her puppies. Mrs Hazelwood also said that, late one afternoon recently, she saw a man on the opposite side of the road to Thornstead. She described him as "lurking" and she didn't like the look of him at all. After Mrs Hazelwood had gone, I remembered that the word "thief" had been painted on the gatepost of Thornstead. Richard noticed it and pointed it out when we were out walking on Sunday.'

'If I remember correctly, the first of the messages left on the bank accused Sutton, or at least the bank, of being a robber and a thief,' said Mr Harriman.

'Perhaps it was a customer of the bank, like Mr Perceval, unable to repay a loan,' suggested Eleanor. 'Mr Hartshorn, do you think?'

'It's possible, I suppose. That reminds me,' said Mr Harriman, 'Superintendent Johnson wants to know what the bank's position is in relation to the mortgage over Clough End Farm. He spoke to Mr Pidcock, Mr Pidcock referred him to head office, and head office referred him to us. Could you go to the station tomorrow and fill him in?'

'Yes, of course.'

'He suggested half past ten? Is that convenient?' Eleanor nodded. Mr Harriman sipped his sherry thoughtfully and then he looked at Eleanor and asked: 'Was the word painted on the gatepost at Thornstead spelt correctly?'

'Yes, it was, as a matter of fact. You're thinking of the other messages which were not.'

'That's right but I'm not sure what to make of it all,' said Mr Harriman.

'Perhaps the message on Thornstead has got nothing to do with the bank, at all,' said Eleanor. 'Perhaps it's about Mr Sutton personally. What could he have stolen, I wonder?'

'There seems to be a lot of stealing about at the moment,' said Mr Harriman. 'Mr Dawson telephoned Edwin this afternoon to tell him that when he opened up the shop on Saturday morning, he found that the two-wheeled handcart he uses for deliveries was missing. He thought someone must have taken it after he had shut up shop on Friday. Then it occurred to him that it might be Charlie Perceval, still angry about Sarah being sent away, and trying to get his own back. Of course, Charlie being the delivery boy knew exactly where it was kept. Mr Dawson asked Edwin if there was anything he could do about it.'

'What would Charlie want with a handcart?'

'Edwin suggested that Mr Dawson should report it to the police.'

Napoleon got up from in front of the fire and went to the door of the sitting room, having heard the door-bell and then heard Mrs Clayton going downstairs.

'That will be Philip,' said Eleanor. 'He's bringing the Chinese vases.'

Mr Harriman got up to pour a glass of sherry for Philip.

~O~

When the vases had been examined and admired and Philip had gone home to his parents' house, Mr Harriman and Eleanor sat down to their dinner. Mr Harriman said:

'I didn't have chance to tell you before Philip arrived but I thought you would like to know, Dr McKenzie telephoned late this afternoon to say that he had now had chance to examine Sutton's body properly and he gave me his opinion, unofficially of course.'

'Has he determined the cause of death?' asked Eleanor.

'No, not yet. He said that would have to wait for the post-mortem. However, he did say that there was evidence of a blow to the left side of the jaw, and also a gash at the back of the head, possibly caused by a fall. Also there was some bruising and discolouration consistent with the body having been moved. He said it was pretty clear that Sutton did not die in the barn where you found him.'

Eleanor thought for a minute, recalling the scene, and then said: 'When I saw the trousers and the shoes I knew they belonged to a town person and not a farm person. I didn't think of it before but now that you have drawn attention to it, I don't recall seeing any mud on his shoes. There would have been if he had been walking around at the farm, wouldn't there?'

'So, we need to revise our thinking as to where Sutton was killed and by whom.'

'Yes, it opens up the field considerably, I think,' said Eleanor.

'What I don't understand,' said Mr Harriman, 'is why Sutton was at Clough End Farm at all. What possible reason could he have had for being there, at any time, let alone in the early hours of Saturday morning?'

'It makes no sense,' said Eleanor.

'Does anyone know where he was on Friday night?'

'Yes, I do,' said Eleanor and she told her father about the walking club meeting. 'I have been thinking about that evening and wondering where Mr Sutton was in the time between when he left me and when he was killed.'

'Well, let's think this through. You left the Sunday-school Hall and walked across the Market Place to Hall Bank and Sutton was seeing you home.'

'No, he didn't offer to accompany me home. In fact, it was rather the other way round. I was trying to avoid Mr Norman. I knew Mr Sutton would be walking towards Hall Bank so I made sure that I left when he did. When we reached the Market Place, Mr Sutton said he would come with me down Hall Bank so I assumed that he was going home via Broad Walk.'

'Perhaps he was not intending to go straight home,' said Mr Harriman.

'I suppose that is possible. He didn't actually say. But where would he have been going at that time of night?' said Eleanor.

'He didn't mention that he was meeting someone?' asked Mr Harriman.

'No,' said Eleanor, 'I assumed that he was going straight home because he told me that he was going to Chester the next day and was intending to take the early morning train to Manchester.'

'Which he obviously did not do.'

Eleanor thought about the last time she had seen Mr Sutton. She was still getting used to the idea that he was dead. Eventually she said: 'I wonder if he was intending to go past the bank and check that the walls were clear of messages.'

'Ah, yes,' said Mr Harriman. 'Don't you remember? When we were at dinner at Brook House, Mondo said Sutton was at the bank that evening keeping watch because the committee wanted to be sure that there were no messages left during the Royal Visit. On Friday night, when you last saw him, that was the night before Princess Mary came. Perhaps he was making a detour past the bank on his way home.'

'And, in fact, somebody had daubed words on the bank wall.'

'Were they already there when Sutton reached the bank, I wonder? Or was the wall still clean at that time?' said Mr Harriman.

'If the words had been there, surely he would have done something about having them removed but it was Mr Pidcock who found them the next morning and had them cleaned off,' said Eleanor.

'Which suggests that Sutton did not go past the bank, or that he did but the words were not there when he passed it,' said Mr Harriman.

'…Or that someone was in the process of putting them there…' added Eleanor, frowning. 'The message was unfinished. Do you suppose Mr Sutton saw whoever it was, caught them red-handed, and confronted them?'

'And then got into a fight? It's possible,' said Mr Harriman.

'And the obvious suspect for that is Sam Perceval, who is known to have left messages on the bank wall before.'

'Of course, it might not have been Sam Perceval,' said Mr Harriman. 'I know everyone automatically blames him because he had a grudge against the bank in the past but what new reason could he possibly have for being angry with the bank?'

'And there are plenty of other people who are currently in straightened circumstances who might want to have their say about the bank,' said Eleanor 'But who? Perhaps it was Pauline's father.'

'Or his brother. Perhaps Frederick is telling the truth and he blames the bank for not stopping his brother from mortgaging the farm without his consent.'

They contemplated these suspects and then Mr Harriman, seeing the worried look on Eleanor's face, said: 'What's the matter?'

'I've just realised that I might have been the last person to see Mr Sutton alive, apart from his killer that is.'

Mr Harriman said, pensively: 'Yes, you may very well be right.' He paused. 'At least you have the comfort of knowing that, whatever happened to him afterwards, while he was with you and previously during that evening, he was in pleasant company and was doing something that he enjoyed.'

~O~

The next morning, when Mrs Clayton served breakfast, Eleanor thought she seemed a bit distracted. She was unusually silent, although several times she seemed on the verge of saying something. When Mr Harriman had left the dining room, Mrs Clayton said to Eleanor: 'Miss Harriman, can you spare a moment, please?'

'What is it Mrs Clayton? Is something wrong?' asked Eleanor.

'Oh no, Miss Harriman. That is, there is nothing wrong as far as I am concerned. No, thank you. No, it's Mrs Perceval. Charlie was in trouble last week with Mr Dawson and now he and Sam are both in trouble because of the dog fighting. Superintendent Johnson has Charlie locked up because he absconded and Sam's being questioned about Mr Sutton being found at Clough End. Mrs Perceval came to see Alf last evening, Alf did Mr Perceval's funeral, and she said she knows something that will help Sam and she wanted Alf's advice and Alf said he couldn't help because she needed to speak to someone legal and he said she should come and see you but, of course, she doesn't like to because, well…' Mrs Clayton had been clearing the table and, in her embarrassment on behalf of Mrs Perceval, she began putting things down and picking them up again at random. '….well, because she can't afford to pay to see anyone legal and Alf said he knows as it's taking a liberty but he was wondering if you would see her anyway and put her mind at rest, like. And, naturally I couldn't say anything about what happened to you out at the farm so, of course, Alf doesn't know about you being hit on the head by Charlie because if he did he wouldn't have dreamed of asking and I can't tell him and I don't suppose that Mrs Perceval knows either because she would be that ashamed if she knew, and she wouldn't think it right to ask you for help, so I just said I would ask you.' Mrs Clayton paused for breath. 'And I have and if you don't want to see her, I quite understand.'

'Oh dear, it is very complicated isn't it?' Eleanor smiled at Mrs Clayton. 'Of course, I would like to help Mrs Perceval but I don't think I can. You see, I'm too closely involved.'

Even if there had been no question of a conflict of interest, Eleanor was not inclined to look favourably on the Perceval family after being hit on the head by one of them. She explained: 'I shall have to give evidence against Charlie when he is charged with assault. If Mrs Perceval has information about the dog fighting, she really should go to the police and tell them what she knows.'

'Well,' said Mrs Clayton, hesitating, 'I gather from what Alf said that it wasn't about the fighting.'

'Oh, do you have any idea what it is about?' asked Eleanor.

'Not really, except that it's something about Albert, her husband, something she knows but has been told not to tell. She thinks it will help Sam, but she is afraid that if she does tell, it might make things even worse for him. That's why she wanted advice. She's in a right state according to Alf and he was very sorry that he couldn't help her.'

'I see,' said Eleanor. 'Well, perhaps you could explain to her that I cannot talk about anything to do with the trouble that Charlie and Sam are now in, but if the advice that she needs relates to her personally, I will see her. Would that do?'

'Oh, I'm sure it would,' said Mrs Clayton, 'and thanks ever so, Miss Harriman. I know it is an imposition but I am sure Mrs Perceval will be very grateful.'

'All right, then I'll see her first thing tomorrow before the office opens if that suits her. Shall we say nine thirty, and you can let her know tonight.'

'I will, and thanks again, Miss Harriman.'

CHAPTER TWENTY-NINE

When Mrs Perceval arrived the following morning, Eleanor saw that she was very nervous and she imagined that it was only Mrs Perceval's anxiety for her sons that was providing her with the necessary courage to come to Hall Bank. Eleanor took her into the sitting room instead of her office, thinking that this would be less intimidating for Mrs Perceval. Nevertheless, when Eleanor directed her to an armchair, Mrs Perceval sat on the edge of the seat not daring to relax. She politely refused the offer of tea, knowing that the ritual involved in juggling a cup, saucer and teaspoon was beyond her shaking hands.

'Mrs Perceval, I hope that I can be of some help to you and I shall certainly try but I am sure Mrs Clayton has explained to you that I can't talk about anything relating to the trouble that Charlie and Sam are in at the moment?'

'Oh, yes. And I do understand. It's very good of you to see me, Miss Harriman, and I do appreciate it very much.'

'I should also tell you, Mrs Perceval, that if you know someone has committed an offence, you must go to the police with that information. Also, depending on what you tell me, it might mean that I too have an obligation to do so. I need to be sure that you have understood the situation fully before you tell me anything.'

'Oh, yes, Miss Harriman. It's not that I want you to keep any secrets. I want to go to the police myself because I want to save Sam from further trouble but I need to know where I stand and whether or not I've done wrong. I've got to think of the girls as well as Sam.'

'I see,' said Eleanor. 'Perhaps then, if you tell me what you know and I will see if I can help.'

'Sam's not a bad boy, Miss Harriman, but he's not been the same since his father died. He ran away from home afterwards and he's got in with a very bad crowd. I did try to find him but I haven't heard anything of him until now. And now he's involved with this dog fighting business. Charlie told me the dog fighting people from Sheffield sent Sam to Clough End Farm and now they've got Charlie into trouble with this business at Mr Dawson's. He's been doing something with the weights.'

Now that Mrs Perceval was speaking about her family she was on familiar ground and she began to relax a little and became more confident. Eleanor was concerned that the topic was straying in a direction she did not want to go but she decided to let Mrs Perceval continue for the moment.

'Charlie was supposed to stay with me and report to the police but he went off without a word and I didn't know where he'd gone although I guessed he had probably gone to find Sam. Those two were always together as little boys, always getting each other into trouble. And now the bank manager has been found at the farm where Sam works. I don't want Sam to be in trouble again about that. And that's what I need to talk to you about.'

'But, Mrs Perceval, you must understand. I can't possibly talk to you about that, particularly if Sam is involved.'

'No, no,' said Mrs Perceval urgently, 'it's not about Sam, it's about Albert.' Before Eleanor could say anything further, Mrs Perceval continued, speaking rapidly. 'You see, Sam was the one who found Albert, that's my husband, and the police were very rough with him, questioning him and that. They didn't believe Albert had taken his own life and they were trying to make out that Sam had something to do with it. And, seemingly, it was all because the police thought Albert didn't leave a note explaining, which they said he would've done if he'd killed himself. And I didn't know that at the time, and if I had known I could have told the police that he did leave a note and things would have been different. That's why Sam ran away. And now I'm afraid that it'll be the same thing all over again.'

Eleanor remembered the conversation with Dr McKenzie during dinner at Brook House about the absence of a suicide note and wondered if Mrs Perceval had information which was relevant to her husband's death that had not been disclosed at the inquest.

'But I don't understand, do you know something about a suicide note?' said Eleanor, feeling that she was on safer ground now and could risk asking questions.

'Everyone knew Albert did what he did because of the bank. He couldn't pay what he owed and he could see no way out. But the police wouldn't have it that way. They kept Sam at the police station and questioned him for hours about how he found his father and what he was doing beforehand and it was as though they blamed him for his father's death. Sam was only sixteen at the time. He was frightened out of his wits and now there's been another body found and it will be the same thing all over again. You know how it is, once the police have it in for a person, that's the end of it. They'll be questioning him and blaming him again, all because they wanted a note from Albert explaining what he had done.'

'But are you saying that there was a note?' said Eleanor.

'Yes, Albert left a letter for me. He explained about the bank and said he was taking his own life because it was best for all of us. The letter said I was not to tell anyone and I was to destroy it once I'd read it. I didn't understand why but that's what Albert said I was to do. So, of course I did what he wanted. And I've never told a soul about it until now.'

'And Sam didn't read this letter?' asked Eleanor.

'No, he didn't know anything about it. No-one did. It's what Albert wanted.'

'And do you have any idea why Mr Perceval didn't want anyone but you to read the letter?'

'No, I thought he just wanted to keep things private like, about not being able to pay the bank.'

'Did Mr Perceval have any life insurance?' asked Eleanor.

'Oh, yes. He took it out when we were married.'

'And did you make a claim?'

'No. The lawyer who came for the bank said they wanted the insurance money but Albert hadn't paid the subscription or whatever you call it, for the last three months so it was worth nothing. I didn't know whether the money had to be paid or not.'

'So, you intend to tell the police about the letter because you think it will help Sam?'

Mrs Perceval nodded. 'Yes, then they will believe Sam when he says he had nothing to do with his father's death and also with the person they found at the farm.'

'And you want to know what the consequences might be for you if you do go to the police?'

'Well I'm not worried about myself. I'll take whatever is coming as long as it doesn't take me away from my girls. But it's more that I don't want to make matters worse for Sam. The police might not believe me. They might think Sam destroyed the letter.'

Eleanor reflected briefly on the subject of a mother's devotion towards her son and wondered irreverently whether, in this particular case, either of the sons deserved it. She felt for Mrs Perceval having been left in this situation and she feared that nothing could be done to help her sons. Mrs Perceval was very likely to suffer yet more heartache.

'Mrs Perceval, destroying that letter certainly was an offence but it could have been worse if you had made a claim and the insurance company had paid on the basis of the coroner's verdict of accidental death.' Eleanor paused to make sure that Mrs Perceval had understood the explanation. She continued: 'Perhaps no-one will want to take the matter any further, but you should tell the police about it and you should also realise that doing so could possibly have serious consequences for you. As to the treatment of Sam after Mr Perceval's death, he was the one who found your husband, so he would be the one most likely to have found a suicide note and, therefore, would have had the best opportunity to destroy it. So it is possible that the police were questioning him because they thought he had destroyed evidence of suicide in order to defraud the insurance company and not because they thought he had anything to do with his father's death.'

Mrs Perceval frowned as she thought about this new explanation and Eleanor waited to see if she would ask for further information.

Then Mrs Perceval just nodded and said: 'I see.'

'No doubt Mr Perceval did not want to leave you without any explanation for his action and without saying good-bye and, therefore, he took the risk of writing the letter and he no doubt knew that he could trust you not to tell anyone about it and to destroy it as he asked.'

'But do you think it will help Sam if I tell the police about the letter?'

'I'm sorry, Mrs Perceval. I'm afraid I don't know enough about the police investigation to be able to judge whether or not this information will help Sam. I don't know what he is being questioned about. If he is innocent of any wrongdoing, he has nothing to fear but it may help the police if they know about the suicide note. At least they would then know that Sam had nothing to do with Mr Perceval's death and they could put that to one side and just deal with the current issues.'

'Thank you Miss Harriman, then I shall go to the police.'

Mrs Perceval stood up to leave, evidently intending to go to the police immediately in an attempt to intervene on behalf of her son. Eleanor could see that further explanation would be wasted and she also stood up. She accompanied Mrs Perceval downstairs as Mrs Perceval thanked her profusely.

~O~

After Mrs Perceval had left, Eleanor went to the kitchen in search of Napoleon and a cup of tea. Mrs Clayton thanked Eleanor for seeing Mrs Perceval but, discreet as ever, asked nothing about her visit. They chatted about the sale of poppies for Remembrance Day. James was making sure that all of the clients who came through the door at Harriman & Talbot went out wearing one. Mrs Clayton had just finished counting the money from the box for the last few days ready for collection by one of the British Legion officers that morning. Eleanor was cheered by the level of support being shown to the Legion's appeal and this gave her the energy to go back to her office and start work.

Eleanor sat thinking about Mr Sutton's body at Clough End Farm. Someone had known that it was there because that was why the venue for the dog fight had been changed. Sam worked at the farm and it was possible that, as Mrs Perceval feared, it was he who had made the discovery. She wondered if Sam realised whose body it was. She also wondered whether, when Pauline's cousin dragged her into the barn, he knew that Mr Sutton was there. And now that she knew Charlie was in contact with Sam and the "bad crowd" in Sheffield, it confirmed her suspicions as to the source of the false weights that Charlie had used in Mr Dawson's shop. She made a note of several questions to which she wanted answers. There were too many questions and she didn't have the energy to deal with them so she opened a file and got on with her work instead.

At ten thirty, Eleanor went to the police station to keep her appointment with Superintendent Johnson. He greeted her with his usual polite reserve. He did not appreciate members of the public interfering in police matters but he had to admit that Eleanor was useful. She had played a vital role in solving a murder the previous year and he was prepared to listen to what she had to say about the current incident.

'Now, Miss Harriman, I believe you have been authorised by Chillingham & Baynard's bank to provide some information about the finances at Clough End Farm?'

'Yes, Superintendent. It may not be at all relevant to your enquiries and, of course, that is for you to decide but the bank is concerned about its mortgage at the farm and, in particular, about the actions of one of the owners of the farm, John Hartshorn.'

'I see,' said Superintendent Johnson, making it clear that he was not going to volunteer any information in return.

'Before he died, Mr Sutton sent instructions to us regarding an unpaid loan and a mortgage granted in favour of the bank. The loan repayments had not been made and the bank was intending to exercise its rights as mortgagee when it discovered a problem with the documents relating to the mortgage. The security for the loan is Clough End Farm which is owned by two brothers, John and Frederick Hartshorn. The documents have been signed by both brothers but it seems that the signature of Frederick Hartshorn may have been forged and, if so, the loan was obtained by deception. As a result of advice we gave Mr Sutton, he cancelled the mortgagee sale and was about to commence proceedings against John Hartshorn. As far as I am aware, John Hartshorn has not yet been informed that the mortgagee sale has been cancelled. I am not alleging that he or his brother killed Mr Sutton. I am simply saying that Mr Sutton's death may have been of some benefit to them.'

'I shall add that information to the file,' said Superintendent Johnson, his face a mask of neutrality. 'Thank you for coming to see me, Miss Harriman. Just one thing before you go, I read the statement which you provided to Constable Goodwin. Other than the person who attacked you, did you see anyone else at Clough End Farm when you were there?'

'No,' said Eleanor. 'You're sure?'

'Perfectly.'

'What about Miss Hartshorn?'

'Oh, I'm sorry. I thought you meant anyone working at the farm. No, no-one other than her.'

Eleanor had explained to Constable Goodwin that she had gone to Clough End Farm looking for Pauline and had found her there but Eleanor had not mentioned the fact that Pauline had been locked in and had to be rescued through the window.

'I understand you went to the farm looking for Miss Hartshorn and that you drove yourself there. Wasn't it a bit late in the afternoon for a young lady such as yourself to be driving out alone into the countryside?'

Eleanor bridled at this but, sensibly, chose to look unmoved. She said, as evenly and politely as she could: 'I went there at the request of Miss Pymble. She was concerned about Miss Hartshorn and with good reason. As to going alone, there was, at the time, no-one I could have taken with me even if I had considered that necessary, which I didn't. Before I left Buxton I calculated the distance to the farm and knew that I had enough time to get there and back well before dusk. And I should have done so had I not been prevented by the people you now have in custody.'

'The top floor window of the farmhouse was damaged, well, destroyed would be more accurate. Do you know anything about that, Miss Harriman?' The Superintendent's voice was neutral but his eyes regarded Eleanor keenly.

'Yes, Miss Hartshorn had been locked in her room for several days. She did not wish to remain there and there was no other way to get her out.'

'And you chose not to mention this in the statement you gave to Constable Goodwin.'

'I'm sorry. I thought that you would only want to know about Mr Sutton and the person who attacked me. I didn't think it was relevant.'

'I will decide what is relevant,' said the Superintendent, rather ominously. 'I shall be taking a statement from Miss Hartshorn in due course, because it will be necessary to verify the statement you have provided.'

'I have nothing to hide, Superintendent. I am sure Miss Hartshorn will be able to corroborate what I have said.'

'Yes, well, thank you for coming, Miss Harriman. If I need any further information about the mortgage documents, I shall let you know.'

Eleanor left the police station with the distinct impression that Superintendent Johnson considered her a suspect, no doubt on the principle that the person who finds the body is the guilty one. She wondered if he thought Pauline had been her accomplice. She also wondered if he thought the purpose of her visit to see him was to blacken the character of an otherwise perfectly innocent man in order to put the blame on him and provide the Superintendent with a ready-made suspect and motive for the murder of Mr Sutton. She came away feeling less than satisfied with her attempt to help and wondered if she was in danger of being arrested. She laughed, but she was also aware that it was no laughing matter. The Superintendent had been known to arrest the wrong person before.

CHAPTER THIRTY

When Eleanor arrived back at Hall Bank, Mrs Clayton was taking a cup of tea in to Mr Harriman's office. Edwin, having just returned from a meeting, was already in Mr Harriman's office and Eleanor joined them.

'Well,' said Edwin, as he pulled up an extra chair for Eleanor. 'I had some sympathy for those two Perceval lads, losing their father in the way they did, but now I am convinced that my feelings were misplaced. My opinion began to change when I learnt that Charlie had attacked Eleanor but what I heard this morning convinces me that they are a pair of heartless and very callous individuals. I met Mr Dawson in the Market Place this morning. He told me he had mentioned to one of his customers that his handcart....'

'One? All, more like. I doubt there's a customer who hasn't heard about that handcart. He's very cross about it,' said Mrs Clayton.

Edwin laughed. 'It's probably just as well that he did because this particular customer told him that she had seen two lads pushing what was almost certainly Mr Dawson's handcart up London Road last Friday night. She's a midwife and she'd been called out around midnight. She was hurrying along London Road but on the other side from the two lads and, of course it was very dark, so she didn't see who it was. She was anxious to get to her patient so she didn't pay much attention to them. Apparently, one of them called out "Penny for the guy" as she drew level with them.'

'Brazen, that's what they are. And unfeeling,' said Mrs Clayton.

'Very disrespectful,' agreed Mr Harriman.

Edwin continued: 'The midwife thought they must have been on their way home from going round the public houses begging money for Guy Fawkes Night so she didn't think any more about it until she was in Mr Dawson's shop and he was complaining about his handcart. Mr Dawson has now added that piece of information to his original report to the police so the trail regarding his handcart has led well and truly to the two Perceval boys.'

'The more I hear of that Sam and Charlie Perceval, the less I like them,' said Mr Harriman.

'But, are you suggesting that the handcart was being used to take Mr Sutton to Clough End Farm? That's appalling,' said Eleanor.

'Well, it does seem a likely explanation, doesn't it? We could think of no good reason why Sutton would have been out at the farm so it is highly likely that he did not go there of his own accord. Nor could we explain how he got to the farm and why there was no mud on his shoes. Unpleasant as it may seem, this does seem to provide the answer,' said Edwin.

~O~

In the last delivery of post that day, there was a letter requesting an appointment to see Eleanor. Mr Harriman asked James to take it to Eleanor and arrange a time.

James said: 'Miss Eleanor, Mrs Sutton, that's Mr Sutton's mother, has written asking for an appointment to see you at ten thirty on Tuesday next. Mr Harriman asked me to refer it to you.'

'Yes, of course, I shall see her. I think I am free then.'

'There is nothing in the diary. I have checked.'

'Does she say what it is about?'

'No, she explains that she was briefly in Buxton last

Wednesday to see the police and has now returned to Chester. She will be returning here on Tuesday to make the necessary arrangements for Mr Sutton and to see Mr Sutton's housekeeper. She particularly asks to see you.'

'Hmmm. Perhaps she just wants to talk to someone who knew Mr Sutton.'

'Very possibly,' said James. 'Shall I write and let her know you will see her?'

'Yes. Thank you, James.'

~O~

Philip was dining at Hall Bank that evening. Mr Harriman was at his club and was due back in time for dinner. It was already dark and the curtains had been drawn, excluding the cold, damp air of the dreary November evening. In the sitting room there was a well-banked up fire and Napoleon was sprawled on the hearthrug, snoozing contentedly. Eleanor was in an armchair on one side of the fire, reading *The Times*. When Philip arrived, Mrs Clayton answered the door, brought him upstairs, and then went back to the kitchen. Napoleon got up and greeted Philip and then reclaimed the hearthrug. Philip sank into the other armchair beside the fire and looked across at the large vase of flowers on a side table.

'It was kind of Mrs Hazelwood to bring you those flowers,' said Philip. 'I assume that the chrysanthemums are some of her own.'

'Yes,' said Eleanor, 'she came to thank me for retrieving her puppies but really it was all thanks to Jon Jon. I did tell her that.'

'He probably saved their lives. No doubt whoever stole them intended to use them eventually for fighting,' said Philip.

'I am pretty sure it was the man at Red Farm and I think his name is Gerard Wilkinson. When I went to Red Farm looking for Pauline, he was there with his brute of a dog. It certainly looked as if it had been in a few fights. I didn't think anything of it at the time but I should have made the connection. Apparently a dog fight had been arranged at Clough End Farm last Monday night but it was moved to Flagg and that is why...'

'I say!' interrupted Philip. 'You mean on the day you went out there! If it hadn't been moved, Eleanor, you would have been caught up in it.'

'Oh, but it had been moved. Because of Mr Sutton, I suppose.'

'Even so...I didn't approve of the treatment you received at that farm but I realise now it could have been far worse.'

'Yes, because Superintendent Johnson got to hear of it and went out to Flagg and he and his men arrested quite a lot of men. If it had been at Clough End, I probably would have been arrested with the others,' laughed Eleanor.

'It's not a joking matter,' said Philip sternly.

'Anyway, that chap Wilkinson was arrested with the others so you were probably right about the reason for stealing the puppies. Dog fighting is so cruel. It makes me very angry just thinking about it. I can see absolutely no way that it can be justified. How can they deliberately put dogs together like that and force them to fight, knowing that one of them is going to be killed? How can they bear to watch the dogs tearing each other apart just for sport? Or worse, for money. It's barbaric. These people must be so unfeeling, so callous, and it's all for their own benefit. The poor dogs have no choice but to fight for their lives.'

Philip looked at her with concern and he paused a long time before he spoke.

'I understand how you feel, Eleanor, and I do agree with you wholeheartedly about the dogs, but unfortunately what you have just described applies equally to what most of these men endured for four or so years at the Front. It was no

261

different in the trenches. They had been set to fighting in the same way that the dogs are, except that they were not fighting for someone's entertainment. War may have made many of them callous or, at best, indifferent to suffering because it was the only way to survive out there. Don't think that I condone what they are doing. I don't, not for one minute, but I do understand how easy it is to become detached, just to watch the destruction of another living being without letting oneself feel any sympathy.'

'Philip, I'm sorry. You never talk about the War and I am sure that it is impossible for those of us who were not there to understand what you endured. And I am sure that it is just as difficult to assess what effect that experience is continuing to have on some of those who have returned. The newspapers are full of reports of violent crimes and assaults and wife beatings. The editorials all point to this as evidence of an increase in moral perversion and a lust for violence and blame it on the brutalising effect of the War. I thought perhaps the newspaper editors were just reporting violence for the sake of attracting readers. But do you think things are worse?'

'No, I don't think things are any worse than they were before the War. The violence was always there. For centuries, men have claimed the right to beat their wives and their servants in order to discipline them and they have always been ready to resort to fisticuffs to settle a dispute. It's seen as being manly. And they have been cruel to animals as well. Perhaps the War has just made us more aware of the violence within ourselves and our own society and the newspapers have realised that reporting this violence sells newspapers.'

'Yes, I suppose crime is something that many people find interesting to read about and it is easy for the papers to sensationalise things.'

'And it is equally easy to blame violence on something as obvious as the War rather than examining the question more deeply and trying to understand the real causes.'

'Such as human nature, you mean? Or original sin? Philip, can I ask, but don't answer if you don't want to. Why don't you talk about the War? Is it that you don't want to remember or is it because you have been able to put it behind you?'

'I think I have almost managed to put it behind me. Lately, the newspapers have started reminding us of it again because of Remembrance Day but that has made me realise that I am one of the lucky ones. Yesterday I read an interview with a chap who was asked what effect the War had had on him and he described the War, quite accurately in my opinion, as days of inaction and nervous waiting in between days and nights of terror under bombardment. He explained that while he was out there, he had no choice, no control over what he did from day to day. He went where he was sent even when he knew he was likely to be killed. He simply obeyed orders. One learned not to think too much and just to live in the present because there was no point in planning for a future that might not exist. And then, as this chap pointed out, after several years of living like that it was difficult to come back here and be expected to make choices. When he applied for a job, the employer always asked what his plans were for the future and he said he still hadn't got used to the idea of having a future, let alone planning for it.'

'But why do you think you are lucky? You went through all that too.'

'Yes, but you see, ever since I was a small boy, I've known what I wanted to do in life. My plan for the future was interrupted by the War but it wasn't destroyed by it. And I was far luckier than some of the chaps out there. After my lungs were damaged, I wasn't much use on the front line, so they sent me back to the supply lines. That meant sometimes going into towns and villages, being away from the fighting, and being able to talk to the local people. They showed me their handmade furniture and valuable pieces of china, and I learnt a lot about how these things were made and where they had come from. All the time I was gaining knowledge that I knew I could use when the War was over. I know it took me a couple of years to find the opportunity that I have now but I never lost hope. I shall never be able to forget the War, of course, but I think I have been able to put it behind me, at least most of the time. It's only when I think of Alistair that I have any doubts about whether what I am doing is worthwhile.'

It was the first time for many months that they had referred to their mutual loss. They lapsed into silence, each with their own thoughts, staring into the flames of the fire. Then, by unspoken consent, they each took up something to read. For some time, they sat either side of the fire-place, absorbed in what interested them, with the crackling of the fire and the snoring of Napoleon forming a comforting background. Philip was reading an auction catalogue, making notes in pencil in the margin next to the pieces worth investigating further. Eleanor had gone back to her newspaper and was reading the notices. This was a pastime she had indulged in since the age of about six, her favourites being the In Memoriam column and the Personal column. People placed announcements there which provided a small glimpse of their private lives. The messages were often cryptic, sometimes highly amusing, sometimes just curious and they appealed to Eleanor's investigative mind and lively sense of humour. The rest of the Harriman family had always thought it a rather macabre hobby and teased her about it but Eleanor enjoyed imagining the people behind the announcements and inventing personal histories for them.

'How odd,' said Eleanor, breaking their long silence.

Philip looked up from his catalogue, pencil poised. 'What, old thing? Are you reading the In Memoriam again?' he asked, accusingly. 'Or the personal announcements? What is it this time? "Chelsea Bridge, ten past midnight on the fourth. Bring goods as agreed." Or maybe "Come home, Reggie. All forgiven." Or just the usual: "Anyone knowing the whereabouts of Ermintrude Dash, etc., etc."'

'No. Look,' said Eleanor as she held out the newspaper.

'A Tired Nation Suffering from Nerves. Dr Cassell's Tablets offered Free to the Public,' intoned Philip, perversely reading an advertisement instead of the item to which Eleanor was pointing. Eleanor shook the paper impatiently and Philip read the item out loud.

> Leo,
> My companion of 27 years.
> Our revels now are ended.
> My comfort is the memory of
> our time together, Soap.
> 11.9.1894 to 29.10.1921

'It's just that it is so unusual, that's all. That's why it attracted my attention.' said Eleanor.

'It's certainly heartfelt.'

'It sounds as if someone has died but, if that is the case, it should be in the In Memoriam column but it's not, it's in the Personal column. So, that suggests that it is addressed to someone still alive.'

'Not necessarily,' said Philip. 'Perhaps whoever placed the notice subscribes to my theory that dead people read the newspaper.'

'What do you mean?' said Eleanor, frowning.

'Well, they must do, mustn't they, because people persist in putting announcements like that in the In Memoriam column every day, messages addressed directly to their dead relatives. "Johnny, why did you leave us? We are lonely and sad without you." That sort of thing. Why go to the expense and bother of a message like that unless you think little Johnny is going to read it in the paper and know how sad you are?'

Eleanor laughed and said: 'You are callous and unfeeling.'

'Possibly,' said Philip, 'but as far as I'm concerned the sentiment in those columns is maudlin. It's like those music hall songs about lost children who have gone to live with the angels.'

Eleanor read the announcement out, slowly.

'It is a curious announcement, though' said Eleanor. 'Definitely my best find so far.'

'Perhaps there's been a falling out and they have parted forever and Soap feels the need to announce it to the world in general.'

'Yes. Perhaps the message isn't addressed to a person, dead or alive. Perhaps it is an announcement and that is why it is in the Personal column.'

'Anyway, the dates don't make sense if it relates to someone who has died,' said Philip. He watched as Eleanor counted on her fingers.

'Yes,' she said. 'If this is someone who has died, the two dates would be the date of birth and the date of death but 1894 and 1921 are only twenty-seven years apart.'

'Which presumably is the twenty-seven years referred to in the message. The years they were together, I suppose.'

'So, if Leo was twenty-seven when he died, he couldn't have been the other person's companion for twenty-seven years. Unless they had known each other from birth.'

'Perhaps they were twins,' said Philip facetiously.

At this point, Mr Harriman arrived home and poured them all a pre-dinner sherry so the meaning of the message was left unresolved.

The following afternoon, Eleanor and Mr Harriman had just gone into the dining room when Edwin arrived back at the office for lunch bringing further news.

'You will be interested to know that Sam Perceval has now been arrested and charged with Sutton's murder,' he said. 'Sam denies he had anything to do with Sutton's death and won't say where he found Sutton.'

Mr Harriman said: 'I imagine that Superintendent Johnson is seeing a pattern that seems to be repeating itself. First Sam finds his father in suspicious circumstances and now he finds Sutton in circumstances that are even more suspicious.'

'I gather that inferences are being drawn,' said Edwin.

'Poor Mrs Perceval,' said Eleanor. She thought that Mrs Perceval would probably already have been to the police station to see Superintendent Johnson and she wondered whether or not the information about Mr Perceval's suicide note would make any difference to Sam's position. She explained briefly to Mr Harriman and Edwin what she had learnt from Mrs Perceval about Albert Perceval's suicide note.

'Well, that is interesting but I haven't heard anything to suggest that these two cases are linked in any way,' said Edwin. 'What interest could Sam Perceval have in the bank now?'

'I've been thinking about that,' said Eleanor. 'Sam demonstrated his anger at his father's death by writing messages on the bank's walls but there has been nothing since then until these last two recent incidents. Apparently, Sam has been away in Sheffield but recently came back and has been working at Clough End Farm. The messages have begun again. It could be co-incidence, of course, but don't forget that the same bank is threatening to sell Clough End Farm. Perhaps, Sam knows about the sale and it has reminded him of the business with his father all over again. Perhaps that has prompted him to write these new messages on the walls of the bank.'

'Hmm,' said Mr Harriman, 'I see your point. I suppose it's possible that this whole unfortunate business is about revenge. Even so, murder is a long step further on from damaging the walls of a bank.'

'Revenge does seem to be a Perceval family trait,' said Edwin, 'because that apparently is what motivated Charlie to behave the way he did against Mr Dawson with the false weights. And I am sure he blames you, Eleanor, for Sarah being sent away, in which case revenge could have been his motive for hitting you. He has admitted to hitting you apparently.'

'Probably only because he realised that Pauline's cousin saw him do it and was likely to identify him to the police to avoid being accused of the crime himself,' said Mr Harriman.

'There is some good news, though,' said Edwin. 'Mr Dawson told me that he went to see Sarah on Sunday and explained to her what had been happening in the shop. Sarah knew nothing about the false weights and the fiddling with the scales and when she heard what Charlie had done she declared she wanted nothing more to do with him. Mr Dawson says Sarah intends to remain in Bolton with her Aunt for the moment. He's very pleased.'

'No doubt that will provoke another act of revenge when Charlie hears Sarah's opinion of him,' said Mr Harriman. 'I think Sarah has had a lucky escape thanks to you, Eleanor.'

'I think I am beginning to tire of the Perceval brothers,' said Edwin.

'I feel sorry for Mrs Perceval though,' said Eleanor, with a sigh.

'I suppose it is possible that Sam killed Sutton in revenge for the action taken by the bank over Clough End Farm but the connection between him and the bank is rather tenuous, far more remote than the connection was when his father died,' mused Edwin.

'Also,' said Eleanor, 'the situation with Clough End is completely different, although Sam is not to know that, of course. If Pauline's father forged Frederick's signature on the bank's documents, surely John Hartshorn would have had a far greater motive for killing Mr Sutton than Sam would.'

'I wonder if John Hartshorn was aware that Sutton had discovered the forgery,' said Mr Harriman. 'After he received our advice about the mortgagee sale, Sutton would have had time to contact Hartshorn and ask for an explanation of brother Frederick's letter. Perhaps I should have a word with Mr Pidcock. He will know.'

'Yes, it is important to know that,' agreed Eleanor. 'And, when you speak to him would you ask him, please, for details of the words that he found on the wall of the bank on the morning of the Royal Visit. I would like to know exactly what was written, if he can remember.'

'Have you decided to do some investigating yourself?' teased Mr Harriman, raising his eyebrows at his daughter.

'Just a little. I would like to know more about what happened.'

Although she was mindful of Superintendent Johnson's warning against meddling in police business, Eleanor had lots of questions in her notebook and she knew she would not be happy until she found some answers.

One of her questions was answered quite quickly. Mrs Clayton arrived back at Hall Bank having made a short trip to Mr Dawson's shop because she had unexpectedly run out of onions. Mrs Clayton was generally so efficient that shortages of any kind were unknown at Hall Bank so Eleanor suspected that this was really an intelligence gathering operation. Mrs Clayton was able to report that Mr Dawson's handcart, abandoned in a ditch, had been spotted by the Longnor carrier and recovered by the police not far from Clough End Farm.

~O~

Just before the office closed that evening, Superintendent Johnson telephoned Mr Harriman to let him know that the Post-mortem Report on Mr Sutton was now available and he explained to Mr Harriman the current state of enquiries. When he had finished the telephone call, Mr Harriman went up to Edwin's office and called to Eleanor to join them.

Mr Harriman said: 'The Post-mortem Report on Sutton is in and Superintendent Johnson is sending a copy to me tomorrow morning. He told me that, as a result of the information given to him by Mr Dawson he questioned Charlie Perceval. Charlie blustered at first…'

'That sounds familiar. Obviously it is the way he deals with every challenge,' said Edwin.

'Well, his bravado didn't last long. He was told that he was going to be charged with perverting the course of justice and probably also with murder. He then confessed to stealing Mr Dawson's handcart and admitted that he had helped Sam move Sutton's body to the barn at Clough End Farm but he says that that is all he did and that Sutton was already dead when he saw him. Sam was told that Charlie had confessed to moving the body and that he, Sam, was also going to be charged with perverting the course of justice. Then he decided to change his story from his previous one. He now says that he found Sutton at the bank. He admits to defacing the walls of the bank and says he left off part way through to go and have a pint with one of his friends at The King's Head.'

'The Kings' Head?' said Edwin. 'Surely that is not his kind of drinking establishment? I can't see him fitting in there.'

'Well, that is what he said,' continued Mr Harriman. 'When he came back just after closing time to finish the job, he found Sutton lying beside the wall of the bank. Remembering his experience with the police over this father's death, he decided it wasn't safe to report it, so he went home to get Charlie to help him.'

'He is still not admitting to murder then,' said Eleanor. 'So what did happen to Mr Sutton?'

'I think we shall have a better idea tomorrow when we get the post-mortem results,' said Mr Harriman. 'I don't think we can achieve anything further this evening.'

Edwin said goodnight and went home. Mr Harriman went to his club and Eleanor went back to her office. She still had many unanswered questions and, as there was still plenty of time before dinner, she settled down at her desk and reviewed what information she had so far. She began to formulate a picture of what had happened and then she telephoned to Philip and asked him to come to Hall Bank that evening after dinner. She wanted him to help her with a reconstruction of the events which had led to Mr Sutton's death.

CHAPTER THIRTY-ONE

Eleanor and Philip were standing outside Chillingham & Baynard's bank, watched attentively by Napoleon. They had walked down Hall Bank, as Mr Sutton had done on the Friday evening before the Royal Visit when Eleanor had last seen him. At the bottom of Hall Bank they debated which way to go and decided that Mr Sutton would probably have gone past The Square rather than The Crescent. They walked past the George Hotel and along the lane beside the bank.

'That's seven minutes,' said Philip, who had been timing their walk, 'so what time did Mr Sutton leave you at Hall Bank?'

'Let me think. The meeting finished just before ten.' Eleanor stared across the road at The Quadrant as she tried to remember that evening. 'Yes, afterwards, a few of us stood outside the hall talking and I remember hearing the Town Hall clock striking the hour. Then, probably after about ten minutes or so, we started walking home. Mr Sutton and I left Catherine outside the meeting hall and walked back to Hall Bank'

'Across The Slopes?'

'No, via the Market Place. I'd say it must have been about quarter past ten when Mr Sutton left me.'

'Right, so that would put his arrival here at around twenty past ten, twenty-five past, perhaps. So, what happened when he got here? What did he find?'

'Well,' said Eleanor, 'Sam's story is that, just before closing time, he left off painting the message on the wall and went to have a drink with a friend at The King's Head. Then, straight after closing time he returned to the bank, intending to finish the message. He found Mr Sutton lying beside the wall of the bank. This wall.'

'Suppose for the moment that Sam is telling the truth. He comes here and starts to paint his message. Then, he realises the time. Perhaps he heard the Hospital clock striking the quarter hour and realised it was nearly closing time. So, he rushes off to meet his friend. Do we know who that friend was?'

'No name has been mentioned as yet, no.'

'All right, Sam comes back here shortly after closing time and finds Mr Sutton lying here. Assuming he left The King's Head at closing time, that puts him back here at about ten minutes past ten or quarter past perhaps, at the latest.'

'But if my estimate of the time is right, Mr Sutton hadn't arrived here yet?' said Eleanor.

'Exactly. He wouldn't have arrived at the bank for another ten minutes.'

'So, if Sam really did find Mr Sutton here, he must have returned after twenty past ten. If Sam left here at about a quarter to ten and didn't get back from The King's Head until twenty past ten, that leaves forty-five minutes between starting to paint the message and coming back and finding Mr Sutton. So what was he doing during that time?' asked Eleanor.

'And another thing,' added Philip, 'assuming that he came down Hall Bank from The King's Head, which is the shortest way back to the bank, why did you and Mr Sutton not see him?'

'He isn't telling the truth, is he?' said Eleanor.

'Absolutely not,' said Philip. 'In concocting his story, he obviously was not aware that Mr Sutton was walking down Hall Bank that evening. I think the story of beginning the painting, going to meet a friend, and then coming back is pure invention. It is more likely that Sam only came here once and that was after closing time. There would have been people in the street before ten. Surely he would have waited until the coast was clear before beginning.'

'Also,' said Eleanor, 'didn't you tell me that someone had passed the bank on his way home and had not seen any message?'

'Ah, yes. You're right. I had forgotten that. It was Mr Furniss,' said Philip. 'I think he said he passed the bank a few minutes after ten. He was on foot so he certainly would have noticed if there had been anything on the wall then, let alone a half-finished message.'

'That settles it. Sam is lying. Let's assume that he came here only once, at some time after closing time.' Eleanor pointed to the left of the side wall of the bank. 'This is where the message was. There were three words and the fourth was unfinished. Sam would have been standing about here when he stopped painting.' Eleanor moved further to the right. 'If he is lying when he says he broke off to go to The King's Head, something else must have caused him to stop halfway through painting the message. What?'

'It wouldn't take long to write those few words so if he had started at about ten twenty, he would have been in the middle of his painting when Mr Sutton arrived. So it would have been Mr Sutton's arrival that stopped him,' said Philip.

Eleanor nodded slowly and Philip asked: 'What happened next?'

'Well, Dr McKenzie said there was a blow to the left side of Mr Sutton's jaw, and a gash on the back of his head, which was possibly caused by a fall.'

'Right, I'll stand here,' said Philip, 'and pretend to be painting the wall. I'm facing the wall so I don't see you coming. You are walking along towards the bank. You see me and realise what I am up to. Your natural reaction would be to call out or attract my attention in some way, wouldn't it?'

'So, I call out something like "I say, you there! What do you think you're doing?" and I probably stop a couple of feet behind you.'

'I turn around from the wall to see who is behind me. I'm holding a brush or something so before I can hit you I have to drop it and then aim a blow at your jaw. That might give you a second or two to realise what was happening and perhaps step back out of the way.'

Eleanor looked at where Philip was standing and said: 'If you lashed out and hit me on the jaw, I would most likely fall backwards, away from the wall...'

'... or perhaps sideways. But, either way, you cannot hit the back of your head on the wall because the wall is behind me not you,' added Philip.

'Suppose there was a scuffle. Perhaps Mr Sutton tried to grab hold of Sam or the brush or whatever he was using and their positions were reversed?' said Eleanor.

'That's possible, I suppose, but Mr Sutton was quite slight and Sam is a very big lad. I think Sam would have stood his ground.' Philip moved towards Eleanor and then pivoted leaving Eleanor with her back to the wall. 'Besides, if we are scuffling with each other, I am too close to you to be able to swing a punch.'

'Is it possible that Mr Sutton fell backwards and hit his head on the road and not the wall?'

Philip considered this suggestion and then said: 'I suppose that's possible but for that to happen, wouldn't he have had to be rigid, falling like a ninepin. If someone hits you on the jaw, I think it's more likely that your knees would buckle and you would sort of crumple sideways away from the direction of the punch.'

'Yes,' said Eleanor, 'I see what you mean.'

'Dr McKenzie did say a gash and not a blow to the back of the head, didn't he?'

'Yes,' said Eleanor.

'I was wondering whether the gash could have been caused by Mr Sutton being hit on the head by someone, the way you were,' said Philip.

'Oh, you mean from behind. Hmmm…but for that to happen, Mr Sutton would have to be in front of the wall with Sam behind him. And Sam then couldn't have punched Mr Sutton on the jaw because he would have been standing behind him.' Eleanor sighed. 'This is not getting us anywhere, is it? I thought it might help if we came here and tried to reconstruct what happened.'

'Oh, I think it has been very helpful. Apart from the problem of how Mr Sutton hit the back of his head, another thing strikes me. Let's do that manoeuvre again and I'll mime it this time to show you what I mean. Right, I'm busy painting the wall.' Philip turned around to face the wall. 'You walk up behind me and attract my attention.'

Eleanor called: 'Hey you!' Napoleon looked at her, startled, wondering if he had done something wrong.

Philip turned around saying: 'I turn around, surprised. I see you, I drop the brush, perhaps you say something threatening. I take a swipe at you and hit you on the jaw.'

Philip suited his actions to his words and lunged forward pretending to aim a blow at Eleanor's jaw. Napoleon now moved quickly forward and gave a low warning growl thinking that Philip was attacking Eleanor.

'It's all right, Napoleon,' said Eleanor as she bent to stroke him. 'Philip won't hurt me.'

'No, in fact, I can't even reach you. Unless you come right up behind me, which I think is unlikely, I would need to take at least one step further forward towards you in order to connect with your jaw.'

'Which leaves both of us even further away from the wall,' said Eleanor.

'You were right. This demonstration is not getting us anywhere.'

276

'No, you're wrong. It is. It has been very helpful. Mr Sutton was hit on the left side of his jaw. As I was watching you just then, I realised that to hit me on the left side of my jaw, you would need to be right-handed.'

Philip looked at Eleanor and moved his left fist through the air towards her.

'See what I mean,' said Eleanor. 'You're left-handed and when you took a swing at me you naturally used your left hand, without thinking about it. So, even if you had been able to reach me, you couldn't have hit me on the left. You would have hit me on the right side of my jaw.'

'Hmmm,' said Philip. 'Of course. So, does that mean that whoever daubed this wall is right-handed?' asked Philip. 'How do we find out?'

'I'm sure a handwriting expert would be able to tell us by looking at the way the words were written but unfortunately we no longer have the words for him to examine.'

'Perhaps our next step is to find out if Sam is right-handed,' said Philip. 'How do we do that?'

'I could ask his mother, I suppose, but it would sound a bit odd, wouldn't it?'

'I think so. Then, let's get back shall we?' said Philip.

'No, wait,' said Eleanor. 'Let's think about Sam's version a bit more. If Sam didn't attack Mr Sutton and he really did find him here, that means someone else must have attacked Mr Sutton. And that must have happened sometime between about ten fifteen when Mr Sutton left Hall Bank and whatever time it was after that that Sam got here and found Mr Sutton.'

'Hmmm, but none of this gets Mr Sutton lying next to the wall, does it? Surely, Sam would have no reason to lie about where he found Mr Sutton. What could he hope to gain? So, perhaps we can accept at least that part of the story as being true. Let's have one more try at understanding Sam's version, shall we?'

'All right. Sam comes along and finds Mr Sutton.'

'Where has he come from and why?'

'From home or the public house, and to paint the wall,' said Eleanor.

'But he must have already painted some of the words beforehand, mustn't he? Because if he came along and found Mr Sutton already dead surely he wouldn't just start painting the message with Mr Sutton lying here. It would be a pretty callous thing to do. And if he did start to paint the message, why not finish it? There would have been no reason to stop.'

'So, at least some part of his story must be true. He started the message, yes, and then he stopped, yes. He says he stopped of his own accord but, more likely, something happened to stop him. But, what? It *must* have been because Mr Sutton arrived.'

'All right,' said Philip. 'Let's assume Sam is right-handed. He's painting the message and, after being interrupted by Mr Sutton, he swings out at him and hits him on the left jaw. Mr Sutton falls backwards, away from the wall, and is lying where you are standing, several feet away from the wall. Sam runs off. And then later comes back, for some reason…'

'…such as, what?'

'I'm not sure.' Philip paused and frowned.

'Perhaps he had dropped something and came back to find it? Something that would incriminate him.'

'Yes, that's plausible. So, he comes back, he finds Mr Sutton lying next to the wall. Why did he not find Mr Sutton lying where he had left him, several feet away from the wall?' asked Philip. 'Something else must have happened in between Sam hitting Mr Sutton and Sam returning to the scene.'

'Ah, yes. I see what you are getting at. But what?' said Eleanor.

They stood in silence for a minute or two, staring out at nothing in particular, each trying to picture the scene.

Napoleon who had been sitting up watching them, now lay

down and rested his head on his paws while he waited.

Then Eleanor turned to Philip and said: 'It's simple really. There are only two possible explanations. Either, someone moved Mr Sutton, or he moved himself.'

'Yes, I'll accept that. So, who? And why?'

'If someone had come along and found Mr Sutton injured or dead, surely they would have either helped him or raised the alarm. They wouldn't just move him and then leave him there.'

'Surely not. So, that leaves the other alternative,' said Philip. 'Mr Sutton moved himself which means that either the blow to his jaw caused him to fall but did not knock him out, or he was knocked out and then regained consciousness…'

'…which would mean Sam's blow didn't kill him,' finished Eleanor.

'Yes,' said Philip. 'That's interesting, isn't it?' They considered this proposition for a minute.

Philip said: 'Suppose Mr Sutton was temporarily stunned and then got to his feet, probably a bit confused…then what?'

'He moves towards the wall, perhaps to steady himself,' said Eleanor going to stand beside the wall. Napoleon got up again to watch. 'Now the wall is behind him. Sam strikes Mr Sutton a second time or pushes him and Mr Sutton falls backwards against the wall, hence the gash on the back of his head.'

'That's plausible,' said Philip, 'and that would mean that Sam was the killer after all. If that is what really happened, Sam's story of going away and coming back again has to be discounted because it would leave Mr Sutton staggering about for forty minutes or so waiting for Sam to come back and hit him for the second time.'

'I think the only thing we can definitely conclude at the moment is that Sam is not telling the truth,' said Eleanor.

'So, where does that leave us?' said Philip. Eleanor didn't reply. He continued: 'If Sam didn't kill Mr Sutton and really did just find him here, he went to an awful lot of trouble to conceal his body. Why?'

'Yes, well, apparently when Sam's father killed himself the police thought the circumstances were suspicious. Sam was questioned rather forcefully and he was only sixteen at the time and he ran away from home as a consequence. So it is just possible that his motive in moving Mr Sutton was simply that, through no fault of his own and just by bad luck, he had found a second person dead and he remembered what happened the first time and thought he would be blamed for killing Mr Sutton.'

'It's not a very convincing story, is it?'

'No, it is not, said Eleanor, 'and I think there must be some other really compelling motive to have warranted all that trouble. Perhaps Sam did attack Mr Sutton out of anger, or even in self-defence, and that had consequences he didn't intend, which is why he decided to move the body.'

'But I know from experience that moving a body is not an easy thing to do on one's own, so he must have had help.'

'Yes, he did. Brother Charlie,' said Eleanor.

'I see.'

'They took Mr Sutton all the way to Clough End Farm on a handcart.'

'Good grief!' said Philip.

'It made me very angry when I heard that.'

'I'm not surprised. That is appalling. Were they hoping to delay discovery of the crime, perhaps? Or, just to deflect attention from themselves?'

'Probably both. If Mr Sutton had been found here, the message painted on the wall would point all too clearly to Sam as the culprit, which reinforces our theory that Mr Sutton interrupted Sam as he was painting the wall,' said Eleanor.

'It's an awful long way, though. On foot, pushing a handcart....Two hours, maybe?'

'They were seen on London Road so I suppose they were going via Harpur Hill along the lane past Diamond Hill rather than on the main road which is the way we went. It's much shorter. I estimated that it would take about an hour.'

'Why choose Clough End Farm, though?'

'Well,' said Eleanor, 'Sam was working out there so he would have known about the barn and the farm is well out of the way. Perhaps they hoped to delay discovery long enough for them to attend the dog fight and then get well away.'

'And they would have succeeded if you had not gone to look for Pauline.'

'No,' said Eleanor, 'I only discovered Mr Sutton because someone put me in the barn where he was. If they had put me somewhere else, I would not have known anything about Mr Sutton. And, the only reason they needed to put me anywhere was that Charlie very rashly hit me over the head. If it had not been for that, I would have just left the farm and been none the wiser. It was Charlie's fault that Mr Sutton was discovered so soon. I suspect that he hit me more out of revenge than to stop me snooping so he really has brought all this on himself.'

'I shudder to think what they were planning to do with you.'

'Nothing, probably. Once the dog fight was over, Pauline and I would have been released. Of course, they may have thought that it was too dark in the barn for me to see anything. They did put me at the opposite end of the barn. They probably didn't expect me to go exploring and looking for something to force the door open with.'

'That's highly likely. They probably thought, to their undoing, that they were dealing with some meek little woman who would just stay where she was put and be too frightened to meddle. They picked the wrong person, didn't they?' Philip smiled at Eleanor.

'They certainly did and I mean to get to the bottom of this. I've just thought of something else and I should have thought of it before. If Charlie helped Sam with the handcart that probably means Charlie was up here at the bank with Sam.'

'That's a point,' said Philip. 'We have been assuming that Sam was alone when he was daubing the wall. How does that fit in?'

They stood staring at the wall, hoping for further inspiration but none came.

Then Philip said: 'I think we really have gone as far as we can with this line of investigation. What have we achieved?'

'Well, we can be certain about some facts, I think,' said Eleanor, demonstrating with her fingers as she counted them. 'One, Mr Sutton didn't arrive here until about twenty past ten or just after. Two, when he did arrive, someone was in the process of painting the message on the wall. Three, Mr Sutton was attacked, probably by the person painting the wall. Four, he was killed here and not out at Clough End Farm. Five, Sam and Charlie took Mr Sutton to Clough End Farm on the handcart.'

Philip had nodded in agreement at each fact. 'Right,' he said, with satisfaction, 'we have made some progress then. Time to go back to Hall Bank, I think.'

~O~

The trio had moved away from the bank intending to return to Hall Bank when Eleanor noticed someone further along the street on the other side of the road, walking slowly in their direction. Napoleon bounded across the road to meet him.

'Ah,' said Eleanor, 'it's Jon Jon. Let me see if I can clear up his story about the man who fell down.' She crossed the road to greet him and Philip followed her. 'Good evening, Jon Jon. How are you?' Jon Jon continued patting Napoleon, not looking at Eleanor. 'Jon Jon, the other day you were telling me about a man who fell down. Do you remember?'

Jon Jon nodded, still not looking up. 'Fell down,' he

repeated.

'And do you remember where you were when the man fell down?'

Jon Jon looked around him and then at Eleanor as though he was surprised that she should have to ask.

'Were you here?' Jon Jon nodded.

'And you told me about the man with the puppies. Do you remember the man with the puppies?' Jon Jon nodded. 'I didn't understand you properly when you told me the first time. Can you help me again? Do you remember who you saw that time?' Jon Jon nodded. 'Was the man with the puppies by himself?' Jon Jon frowned and looked from Eleanor to Philip, searching for the answer. Then he looked at Napoleon and patted him. Eleanor waited patiently. Jon Jon looked up and smiled, shaking his head. 'Was it the man with the puppies who fell down?' Jon Jon slowly shook his head. 'I see. Thank you, Jon Jon. You have been a very big help.' Jon Jon patted Napoleon again and then, losing interest in the conversation, lumbered away.

Eleanor turned to Philip and said: 'I think we are on the right track. I misunderstood Jon Jon previously. You see, I think Jon Jon saw who stole Mrs Hazelwood's puppies. That is how he knew where they were. I also think it was someone he knows and that he saw that same person outside the bank, which is why he referred to him as the man with the puppies. When I tried to understand what Jon Jon meant, I thought he had seen the man who stole the puppies fall down but I think what he actually meant was that he saw two men, the man who stole the puppies, and another man, the man who fell down.'

'And you think Sam Perceval was the man with the puppies? So, Jon Jon saw him and also saw another man fall down?' asked Philip.

'Yes. Jon Jon's aunt lives only a few doors up from where

the Percevals live so he's bound to know Sam.'

'So, the man who fell down must have been Mr Sutton, which would put Sam Perceval and Mr Sutton in the same place at the same time.'

'Yes, and if only two people were here when Mr Sutton was attacked, that means that Charlie must have arrived later,' said Eleanor.

'But we would need to find a more reliable witness than Jon Jon,' said Philip.

'I agree, but at least we now have an idea of the kind of witness we are looking for.'

CHAPTER THIRTY-TWO

On Saturday morning, the report of the post-mortem examination of Mr Sutton was delivered to Mr Harriman as promised. Mr Harriman read through the report and then went to discuss it with Eleanor and Edwin.

'Dr McKenzie's preliminary opinion as to the time of death has been confirmed and also the fact that Sutton's body had been moved from wherever it was he died,' said Mr Harriman. 'Dr McKenzie noted a small gash on the back of the head, bruising, and evidence of a blow to the left jaw, but according to the post-mortem the cause of death was a blow to the right temple, which may have been inflicted after the blow to the jaw. According to the report, a blow to the temple does not always leave any outward signs so the cause of death is not apparent until there is a post-mortem examination.'

Eleanor said: 'I feel very angry that Mr Sutton should have died in this way.'

Mr Harriman nodded. 'Yes, it is hard to accept. He was not a violent man and it is not possible to imagine him initiating a fight.'

'Perhaps before the inquest, Superintendent Johnson will be able to find a witness, someone who saw Sutton on the night he died. There must have been someone around,' said Edwin.

Eleanor said: 'I do have a little bit of information about that but I'm afraid it's not very helpful.'

She went on to tell them about Jon Jon's story of a man who had fallen down. Then she described the efforts at reconstruction that she and Philip had made the previous evening. When she had concluded her description, she said: 'It all just seems so wrong, so hard to believe.'

Mr Harriman and Edwin nodded their agreement.

Mr Harriman said: 'It's just after eleven, and there are no appointments this morning. I think we all need cheering up. I propose that we leave James and Mrs Clayton to hold the fort and give ourselves a holiday for half an hour. Let's walk up to the Town Hall and look at the Chrysanthemum Society show. The trophies are being presented this evening so the results will have been published by now.'

~O~

The Ballroom at the Town Hall was filled with chrysanthemums and the sound of conversation. Participants, proud relatives, and onlookers all gathered in excited groups to view the results. Eleanor noted with interest that most of the entries in the cut blooms and the plants section were from men, many of whom were still at their place of work and, as yet, ignorant of the results. However, their female relatives were milling about eagerly, hoping to see a familiar name on the card announcing an award. By contrast, the entrants in the floral arrangement section were mainly women although three men had been bold enough to enter the fray. This section was attracting a large crowd of ladies either highly critical of the winners or seeking inspiration for their own arrangements at home.

Eleanor, Edwin and Mr Harriman were in front of the cut blooms section. There were forty three vases, each one containing five specimens, identical circles of perfect petals in a dazzling variety of colours. The Hall Bank trio admired *Red Fireball*, in third place, then *Bronze Beauty*, in second place.

'Look,' said Mr Harriman. 'First prize. *Autumn's Peak*.

And the Mayor's Trophy as well. That's the flower Mondo mentioned at dinner.'

Eleanor looked at the perfect flowers, the petals a masterful mixture of the colours of autumn. Hints of bronze, orange, red and yellow, all blending into one another so it was hard to decide which colour was predominant.

'Yes,' said Eleanor. 'That's Mr Sutton's entry. The one Mondo said wouldn't be ready in time. I am so pleased that he has won. Someone must have entered his flowers for him.'

This was the section in which Mondo usually excelled. Eleanor, remembering how confident he was of winning, wondered why he had not been awarded a prize and could not see an entry from him. While Mr Harriman and Edwin were chatting to a client, Eleanor paused to look at the entries in the new variety section and noticed that the prize had been won by a new chrysanthemum aptly named, *Princess Mary* and bred by Sam Fidler. Eleanor thought that Mrs Fidler would be relieved. Then Eleanor overheard a conversation which intrigued her. The speakers were behind her and she could not turn around to see who they were without risking them stopping talking or moving away.

'I notice Mondo hasn't won a prize this year,' said a female voice. 'That's odd because I was talking to him before the last meeting and he was very pleased with the way his plants were coming on. He was quite confident that he was going to win the Mayor's Trophy this year.'

'Yes, it is a surprise,' said a second female voice, 'he always enters, every year without fail.'

'Of course, there was that attack on his greenhouse. Maybe that damaged all the plants he was intending to show.'

'Yes, I heard about that incident. Someone told me that it was Mr Sutton who did it.'

'Oh, I didn't hear that. Well, everyone knows that they didn't get on but I think that is going a bit far, don't you?'

'Well, yes. I do. And I know one shouldn't speak ill of the dead but if Mr Sutton did damage Mondo's plants, I don't think he should have been awarded those prizes even if his flowers are the best in the show.'

'No, it doesn't seem fair, does it. Although, I have to admit that I think his entry is undoubtedly the best this year.'

'Did you ever hear what the feud between them was about?'

'Well, what I heard was that…'

The voices started to move away and Eleanor turned around very slowly to see who the speakers were. There was quite a crowd behind her, mostly with their backs turned and she couldn't tell who had been speaking so she re-joined her father and Edwin. The half hour which they had allowed themselves had turned into an hour and it was time to leave. Refreshed by their contact with beautiful flowers and friends, they were all in a more optimistic mood when they returned to Hall Bank. Eleanor suggested that Mrs Clayton might want to take time off to go and look at the show but she declined.

'No, thanks very much all the same,' she said. 'I'm off to the pictures with my sister-in-law this afternoon. They're showing a new film. That'll set me up just fine. Besides, I've heard enough about chrysanthemums from Sam Fidler to last me well into next year. I'm pleased Mr Sutton won, though.' So after lunch Mrs Clayton went off to join the Saturday matinee queue at the Picture House where Mary Pickford was starring in *Pollyanna*.

James was getting ready to close the office and also expressed his pleasure at the news of Mr Sutton's success.

'And Mr Norman?' he asked, one eyebrow raised in interrogation.

Eleanor then realised that she had not seen Mr Norman's name on any of the entries. That made two missing entries.

~O~

After he had closed the shop for the day, Philip looked in at the

Chrysanthemum Society Show and then called at Hall Bank. Mr Harriman had gone to golf and Eleanor and Napoleon were just setting off for a walk so Philip said he would join them. Although it was cold, the air was clear and crisp, a perfect day for walking. They decided to walk to Fairfield and headed down Hall Bank towards Spring Gardens. By the time Eleanor and Philip had discussed the chrysanthemum awards and expressed their satisfaction at Mr Sutton's trophy and their regret at his absence, they had reached the top of Spring Gardens. The shops were now closed but there was quite a bit of traffic in Spring Gardens, so Eleanor put Napoleon on his lead.

Eleanor said: 'The post-mortem report arrived at the office today. Father telephoned Dr McKenzie this morning and discussed it with him. It seems that Mr Sutton was actually hit twice, once on the left side of his jaw and then a second blow on his right temple. It was the blow on the temple that caused his death. Do you remember, last night we decided that the blow to the jaw must have been struck by a right-handed person. Wouldn't that mean that the blow to the temple must have been by a left-handed person? I don't know enough about boxing to be able to judge whether one person could inflict both injuries.'

'Someone with a bit of experience in boxing could certainly do so. You hit the jaw from the right and then follow it with a blow to the temple with your left.' Philip paused miming the action of a boxer and then added: 'Although, I am inclined to think that if the sequence was "blow from the right" followed by "blow from the left" the assailant would be more likely to be right-handed than left-handed. One is likely to lead with the stronger hand and that would be the first blow, then follow with the weaker hand. Well. I would do that anyway.'

'The post-mortem report didn't say how much time there would have been between the two blows so we don't really know whether they were inflicted at the same time or at different times with a delay between. You see, when I thought back to our attempt at reconstruction last night, we did consider a delay and I wondered whether we are actually dealing with two people. A single blow each administered by two different people, one right-handed and the other left-handed.'

Philip stopped walking and looked at Eleanor. 'That is a very clever suggestion. Let's reconsider and see if it works. Mr Sutton interrupts Sam Perceval at the bank, calls out to him, Sam turns around and hits out at Mr Sutton, landing a right-handed punch on his jaw. Mr Sutton staggers and, perhaps, momentarily loses consciousness.'

'I wonder,' said Eleanor, 'if he fell down at that point or just stumbled. But let's imagine that he moved towards the wall in order to steady himself and that is how he came to be standing with his back to the wall.'

'Yes, that would fit. I am trying to visualise the scene.' They started walking again.

Philip continued: 'Assume for the moment that Sam then runs away...'

'If he ran off straightaway, perhaps he didn't see Mr Sutton fall or stagger and doesn't know what happened after that.'

'So then a second person comes along,' said Philip. 'He hits Mr Sutton on the right temple...'

'... because he is left-handed. Mr Sutton falls backwards and hits his head on the wall, and that is how the gash to the back of his head occurred.'

'Yes....that would certainly work. Then what?'

'Sam comes back to retrieve his brush and pot or whatever it was caused him to return and finds Mr Sutton lying there as a result of the blow to the temple. We know what happens from there.'

'Yes,' said Philip. 'And if that is the explanation, it means that Sam isn't Mr Sutton's killer after all and he has been wrongly arrested.'

'Well, for murder, yes. Certainly not for assault and battery, or possibly for attempted murder even.'

'But, if Sam didn't see this other person hit Mr Sutton and simply came back and saw Mr Sutton lying next to the wall, it is quite conceivable that he thought that he had killed Mr Sutton with the blow to the jaw. If he thought that, it would explain why he went to all that trouble of hiding Mr Sutton's body' said Philip.

'So where was the second person when Mr Sutton was hit the first time? Surely he must have been close by because otherwise Mr Sutton would have had time to recover and move away to safety.'

'Perhaps the second person hit Mr Sutton straight after Sam did?'

'But Sam would have seen him,' said Eleanor.

'Not if Sam ran away immediately without stopping to see what happened to Mr Sutton. If Mr Sutton was facing the wall when he was hit by Sam and then staggered and moved towards the wall to steady himself, that would have taken a few seconds, so Sam could easily have disappeared during that time.'

'And person number two then steps in and hits Mr Sutton,' said Eleanor.

'And Mr Sutton hits his head on the wall as he falls. So who is person number two, the left-hander?' asked Philip.

'How many left-handed people do we know?' asked Eleanor.

'Apart from me, you mean!' Philip thought for a minute and added: 'Mondo is left-handed.'

'Are you sure?'

'Yes, we left-handers tend to notice each other. I can picture him now the last time we were at Brook House for dinner. He took down that book from his shelf, Chaucer remember, when we were discussing people in glass houses. Also, I can visualise him pouring whisky. Yes, definitely left-handed.'

Eleanor said nothing.

Philip said: 'It's odd, don't you think, that Mondo seems to have disappeared? And why didn't he enter his chrysanthemums in the show? He always enters.'

'Yes,' agreed Eleanor, 'but I don't...I can't believe that there is a connection.'

'No, you're right. I cannot believe that he would have killed Mr Sutton, even given their notorious feud. He is just not capable of something like that. Let's try another route. Who do we know who disliked Mr Sutton?'

'Well, someone wrote the word thief on the gatepost at Thornstead and obviously did not think much of him,' said Eleanor.

'Could that just have been Sam again, do you think?'

'Well, father and I thought it might not have had anything to do with the bank. It might relate to something more personal. What can you steal?' asked Eleanor.

'A man's reputation?' suggested Philip. 'Someone's wife or sweetheart? Mr Sutton was a very popular man and a much sought after dinner guest but I don't recall his name ever being connected romantically with anyone, do you?'

'No. He was considered a very eligible bachelor but no-one ever seemed to make any impression on him.'

'We are not getting anywhere with that train of thought,' said Philip. 'The plum role in the next amateur theatre production? A secret formula that makes the plants bloom?

'Now you are being absurd,' said Eleanor,

'The first prize at the Chrysanthemum Society?'

'Well, Mr Sutton has actually done that.'

'Maybe it was something to do with the bank after all. Perhaps he refused the killer a loan.'

They walked along without talking for a while, each mulling over theories.

'Hmm,' said Philip, 'I've just thought of someone else who is left-handed and I don't like what else I am thinking.'

'Who?'

'Norman.'

'Mr Norman!' Eleanor paused. 'Oh, yes, you are right. He is left-handed. But what could Mr Sutton have stolen from him? As far as I know they weren't even friends.'

'No, the thing that Norman had, in his own mind at least, was his expectation of a relationship with you.'

'But that's nonsense!' said Eleanor, angrily. 'I would never consider such a thing.'

'I know that, but he certainly did not.' Philip thought for a minute and then added: 'Remember that conversation that he had with his friend in the shop that I told you about? I could see how deluded he was, but I don't think he could.'

'If that is what Mr Norman thought he was just being ridiculous. Whatever could have given him that idea?'

Philip did not respond.

~O~

Eleanor and Philip walked in silence until they reached Sylvan Park at the bottom of Spring Gardens and stopped to sit on a seat in the park. Napoleon settled down beside Eleanor and watched the passers-by. Angry thoughts were whirling around in Eleanor's head. Then she forced herself to overcome her distaste for the whole subject of Mr Norman and consider the facts objectively and without emotion. As she remembered her most recent encounters with Mr Norman, she began to wonder if Philip was right although she did not want to believe it.

Eventually, Philip said: 'I've been thinking about left-handedness.'

'Oh?' said Eleanor. 'What about it?'

'Well, think back to the tennis competition this season.

In the mixed doubles this year, you were partnered with Norman quite a few times but you haven't played with him in previous seasons. This was the first time and this year he was more successful than usual and certainly more so when he was partnered with you than with any of the other ladies. He had a very good season and finished much higher up the rankings than usual. His tennis hasn't improved all that much and I think his success was partly due to the fact that you are a very strong player but, possibly more importantly, it was due to the fact that you are used to playing with someone who is left-handed.

As you well know, when a right-handed person and a left-handed person are on the court together they have to concentrate particularly hard. It is easy to get in each other's way. You are used to partnering me so, unlike his other partners, you had no difficulty playing with him. Hence, his unusual success. Maybe he read more into it than was warranted. He is pretty odd, and socially a bit naïve. Perhaps he saw your compatibility on the tennis court as a sign that you would be a suitable partner in life.'

Eleanor looked at Philip, speechless and horrified. She didn't want to think about the implications. Echoing in her head were phrases that Mr Norman had used about partnerships.

Philip said: 'I've just thought of something else. You remember I told you that Norman had telephoned to say he no longer wanted that brooch he had asked me to put aside. He said "it's been stolen" and we thought he was referring to the brooch. Perhaps what he meant was that you or your affection had been stolen. I'm sorry to keep finding reasons, Eleanor, but I think we have to face the possibility that, in Norman's eyes, Mr Sutton had stolen your affection, stolen you from him.'

'But I didn't even know Mr Sutton all that well, he was a business acquaintance, not a friend.' She considered the problem further, then added: 'I wonder if Mr Norman was the man Mrs Hazelwood saw in Burlington Road outside Thornstead. She told me she thought she had seen someone spying.'

Eleanor was silent for a while and then she steeled herself and said firmly: 'All right. Let's go back to the scene as we imagined it. Mr Norman is somewhere close by when Sam hits Mr Sutton. Sam runs off. Mr Norman attacks Mr Sutton. Was he provoked in some way or did he just take advantage of an opportunity which presented itself? Mr Sutton, having been stunned by the first blow to his jaw, was an easy target.'

'Norman does not seem to me to be a coward,' said Philip, 'so I think he would not hit someone just because they were vulnerable. I think it is more likely that something happened to make him angry, angry enough to hit Mr Sutton. And then, he walked away leaving Mr Sutton lying beside the wall where Sam found him later on. The thing about a blow to the temple is that it doesn't have to be very hard to be fatal.'

'You mean, he might not even have realised that he had killed Mr Sutton.'

'That's entirely possible. He may only have intended to hurt him,' said Philip. 'Punish him for stealing you.'

'If that is the case, he may not have known until Tuesday that Mr Sutton was dead.'

Eleanor sat thinking things over and then said: 'Philip, I have remembered something about that last evening with Mr Sutton. It is only a vague impression and I certainly couldn't swear to it so you mustn't take too much notice of it. When Mr Sutton left me at our front door, I glanced back across The Slopes before I went inside and I saw a movement. I thought someone had moved quickly into the shadows. It was only a fleeting impression but I did think at the time that it might be Mr Norman because he had offered to see me home and I had refused. I remember being annoyed at the thought that he might have been following us.'

'So he could have followed Mr Sutton after you had gone inside and he would have been only a few yards behind him. If so, he would have seen Sam Perceval at work on the wall.'

'But surely that had nothing to do with him and there was nothing in that message that could have provoked him to attack Mr Sutton. What could have made him angry enough to hit out at him?'

'Perhaps it had nothing to do with Sam Perceval. Perhaps it was connected with something that had happened earlier. When you were walking with Mr Sutton perhaps. If Norman was following you he could have heard what you were talking about.'

'We were laughing about one of the speakers who objected to ladies walking about the countryside with men. He thought they should all be confined at home in the kitchen. We were rather making fun of him, I'm afraid. And we were certainly enjoying ourselves and laughing. I suppose if Mr Norman heard us that could that have made him angry.... angry enough to want to punch Mr Sutton, perhaps, but angry enough to kill?'

'It might have made him jealous. One might be prepared to harm a rival if one were a jealous suitor,' said Philip. 'The description fits Norman perfectly, I'm afraid.'

'Oh, surely not!'

'Norman must have realised by then that he was wasting his time with you. He may have been angry enough.'

Philip's words had set off another unwelcome train of thought in Eleanor's mind and instances came flooding in when Mr Norman and Mr Sutton had been present and Mr Norman had tried unsuccessfully to claim her attention. She could understand that, from Mr Norman's perspective, this must have been very distressing.

'Philip, I am horribly afraid that you are right about Mr Norman being jealous. I think I should go and see him.'

'I would strongly advise against it.'

'No, I've got to know the truth. Besides, if Mr Norman did hit Mr Sutton and didn't mean to kill him, he must be feeling dreadful at the moment. And it wouldn't have been murder so he would not be hanged. He may not realise that. I might be able to help him.'

'Eleanor, I don't think you should go anywhere near Norman,' said Philip, firmly.

'But, if what we suspect is true, he must be suffering terribly at the moment. I feel responsible. I really should go. He may still be at his office.'

Eleanor stood up and Napoleon followed suit.

'Then, if you insist, I'm coming with you. You must not go alone,' said Philip as they left the park and started to walk back along Spring Gardens.

CHAPTER THIRTY-THREE

Eleanor, Napoleon and Philip walked along Spring Gardens until they reached the building where Mr Norman had his office. There was a shop at ground floor level and, to the right of the shop, was a door with Mr Norman's name on it. The sign on the door directed clients to his office on the first floor. Eleanor tried the door and it was unlocked. She gave Napoleon's lead to Philip.

'I will see if he is in his office,' she said.

Philip looked at the flight of stairs and said, 'We'll be right here, within listening distance. Are you sure you want to do this?'

Eleanor nodded. She was shaking and she tried to control her hands. She walked quietly up the stairs and saw that the door to Mr Norman's office was open. He was sitting at his desk with his head in his hands.

Eleanor said: 'Mr Norman, I have come to...'

Mr Norman looked up, startled, and then shrank back as though fending off a blow.

'...to apologise and ask you about Mr Sutton.'

Mr Norman stood up, his courtesy in the presence of a lady automatically taking precedence over his emotion. His face was gaunt and his eyes red as though he had not slept for days. His clothing was dishevelled and his suit sagged, giving him a shrunken appearance. Eleanor was shocked at the change in him. She feared that what she and Philip had suspected was true.

'Mr Norman, I am sorry if I caused you any unhappiness or if I led you to believe that I had feelings for you.'

'Unhappiness, you call it!' Feelings! You have no feelings.'

Eleanor did not know what to say. Mr Norman had remained standing and was clearly very angry. He seemed to regard her presence as an intrusion. His face was distorted with emotion and she wondered if she had been rash to come. She began to be afraid of him. She decided to stand her ground but she was glad Philip was not far away.

'I was blind but my eyes have been opened and I thank God for that. And my mother was right. You are a harlot! A Jezebel! Not fit to be a wife and mother. You are nothing to me,' he said vehemently.

During this speech, he had become more and more agitated and he almost spat out the last few words. He had moved away from the desk and was now standing behind his chair. His hands were gripping the top of the chair and his knuckles were white.

Eleanor said, as calmly as she could: 'But if you thought that I had feelings for Mr Sutton you were mistaken.'

'Oh, I know what he was doing. He was turning you against me. He wanted you for himself.'

'Mr Norman, that is simply not true. Mr Sutton had absolutely no interest in me in the way you suggest. He was just a business acquaintance. Nothing more.'

'Well, it's settled now. I have dealt with it.' He let go of the chair and began clenching and unclenching his fists. He stared directly at Eleanor.

Eleanor looked at him steadily, holding his gaze. 'I know,' she said, quietly. 'I know what happened to Mr Sutton.'

Mr Norman continued to stare straight at her, his eyes wide and unblinking, but he did not actually seem to be looking at her. He suddenly grabbed the back of the chair again, feeling for it with his hands rather than looking at it. With an impatient gesture, he pulled the chair away from the desk and the chair legs scraped loudly against the floorboards. Eleanor flinched, startled by the sudden harsh noise.

'Get out!' he hissed. 'The scales have fallen from my eyes.

Leave me alone! Stop tormenting me!'

As Eleanor turned to go, Mr Norman slumped down onto the chair, his elbows on the desk, and his head in his hands.

~O~

Philip and Napoleon were waiting on the landing, half way down the stairs. Philip had heard everything. Eleanor looked shocked and was still shaking and he guided her away. They walked back along Spring Gardens and when they reached The Crescent, Philip steered Eleanor towards a seat. Napoleon sat down beside Eleanor and rested his chin on Eleanor's knee. He and Philip waited until Eleanor was ready to speak.

'It is true, isn't it?' she said, at last. 'I feel responsible. It is horrible to think that I have caused Mr Sutton's death. Or that I could have done something to prevent it. And what has happened to Mr Norman is my fault.'

Philip took her hand and said gently: 'Eleanor, look at me.' Eleanor refused to look at him 'Eleanor, none of this is your fault. You didn't invite Mr Norman's advances. I have thought for some time that he is mentally unstable and Catherine agrees with me. I also know that your father has been worried about his persistence. There is nothing you could have done or said to make him behave any differently. His mind was fixed on what he wanted and he would not have taken any notice of the fact that his feelings were not returned. He was being very, very selfish. He refused to understand the positon and there was nothing more that you could have done to persuade him that what he wanted was just not possible. If what we suspect is true, you must not think that you are in any way to blame.'

Eleanor sat very still and silent. After a few minutes, Philip said: 'Norman was probably consumed with jealous rage which affected his judgment and that caused him to act without thinking of the consequences. That passage of Chaucer that

Mondo read to us after dinner, do you remember? Chaucer's warning was right. Those who are not strong enough to cope with the consequences of love should have nothing to do with it. He has brought all this on himself.'

Eleanor nodded and then stared at the ground in front of her, lost in thought. Philip waited patiently but then he heard the clock strike and that reminded him of the time. He was concerned because he knew Mr Harriman would not be home for some time yet. He did not want to leave Eleanor alone at Hall Bank but he could not stay.

'Eleanor, my mother has people coming for bridge this afternoon and this morning someone dropped out. I promised to make up the numbers so as not to put her tables out but I don't want to leave you like this. Let's go back to Hall Bank so that I can telephone her and let her know that I can't come. I am sure she will understand.'

Eleanor smiled at Philip and shook her head slowly. 'No, Philip, thank you. Don't disappoint your mother. I shall be perfectly all right.'

'I don't think so and I am certainly not going to leave you like this. Why don't I walk with you to Oxford House and you can spend the rest of the afternoon with Cicely. You can explain to her what has happened and get her opinion.'

'Yes, that's a good idea.' She stood up and let Napoleon off his lead.

They walked back along Broad Walk, in comfortable silence, not feeling the need to talk. Philip left Eleanor safely with Cicely and, to his mother's relief, arrived home in time to change and take his place at the bridge table.

~O~

As Richard was out playing with one of his friends, Eleanor and Cicely could talk freely. Cicely listened with interest and growing indignation as Eleanor described the reconstruction that she and Philip had imagined and the conclusion they had come to. Cicely, like Eleanor, was angry at the thought of Mr Sutton being killed in this way. Eleanor described the occasions when she had encountered both Mr Norman and Mr Sutton at the same time, and she and Cicely analysed these meetings at length and went over the implications of what Eleanor had said or done. Eleanor particularly remembered the expression on Mr Norman's face at the bank when she had last seen him. Once again, she arrived at the conclusion that it was all her fault. Cicely then spent a good deal of time explaining to Eleanor why it was not her fault, assuring her that she was not responsible for the fact that Mr Sutton had decided to go past the bank on that Friday evening. That had been entirely his own decision.

Finally, Cicely said: 'If it is true that Mr Norman killed Mr Sutton, there is nothing you could have done to prevent it. I cannot imagine what could have triggered such a violent act except the motive of jealousy. But I know how you feel about Mr Norman so I know that you would never have deliberately done anything to attract his attention or try to make him jealous. It was all in his head.'

By the time Cicely had reached this point, Richard arrived home, hungry and excited. It was Guy Fawkes Night. It would soon be dark and the bonfires would be lit. Richard had been looking forward to tonight because it meant that he was allowed to stay up later than usual and more importantly fireworks, which had been absent during the War, had started to return. He had even been allowed to buy some sparklers and he brought them out proudly to show Eleanor. Napoleon was not keen on fireworks so Eleanor said she would take him back to Hall Bank. Before allowing Eleanor to leave, Cicely telephoned to Hall Bank to make sure that Mr Harriman had returned home.

After dinner, Eleanor and her father were in the sitting room either side of the fire. Although Eleanor had closed the shutters and the curtains to reduce the noise of the fireworks, Napoleon had abandoned his usual place on the hearthrug and was sitting at Eleanor's feet. Mr Harriman and Eleanor had a long discussion about the death of Mr Sutton and Eleanor's visit to Mr Norman that afternoon. Mr Harriman listened to the theories that Eleanor and Philip had put forward, commenting or asking a question occasionally. He was inclined to agree with Eleanor's conclusions. Towards the end of their discussion, Mr Harriman told Eleanor about the two anonymous letters he had received and their likely source. He hoped that this would help Eleanor to understand the factors which influenced Mr Norman's life and the pressure to which he was subject.

'Perhaps,' said Mr Harriman, 'instead of discouraging him as his mother intended, her disapproval had the effect of making his plans seem more attractive. I think Mr Norman is a very troubled man and it is probable that his mother should take some responsibility for what has happened to him.'

Eleanor was grateful for her father's support and she smiled at him, although rather sadly.

'Now,' he said, 'in order to take your mind off things, I prescribe a game of chess. You always want to win and to do that you will have to concentrate so that will prevent you from brooding and thinking any more dark thoughts.'

That caused Eleanor to laugh and Mr Harriman was relieved. Eleanor got out the board and set out the pieces.

Most of the town was gathered around the various bonfires that had now been lit. Many of the children had made guys and others, like Richard, had a few fireworks bought with pocket money saved up over many weeks of anticipation. Among the noise and general merriment, no-one noticed the sound of a shot from a service revolver as Mr Norman ended his own life.

CHAPTER THIRTY-FOUR

On Sunday afternoon, Philip called at Hall Bank to check on Eleanor and joined her and Napoleon on their usual walk with Cicely and Richard. While they were out, Mr Harriman, as Coroner, had been informed by Superintendent Johnson of Mr Norman's death. When Philip and Eleanor returned to Hall Bank, Mr Harriman told them the news.

~O~

On Monday the office at Hall Bank had a sombre air. Because Eleanor was the one who had found Mr Sutton, Mr Harriman could not act as Coroner at his inquest and he was arranging for someone else to conduct it. Superintendent Johnson telephoned Mr Harriman to discuss the alternative arrangements for the inquest and informed Mr Harriman as to the present stage of the enquiries. Afterwards, Mr Harriman went up to Edwin's office, where Eleanor and Napoleon joined him, and they mulled over the facts.

Mr Harriman said: 'Superintendent Johnson has told me that, after he received the post-mortem results on Saturday, he confronted Sam Perceval with a few facts and questioned him about the blow to Sutton's temple. Sam eventually admitted that he had hit Sutton on the jaw but denied striking him a second time. He showed surprise on being asked about the second blow and the Superintendent is satisfied that the surprise was genuine.'

'So, has Sam now explained what happened?' asked Eleanor.

'Yes,' said Mr Harriman. 'His latest story, which at last has the appearance of truth, explains his motive for painting a message on the wall of the bank. According to him, when he went into the kitchen at Clough End Farm recently he saw a letter from Chillingham & Baynard's bank lying on the kitchen table. He apparently has no reservations about reading other people's letters and so he learnt that Sutton was warning John Hartshorn that Clough End Farm would have to be sold. Sam was already aware that the farm was in financial difficulties and the letter made him very angry. And, of course, it brought back memories of what had happened to his father when a similar demand had been made by the same bank. So, he took out his anger at the bank in the same way as previously by daubing the bank's walls. It was Sam who painted the first message and apparently Pauline's cousin was also with him that night. Sam blames him for the poor spelling.'

Edwin shook his head in dismay.

'And what about Mondo's greenhouse?' asked Eleanor.

'Sam insists that it wasn't him,' said Mr Harriman.

'So, it sounds as though your theory was correct, Eleanor,' said Edwin. 'On the night he was killed, Sutton must have come upon Sam painting the wall. Sam hit out at Sutton, catching him on the jaw.'

'Yes,' agreed Mr Harriman. 'According to Sam, Sutton staggered as a result of the blow and, fearing that Sutton would retaliate, Sam ran off immediately without looking back. Then he realised that the pot for the lime wash that he had abandoned at the bank would provide evidence of his presence there. The pot had the name Perceval's Motor Garage on it.'

'Oh, dear,' said Edwin. 'Such a simple error. Sam is clearly not a hardened criminal who knows how to cover his tracks. Perhaps there is still hope for reform.'

'Yes, it seems that the only thing he planned was painting the message on the wall. Nothing else. And he did not anticipate the consequences of what he did when he hit Sutton. He thought Sutton was still alive. He loitered about for a while to make sure Sutton had gone, then he began walking back to the bank in order to retrieve the pot. On the way, apparently bravado took over and he decided to finish the message when he got there but when he arrived at the bank, he found Sutton dead. Not unnaturally, he thought that he had killed Sutton and he panicked. He ran home to get brother Charlie and Sam says it was Charlie who had the bright idea of moving Sutton to avoid discovery.'

'Not a very sensible idea on Charlie's part,' said Eleanor, dryly. 'About as clever as his plan for winning Sarah Dawson.'

'In his interview with Superintendent Johnson, Sam didn't cover himself in glory either. When he told his story the first time, he tried to give the impression that, in striking Sutton, he was acting in self-defence. He said that when Sutton found him at the bank, Sutton was angry and had threatened him. Sam claimed that he had only struck out with his fist in order to ward off a possible blow from Sutton and hadn't actually intended to hit Sutton. However, his story did not withstand the Superintendent's questioning and, eventually, he admitted that he had initiated the dispute. Sam's excuse is that he was very angry with Sutton.'

'But what had he got to be angry about?' asked Edwin. 'John Hartshorn was the one who was about to suffer as a result of the bank's demand for payment. Sam had nothing to do with Clough End Farm apart from being employed there.'

'It seems that there were several things causing this anger,' said Mr Harriman. 'He was still angry with the bank because of what had happened to his father, he was angry with Sutton for sending the letter threatening to sell Clough End Farm, he was angry at the prospect of Clough End Farm being sold because he would be out of a job and also it would upset his relationship with the people in Sheffield who were organising the dog fights and providing him with money, and this is the more disturbing part of Sam's story, he was angry with us because this firm acts for the bank but, more particularly, because you both acted for Mr Dawson. Sam is particularly angry with you, Eleanor, because of the part you played in what he described as "ruining his brother Charlie's life" and he wanted revenge. Superintendent Johnson questioned him very closely as to every detail of the events on the evening Sutton was killed. Eventually, Sam revealed that, as he was aiming his punch at Sutton's jaw he yelled out: "You and that Harriman woman. You ruin people's lives." Now, if Norman had been following Sutton, as you suspect, Eleanor, he would have heard those words and that might explain his subsequent action.'

'You mean, Harriman, that he would have interpreted those words in terms of his own obsession and made more of them than was intended by Sam,' said Edwin.

'Exactly,' said Mr Harriman. 'Probably in his tormented mind, the linking of the two names, Eleanor's and Sutton's, in the mouth of a third party amounted to proof of Sutton's intentions towards Eleanor. Those words might have convinced him that what he feared was true. Perhaps they provided a flashpoint for Norman's jealous anger and produced in him a sudden hatred so intense that it was uncontrollable. Perhaps he was overtaken by a blind rage and simply lashed out at Sutton without thinking.'

'The whole episode stems from the fact that Sam Perceval decided to daub the walls of the bank,' said Edwin.

'It has been a very unfortunate series of events,' said Mr Harriman.

'But,' said Eleanor, 'it leaves us with this question: did Mr Norman intend to kill Mr Sutton?

'We shall probably never know,' said Mr Harriman, sadly.

'And, perhaps, it is better that way.'

Although Mr Harriman didn't say so to his daughter, he was relieved that they would never know and that Mr Norman had chosen to end his own life. If Mr Norman had been tried for murder or manslaughter, his daughter's name would be bandied about by the press and the town gossips. He knew how easily an innocent person could become the subject of false stories and salacious gossip. She would become the subject of rude jests in the pubs and ale houses. He was horrified at the idea of his daughter being slandered in that way and knew that he would be powerless to prevent it, no matter what the truth might be.

CHAPTER THIRTY-FIVE

On Tuesday morning, Eleanor got ready for her appointment with Mrs Sutton. She was puzzled as to why Mrs Sutton had made the appointment but she was also aware, from her own experience, that sometimes there is a need simply to talk about the person one has lost. Eleanor was quite happy just to listen and let Mrs Sutton talk if that was what she wanted.

Mr Harriman had asked James to let him know when Mrs Sutton arrived and he greeted her and expressed the firm's condolences on the loss of her son. They chatted for a minute or two and then James took Mrs Sutton up to Eleanor's office. Napoleon had been banished and was sitting at the top of the stairs. From there he could watch the comings and goings of the office unobserved.

Mrs Sutton was a petite, elegantly dressed woman of about sixty. Her manner and her neat, precise appearance and stylishness reminded Eleanor strongly of Mr Sutton. After Eleanor had expressed her sadness over the death of Mr Sutton and they had chatted for a few minutes about the situation, Mrs Sutton said: 'Miss Harriman, I am a friend of Mr Aubrey-Mere and he has recommended this firm, and you in particular, most highly.'

Eleanor hoped that her surprise at this statement did not show. She was puzzled to think that Mr Sutton's mother would be a friend of Mr Aubrey-Mere when Mr Sutton himself was not.

'I hope you will understand,' Mrs Sutton continued, 'when I say that I was a little uncertain about seeing a young woman and not a man but I know from experience that I can rely on Mr Aubrey-Mere's judgment. And now that I have met you, I think we shall get on splendidly.'

'That is very kind of you to say so, Mrs Sutton. How can I help you?'

'Perhaps I should explain my connection with Mondo, that's Mr Aubrey-Mere. He is our house guest at present. When my son disappeared, he had been intending to visit us for a family christening and, naturally, as his closest friend Mondo knew of Lionel's plans.'

Eleanor could not hide her surprise this time. She said: 'But I thought...I have to confess to being rather confused at the moment. I did not realise that Mr Sutton and Mr Aubrey-Mere were friends. Quite the contrary, in fact. It is common knowledge that they were not on good terms at all.'

Mrs Sutton laughed and said: 'They boasted to me that their subterfuge had been successful and I didn't believe them.'

She paused and looked down at her hands and, for a moment, she was lost in thought. Eleanor waited and eventually Mrs Sutton looked up.

'Miss Harriman, I came here today to ask for your help but I think that, first, you are owed an explanation. Of course, what I tell you is in the strictest confidence. I would not want anyone to think less of my son, nor would I want people to feel animosity towards him or to Mondo because they resent having been fooled. Mondo assures me that I can rely on you and everyone else in this firm.'

'Of course,' said Eleanor. 'Please tell me whatever you feel is necessary for me to be able to help you.'

'Lionel and Mondo have been friends for nearly thirty years. They met when they were undergraduates. Mondo often comes to stay with us in Chester and that is why he is with us at the moment. They were up at Oxford together, you see, and they became very good friends. They joined the same clubs and shared the same interests, mainly climbing and collecting fine things. In the summer vacation, they would go with their club on climbing expeditions, mostly in Switzerland, and then the two of them would go on to Italy for the rest of the summer. On their last climbing expedition, the year they went down from Oxford, there was a fatal accident. Their group was on a glacier and two of the party were killed falling down a crevasse. Lionel survived only because of the quick thinking of Mondo. He was very brave and he risked his own life to save Lionel. As you can imagine, their friendship became even stronger after the accident.'

'Is that why they became neighbours?' asked Eleanor.

'No, that came about later on and for a different reason. Mondo came to Buxton first. He moved into Brook House as soon as it was finished. His people are in Yorkshire, very wealthy landowners of the hunting, fishing type. Very different from Mondo. Despite the fact that Mondo breeds gun dogs, he and his family have very little in common. His family cannot understand his passion for fine things so they have almost nothing to do with each other. Fortunately for Mondo, he has an older brother to inherit his family's estate and he is free to live here in Buxton and indulge in all the activities he enjoys.

Lionel, on the other hand, went to London and was employed in a family-owned bank there. He and Mondo remained friends though and whenever Lionel could get away they continued to go climbing together. After a year or two, Lionel became engaged to one of the daughters of the family. I went to London to meet her. Lilian was a delightful girl but, for some reason that was never explained, she broke off the engagement after only a few months. She and Lionel were both very young and perhaps they didn't really know their own minds. It was probably for the best. Naturally it was impossible for Lionel to continue working in the family bank so he joined another firm. Then he had the opportunity to join Chillingham & Baynard's bank here in Buxton. By then, Thornstead had become available and he moved there.'

'And that was when their friendship stopped? There was a dispute about the boundary between their two properties, I believe,' said Eleanor.

'Oh no, they have never ceased to be friends. They have just made people think that they have.'

'But why?'

'For protection. And for the sake of being able to continue in their chosen professions.'

'I don't understand,' said Eleanor.

'At first, they did not try to hide their friendship. They went walking on the moors and went climbing and they pursued their collecting interests together. Lionel was particularly good with dogs and, over the years, he and Mondo have bred and trained many champion gun dogs together. They were just very comfortable in each other's company. But some people are, shall we say, over-zealous in their opinion of others and take it upon themselves to judge, often in ignorance of the facts, and to comment unfavourably on other people's lives. Mondo received an anonymous letter accusing him of improper behaviour and referring to Oscar Wilde. I am sure, Miss Harriman, you will understand what was implied by that.'

Eleanor nodded and said: 'Oh, I see.'

'Mondo chose to ignore the letter but then he received a second one and several others followed. All the letters contained a quotation from the Bible and their tone became more and more insulting and eventually threatening. After a month or two, Lionel and Mondo began to realise that it was no longer possible just to ignore the letters. They were afraid that the accusations would be made publicly and that their professional lives would be affected. They came to Chester to consult my husband and ask for his advice. We all discussed the situation at great length. The anonymous letters were cowardly and they made me very angry.'

'I can imagine,' said Eleanor, thinking of the letters sent to her father. 'I should feel exactly the same way.'

'Lionel and Mondo feared that if they took no action, the accusations would just continue and perhaps become more forceful. On the other hand, they knew that if they made the situation public, some people would be only too ready to believe the accusations, or would pretend to believe them for their own purposes.'

'Yes,' agreed Eleanor, 'the fact of the accusation is enough in itself to condemn. That is all that is required. People will then say: "There is no smoke without fire" and will accept the accusation as the truth even when there isn't the slightest whiff of smoke. It then becomes impossible for an innocent person to be believed.'

'You have understood the situation exactly. That sort of accusation was of very grave concern to Mondo, and to Lionel too, for that matter. But for Mondo, it was extremely difficult. Society has certain expectations of him as a magistrate and that makes him particularly vulnerable. He is required to sit in judgment on other people. He was afraid that he would be regarded as a hypocrite. Naturally he has enemies amongst those who think that they have been dealt with too harshly and also amongst those who think he should have been harsher in punishing some offences. Given the slightest excuse, they could have become openly critical and his authority would have been undermined.'

'So the solution was to pretend that they had a falling out?'

'Which developed into a feud, yes. They resented the idea that they should have to give up their friendship for no reason so their solution was to remain friends in private. They came up with the idea of having a dispute so public that the whole town would hear about it and, from then on, would think they were sworn enemies rather than friends. It all happened many years ago. Your father would remember the dispute because he acted for Mondo but I imagine you were too young at the time to have known anything about it.'

'Yes. All I have ever known is that Mr Sutton and Mondo never have anything to do with each other. Father told me recently about the boundary dispute but I got the impression that he too thinks the dispute was genuine.'

'Oh, he would. No-one was let into the secret other than Rowland and Mrs Rowland. Lionel and Mondo were quite pleased with themselves at the success of their ploy.'

'And did the letters cease?'

'Yes, they did. Then the feud became a sort of game to them. I think they actually began to enjoy leading a secret life and teasing their critics. I suppose in a way it was a kind of revenge on them. Over the years, when it seemed necessary, they have manufactured several minor incidents to remind people of their mutual animosity. They have had tremendous fun and so have I listening to their stories. And, of course, they have always pretended to be rivals at the Chrysanthemum Society.'

'Yes, Mondo's greenhouse was daubed with lime wash last week in an attempt to damage his plants. One of the local young lads was suspected but some people blamed Mr Sutton on the grounds that he intended to damage the plants of a rival.'

'They were correct. That was Lionel and that was exactly the impression he wanted to create. A few days previously, he and Mondo had been out on the moors together. They had been climbing and were taking their equipment back to Mondo's car. They always chose places where other people don't go, but they unexpectedly came across one of the town's carriers. He was well out of his usual way because the road he normally took had been blocked by a rock fall overnight.

315

He had decided to make a detour via a track that proved to be unsuitable and his cart had become stuck. Lionel and Mondo spotted him before he saw them and they could see that it would take all three of them to get the cart free. They were reluctant to be seen together but naturally they did not want to abandon the carrier.'

'No, out there alone on the moors he would have been quite helpless. There would have been little chance of anyone else passing and it gets very cold up there at this time of year.'

'Naturally, the carrier was very grateful for their help but they knew he would be bound to tell everyone about the incident. It would not take long for the tongues to begin wagging again so they agreed to try to confuse the gossips by reminding them of the feud. Lionel thought up the idea of the greenhouse but he didn't tell Mondo beforehand what he was planning to do. He left a statue in Mondo's garden as a clue so that Mondo would know who had whitewashed his greenhouse. He didn't want Mondo wasting police time trying to catch the culprit.'

Talking about these events and seeing the funny side of them had temporarily diverted both women from the reality of more recent events but then they sat silently unable to continue.

Eventually, Eleanor said: 'Mrs Sutton, I am so pleased that you have felt able to share this information with me. It has helped me to understand the situation so much more clearly. We have all been deeply shocked and saddened by what has happened. I am not sure that there is anything that I can do to help but if there is, please don't hesitate to ask.'

'Thank you Miss Harriman. Let me explain. I came here to Buxton last Wednesday as soon as we received the news about Lionel and I saw Superintendent Johnson. He was most kind but, at that time, enquiries had only just begun and there was very little he could tell me, apart from the fact that you were the one who found Lionel and that they were questioning the man who owns the farm where you found him. I wrote to you asking for an appointment with the intention of asking you to find my son's killer. Mondo has told me about your success last year. There will be an inquest, of course, but Mondo thinks that there probably will not be very much evidence given at that. For my own peace of mind, I need to know. I need to understand how my son died but more importantly, why. And, of course, Mondo also needs to know. I am sure that there is more that has not been revealed. I went to Lionel's house today to deal with his post and to see his housekeeper. I found this letter which the housekeeper said arrived last Saturday. It hadn't been opened. It is clearly one of the anonymous letters that I was telling you about. I thought at first it was related to the incident on the moors with the carrier but I couldn't quite see the relevance of it.'

Mrs Sutton took an envelope from her bag and handed it to Eleanor. Eleanor noted from the post mark that the letter had been posted on the day before Mr Sutton died. She slid out a folded piece of paper. It contained two quotations from the Bible.

Treasures gained by wickedness do not profit, but righteousness delivers from death. Proverbs 10:2

Bread obtained by falsehood is sweet to a man, but afterward his mouth will be filled with gravel.
Proverbs 20:18

Eleanor mentally compared this with the anonymous letters received by her father which had been typed. This letter was handwritten and on different paper. Given the subject matter and the post mark she felt sure that this had come from Mr Norman.

317

'Mrs Sutton, I do understand and I can sympathise with your need to know. I have experienced it for myself,' said Eleanor.

She remembered her own desire to know the details when Edgar and Alistair died and of Cicely's desperate pleas for the facts about Wilfred's death rather than just the citation which accompanied the award of his medal. However, Eleanor was still dealing with her own feelings of guilt about recent events and, although she wanted to help Mrs Sutton, she was reluctant to discuss Mr Norman's infatuation and need for revenge. To give herself more time, she decided to concentrate on the legal process where she would be on familiar, unemotional, ground. Also, although she was sure of the accuracy of the theory which she and Philip had proposed, there were missing details that Mrs Sutton would be able to supply which would confirm or contradict parts of that theory.

'Mrs Sutton, there is, I think, a great deal of information that I can give you which will help but I would like, first of all, if you don't mind to have a little more information from you.' Mrs Sutton nodded her acquiescence and Eleanor continued. 'Did Mondo ever find out who sent the anonymous letters?'

'No,' said Mrs Sutton, 'although it was clear from the letters what sort of person was writing them. People of that kind have such fixed ideas. This is particularly so when they have strong religious beliefs and it became clear from the letters that the writer's beliefs were rather extreme.'

'Yes,' agreed Eleanor. 'I have noticed that some ardent church-goers are very willing to read more into a situation than is warranted by the facts. They can sometimes be guilty of making false accusations and scandal mongering while at the same time believing totally that what they are doing is right.'

'Sometimes,' said Mrs Sutton, energetically, 'I think that their unkind comments only serve to betray the sordid imaginings of their own minds and, if they realised that fact, surely they would remain silent. Their comments reveal more about themselves than about the people they criticize.'

'I couldn't agree more,' said Eleanor. She decided to delay identifying for Mrs Sutton the likely source of the anonymous letter and she went on with her questions. 'Mrs Sutton, I believe Mr Sutton was intending to visit you in Chester for a family christening. When was he planning to arrive?'

'Lionel was intending to leave here early on Saturday morning and we were expecting him to arrive by about ten thirty. Mondo telephoned at about eleven thirty to ask Lionel about something and we told him that Lionel had not yet arrived. We thought perhaps that the train had been delayed or that he had missed his connection in Manchester. My husband went to the station to meet the next train that was due but, of course, Lionel was not on that train either. Mondo telephoned again just before lunch to see if Lionel had arrived and said that he had checked at Thornstead and Lionel was not still there. Mondo thought that perhaps Lionel had been taken ill on the journey. He said that he couldn't bear just sitting and waiting for news so he rushed to the station and, rather impulsively I thought, took the next train and followed the route Lionel would have taken, making enquiries as he went.'

Eleanor interrupted Mrs Sutton, saying: 'So that is why Mondo was not at the Thermal Baths on Saturday with the other officials to meet the Princess.'

'Yes, he was with us in Chester. We began to be worried and eventually, my husband telephoned the police. Mondo very kindly decided to stay with us while we waited for news. And then, of course, we were informed that Lionel had been found…'

Mrs Sutton stopped and fought for control of her emotions. Eleanor too was trying hard to retain her composure. They sat in silence for a moment. Eleanor gazed, unseeing, out of the window and Mrs Sutton concentrated on her gloved hands, neatly clasped on her lap.

319

When Mrs Sutton was able to continue, she said: 'Naturally, Mondo feels the loss as much as we do and he is going to stay with us in Chester for the moment. I'm taking Jasper back with me when I return home later today because it may be some time before Mondo is ready to return. When I told Mondo I was coming to Buxton, he asked me to come and see you. He was confident that you would be able to help us.'

'Please give him my best wishes and those of my father and Mr Talbot. I know they would want me to add theirs.' Eleanor paused. She considered that Mrs Sutton had a right to know the truth about her son, even if the story she had to tell reflected badly on herself.

'Mrs Sutton, I think I do already know what happened to your son.'

Mrs Sutton looked at her attentively, surprise mingled with hope.

Eleanor said: 'There will be an inquest, of course, but there will not be a trial because it seems that the person who killed your son has since taken his own life. You must understand that when I say that I think I know what happened, it is only my speculation based on the facts that I have been able to establish. It is not by any means the official version; however, I think it is probably accurate.'

Eleanor took a deep breath and began her narrative. She explained how she came to find Mr Sutton in the barn at Clough End Farm and went on to describe the events of the evening when Sam Perceval had been painting his message on the wall of the bank. Finally, she came to Mr Norman's role in these events and the cause of his jealousy and she described for Mrs Sutton the anonymous notes her father had received and their likely source. She ended by apologising to Mrs Sutton for the part she had unwittingly played in Mr Sutton's death.

Mrs Sutton was silent as she absorbed the information Eleanor had given her and eventually she said: 'Miss

Harriman, I cannot thank you enough for what you have done. You have clearly spent a lot of time trying to understand what happened to Lionel and it is a great comfort to me to have that knowledge. I am sure that, later on, I will have questions to ask, things I want to clarify, but at the moment I am just trying to take it all in. I am very sorry that you have been put through this ordeal. I am sure you are not responsible in any way for what happened. Mr Norman was clearly infatuated with you and no doubt reacted violently to something he overheard. I am certain that his lack of control is entirely his own fault.'

'Thank you, Mrs Sutton, you are very kind. I am afraid that I keep asking myself whether I could have done something to avert the situation.'

'I don't see what you could possibly have done in the circumstances. You were not to know what was in his mind. You must not blame yourself.'

'But it was all so unnecessary,' said Eleanor, sadly.

'Yes, my dear, it was and, unfortunately, we have all learned over the last few years to accept with fortitude the unnecessary death of our loved ones.'

Eleanor nodded in agreement.

'Now,' said Mrs Sutton, briskly, 'there is one other thing I would like to ask of you, if I may.'

'Of course. What would you like me to do?'

'I would like you to deal with my son's affairs. I collected the Will from the bank this morning.' Mrs Sutton took a large brown envelope from her bag and handed it to Eleanor. 'I haven't read it but Lionel discussed it with me so I know its contents. He has left almost everything, including his furniture and other valuable items, to Mondo. Mondo does intend to come back to Buxton and he wants to leave everyone believing in the fiction of their dispute. I know you will be discreet in dealing with Lionel's estate and keep their secret.'

'I can assure you of that and I feel privileged to share in the continued teasing of those responsible for the anonymous letters.' Eleanor paused. 'Mrs Sutton, in the circumstances, this probably seems very trivial but I was very pleased to see that *Autumn's Peak* did so well in the Chrysanthemum Society Show.'

'Ah yes, that was Mondo's doing. He telephoned to Rowland and made arrangements for Lionel's best blooms to be prepared for showing and had them delivered to Mr Wentworth-Streate in time for the judging.'

'And what about Mondo's flowers?' asked Eleanor. 'I did not see his entry. He is usually a prize winner.'

'No, he didn't enter this year. He wants his flowers for the funeral. It will be in Chester, of course. I have been making the necessary arrangements today to bring my son home.'

CHAPTER THIRTY-SIX

After Eleanor had accompanied Mrs Sutton downstairs and said goodbye, she went back to her office but she did not feel like returning to work so she climbed the next flight of stairs to where Napoleon was waiting patiently. He was lolling on the top step, paws dangling over the edge, chin resting on paws, and watching through the stair railings. Eleanor sat down beside him on the top step and said: 'What do you think about all this?'

Napoleon sat up onto his haunches and then leaned against Eleanor, in sympathy with her mood. They propped each other up as she sat thinking over what Mrs Sutton had told her. She began remembering things about Mr Sutton and Mondo, little things, inconsequential things that each had said or done, and gradually these incidents started to fall into place and she formed a picture of them both as they really were. She liked both Mr Sutton and Mondo very much and now she found that she liked them even more and she was filled with sadness for both of them. After a while, Eleanor roused herself.

'Come on, Napoleon. We need a walk.'

Napoleon, who knew that a walk was the cure for most troubles, was already half-way down the stairs before Eleanor had even stood up. She went to her office and put on her hat and coat. When she got down to the front door, she found Napoleon sitting beside James' desk, waiting patiently.

Eleanor and Napoleon returned from their walk half an hour later and Napoleon went to the kitchen door to supervise Mrs Clayton who was preparing lunch. Eleanor went back to her office to consider what she had learnt from Mrs Sutton. Eventually, she turned her attention to Mr Sutton's Will. She slit open the large envelope that Mrs Sutton had given her and took out a large foolscap document folded in half, lengthwise. She opened it out and read it through carefully. Mr Sutton had made provision for his housekeeper and a gift to his parents and had left everything else to "my friend, Ormond Montague Ottiwell Aubrey-Mere. Eleanor was surprised because she had only ever heard Mr Aubrey-Mere referred to as Mondo and she had just assumed that he had a rather unusual first name. Now she realised that Mondo was short for Ormond. There was a second envelope inside the larger one that the Will had been in and Eleanor shook it out. It was a small square envelope of good quality paper. On the back of the envelope, the flap had been sealed with sealing wax. On the front of the envelope was a handwritten direction.

> To O.M.O. Aubrey-Mere, Esq.
>
> To be given to him on my death or destroyed unopened in the event that he predeceases me.

'O-M-O,' said Eleanor as she read out each of the initials separately. 'OMO,' she repeated and then laughed. 'Those three very impressive Christian names add up to nothing more than a brand of laundry soap....soap...now where...Ah, yes. *The Times*...That notice I read out to Philip. I've forgotten the exact words.'

Eleanor went into the kitchen and retrieved the newspaper from the pile waiting to be used to wrap rubbish and took it back to her office. She found the notice again and re-read it. 'Soap must have been Mr Sutton's nickname for Mondo,' she said 'So why was Mr Sutton, Leo?' Then she remembered something Mrs Sutton had told her and she thought: 'Of course, L-I-O-N, the first four letters of Mr Sutton's name. Lions are often referred to as Leo, like the constellation. Leo was Mondo's nickname for Mr Sutton. That was the clue he left in Mondo's garden after the whitewashed greenhouse affair. A stone statue of a lion. And the twenty seven years, that was the length of their friendship. Now the announcement makes sense.'

As Eleanor thought about the message she realised that wagging tongues had made it impossible for Mondo to express publicly his sadness at the loss of his friend. Eleanor now realised how poignant that notice in *The Times* was. His feelings had to remain private to the end and this was his way of making a declaration of his friendship. She sat for a long time reflecting on Mondo's loss and then she put the sealed envelope back with the Will thinking that, at least, Mondo would have the comfort of this last letter from his friend.

~O~

The following Friday was Armistice Day. The two minutes' silence would begin at eleven o'clock but earlier in the day many of the town's residents had already marked the occasion in an unofficial, private way by visiting the war memorial which had been unveiled in September of the previous year. This tall sandstone obelisk with its bronze figure of "Winged Victory" holding out a laurel wreath dominated The Slopes and was the only focal point the bereaved had for their lost sons, brothers, husbands or fiancés who had been buried in graves overseas or who were missing presumed dead, their

325

whereabouts unknown. Since early morning, visitors had been to the memorial in groups or singly to lay a wreath, a bouquet, a small posy of wild flowers, or a single bloom, according to their means. Some just laid the poppies they had bought from the Legion's poppy sellers. Eleanor and Cicely went with Richard and together they laid three small bouquets of marguerite daisies and rosemary which Richard had collected from the garden at Oxford House, one for Wilfred, one for Alistair, and one for Edgar. Eleanor noticed that there was no inclination among the visitors to talk. They laid their flowers, stood for a moment, heads bowed, alone with their thoughts and memories, and then slowly turned away to face another day.

Just before eleven o'clock, Eleanor and Philip were standing on the pavement in Terrace Road at the top of Spring Gardens. The air was cool and crisp and flags were waving in the slight breeze. Groups of people had started to form and the horses and carts, delivery vans, and motor-cars, had slowed in anticipation of being stopped by the policeman on point duty at the junction. At the first chime of eleven o'clock, the policeman came to attention and saluted. As the flags were gently lowered to half-mast, the crowd fell silent and the men and boys removed their hats and caps. As they stood in silence, Eleanor and Philip thought of the missing friends of their youth. Then came the sound of The Last Post. The air was so still and clear that the notes floated eerily out over the silent crowd from some unknown source, the bugler being hidden from view in the window of the offices of the Buxton Lime Firms. As the Reveille sounded, Eleanor thought of Lionel Sutton and Mr Norman and sighed. Two more names to be added to the remembrance of the dead.

Mondo eventually returned to Buxton and a stone statue of a lion appeared in the flower bed next to the front door of Brook House.